# WOES OF IKENGA

Ndubuisi George

**Copyright © 2014 Ndubuisi George**

First Published, 2014
**Kraftgroits Publishers, Nigeria.**

Digitally Published, 2015
**GiPi Publications, Abuja**
Plot 701 Mabushi, Cadastral Zone B6,
P.O. Box 7881 Wuse,
Abuja

All rights reserved.

ISBN:-10: 150856311X
ISBN-13: 978-1508563112

# INTRODUCTION

The indispensable place of literature as a veritable instrument to capture social, political, economic and religious realities in the society, for purposes of exposition, commentary, information, criticism, education and evaluation is profoundly demonstrated by the author of Woes of Ikenga. The plot and setting of the novel, the characters and characterization go a long way to show the superlative degree of what literary artists call "Realism" in literary parlance and also accentuate the view that, truth sometimes can be stranger than fiction.

In the novel, the protagonist, Ikenga, symbolically represents the strong breed that can withstand all forms of social challenges, hardship, persecution, prosecution, intimidation, harassment and suffering. He symbolizes the shortest of the five fingers, but the strongest and the most indispensable. Ikenga is indestructible and invincible. He represents victims of war, peace, discrimination, marginalization and elienation.

In specific terms, the novelist gives the reader, a sordid and profound insight into the ordeals and inhuman experiences often undergone by young African men and women who erroneously perceive Europe and other western countries as the destination and the "promised land." In achieving this objective, the Youths take unimaginable risks by travelling through deadly and dangerous rivers, seas, oceans and deserts to get to their dream countries. In the process, many perish on high seas and deserts and their dead bodies nibbled clean by vultures, fishes and other wild animals.

The very few survivors who get to the "promised land," discover to their chagrin and utmost disappointment that all that glitters is not gold, as they face stiff immigration laws and challenges with particular reference to the near impossibility of obtaining Permanent Resident Permit (PRP); a paper that guarantees the holders, the freedom and opportunity to move about, work and earn a living without tears, fears, and police harassment. The extreme difficulty in getting the permanent resident permit compels aliens or migrants to embark on drug trafficking and usage, prostitution and many ill-fated, unsuccessful and catastrophic marriage arrangements with young girls from the host and hostile countries.

The ultimate results of the social and economic challenges on the migrants or aliens include: constant police surveillance and harassments which consequently lead to frustration, dejection, lawlessness, isolation and loneliness, loss of focus and identity, drug addiction and abuse, emotional and psychological deterioration and degeneration. It is on the basis of the above premise that the novelist informs the reader that,

"Life outside one's country can be adventurous but life as an economic migrant in the Western World is best understood by those who have lived it."

As a further accentuation of the main message of the novel, the author tells the reader that:

"The impact of the inglorious adventures across the Atlantic might be difficult to access among adventurers, and those who made the journey and still lived to tell it admit that one's components in their cerebral hemisphere had been tampered with."

A critical reader would notice that characters such as the Law Professor who had overstayed his welcome in Germany and went about speaking "grammar"; Pastor Raymond who started "Ray Power Miracle Fountain Church" as the last resort for economic survival in Germany; Eze, who went to the office of Pastor Ray and nearly strangled him for using religion to exploit him and Ikenga, who was declared a psychiatric patient and thrown into the prison at Balthazar, all gave obvious symptoms of emotional and mental breakdown and degeneration.

Among the outstanding messages in Woes of Ikenga is that the selfish, inhuman and poor leadership of African political, economic and religious "Rulers" is squarely responsible for the brain-drain and mass exodus of African Youths and intellectuals to Europe and other continents, where leaders are altruistic, humane and achievement inclined. It is therefore not surprising that the novelist informs the reader that:

IV

"Life in Balthazar (the German maximum security prison) was far better than freedom in their own (aliens) countries. There was no issue of lacking the basic three square meals and there was the pleasure of having a television or a radio set for contact with the outside world."

This is an indictment on African leaders who act as rulers. On the basis of the currency and relevance of Woes of Ikenga to social, political, religious and economic realities of life in Africa and in the Diaspora the novel is unhesitantly recommended as a companion literary text for African students in the secondary and tertiary institutions, parents and Africans in Diaspora. The objective is to expose Africans and African Youths to the hard, sad and unsafe realities of life in Europe and other Western Nations as it concerns aliens or migrants, who perceive the West as the Promised land and the Eldorado where dollars and pounds are littered on the streets and can be freely picked by anyone who cares.

The essence is to discourage African Youths who die in transit, suffer in silence and perish unsung in their bid to graze in greener pastures that habour lots of poisonous snakes, deadly grasses and inedible herbs. By reading the fictional truths of the unenviable experiences of African Youths who perish in their adventures in foreign lands, many would be positively discouraged from embarking on suicidal trips to unknown lands.

Echezona Ifejirika (Ph.D)
Department of English
Anambra State University.

# DEDICATION

"Until the lions have their historians; the stories of the hunt will always glorify the hunter."

This work is solely dedicated to the Dead. Yes, countless of them roasted under the baking sun of Sahara desert and similar numbers soaked everlastingly in seabeds enroute greener pastures.

An overdue dedication as well to the children of my generation, a million of them whose lives were cut short by artificial hunger during the Biafran struggle.

And to late Mrs Priscilla Afuecheta, a warm-hearted woman, popularly known as Mama-Ogoo. She was a sister that stepped into the shoes of the mother I never knew ... Her *chi* certainly knows why she submitted to death so untimely.

# ACKNOWLEDGEMENT

As branches that bear most fruit bend themselves thankfully towards Mother Earth, I seize this opportunity to express my appreciation to my family; my wife Ozioma, Justin, Henry, Benny and Nora.

A keg of palm-wine in thanks goes to a unique apostle, Rev. Fr. Ositadimma Amakeze, for all his selfless assistance.

A genuine acknowledgment as well to Mrs. Amara Chimeka, the Executive Editor for her constructive criticisms and contributions to the perfection of this work.

-Ndubuisi George

# Chapter 1

Chukwuma could not help but get himself a third wife when his second wife failed to give him a male child by the fifth delivery. He was well known and respected in Umuafor and beyond, and had taken over the leadership of the family when his father died shortly after the civil war. *Chukwu-ma-onye-uka* was the name his father had christened him as he had been born during a period of religious tussles in Umuafor, in the days when righteousness was measured by the number of attendance to houses of worship. His elder brother, Eloka, had joined the missionaries and had neither been seen nor heard from for many years. Actually it had been a ploy by their father who did not want to risk losing two sons, should events get ugly during the civil war.

The desire to rule and govern themselves had led Umuafor and all her twelve clans into arms struggle with their dominant neighbours. Motivation was the only thing that was not in short supply. The poorly equipped rebellious movement with dwindling number of men of fighting age implied that young men were being rounded up at random and conscripted into the army. There had been a mandatory contribution of manpower for every family with young men of fighting age. However, people whom the gods had marked for death or banishment were easy recruits.

Exile and banishment were integral to the Umuafor religious and cultural practices. The people wisely preserved the dreadful punishment of exile for equally dreadful sins against their powerful earth goddess, *Ani*, and offences that should have merited death were converted to banishment. The traditional and the ever changing religious norms in the Umuafor cosmology favoured the expulsion of a serious offender over his or her death or execution due to the fact that blood was regarded as sacred. Therefore, rather than sentence a habitual thief to death, he would simply be banished permanently, or for a certain number of years from his clan.

Since bloodshed was against the commands of Chukwu, the

Great Being and against the moral code of *Ani*, those who merited such forms of punishment were handed over to the army commanders. Fathers who saw themselves as noble and patriotic citizens also took their sons and daughters to the camp as soon as they were old enough to carry arms, or help in transporting supplies through the dense jungles of Umuafor and the surrounding towns and villages.

Chukwuma grew up to become a man and a soldier to be reckoned with. His father gave him up at an early age because he was not the best of sons. Eloka was their father's pride and would definitely be the one to succeed him whenever he joined his ancestors. Though their father did not see eye-to-eye with latterday missionaries and their religion, he handed Eloka over to Reverend Klaus with hopes of recalling his son as soon as the war ended.

Reverend Klaus belonged to the generation of European missionaries who continuously waged war against the oracles, deities, ancient trees and rivers regarded as sacred in Umuafor. He had been sent over to assist a group of foreign experts who steadily sniffed round the bottom holes of Umuafor's resourceful landscape. His job being to evangelise while helping to pacify the populace in matters of religious sensitivity, whenever the treasure hunters ventured into areas considered sacred by the people. The unfortunate ones though paid the ultimate price at the hands of the local extremists, the *gods' warriors* who had vowed that the abomination by intruders would not go unchecked.

Shortly after the colonial era, the white men realised that they had left Umuafor too early. Just on their way out, they had stumbled upon one of the storage chambers of Mother Earth's abdomen as they were smiling home with an elephant load of the loot they had already acquired. Their next viable option was to stage a comeback based on mutual relationship and equality or partnership. This time, they sent some long-nosed breed of intellectuals to not only sniff out whatever mineral resources Umuafor was endowed with but ignorant of, or had no way of exploiting, but also to secure a profitable deal with the elders of the land. While these men vigorously crawled with their long noses over the hills and valleys around Umuafor in search of elements, Reverend Klaus, a devoted missionary, was busy learning about the people; especially those to be consciously mindful of, as well as those whose feet it would be unwise to intentionally step on. He preferred to live among the people, and cared less about the resentment or suspicious reception that many accorded him.

The white Reverend encountered the first stumbling block when the treasure hunters made the vicious move of attempting to purchase the flourishing parcel of forest overlooking Ogba Lake. The old men of Umuafor could vividly recall that the forest was an exclusive preserve of Eke-Ogba, the giant python that dwelt beneath the earth's surface. Its head was reportedly positioned in the middle of the forest while its lengthy body ran deep down into the lake. That explained the occasional landslide that Umuafor had to deal with whenever the beast moved her massive body. In the early months of the year when Harmattan is at its peak, white smoke could be seen emitting from the grounds surrounding the forest as millions of air bubbles continuously escaped from the lake. The only explanation given by Umuafor soothsayers and great thinkers for the unnatural phenomenon was that the beast annually wore off its old skin for a new one, and that the white plums and air bubbles that escaped from the ground could be the heat generated as it struggled to pull off the old skin. In the olden days, people were advised to pour red oil inside the holes and cracks from where white smoke was released, as it was believed to aid the lubrication of the python's body and consequently bring goodluck and blessings to those who bore with Eke-Ogba.

The cries of foul by the *omenani* custodians of Umuafor fell on deaf ears. Not only did the treasure hunters fish from the lake and pitch their mobile tents inside the forest, they also insisted on having the sacred piece of land at all cost. Since Ogba Lake and its surroundings were jointly owned, the twelve clans of Umuafor separately appointed leaders and elders to represent them in the crucial land negotiations. Their first meeting had yielded no results because Umuafor had blatantly refused to give up that sacred piece of land.

"You dare not close your eyes when the white wizards conduct their prayers," Chinua warned his team on the second leg of the negotiation. "My father told me how their lands were swapped as soon as they closed their eyes for prayers."

"Are you still insisting that we reject their offer?" Mr. Ubanese asked.

"They should keep their money," Chinua replied without hesitation.

"That money is enough to buy three bags of rice for each family in the whole of Umuafor kingdom."

"We are not starving yet."

"From Ogba we have profited nothing but land erosion."

"*Nso ani!*" Chinua exclaimed. "Your father would turn in his grave to hear you say a thing like that."

"My father and I were born in two different times," Ubanese defended.

"Whether you were born in three or four different times," Chinua lambasted: "*Omenani* is timeless."

"If Umuafor insists on retaining Eke-Ogba, so be it," Ubanese replied conceding defeat.

"Mother Earth has her reasons for harbouring the giant creature in our land." Chinua preached on: "Selling it off to foreigners is to lose an integral part of our identity. What will I tell our ancestors should they ask me what happened to Ogba?" He wondered aloud.

The issue of identity and eventual calamity for whoever took part in giving away the Ogba sanctuary discouraged most of the Umuafor delegates from opting to sell the piece of land. How would Umuafor have envisaged in those early days of their scientific development that what they referred to as a beast inside the ground were actually treasures reserved by the generous Mother Earth for them, their children and their children's children.

Umuafor needed more men like Chinua at this

## WOES OF IKENGA

transformational stage. He had adamantly stood against all mis-educations of the intruders. Among the subsequent disgraceful declarations presented to Umuafor elders was that the lake in which they had washed their *abacha* and *onugbu* leaves for ages, should cease to be known as Ogba Lake but to be known as Lake Clinton, in honour of the young adventurer who unravelled the mystery of the underground beast.

*     *     *     *     *

The prosperity and potential power-shift witnessed in Umuafor soon after the exit of the colonial masters made her an object of envy among her neighbours. The strangers, who felt affronted when the elders refused selling them the small piece of land, consciously but indirectly fanned the flames of aggression among Umuafor's neighbours with the intention of bringing the stiffnecked tribe to her knees. This wind of animosity rapidly evolved into an ugly and a long protracted tribal segregation and arms conflict, and Reverend Klaus was about to be caught up in a bloody civil war that he genuinely wished had never occurred.

When the team of treasure hunters packed up their sniffing equipment and fled the land as the drums of war sounded louder, the white Reverend together with some natives who were his followers and had offered to protect him from the hostile communities, left their camps at the bank of the river and made their way through the dense jungle to the strategic town of Umuafor.

The decision to settle in Umuafor was not reached because the town was the most welcoming for intruders, but because the ruling authorities wanted a medium to eradicate a number of defiant shrines that still commanded the people's loyalty. Hence, the then District Commissioner had given Reverend Klaus a piece of land, that had been forcefully seized from two warring families, on which the Reverend's followers had erected a bamboo house of worship and two other separate mud houses for their leader. Because of his dedication to his mission and love for nature, the

5

white Reverend gradually began to love Umuafor and its people for reasons best known to him, regardless of the visible threats posed by the *omenani* custodians. A practical preacher indeed, he was able to master the culture and local language of the people; their food became his food, and their drink became his drink. The merciless sun beat him till the fat tissues under his skin melted away leaving only a dried reddish leather-like skin hanging over his skeletal form.

Well into his late seventies, the Reverend had neither wife nor children. Therefore the women of his congregation took it upon themselves to cater for his feeding, laundry, and the cleaning of the church premises. It was believed that the white Reverend knew everything. His followers thence referred to him, as the white Jesus and indeed he became all things to many.

Though Reverend Klaus had found favour with the government forcibly imposed on Umuafor, he continually communed with the locals and their leaders to convince them that arms struggle was not the way forward. He usually went around with his toolbox to repair the leaking roofs of the houses of church members and non-members; derived the joy of humanity when in the company of Umuafor market men and women whose bicycles and wheelbarrows he freely repaired; and with the same toolbox responded to emergency calls from families with dying persons, and parents whose children sickness was almost snatching away.

With this uncommon exemplary life from a stranger, it was not long before the people of Umuafor began to listen and pay attention to his teachings, and regard him with respect and admiration. The rectangular wooden box that he carried everywhere was said to have solutions to all their immediate problems as many who had abandoned *omenani* for the white Jesus and his new religion claimed to have benefitted from the unending magical powers deposited inside the mysterious toolbox and his wooden cross. Umuafor with her twelve clans finally became the last to fall for the new religion long after the advent of its first missionaries.

A woman who had run to him in the dead of the night for fear of losing another child could not control herself when her dying baby suddenly regained full consciousness.

"The white Jesus brought out his toolbox and made my child well again," she testified loudly to neighbours who had run out from their houses to see what the shouting had been all about.

"Yes," echoed a man from the crowd. "I watched him talk to flowers and plants. With his tool box, he makes them give up their secrets whenever he is seated under their shade."

"Open your eyes my people!" Another shouted. "The white wizard is after our land. He who does not know where rain started to beat him would definitely not know where it stopped."

"Those held hostage by *Ogwugwu* are blind." The woman whose child had just been brought back to life shouted back at the last speaker.

The prolonged conversation went on till daybreak, between Reverend Klaus's converts and the staunch allies of *omenani*; each making his or her argument for or against why the uninvited guest should be allowed to stay on or be evicted from Umuafor.

Many who had found love and comfort with the new religion embraced the white Reverend as God-sent and always called on him whenever they needed assistance for one challenge or the other. They secretly nursed hopes that the looming war would not get to Umuafor, believing partly that the white wizard had all it took to reroute or quench the war. But to many undecided believers who still paddled between tradition and the new faith, his teachings and the way he called on his God every now and then for blessings and mercies became a mental balm to comfort their souls while the world rode on in its same old destructive process.

$$* \quad * \quad * \quad * \quad *$$

To Chukwuma, a brave soldier who had chosen to live and die by his Russian made gun, religion was only a man-made medium for reducing anxiety and uncertainty, while a very sceptical few, who did not like to air their views, believed that religion and its practical effect was designed to keep the poor happy in their state of poverty and prevent them from any act of revolt that might make life uncomfortable for the wealthy.

Since going publicly to evict the white Jesus would attract the wrath of the Governor and a revolt by Umuafor youths and market women, the traditionalists resorted to discussing their grievances in private while pointing fingers at Reverend Klaus and the team of long-nosed white men as a thorn in the flesh that must be gotten rid of. The Reverend had discouraged people who regularly took sacrifices of goats and fowls to shrine keepers for divinations or consultations.

Udeaja had lost many of his clients to the white wizard and his God, but still thought it wise to hand Eloka over to him.

"At least he can be useful for one thing." Udeaja told Chinua as they drank palm-wine in front of *ndi-ichie* family shrine.

"That is a wise decision my friend," Chinua replied. "But the boy must come back to the village as soon as the war ends."

"*Ndi-ichie* will not allow them to keep him a day longer." Udeaja promised. "The white Jesus will be coming tomorrow morning to pick him up."

"Is that?" Chinua asked.

"Yes!" His friend replied: "That is our arrangement."

"I would not have been a castrated man if I were as clever as you." Chinua said, referring to an ugly incident that had taken place at Ovuvu junction where his two sons had been butchered in a failed ambush during the early stages of the war. Udeaja, who did not like to re-open old wounds spoke briefly and quickly changed topics.

The two talked lengthily about the events in their village; the activities of the new religion and the havoc it had brought to the land and its people. The rainy season had come late that year; worse still, grasshoppers would not allow the sprouting grains produce any green leaf. The palm trees as well, for one reason or the other would not produce enough wine. Consequently, the yearly harvest had been very poor.

*Ndi-ichie* shrine was slowly running out of stock and the chief priest now visited Afor market once in a while to buy items for sacrifice since the cheerful givers had all gone astray, yet those who brought these calamities on the village still walked about freely and the gods had refused to strike them down. The old men were greatly baffled.

"Why has the ground not opened to swallow them?" Chinua asked his friend.

"That I cannot explain," Udeaja replied. "But I will not accept that the white man has seized the powers of *Ani*."

"Far from it," Chinua corrected sharply. "Would they seize the powers of *Amadioha* too?"

"But we are yet to see the white Jesus brought down to his knees by thunder," Udeaja unknowingly challenged.

"Do we fold our hands and watch then?" Chinua asked.

"The gods will always fight for themselves," Udeaja explained. "My father grew feathers before death took him. He always forbade Umuafor from taking revenge or fighting for the gods, lest one went into unjust war."

"Let us sit and watch then, if you say so." Chinua concluded.

"Our ancestors have not fallen asleep," Udeaja assured. "He who knows his father knows his ancestors."

The two were among the eldest in the village and for sure among those hit hard by the advent of the new religion and the looming war. They had formed the habit of sitting around the shrine; to share stories of the good old days with whatever was left of the palm-wine that Chinua had taken to the market. The cloud was heavy and the future far from certain. As pillars of the sacred *omenani*, the two knew that they would not escape queries from their ancestors should their ancient tradition with the steady influence of white man's culture, breakup in their hands.

The war was already raging in towns and villages not too far from Umuafor, and noble men like Udeaja and his friend Chinua, who had struggled to uphold the moral principles of *omenani* could only hope and pray that the fallout would not happen in their lifetime.

* * * * *

Reverend Klaus arrived Udeaja's compound early the next morning as previously discussed. He had mastered the nooks and crannies of the village and was used to moving alone even in odd hours without fear of attack from any human or spirit.

"What do you intend to do with my son?" The old man asked as Reverend Klaus cleaned the three-legged wooden stool he had been given to sit on.

"I intend to help him get the best education," the Reverend answered calmly.

"How are you certain that the white man's education is going to do him any good?"

"Education is the key to survival," the Reverend replied.

"You have failed it this time, Mr Know-all," Udeaja retorted in mock triumph, happy to have confounded the white wizard. "Our forefathers survived without your education and we are still surviving."

"That might not be for long, friend," the Reverend prophesied. "When your wives and children go to the bush to collect firewood and find none, education will be the key to unlocking alternative means of boiling your yam and cassava."

Udeaja emptied the remaining pieces of alligator pepper in his left palm into his mouth, and stared at his visitor, cogitating on the possibility of firewood drying up in the bushes. He did not need to ponder much before telling himself that the white Reverend was not far from the truth. Even the unthinkable was a possible scenario, judging from the pace at which bushes and evil forests were fast disappearing.

"*Ndi-ichie* want him back in Umuafor," Udeaja emphasised.

"He will be back."

"Please let him return!"

"We have to give him this opportunity." The Reverend preached. "Eloka, your son, might be a future political leader in Umuafor when the guns must have gone silent. He may also want to assist in the work of evangelism if he is not interested in politics."

"*Mbaaaa...*" Udeaja abruptly objected to the notion that his son might be used as a tool to propagate what he deemed as false news. "You are still alive because *Amadioha* spared your life." He continued: "The young man I am entrusting to your care will take over the *Ndi-ichie* and *Ogwugwu* shrines when my time is over. *Anyanwu,* the sun god, along with our ancestors will always keep their eyes on you and that God of yours."

"My God who created them all is keeping an eye on them as well." Reverend Klaus replied casually.

Eloka came in with a bowl of water and a wooden tray containing kola-nut, alligator pepper and a moulded clay chalk. The items with its significance as a mark of spiritual purity and hospitality was not new to Reverend Klaus and so both men washed their hands and prayed over it. Udeaja chewed and watched as Reverend Klaus repeatedly washed his own share of the kola-nut, and hastily made a quick sign of the cross before throwing it into his mouth.

The cock was yet to crow when Eloka bid farewell to his mother and the rest of the family members that came out to see him off. Udeaja walked with them a little way down the road and both men shook hands, after which Eloka passionately hugged his father. The old man stood and watched as the two disappeared into the morning dew.

"Stray bullets will not locate you in the hands of that white wizard my son!" He prayed. "Chukwu Okike will give you victory in the face of your adversaries. In honour of our ancestors, you will come back to take up your role as the custodian of *Ndi-ichie* and the leader of your people." He was still talking to himself as he took the left turn towards the farm to go and see if his cornfield had survived the recent vicious attacks on farmlands by those giant grass-cutters that were reported to have wrecked much havoc in the past few days.

* * * * *

The brutal war finally reached Umuafor. Then, the supply corridor had been completely cut off and hunger constantly snuffed life out of young children and their helpless parents. At that stage of the war, Umuafor's brave fighters were paired two men to one rifle so that if one fell, the other would pick up the firearm and fight on. Such was the bravery of a kind exhibited by Umuafor warriors. While everyone else ran helter-skelter for safety amidst the ever-raining bombshells of the enemy, the white Reverend took to town crying, as he was determined to alert the world or whoever cared to listen that there was a systematic tribal cleansing going on around him.

He had turned St. Patrick's Mission into a refugee centre and was also providing the last comfort with hastened burial rites to scores of children and adults who had lost their lives to hunger. When those who survived the war returned to discover that the reverend survived the onslaught, rumours began to fly that the toolbox, which the preacher carried around, housed some supernatural powers. Umuafor had no way of verifying this and other news going round that the white wizard had given his life to a certain white goddess in exchange for the mysterious toolbox; hence, death would not locate him easily.

For the number of years that the bloodshed lasted, the lives and livelihood of the entire Umuafor populace was brought to ruins. Those who were lucky to escape to a reserved forest deep in the jungle had been sheltered in camps while many others had not lived to tell of their ordeal and struggles to escape. The movement leader, hoping to live and fight another day had fled into exile when he realised that he and his poorly equipped men could no longer stand the heavy bombardment of the much stronger aggressor and their allies. As for the rest of the field soldiers, it had been a case of *"Oke na ohia, ngwere n'uzo."*

The arms hostility ended only to be replaced by stringent and crippling economic measures aimed at ensuring that the vanquished were kept on their knees. By far, the most destructive of the administrative policies was the Abandoned Property Decree. This edict transferred landed properties and businesses from the hands of the weak to the hands of the mighty. Post-war poverty and suffering eventually turned the people of Umuafor to adventurers and religious bigots, clinging to worship houses where signs and wonders were ever present. The deities that protected their ancestors suddenly lost potency or had been swallowed up by a greater unseen force that made the people of Umuafor quickly turn their backs against them. Education and the everchanging lifestyle, which the youths of Umuafor were quick to identify with, also implied that Reverend Klaus, his culture, and new religion had come to stay.

Chukwuma returned to an empty family with only a pair of black leather boots, an Old Russian-made double barrel gun and a bunch of chewing sticks, to show for many years of service in the defeated army. While he had been away, his father had spotted Ozioma; a beautiful girl from a well cultivated family in a neighbouring village, paid her dowry and sent her to join Chukwuma in the camp. Chukwuma had however married a second wife as tradition demanded to secure an heir to the compound when he discovered that Ozioma could not bear him a child. His actions had been purely in line with the laid down principles of the Umuafor hereditary system. However, by the time his second wife gave birth to the fifth baby girl, he knew that a third wife was inevitable.

Besides returning to an empty family, Chukwuma was also saddled with the responsibility of fending for and taking care of three wives, five daughters and his aged father. Udeaja, a much weaker and aged man was terribly affected by the defeat since he had given everything he had to support the young men and women fighting for their fatherland. He had sold two parcels of land and handed over the proceeds to the army commanders. The soldiers had also visited every now and then to empty his yam barn. He attributed Umuafor's defeat to their neglect of an important tenet of their indigenous religious practice; a sacred traditional rite for warriors and hunters where they were not only taught physical methods, but also the respected spiritual aspects of a war, and the use of supernatural magical means to obtain compliance from an opponent or the animal hunted. Most young men of fighting age had disregarded *nso-ani* to embrace man-made edicts, for that, Umuafor had lost a battle for the first time in their entire history. But the one that continuously gave him sleepless night was that Reverend Klaus would not bring Eloka back as agreed.

Chukwuma who had recently returned from camp was taking a tour of his father's compound to see what was left of it after his long absence. The onus now rested on him to pick up the pieces and move on. The horns cannot be too heavy for the head of the cow that must bear them. Experiences gathered during the war had not only tamed his wild nature, but also taught him to run away from a problem before it went for his head. His views were now more constructive and this greatly impressed his aged father. At least, there still seemed to be a reason to live on.

"But why did you hand Eloka over to the white wizard?" Chukwuma demanded from his father as he stepped into his *obi*.

"I was afraid my son," the old man replied; "Afraid of losing both of you to the war."

"I am going to bring my brother back," Chukwuma said emphatically to his father. "Men have fallen under the nozzle of my gun and the stiff-necked ones who refused to fall, I slaughtered with my *obejili*. Children will play with snake like a toy only if it chooses not to reveal itself. I will come back with the head of that white rabbit if he refuses to hand my brother over to me. Whether dead or alive, the tail of a lion must not be touched."

Udeaja became very afraid, as he perceived fire coming with those words out of his son's mouth. He knew Chukwuma meant every word of what he said. For the first time in so many years, he saw his son's old nature, and was reminded of a wild cat in attack mode. Silently he consoled himself that he had done right by risking Chukwuma at the war and was deeply grateful that the gods had spared his life.

"Do not send my grey hairs to the grave with sorrow, I beg of you," the old Udeaja pleaded with his son. "How can you take over a curse placed on someone else's head? That man has dug a grave for himself in the church compound as I heard. No right thinking man digs his grave while alive and beckons death to come and take him. He stayed behind waiting for death when everybody was running from the war and we all came back to discover that death also avoided him. His parents and kindred must have placed a curse on him and that is why he is willing to accept death in a foreign land."

Chukwuma did not make any sense of what he heard from his father. He had never trusted those intruders; not the Reverend, and certainly not those treasure hunters with their dubious ambitions. He was determined to retrieve his brother. Belief in charms or white and black magic to him signified weakness of the spirit. As far as he was concerned, death is a debt and it made no difference if he died today or tomorrow, be it from a mosquito bite or the deadly blow of *Ogbunigwe*.

"I am not afraid of their impotent charms," he asserted as he sprang up on his feet. "The death that will kill a man begins as an appetite. When the blade of my *obejili* goes over his neck and his head refuses to fall off, then I will know that the gods are against my moves."

"You have said it right, my son," his father cried loud. "The gods are against your moves. The bird that remembers its flock mates never misses its way. Taking a man's life is no crime against the man himself or his family, but against *ani*. It is an abomination in the eyes of our people. I have made several appeals to white Jesus to bring back Eloka but he keeps telling me that my son is in good hands and will be back as soon as he is through with his education. Udeaja your father is not the type to sit and watch while the she-goat suffers the pain of giving birth while on tethers. I have gone far and wide with my inquiries. I have consulted the native doctors of our land and the powerful oracle of *ndi-ichie*. My enquiries have also taken me to *Udo* and *Ududonka* shrines, I have been reassured each time that the white wizards do not eat human flesh. Eloka, your brother, is still alive and will one day make his way back to Umuafor where he came from. You dare not doubt the gods my son. Our ancestors have never let any son of the soil go astray. Eloka's fate should be left in the hands of the gods. Your worries for now should be over Ogochukwu, your pregnant wife. When a dying man cries, it is not because of where he is going which he knows nothing about, but because of what he wishes he would have done in the world he is leaving behind."

The more the old man tried to talk sense into his son, the more furious Chukwuma grew. The white Reverend had stepped on his toes and the ear that refuses to hear is sure to go off with the head when it is cut off. He sprang to his feet and walked out of his father's hut without giving the old man any chance to say another word. A cold shock ran through Udeaja's veins and the old man stood gazing until his son disappeared out of sight.

Chukwuma went straight into his *obi*. Small round huts made of clay and grass roof dotted the big compound. The men had their huts or *obi* close to the entrance while the women had theirs in the middle of the compound in a semicircular form. The *ndi-ichie* family shrine with three ancient *Ogilisi* trees was situated close to the entrance to greet whoever entered the compound. He mounted a wooden chair, brought down his long forgotten double barrel gun, opened its cartridge chamber, blew out thick dust, and within seconds the gun was loaded and alive again. With his long *obejili* dangling round his waist, Chukwuma set out. Whenever the dusty Dane-gun was well fed, nobody dared stand before it. He was determined to come back with either his only brother Eloka, or the head of "that white rabbit" and nothing was going to stop him.

As he marched towards the gate of their compound, Ozioma, his childless first wife who everyone fondly called Nne, rushed towards him and whispered something into his ears that made him immediately abandon his mission and follow Nne to her hut.

They returned in the early hours of the next day. A new dawn had come over the entire family. Ogochukwu, his third wife, had successfully been delivered of a set of twins; a boy and a girl. The day before, she had been rushed in the family wheelbarrow to the village clinic when Ozioma notified their husband that the labour was intense. The whole family had escorted her, leaving their aged father all alone in the compound, and oblivious to the recent happenings. They had all stayed awake all night waiting for good news, but that was the least of their problems. Had it not been for the works of Reverend Klaus and the early harbingers, the babies would have been taken to the evil forest where they belonged, straight from the delivery room. Myth and superstition had it that twins were devil incarnates sent by evil spirits to torment their parents and bring pain and agony to people around them. It was also believed that they would eventually die at a young age and return to their sender, leaving their parents in grief. Thus, single births were regarded as normal while multiple births were seen as atypical. Before the advent of the white man's religion, twins in Umuafor were thrown into evil forests as soon as they were born. Children born with teeth and breech babies also suffered the same fate. Fortunately for Chukwuma, the new religion had already made people understand that twins were not evil as they had thought but instead a double blessing from *Chukwu-Okike,* the God of creation.

* * * * *

The family did not want to disturb their aged father, as it was still very early when they returned from the village clinic. Nneamaka waited till the second crow of the cock before going out with the usual bowl of water. She was the eldest of Chukwuma's children and this practice was a family ritual. Every morning she took a bowl of water to her grandfather to wash off whatever encounter he may have had with any spirit during the night before the daily breaking of kola-nut. This was normally followed by the sprinkling of drops of *kai-kai,* to *Ani,* the mother earth, and to the ancestors in appreciation for the new day.

"*Nna anyi Ututu oma,*" Nneamaka greeted as she entered her

grandfather's *Obi*.

As the small hut was still in darkness, she took the *mpanaka* from its stand and went out to light up. "The old man must have taken more than his usual dose of palm wine the previous evening." She thought to herself. But one could have heard him snore even from the neighbouring compound if he was asleep. The whole thing baffled Nneamaka. Sleep should have left her grandfather at this time of the morning. He usually slept like a dog and everybody knew that he opened his eyes at the slightest movement of an ant, even in deep slumber.

"Grandpa, your water is here," Nneamaka called again. And again there was no response.

The more she gazed at her grandfather asleep at this time of the day, the more confused she was. Then she knelt down by the side of the wooden bed and pulled down the blanket. The old man usually covered himself from head to toe to ward off the biting teeth of the midnight cold in the middle of the harmattan season. Nneamaka brought over the oil stained *mpanaka* closer to her grandfather's face and was overwhelmed with shock. Frantically, she ran to her father's *obi*, shivering tremendously in fear.

Chukwuma had been helping himself from the bottle of local whisky he opened in the middle of the night when they returned to the house. He was a happy man now. Though he claimed to have no business with religion, his quest for a male child had made him pay tribute to numerous shrines including St. Patrick's Mission and fate had finally granted his heart desires. Now he was soaking himself with joy before his friends and kindred would join him by daybreak. For once, he was grateful to Reverend Klaus and his new religion. The twins were safe and that brought great joy to the family. The double barrel gun had since been unloaded and replaced in its safe. He was almost at the peak of enjoyment when Nneamaka dashed into his *obi* looking bewildered as if an aimless ghost was after her life. Chukwuma grabbed his bottle of whisky in confusion and hid it behind his back as whatever was after her daughter might decide to go for his bottle of *kai-kai* as well.

"What has gotten over you this early morning, Nneamaka?" He queried.

"It … it is … Grrrh … " The young girl was short of words.

"They have sent you again," her father said to her angrily as he returned the bottle of whisky to the table. "Tell them for today, you did not see me."

"Nobody sent me papa," Nneamaka said, trying to get herself together.

"And no spirit sent you either?"

"Yes, Papa."

"So what is your problem this early morning?"

"Grandpa is not well," she finally managed to say.

Chukwuma lowered his tone and paused to gauge the level of the *kai-kai* remaining in his stained glass cup.

"Is that why you want to run over my bottle of Schnapps?"

Nneamaka remained silent with her heart beating loudly as she panted.

"What is wrong with Udeaja?" Chukwuma demanded.

"I don't know Papa," Nneamaka answered. "He is still asleep."

Her father took a deep sip from what was left in the glass, jerked his neck to the right and to the left as if the whisky had problems going down his throat, and with his left hand he scratched his bushy beard. For his father to be asleep at this time meant that the old man was really not well. He reached for his torchlight, grabbed his *obejili*, a trusted defence tool for every Umuafor man and walked towards Udeaja's hut with Nneamaka following carefully behind.

"*Nna m Agu!*" he called out in a loud voice. "The calabash that never gets drowned. The vintage machete that clears the evil forest. The ear that hears the drum beats of the dead."

Chukwuma expected his father's return greetings, but when none came, he turned to Nneamaka trying hard to conceal his worst fear.

"Has he gone out?"

"On the bed"

"Go to Chinua's house!" He ordered. "Hurry up before he leaves to attend to his palm trees, tell him to come over with you immediately."

Chukwuma watched his daughter disappear before entering his father's *obi*. He could sense some strange spirits as he entered the round mud hut. He brought out his torchlight and carefully surveyed all the corners of the room before gently bending down to feel his father's heartbeat.

Okoye Udeaja had joined his ancestors!

Chukwuma sat down on the wooden chair next to his father's lifeless body short of words. He recalled his father's last words the previous evening, shortly before he had stalked away with a burning desire for Reverend Klaus's head and nodded his head in affirmation. The words of the elders do not lock all doors; they surely leave the right one open.

\* \* \* \* \*

Chinua could hear crying from a distance, so he ignored greetings from left and right. He had left for the market with his kegs of palm wine before Nneamaka got to his house, but people were pouring into the road from their houses and heading towards one direction, and even an old woman may run when a goat carries her snuffbox. He cycled as fast as his two-runner bicycle could carry him as if to catch up with the spirit of his best friend and perhaps convince him to abandon his journey.

The peace of the morning had been devoured; the loss of a good man had brought grief to the hearts of many. As if Afor market had been relocated, people filed into Udeaja's compound as cries rang out from different quarters. The women were uncontrollable. Nne cried her eyes out as she rolled and rolled round the dusty compound along with the elderly women who tried hard to console and stop her from rolling off her wrapper and going naked. Nneamaka's *ogene* voice was remarkably touching. She had been raised to take charge of family affairs in the absence of a male child, and was the perfect example of a "black beauty" combined with elegance and bravery surpassing that of a man. Her father sometimes wished that she had been born a boy. *Eke-uke*, the family dog barked in confusion while the fowls ran helter-skelter through the corners with their chicks trying to secure a territory for themselves. Chinua quickly fastened his two-runner bike to the *Udala* tree and went straight to the hut where the lifeless body of his bosom friend was kept. The big compound streamed with mourners when he entered. Men stood in small groups discussing in low tones, and wearing sad faces with their hands behind their backs while some who could not help it allowed tears flow freely down their faces.

Reverend Klaus, who went straight to the compound as one of his church members broke the sad news to him unaware that death had narrowly missed him, had also taken up a corner and was singing praises to his God with some of his church members.

"With whom do you want me to share my stories?" Chinua cried out with a broken voice.

The old man was deeply saddened; most of his age mates who understood life as he did had all gone. Hence, Udeaja's exit signalled loneliness in a completely changed world.

"I would have stopped you if you had told me." He lamented. "But you hid it from me."

He pulled out a snuff-stained piece of cloth to wipe his tears. A kinsman who felt touched seeing the old man shed tears rushed to assist him. Not even the death of his two sons had brought the old warrior to such state of helplessness.

"Allow me to join him!" He pleaded with a man who had thrown his arms round his waist.

"You cannot go with him." The young man implored. "Umuafor still needs you."

Relatives who had come to pay their last respects filed into the small hut and exited after a short while, but Chinua insisted on joining his old compatriot. People were temporary halted from going into the hut till a group of men succeeded in consoling the legendary wine-tapper.

"Why did you decide to leave me behind?" He queried the lifeless body of his friend over and over again. "Together we visited this world, together we held the centre from falling apart and together we planned to give account to our ancestors."

Udeaja, his friend was no longer able to hear or reply but Chinua did not mind.

"Chukwu-Okike, he kept his journey from me." He lamented as he exited the hut throwing his hands open for the sky to bear him witness. Coincidentally, or as the gods would have it, the twins with their mother were being taken out to a relative's house because of the noise and dust that had stormed the air.

Chinua's hands got stuck in the air at the sight of two baskets containing the twins, and his mouth was agape. The remaining white hairs on his shining skull stood straight, and even the smallest *obene* tied to his waist was still. He must have been a warrior in his days judging from the way his two tiny legs stood their ground even with the little strength left in the old man.

Apart from being a distinguished wine-tapper, Chinua had also been bestowed with the title *"Ogbuagu"* as a mark of braveness for the time when he had decisively overpowered two unwelcome strangers from a neighbouring village, who had invaded *Ogwugwu* shrine in the dead of the night for its much-valued vintage statues. He had pinned both men with their loot to the ground till the villagers gathered the next morning and thus confirmed the general belief that wine-tappers saw and knew more than the average man. The sons and daughters of Umuafor had thereafter held Chinua in very high esteem.

For a while, he remained like a statue with open arms. The news of the death had spread through the market like wildfire but many of the mourners were just learning about the arrival of the twins at that moment. Chinua reached for alligator pepper in his goatskin bag and without asking, picked up the baby boy in his hands and examined carefully as he chewed. Then he blew out chewed bits of pepper right into the baby's face.

*"Ezi-oyi nno!"* he exclaimed and did the same to the twin sister.

"Udeaja has returned in a new body," he told the crowd with a suddenly brightened face as he gently put the babies back into the basket.

Reincarnation is a strong tenet of the Umuafor cosmology. In such perfect coincidences as these, where an infant arrives just as an elder departs, the people considered it an extension of life approved by their ancestors and the spirit world.

It was almost noon and the cries were gradually dying down with spontaneous outpours of grief at intervals. Heaps of red earth could be seen flying out of the ground as young men took turns under the heat of the scorching sun in and out of the grave. Chinua had come from the market with six kegs of palm wine and with that paid his first condolence visit to the family of his dear friend.

Proudly, he offered wine to the young men who dug the grave, and drank along with them as he regaled them with stories of the world he was used to. The renowned wine-tapper confirmed to his listeners that he had actually been on a treetop on that fateful afternoon when darkness had suddenly engulfed Umuafor in the middle of a bright sunny day.

People's faces gradually brightened as his stories went on. He also told of how he had fought the whole night with the thieves who had tried to steal *Ogwugwu* to hand over to a white man in exchange for money, and how he had lost seven of his valuable kegs of palm wine in the market in a last minute effort to meet the Messiah.

"They charmed our men and women." He stated, pointing towards Reverend Klaus and his followers who were busy singing praises.

"His people besieged the market square that early morning shouting on top of their voices; "the end is near, the end is near," and that those who wanted to enjoy the abundant wealth of paradise should hurry to meet the Messiah." He paused for a moment so his listeners could digest the information and pass their individual judgments.

"I was not there when the wealth of this world was shared."

He showed up his palms to confirm his story. "I could not afford to be absent when the wealth of the heavens would be shared as well. So I abandoned my kegs and hurried," Chinua said sadly. "And I waited and waited."

People could not help but laugh through their tears, thereby drawing the attention of other mourners towards the circle. This was one story that Umuafor was known for and mocked about. The crowd was delighted to be getting an unedited version from one of the few remaining elders who had actually witnessed the day when the popular Afor market had been completely deserted leaving valuable wares to the mercy of thieves and hoodlums.

"I had never believed them but was forced to run down to that mission when I discovered that I was alone at the market," Chinua continued as the laughter subsided. "At the end I got tired of waiting and begged my kinsmen to help me explain to the Messiah when he comes that I must attend to my wine. On getting back to the market, my seven kegs with fresh palm wine had vanished. And till today, the Messiah is yet to come."

The second outburst of laughter was uncontrollable. For some minutes, people forgot their grief and enjoyed the funny experiences of the old wine-tapper.

"I made my complaints at the Mission," Chinua recalled. "Those kegs must be paid for whenever He shows up before we discuss the heavenly wealth."

"You understood it all wrong, *Ogbuagu*," Mr. Ubanese said to him. "We are all going to meet the Messiah one day when we die."

"You are as confused as your masters," Chinua said to the headmaster. "Why were people tricked to believe that end was going to come with the sunset?"

"That was to get people to be ready at all times," Mr. Ubanese tried to explain.

Mr. Arinze Ubanese was the headmaster of the only primary school in the district and had smooth relations with the District Governor. He had worked with the missionaries since childhood and learnt both their language and ways of relating with their unseen God.

"So is Udeaja now on his way to meet Him or has he already collected his own share of the heavenly wealth?" Chinua asked.

"We all have to give account of our lives here on earth and anybody who is not worthy of paradise will be thrown into hell fire," Ubanese explained.

"Keep your mouth shut before *Ogwugwu* strikes you dumb," the old man cautioned the headmaster. "Okoye Udeaja, half a man half a spirit, is already with our ancestors and has no further account to give to any human or spirit."

The heated debate of life after death raged on for a long while as Chinua was not ready to buy any foreign ideas, especially not that of the white strangers or their confused followers. To give up his *omenani* and *nze na ozo* titles that he had laboured hard to acquire would mean to give up his identity, an *Nso-Ani* and shameful betrayal to all he had lived and stood for. He had strived to live a noble life, observed the moral codes of A*ni,* and was sure to join his ancestors whenever he ended his earthly sojourn.

Before long, the six-feet grave was dug. The last keg of palm wine was shared in a bamboo cup, first among the grave diggers until the last man that came out of the grave received before being passed on to the standing listeners who seemed to be getting the comfort they needed from Chinua's tales.

The lengthy funeral ceremony lasted for several market days; a tradition practiced by Umuafor's ancestors for ages. Udeaja was not an ordinary villager and would not be buried as such. That meant that a drop of rain during the burial ceremony of such a man would be seen as a bad omen. Therefore, all the rainmakers in Umuafor and beyond had been consulted and given whatever requirements they demanded. As custodian of *Ndi-ichie* and *Ogwugwu* shrines, a white he-goat was sacrificed to *Ogwugwu* to guaranty his safe transit to the spirit world, while as an *Ozo* title holder, a cow was made available to *Ndi-Ozo,* a group of titled men who had achieved greatness in their various fields with selfless sacrifice to their respective communities. Different dancing groups with their masquerades came from far and near and each group was given a white cock and a sizeable tuber of yam. Food and drink did not run dry for seven days and many gave up cooking in their homes during that period. For the *Ofeke* and drunkards in the village, it was a feast that would never be forgotten.

The funeral and burial ceremonies of men of such integrity were extremely complex. If his family failed to perform any of the funeral rites, it would be seen as disgraceful to the spirit of the dead and disastrous for the living. However, there were other kinds of death considered shameful in Umuafor and in such cases, burial ceremonies were forbidden. Those who took their own lives were regarded as having committed *alu*, an abomination, and their bodies were thrown into the evil forests with no burial rites. Women who died during labour and those who died in the sacred months also suffered similar fates till the coming of the new religion with its revised versions of beliefs.

On the eight day, people were still coming and going, especially those who for one reason or the other could not make it within the seven days, and those from the deceased's kindred who were helping out in washing the pans and pots, clearing the debris, and sending back the chairs and tables from wherever they had been gathered from. The eight-day was also the circumcision and naming ceremony. Those who were blinded by superstitions surrounding twins still nursed fears that the twins would one day die mysteriously, and calamity would befall their family for harbouring them.

Chinua and Nne were to officiate at the ceremony. Nne had long embraced Reverend Klaus and his unseen God but was ready to perform any of her forsaken traditional rituals if that would save the lives of the twins. Chinua broke the kola-nut after addressing the attendants, and poured a wine libation to share the children's names with the ancestors. With a sharp razor, he beautified the tiny genital of the male child, a practice he very well knew how to perform. This was followed by the name giving and planting of a live *Ogilisi* tree to represent life and survival. The male child was named Ikenga – place of strength – after the horned deity that played a central role in the existence of the twelve clans of Umuafor while the female child was named Chinaza – God answereth. These names were carefully chosen to avert the death of the twins, as the people believed that the gods would not harm their own.

Tragedy however struck exactly three years later when the little Ikenga lost his mother and a brother during delivery. Till this day rumours have it that the gods were really unhappy with the family for harbouring the dreaded twins.

# Chapter 2

Umuafor easily embraced the new religion at a rather fast pace after the civil war and soon laid claim to a historical semblance with the biblical sons of Abraham. A sizeable number of her sons and daughters had been made fugitives and wanderers as a result of the conquest and defeat and a large number of these industrious people who had been engaged in travel and adventures even before the unholy war were soon literally being forced out of their homeland by poverty. Sprouting houses of worship worsened matters with such claims as that material poverty was a form of spiritual bondage or a curse and as such, many were no longer comfortable with the fact that a man could be poor, yet be a friend of his creator or relevant to the society. The alien culture of praises for wealth therefore, plunged many into blind adventures and those who stayed behind to manage with whatever resources they could lay their hands on, battled with the increasing influence of foreign cultures and seeds of retrogression planted by Umuafor's enemies.

The autonomous clans and kindreds that formed primary units of political authority had their respective elders and chief priests who ensured that *omenani* was adhered to. Their system of governance could be best described as theocratic with the central and divine authority being Chukwu, the Supreme Being, and other lesser deities that dealt with the day-to-day activities of mortals through their priests and priestesses. The absence of any religious house for the Supreme Being in the Umuafor ontology before the coming of Reverend Klaus was hinged on the belief of the Great Being being incomprehensibly huge in size and incredibly multidimensional that people could not even begin to contemplate putting up a structure for Him. Instead, they erected shrines for messenger deities and dots of semi-shrines for *ndi-ichie*, the ancestral spirits or personal gods. Sacrifices were regularly made to these lesser gods but Chukwu was conceived in the hearts of the people as the ultimate receiver of all the sacrifices made through

WOES OF IKENGA

the minor deities.

The young Ikenga who was widely believed to be the reincarnation of Udeaja, his grandfather, was being groomed for the great responsibility he would assume when he grew up. With all humility he had accepted to take over his grandfather's position as custodian of *ndi-ichie* family shrine and possibly the sacred *Ogwugwu* shrine of Umuafor, to serve as a liaison between his people and the spirit world.

Chukwuma, his father, had not treated the family's ancestral shrine with regard. His uneven life, he believed, had been full of ups and downs without any noticeable intervention or assistance from any spirit or *agwu*. Right from his teenage years, his double-edged *obejili* and the Russian-made riffle coupled with will power took credit for his life and survival. The quest to encounter the unseen had made him question myths and dare things deemed forbidden by the gods, but he never restrained members of his household from worshipping in any shrine of their preference.

Ikenga and his twin sister followed Nne to St Patrick's Mission where the headmaster quickly enrolled him to learn and assist in church services. His services in the new religion as an Altar boy however did little to diminish his faith in the gods and goddesses of his ancestors. Chinua had handed over the Udeaja family ancestral shrine to him in a mini ceremony when the secrets of the masquerade were revealed to him. Hence, while his sisters cleaned the compound, Ikenga ensured that the small corner where the family shrine was located was always neat as that was the only inheritance he had received from a grandfather he never knew. A man, who Chinua told him, had given his life that the little Ikenga might live.

The gods of Umuafor were not only believed to protect them from danger, but were also trusted to chastise anyone who committed atrocities or went against the principles of human existence. Before Reverend Klaus and his group came with their own doctrine of the Supreme Being, it was unthinkable that mortals could communicate directly with *Chukwu-Okike*, the God of creation, who ordered the theocratic universe. He was believed to have created lesser gods in his infinite goodness through which humans could reach him. The greatest among these gods according to Umuafor credence was the female deity *Ani*, the Mother Earth and goddess of moral and fertility, with her own codes of conduct known as *Nso-Ani*. Along with her husband *Amadioha*, the sky-god, the pair was believed to be the first to be created by Chukwu. While *Ani* was deemed gentle and compassionate in her judgment, *Amadioha,* who spoke through thunder, protected and enforced the law as the revered god of justice, and struck down anyone who committed *Nso-Ani* with deathly thunder or lightening. Bodies of his victims were left unburied or thrown into the evil forest and their properties confiscated by the priest or priestess of *Amadioha*.

Among other gods created by Chukwu were *Ekwensu*, the tempter god who had been given the authority to go against normal rules and conventional human and spirit behaviour. His greatest weapons, which were mostly sin, love for pleasure, and fear of the unknown, was deployed to net mortals in their daily life and whoever succumbed was counted as one of his doomed followers. He retained powers with which he ruled legions of *Agwu* otherwise known as contrary spirits or the chaotic forces of nature. His ways were evil, and his kingdom, though Umuafor had no means to confirm, was believed to be located in the deepest of the ocean and dark corners of the earth.

*Anyanwu*, the sun-god, together with his wife *Agbala*, lived far away from mortals but saw and reported human activities to Chukwu. Even as he gave light to both the righteous and evildoers alike, his purity and brightness were created as a perfect image of what humans should be.

Ikenga, the horned god, was created and endowed with unimaginable strength and purity. Well adored for his steadfastness and honour, he resided on an Iroko treetop from where he watched over anyone or community under his care. Umuafor held the god, Ikenga in very high esteem, for they believed that he was instrumental to their survival and victories, as their vicious enemies had not succeeded in wiping them off and taking over their lands.

Ikenga, a supernatural warrior, was believed to have come down to earth and made for himself a dwelling place on top of an Iroko tree from where he had fought and won uncountable battles alongside Umuafor and her clans. Shortly after erecting the first altar with the ancestral fathers of Umuafor, Ikenga, the god immortalised himself into a wooden totem depicting a well-developed two-horned human figure holding a sword at the right hand and a tusk at the left with a fierce expression.

*Agwu*, which is just below god or deity status, was used to refer to another unseen multitude of spirits created by Chukwu. Since they had no shrines or dwelling places, they constantly sought to occupy humans with vacuum and were also known to have no enemy or friend, a weak point that made it possible for *Ekwensu* to rule over them. On some occasions, *Agwu* served as the god of health and divination and had widely helped or confused humans in understanding superstitions surrounding wealth, poverty, fortune and misfortune. Other times, they struck at random when annoyed and caused their victims to indulge in petty stealing or waywardness that could eventually lead to death if the necessary sacrifice and cleansing were not performed.

Reverend Klaus referred to these legions as contrary spirits and even went further to pinpoint them whenever he spotted *Agwu* in humans. When hunger led any of his followers to steal tubers of yam from a neighbour's barn, the white Reverend blamed it on the spirit of stealing. If poverty pushed Umuafor virgins to succumb to pre-marital affairs with the consequent unwanted pregnancies, he cited the spirit of lust. Chinaza at her early age suffered from one sickness or the other. While Umuafor saw it as the consequences of keeping twins, the white Reverend boldly declared after a prayer session that the little girl was possessed of an ancestral spirit, which must be cast out. His followers had no choice but to draw a conclusion that *Agwu* must be in existence in the white man's land since their leader knew them by their names.

So many other gods and goddesses existed in those early days in Umuafor with their unique stories of origin and mission. Abnormal events or natural occurrences that Umuafor and the soothsayers could not explain were left to fate and to the gods with whom they were more comfortable with. This explained why they regretfully accepted defeat during the war and saw the advent of foreign religion and culture as a form of punishment from Chukwu for their transgressions.

\* \* \* \* \*

Losing their mother was a double blow to the twins. Not only did they have to put up with hunger at a very early age, everything Ikenga did was wrong in the sight of his wicked stepmother. Indeed, a slave boy is blamed no matter what he does: if he does not wash his hands, he will be accused of being dirty and if he washes his hands, he will be accused of wasting water.

Life was tough throughout his childhood. His father had fought in the civil war with a Russian made riffle through the jungles and the trenches, but he battled poverty and hunger with his bare hands on a daily basis. The poverty inculcation soldiers of those days had no exemption. Recruits comprised pregnant women, men, both old and young, and children with swollen cheeks and protruding bellies. Young boys and girls below the age of eight roamed around market-places and refuse dumps with their younger siblings strapped to their backs. These little girls were clearly used to having to bend down at intervals to adjust their baby siblings on their backs, and this showed in the way they retied the wrappers with practiced ease. Whatever decomposing edibles salvaged from market-places and refuse dumps were immediately used to quell their hunger without caring for what disease it could cause them. Boys also went in small groups into the forest to hunt for squirrels, lizards, mice and crickets, as these served as delicacies for the war-torn children of Umuafor.

Kids born during or after the war knew no other form of life apart from famine and hunger, and accepted their fate with all humility even if this denied them aspirations and creativity as they were all bent on solving the hunger problem which was paramount. Umuafor parents, who were not in any illusion about the reality that awaited these children named them accordingly. Therefore children born in that time went by such names as

*Aghaelinam*, war I implore you; *Ogudiegwu*, war is horrible; *Ndubuisi*, life first. These names were given to children mostly born in the farms and bushes where their parents had run to for safety. It was intended that the names and their implied meanings would see them through the deplorable conditions that Umuafor had been subjected to. Severe malnutrition left them with tiny arms and limbs scavenging through gutters and empty cans like vultures in search of any form of comestible, and some ill-fated ones met with their deaths once they stumbled over any unexploded ammunition. Although the warriors looked forward to a cease-fire, a unilateral cease-fire with hunger proved practically impossible.

Being a young boy without motherly care meant that Ikenga had no defence or trenches to run into when confronted with massive firepower in form of hunger as his stepmother only fed her daughters and left Ikenga and Chinaza to starve till whenever Nne returned from the market.

His struggles to survive turned him into an ambitious young boy and he soon began to view those who returned from Congo, Gabon, and Equatorial Guinea, and always carried their battery-powered radios permanently tuned to the unending BBC news as heroes. Before long, he started to believe that their lives would suit his future. From that early period of his life, Ikenga began to cultivate the ambition of travelling around the world like the heroes who went and returned in khaki suits, armed with new languages. As the son of an ex-militia, his father had raised him with iron fists, on the grounds that a piece of iron could only become what the blacksmith wanted it to be. Ikenga turned out to be a very brilliant boy who excelled through primary school, irrespective of the pleasures of childhood that had been denied him.

He regarded children who returned from school and still had

time to play with rotten wheels and worn out tyres as privileged kids as his routine was to go straight to the farm to help his father immediately after school. He woke up early every morning to fetch water from the stream and probably drop off a basket of yam or plantain at the market for Nne before running a few miles to school. Even with all those struggles, it was unacceptable for Ikenga at the end of the school term to not pass in the first, second or third positions.

He never forgot what happened to him after his common entrance examinations at the end of primary six, an event that marked the beginning of his breakaway from the uncountable gods and man-made statues of his ancestors. His father had almost roasted him alive for dropping down to seventeenth position among the sixty-two pupils that had sat for the highly valued common entrance examination. Ikenga had almost not returned to the house to confront his father when he received his report card, but running away from the house would mean a double offence.

Umuafor had come to realise the value and importance of education as the few available employments were only reserved for those with any form of education. Ronasko was one of the first foreign companies to be set up in Umuafor after the war to deal with the erosion menace, and create the much-needed employment opportunities, Chukwuma managed to secure a job with Ronasko, not because of his education but for his exposure and reputation during the war, and had been nicknamed Mayor by Mr Maya, a German engineer, because of his leadership skills.

Other illiterate parents who were mostly farmers struggled to send their children to school in order to secure an easier life for them. There was no pleasure at the time but these dedicated parents went hungry most times to squeeze out school fees for their children.

At dinnertime, Chukwuma remembered the common entrance examination as he waited for his meal.

"You have not shown me your results Ikenga." He said changing the mood dramatically as the little Ikenga, who had prayed that his father would forget to ask, suddenly started to shiver.

"Nne said she would show it to you," Ikenga managed to reply.

"Was she the one that sat for the examination?"

"No, Papa."

"Go and bring me the result certificate."

Nne who sensed that there was a problem hastily fastened her wrapper round her waist and followed Ikenga to collect his result sheet from his school bag. Chukwuma was sitting by the elevated pavement in the middle of the compound awaiting two sets of dinner from his two wives when Ikenga handed the result over to him and moved a few steps backwards in fear as his father pulled the smoky *mpanaka* closer to look at the result.

"So you now go to school to waste your time my son?" He queried. "You should have told me to give you your own portion of farmland." At this point Nne came closer and pleaded with her husband.

"The boy has not been well since few days now. That might have contributed to his poor performance."

"I did not call you here, woman," Chukwuma barked at her.

"You better go back to your hut and get my dinner."

"He is always among the first three," Nne reminded.

"But not this time."

"Pity the poor boy, my husband!"

"There is still enough farmland for him if he is no more interested in school."

Chukwuma was not ready to go through the marks to see how his son fared in the respective subjects but skimmed down to the spot where "17th" was boldly printed and concluded that it was a very poor performance for a son whose school fees he toiled day-after-day to pay.

Ikenga on the other hand, had been warming up for the usual cat and mouse race when his father suddenly sprang like a tiger and seized him before he could throw the third step.

"*Papa, bikoziooh!*" he had cried like a mouse caught in a crude trap but his father who would not heed his cries dragged him towards the back of the house where the goats and sheep were kept and fed, and with the palm fronds collected from the compost flogged Ikenga mercilessly all over his body.

Even his wicked stepmother had run out of her hut flanked by her daughters and was moved with pity for the poor Ikenga but dared not try to free him or she would get a good dose of the beating. Neighbours also knew the rule and none dared ask what was going on. It was only Nne, the childless first wife who mustered courage enough to grab Chukwuma from behind.

"Have mercy on the poor boy," she begged of him. "I have no child to call my own, give him to me instead of killing him."

"Stay out of this woman." Her husband shouted at her.

"Kill me as well!" Nne insisted.

Ozioma, the kind-hearted childless first wife was regarded as the mother of the family and Chukwuma would never lay hands on her. With an open and warm heart she treated children from other wives and those of the neighbours as if they were hers. This explained why they all called her Nne, mother of all.

"I brought him into this world. The children who took the first, second and third positions are not two-headed. I was not a failure in my own time, how can I waste my hard-earned money on a foolish son?" Chukwuma demanded.

"You cried your eyes out before Goodness gave you a male child and you have quickly forgotten that a one-eyed man is still indebted to blindness." Nne reminded him when the flogging would not stop.

Chukwuma loosened his grip and turned to Nne trying to digest what she had just said. The alert Ikenga seized the opportunity to free himself from his father's long and dried fingers, and ran off as fast as his legs could carry him, disappearing through the gate before his father could make a move to go after him.

"Let him go!" Chukwuma bragged, "I can do without him."

"You cannot do without him!" Nne angrily corrected. "Ikenga is the centre of your life and the way you beat that boy makes me afraid. He has run out of the house by this time of the night and you better go and bring him back."

"He will run back the way he ran out." Chukwuma shouted to Nne. "You better go back to your hut woman, and stop telling me how to train my son."

The women brought food to their husband and with their daughters retired to their various huts. After a long wait outside the compound under the *Udala* tree hoping that Ikenga would appear from the bush where he was probably hiding, Chinaza became very much afraid that the evil spirits that roamed around in the night might have harmed her brother. The wicked stepmother however, seemed happy with the turn of events and was having her wish gradually. Since she had not succeeded in giving her husband a son and all her daughters would be married off one day, the thought that a son from another woman would one day take over her husband's properties always made her bitter.

Polygamy was widely practiced by the men of Umuafor who cherished and saw large families and extensive helping hands as part of life. It was when education and the influx of the white man's culture began to have its way that the adverse effects of such practices were brought to light and the whole population began to change their orientation. Feeding of such large families was no longer easy as the young men in the family who normally helped in the farms now preferred to travel out of Umuafor in search of greener pastures. Women emancipation also made men have a rethink when evidence emerged that polygamy was capable of sending husbands to early graves.

It was past midnight, and Chukwuma expected that his son would show up after sometime or try to sneak in like a chameleon to Nne's hut as he always did every time his father gave up on their cat and mouse race. By the second cockcrow, he became really worried. He was quite sure that the boy had not come home because he had kept an open-eye throughout the night and had even taken his torchlight and combed the whole compound hoping that Ikenga had jumped in from one corner of the fence. He had also checked Nne's hut and found only Chinaza lying on the raffia mat. By daybreak, Ikenga was still nowhere to be found.

The gods would never forgive him: Nne would not also allow him return to the house without her son, and for two good days, Chukwuma ran helter-skelter in search of his son. Against all odds, he ran to Reverend Klaus and pleaded with him to consult his magic-box. He had avoided the white Jesus since the death of Ogochukwu, after he had preached to his followers against polygamy and the need for birth control during her burial ceremony.

Chukwuma as a typical Umuafor man saw his children as life insurance. The more children he had, the more his chances that some of them would triumph over hunger and diseases, and consequently the more secured he felt with regards to aging. Umuafor's social welfare scheme was rightfully phased in their pre-historic adage that says,"if your parents take care of you up until you grow teeth, you must take care of them when they lose theirs." It was totally absurd for a stranger from a faraway land to intrude on what he knew nothing about, a tradition that their ancestors had practiced for ages. For the sake of his only son, he had swept those grudges under the carpet and walked into the St Patrick's Mission premises.

Reverend Klaus listened patiently as his august visitor narrated the story of his missing son.

"… He ran out of the house that very night and nobody has seen him since then," Chukwuma concluded with a rather broken voice.

"Why did you stress yourself to visit your enemy to consult his God?" Reverend Klaus teased. "*Ndi-ichie* will be angry with you and your actions."

"I have never believed you or any motionless statue called gods," Chukwuma confessed. "But whoever provides my son will not only have a male cow, but my loyalty as well."

"You can as well sit back at home," the Reverend returned. "My God has no need for a cow."

"The lad is the only heir to the Udeaja family," Chukwuma implored. "Life will lose its value for me if I lose him."

WOES OF IKENGA

"You should have taken your petition to the Chief Priest of *Ogwugwu*," the Reverend maintained.

"When a frog decides to leave the swamp for the mountains, it means that its life is in grave danger," Chukwuma answered without hesitation.

The devout Reverend who had just finished his evening prayers absent-mindedly arranged his prayer books giving the impression that Chukwuma's preference to his God or magic box instead of *Ogwugwu* seemed not to have moved him. The old gentleman handled everyone as his spirit directed with no special regards for his followers or non-followers. Without further conversation, he walked into the tiny bamboo kitchen attached to the living room while his guest patiently waited for him to bring out his magic box and commence consultation. Instead, the skinny Reverend reappeared with two jumbo size cups of steaming black tea.

"Oh! This is not the time to present kola-nut," Chukwuma objected. "A man whose house is on fire doesn't go about chasing mice."

"Calm down, Mayor!" the Reverend beckoned him. "God has brought you here for a purpose."

"Hold it there!" Chukwuma who was gradually losing his patience replied him. "I came to you on my own and not by the order of any Spirit or *Agwu*."

"Tradition demands that we pray over and partake of the kola-nut that I have offered you."

"Is that my tradition or the white man's tradition?" Chukwuma demanded.

"Both traditions," the Reverend replied.

"Thank you for the kola," Chukwuma said to him. "The yam ban is sold off when one encounters that which is greater than the farm."

"All your worries will be over only if you believe," Reverend Klaus preached.

"I believe," Chukwuma replied immediately thinking that the

39

white Reverend was seeking for a deal.

"Worry no more, for the Lord has taken over your burden!" Reverend Klaus replied, still not bothered by his visitor's anxiety. "Your son is well."

Chukwuma stared at the Reverend for a few seconds in confusion. That was what he did not understand about the man; how could the white Jesus so calmly tell him to go back to his house and rest as if the missing boy was having siesta in the next room?

"Ikenga is my only son," Chukwuma reminded as if to convince the Reverend.

"I am aware of that."

"And I should worry no more you mean?"

"My God is about to bring you closer to Him."

"Tell him to hold on till I find my son," Chukwuma retorted already on his feet.

He left Reverend Klaus furious and disappointed. Regretting going to the white Jesus for solution, he staggered out of the mission's compound to the major road where he stood gazing like a ghost that had lost its way back to the graveyard. From his goatskin bag, he produced a long chewing stick, stuck it into his mouth, and headed for *Ogwugwu* shrine, to at least inform them that one of theirs had gone missing.

Ikenga ran through the darkness along the tiny pathways to the house of the village headmaster who was also an extended relative and a good friend of his father's, forgetting to be afraid of the evil spirits that had taken hold of the community since the war ended. The spirits of those who had died during the brutal civil war or those who had suddenly lost their lives and were not given a proper burial were widely believed to be hanging around market places and crossroads at night because they had nowhere to call a resting place.

Ugodi, the headmaster's wife and her children were already asleep while her husband tried to finish up some paper work when he heard someone bang repeatedly on the zinc sheet that served as the compound gate.

"Come in!" He ordered, only to see Ikenga push the zinc sheet and sneak in swiftly like one who had suddenly realised that the spirits of the dead were about to get hold of him.

"My goodness!" the headmaster exclaimed as Ikenga crept closer to his working table. "What have you done? Why did your father do this to you?" he asked in disbelief. There was no question about who was responsible for inflicting those wounds. No human being born of a woman would dare touch Ikenga or any other member of the Udeaja family while Chukwuma was alive without paying with his or her own life.

"Because my result was bad," Ikenga replied still panting.

"No! He got it wrong. You came seventeenth, am I right?" he asked Ikenga.

"Yes, but my father said it's very bad."

Mr. Ubanese quickly put the files away, and took a bucket of water to the makeshift bathroom at the extreme of the compound for his guest. The cane marks became visible all over Ikenga's body by the time he came out of the bathroom with his blood stained T-shirt. Pitifully, the headmaster offered him the food his wife had served before going to bed but the poor boy already lost his appetite right from the very minute he collected his result certificate.

He took Ikenga to his bedroom and spread a rugged raffia mat on the floor for him to sleep on.

"People never value what they have until they lose it," he muttered as he applied locally made palm kernel lotion all over Ikenga's body. For the deep cuts that Ikenga sustained on his right foot, he used the most effective traditional method of dealing with such wounds and prevention of bacterial infection. He roasted a kitchen knife over the *mpanaka* and with a few drops of palm oil on the hot piece of metal, pressed it on the open wound while holding firm Ikenga's right leg. The loud scream from the young lad sent Ugodi out of her bed and she quickly rushed in with a piece of cloth over her chest to her husband's hut to see what was amiss.

"That will stop the bleeding," the headmaster explained to

Ikenga. "You can lie down and sleep, tomorrow we continue."

It was no longer news, the kind of heavy-handed treatment that Chukwuma meted out on the young boy. The headmaster then decided to teach his friend a little lesson and kept the news about his august visitor to himself, his wife and his trusted confidant, Reverend Klaus. The wife ensured that the lad was well fed and rubbed his wounds with palm kernel lotion every morning and evening.

By the second day Ikenga became nervous and restless as the traditional and emotional bond between father and son made him very uncomfortable. He had missed Nne and Chinaza enough and despite the occasional marathon flogging from his father, Ikenga at his young age knew that his father meant well for him. His mother had been dead for twelve years now and his father had proven to be a caring father. Irrespective of his stepmother's cruelty, he made sure his children were well fed even if he had to forfeit his own food and no one pointed a false finger on any member of his family and got away with it.

Ikenga grew up full of strength and with well cultivated morals. He was allowed into the community of elders after taking the *Ozo* title at the age of seven. If a child properly washes his hand, he can dine with elders. The final introduction ceremony into the masquerade cult had taken place shortly before the *Ozo* ceremony and from that age, his presence as mouthpiece of the gods had become vital whenever a consultation or sacrifice was being performed. He was also entitled to carry *akpa-agwu*, the mystic handbag every time they went to a faraway land for divination.

Conscious of his role in the family and society, Ikenga dutifully told the headmaster that he wanted to go home. The caring headmaster did not object but quickly put on his white singlet, filled up the rusty radiator of his car with water and drove with Ikenga to St Patrick's Mission where Reverend Klaus joined them as they headed for Chukwuma's compound.

Again the desire to travel abroad burned as he sat in front of the Mercedes Benz car that had been sent to the headmaster by his son Ogbonnia who had left for Germany to study medicine. The car had come barely six months after Ogbonnia's departure and surprisingly it was only Reverend Klaus who had questioned how the young man could so quickly afford a car. The Reverend had known the headmaster and his family ever since he settled in Umuafor and had renamed Ogbonnia the first son of the headmaster, Raymond, during baptism where he had stood as both the officiating minister of the christening and godfather of the young boy. He had also maintained a warm relationship with the brilliant Raymond Ubanese and had been instrumental to his overseas studies.

The locals could not help but conclude that the Reverend had indeed lost touch with the realities of his own part of the world when he voiced his worries about what Raymond was up to in Germany. From what the local folks of Umuafor understood of the white man's world, cars were randomly abandoned on street corners for whoever was interested and afterwards collected and disposed off as waste when no one indicated interest. Ikenga dreamt of sending this type of car down to his father one day and possibly another beautiful one to Nne.

"When is Ogbonnia coming back?" He asked, admiring the shiny dashboard of the Mercedes Benz car.

"Not so soon my son." The headmaster replied. "He has to finish his education before coming back."

"Is he going to marry a white woman?"

"Impossible," the headmaster objected. "I went with him to our in-laws together with some members of our kindred to pay for his wife's dowry. Your father was also there. He cannot afford to fail us all."

"I would like to travel overseas one day." Ikenga revealed looking straight into the headmaster's eyes. "Can you help me talk to my father?"

"That will be no problem," the headmaster assured him. "But you have to finish your college education first so that you don't end up in the white man's kitchen as a dish washer."

"The white men already have enough machines to wash their dishes," Reverend Klaus threw in casually from behind.

"You see what I mean, my son?" the headmaster said, minding the steering while reading the reaction of the smart young boy sitting right next to him.

"You can be used as common toilet cleaner if you don't have anything in your brain."

Ikenga pulled himself together counting his teeth with his tongue. "The white man's country cannot be that bad," he reasoned to himself. "Those people are closer to God. The headmaster has not been there and the white Jesus for whatever foolish reasons abandoned milk and honey for palm kernel. Ogbonnia has spent less than a year in Germany and even a blind man can see the evidence of good living that is gradually creeping into his family back home. The Ubanese family now owns a coloured television and his father, the Headmaster, who never dreamt of such pleasures, is now a proud owner of a Mercedes Benz car. So what has the Reverend got to tell me? A toilet cleaner in a white man's world is a rich man or better still, I will move around and collect cars and bicycles that have been abandoned by their owners if the white man thinks that there is nothing in my brain."

What a young man cannot see standing atop an iroko tree, the experienced aged fellow already observes squatting in a corner. Ikenga was still engulfed in his fantasies when the white Mercedes Benz pulled up under the *Udala* tree. Everyone rushed out from the compound at the sound of the car engine to see if whoever it was had any clues about the missing lad. There was spontaneous jubilation from friends and relatives who had come to console the family as soon as they saw the occupants of the car. Chukwuma who had been turned into a wanderer also heard of his son's return and rushed back to the house to have a good time with the headmaster and Reverend Klaus under the assumption that the white Jesus had consulted the magic box in his absence to locate his son.

"Greet your God for me," Chukwuma cheerfully told the Reverend as the men stood to leave. "Since you have rejected my cow offering on His behalf."

The whole jubilation took another dimension when the *Ogwugwu* Chief Priest walked into the compound later in the evening. He had also heard of the boy's reappearance and had come to take credit and possibly demand for a sacrifice in appreciation. All other well-wishers had returned to their homes except for Uzuaku who stayed behind to rejoice with Nne. She very well knew the pain of not having a child or having one and losing it. Her husband had been listed as missing in action during the civil war and their only son who had left for Gabon in search of a better life had not sent word for years. All efforts to find her husband to at least give the dead a final resting place had yielded no results and the woman in her old age had been left to mourn the dead whose spirits regularly haunted her.

Ikenga's disappearance had refreshed those wounds, and both women shared their joys and sorrows the whole evening. They were now seated by the hut's pavement with Chinaza who was helping to sort out ripe tomatoes and some vegetables for sale at the next day's market.

With his usual oversize multi-coloured gown, the one-eyed *Ogwugwu* Chief Priest shook rigorously his long traditional religious staff, a long pointed piece of metal decorated with locally made jingles and bells. From outside the compound, he walked in backwards through the gate. His wrists and ankles were painted with white and black clay and a red rag was tied around his head, and one of his eyes with which he claimed to see tomorrow circled with a thick black substance. He stuck his jingled staff at the centre of the big compound and began to walk round the huts reciting strange incantations. The women bowed their heads in silence when the dreadful looking emissary of the gods walked past them. When he got to Udeaja's tomb, he stood for a while and lamented before bringing out another red rag to tie around the *ofor* tree planted by the graveside.

He insisted that the gods had rescued the young lad from the hands of the white wizard, and that the ancestors must be appeased, and charged the spirit of late Udeaja to dispute him if he was telling lies. Graciously he took a tour of the compound, warding off evil spirits as he swung his hands over the air. In front of Nne's hut he made a sudden stop, ran back to pull his religious staff where he had stuck it and pointed it to Uzuaku as he came back.

"The gods are not happy with you, woman," he shouted. "A son has been left to rot in a faraway land."

At the mention of "a son," Uzuaku collapsed with her face to the ground and cried aloud for having unknowingly offended the gods. The wretched and lonely woman had gone through several nightmares and was ready to dance to the tune of anyone that would help her set her eyes on her only son again. She had long waited for God's time as Reverend Klaus always preached but even time was no longer on her side.

The one-eyed messenger from the gods seemed to have the solution as he had been appointed mouthpiece of the gods and custodian of *Ogwugwu* shrine until when Ikenga would grow up to become an adult. He had lost an eye in a mysterious encounter when he had gone in a group with the village *Ogba-agu*, the dreaded night masquerade, to avenge a purported witch-hunt from a neighbouring town. The group had suffered heavy humiliation even with all their charms and talisman but the frightening aspect was that the right eye of the masquerade bearer had completely gone off, leaving a deep hole when the costumes were removed. To the astonishment of the group, he claimed that the gods had plucked off the eye and stored for the future, to enable him predict events and overcome the knowledge of action and reaction preceding "had I known." He boasted that the ultimate knowledge of calculation reserved for the spirit beings to predict the beginning or end of an era was also in his wisdom bag. With such perceived supernatural abilities, he had taken over the staff of authority when Chinua's health condition had taken a drastic nosedive and had since been running *Ogwugwu* shrine as it pleased him.

"You drove away a free-born out of your wickedness," he continued to shout. "The gods have not gone asleep."

"He insisted on leaving," Uzuaku managed to reply through tears.

"Where is the wife we got for him?"

"She went back to her family with my grandson."

"The spirit of your late husband is not at rest," he shouted louder on her. "You drove his son and grandson away and pretend as if all is well."

"All is not well!" Uzuaku pleaded still faced to the ground. "Please help me, great one, my life is useless."

"A curse has been placed on the whole family." The chief priest declared: "You will not set your eyes on them till the yoke is broken."

At this point, Nne also went down on her knees to intercede on her friend's behalf as she felt that the judgment was too harsh for an old woman who had been wrongly deprived of her husband, a son and grandson. Her pain of barrenness was lighter to handle than the agony of her friend who had all but could not boast of any.

*   *   *   *   *

The new religion was no more in its infant stage but believers paddled between it and their traditional beliefs when confronted with fear. There were powerful oracles and deities capable of censuring humans in those days and their verdicts had been deemed upright until evil men began to influence them. Besides, when one's hands are soiled he begins to experience fear and anyone whose personal *chi* is held captive by fear would secretly begin to indulge in an endless search for non-existent problems or one they might have brought upon themselves thereby running from one shrine to the other. *Ekwensu* the tempter god, on discovering this weakness in mortals steadily unleashed his vital weapon of fear to deceive and drag many into the mud.

With the assurance of a steady forgiveness from a loving

heavenly Father whenever one went astray as the white Reverend preached, it became a common occurrence for converts to seek solutions through *omenani*, the traditional way, whenever they ran out of patience for God's time. Little wonder, the first indigenous *Ukochukwu* of Amanze, when found guilty by the white man's court for patronising soothsayers maintained that one does not go about selecting who helps him put out the fire when his yam barn is ablaze.

"Our ancestors will bring them back as they brought back Ikenga," the Chief Priest assured. "I can see the young man searching for his way home."

Then he changed the direction of the jingling staff and pointed it towards the sky. The atmosphere was charged and the vibration from the tiny bells and jingles echoed his words.

"His way back is blurred like the clouds," he repeated again and again. "*Ogwugwu* my ears are open. It is he who owns the corpse that carries it by the head. Your son is languishing in the wilderness. We all agree that a bush trap may mistakenly catch *Ozodimgba*, the gorilla, but *Ozodimgba* will eventually go. Heaven has fallen over your daughter and her entire family. Whatever you tell me is what I will convey to the people."

The uninterrupted loud conversation with the spirits was followed by a dead silence. All the family members remained motionless including *Eke-uke* who ran out from its cage to witness the frightening showdown.

"Get a white he-goat and two trays of tobacco ready for sacrifice," the one-eyed seer instructed.

With those last instructions, the chief priest headed for the gate, and exited the compound with his back without saying another word to anybody.

It was not long before Uzuaku got the requirements together, eager to set her entire family free from any unknown or inherited bondage. Ikenga accompanied her to the shrine, as his presence would ultimately be needed. Before they set out to *Ogwugwu* shrine, Uzuaku made Nne promise that no other member of the St

Patrick's women group would hear of their adventure.

*Ogwugwu* shrine was the most sacred in Umuafor. Beautifully constructed and situated off the village centre by the early ancestors of Umuafor, its thick mud walls and heavy wooden doors were decorated with paintings and carvings of wild animals and other strange creatures. The exquisite appearance was made more awesome by magnificent sacred trees like *akpu, ofor* and *inyi* that overshadowed the compound, while animal skulls and other traditional injunctions made of palm fronds and foul-smelling concoctions were used to keep intruders away from the dreadful shrine. Lesser deities who were quickly swallowed by the new religion were brought to Umuafor to seek refuge at the *Ogwugwu* shrine. A giant *Ekwe,* the slit wooden drum carved out of an Iroko tree, used for communication, stood outside the shrine while the interior was made up of strange objects and deities of different forms.

The compound was bustling with activities when Ikenga walked in with Uzuaku dragging an unwilling white he-goat behind her. They were informed that the one-eyed seer was attending to other guests in his inner chamber as one of the shrine's errand men collected the he-goat from the woman to tie to the *ogilisi* tree and offered them a seat in the waiting room. Some of the rituals were not new to Ikenga who would soon be running the affairs of the gods. He took a piece of white clay from the wooden tray, drew four vertical parallel lines on the ground marking the four market days in Umuafor and poured for himself a cup of palm wine from the wine jar. Uzuaku's youngest brother who had come with them also drank two cups but his sister was not in the mood to take anything till her burden was lifted. *Ogwugwu* did not advocate fasting or exclusion of women from partaking in palm wine but Uzuaku had chosen to tread carefully whenever it concerned her rejected *omenani.* The fowl advised her chicks as a precautionary measure to watchfully look up every time they drank because from up comes their death.

It did not take long before the guests walked out in a single file from the inner chamber. The chief priest followed after them with a string of cowry shells in his hands indicating that he had just finished consultation with the spirit world. He greeted the new arrivals with a more relaxed tone, instructed the servants to get things ready for a special sacrifice, and took some time to take few cups of wine before motioning the next group into his chamber. When they were seated, he asked Uzuaku to knock at the door, a modern day consultation fee aimed at getting uninterrupted attention from the gods, and her brother produced some local currency notes from his pocket and dropped them inside an empty tortoise-shell. The chief priest rang the local jingle, sounded the gong and hit most of the totems and objects with what seemed like a wooden gun, and then threw the long string of cowry shells to the ground when he sensed that the gods were at alert.

"Am I hearing you right, *Ogwugwu?*" he asked calmly as if the oracle was right before him in a human form. The guests also sharpened their ears to hear a spirit reply.

"Speak again to my hearing." The chief priest picked up the string and repeated the consultation with a clear appeal to an invisible spirit before him. "They want to partake of the foreign currency," he barked at Uzuaku pointing at an old piece of leather attached to the string. "The gods demand the fattest part of the sacrifice."

"I have not set my hands on a coin from abroad," the woman swore.

He threw the string again and again and counted, making occasional gestures at a heap of blood stained fowl feathers in the centre of the shrine.

"*Ogwugwu* deals without mercy to those who come before him to tell lies," he reminded.

"The gods should know better," Ikenga threw in. "We are mere mortals."

"The gods know better indeed," the chief priest echoed. "They know that Uzuaku brought calamity upon her entire family by forsaking her tradition to run after a foreign religion. When you lose on the drumbeat of the gods, you lose on the rhythm of life. Be wise, woman."

"I have acknowledged my transgressions, great one," Uzuaku accepted with fear. "Intercede on my behalf and I will throw a great feast to the gods."

The one-eyed seer spent some more time throwing the string and counting the beads. He made some twisting body movements occasionally and invoked or showered praises to a number of other unseen beings and ancestral spirits.

"Swearing to one god in the shrine of another is equally a deplorable offence," he warned. "Be sure to redeem your vows when your petitions are met. Your son is on his way back, no one teaches the paths of the forest to an old gorilla."

He ordered that the he-goat be brought in and two of his men held it down before the shrine while he slit its throat with a well sharpened knife. The poor animal gave up the ghost after a short struggle. Its gushing warm blood was collected with a bowl and Uzuaku with her brother, were instructed to wash their hands in the bowl on behalf of their entire family. The poor animal had been made to put down its own burden to bear the sins of humans. Its lifeless body was buried in the compound and the sacrifice sealed up with light refreshment.

Ikenga watched the whole ritual with a degree of skepticism, especially since after the gods had claimed credit for rescuing him from the hands of Reverend Klaus. He was also taken aback when the chief priest ordered the shrine keepers to unearth the he-goat as soon as Uzuaku and her brother left the shrine. He did not know what to make of the man who had just declared before the deities and his guests that the sacrificial he-goat must be buried whole. Because he was young and inexperienced to question the god's initiatives and the authority of the one eyed seer, he complied with shrine keepers as they prepared delicious yam porridge with the god-sent meat by the orders of their emissary.

It seemed that the gods had become impotent, as they now allowed humans manipulate and dictate judgment for them. That was how the famous Ibini Ukpabi, which once served as the highest court in the land lost its credibility and powers. Not only did it remain silent when the long-nosed white men disrespectfully christened him Long Juju, it also maintained a blind eye when its greedy priests sold men of their kind into slavery. The deity was long known for handling cases of land ownership, murder and witchcraft. However, its emissaries developed preference for selling the losing party into slavery instead of the normal punishments or sentences of property confiscation or banishment. The practice was believed to have lingered on and on while those unworthy mouthpiece distorted judgments in order to procure enough of their fellow men and women to be sold to white merchants. Many who visited the shrine during the slave trade era never made it back and their families dared not to ask what had become of their relatives.

The human-influenced way of sacrifice and divination in *Ogwugwu* shrine was not like that of the days of his grandfathers. Ikenga really had no interest in making a living from poor helpless folks. Chukwuma, his father, always told him that any man who does not end up better than his ancestors is a disgrace to his generation. Thus, he would rather abandon his people with their gods and look for his destiny in a faraway land.

# Chapter 3

Umuafor and her twelve clans were rural dwellers; mostly farmers and fishermen blessed with abundant vegetation and fertile lands. They are also best known for exploration with their nature endowed ability to survive the harshest of conditions and circumstances. While they seemed backward and unsophisticated from a distance, other tribes who happened to have come in contact with them testified that they were a people blessed with wisdom and unique adaptation techniques. The average Umuafor indigene could easily make something out of nothing and en masse they had turned a desert into a vegetative habitation. The traditional Umuafor society was a loving, selfless, and well-structured community with chains of overlapping kin groups known for their unquestionable loyalty to the noble heads of their respective kindred.

Tradition placed women as the organisers of the family. They did a tremendous amount of work in tending the house, rearing animals, raising children, weaving baskets and in some cases nursing the elderly. The men managed the farms and socialised with other men. In order to properly master these social roles, even from infancy, boys began hanging around the father's side while girls helped their mothers with house chores.

Hospitality was also a very important feature of the ancient Umuafor culture. Their generosity compelled them to always assume that a guest was tired, cold and hungry, and to act accordingly. Hence, a visitor would be warmly presented with kola-nut and invited to partake in the meal by a host friend or family.

Chukwuma had proven to be a man. By combining the meagre income from the Ronasko Company with proceeds from his subsistence farming activities, he was able to see all his children through primary school. Moreover, he had raised them to have a decent sense of morality. Although his burdens had been greatly reduced after his three older daughters were given into marriage, Ikenga who had been privileged to attend college in a neighbouring town had eventually dropped out of school as the fees kept increasing. It had been one rare opportunity that Reverend Klaus had secured for him before death snatched the white Jesus away. But with the little exposure he had gathered from the boarding school and English language skills that he still grappled with, Ikenga left the college a more experienced young man. His father was very proud of him and nursed the belief that his only son would one day relieve him of his duties as head of the family when he might have found his place in life.

Ronasko was in its final stages of operations and would be leaving Umuafor as soon as their contract expired. This was bound to cause gross unemployment in Umuafor and its environs. The ancestors had survived on farming but that option clearly offered no future for young men in recent times as farmlands had lost their fertility and mechanised farming seemed to be the only option if it was affordable.

At nineteen, Ikenga was faced with no other option than to follow his mates to town. A friend took him to Port Harcourt where he secured a job in a foreign fishing company and although the salary was a meagre one, they were offered a makeshift accommodation in the company premises, and life in the city of Port Harcourt became his first step to freedom where he could freely act like his mates. The twenty-four hour "earn-as-you-work" labour force comprised mostly of members of different indigenous communities who were taught basic skills like deep-water diving and navigation. Ikenga soon made a name for himself with his strong physique, ability to easily pick up languages, and most importantly, his self-acclaimed knowledge of virtually everything. When admiration from the Lebanese managers brought about vicious envy from his co-workers, he was forced to rent a room apartment for himself in town. The management was also quick to identify the threat and drafted the young devoted worker to night operations.

The elite team made up of mostly workers from Lebanon sailed in groups into the open sea with fishing vessels every evening and returned early in the morning with their catch. This was not only a big relief for the already frightened Ikenga who by now was used to being on his way home before his ex-shift mates arrived in the morning to commence off-loading and processing, but also offered him ample opportunity to hang around the big city during the day when he was not needed at work. He was also quick to make friends with foreigners and his countrymen alike, and from the stories told by his Lebanese colleagues about happenings in their part of the world learned that places like Damascus, Jerusalem, and Philippe, which Reverend Klaus often cited from his Holy Book were not heavenly cities.

"I never knew that countries like yours existed on earth," Ikenga revealed to a Lebanese co-worker as they walked home.

"How can you know if you have never stepped out of your jungle?" his colleague teased.

"I learnt of it through the white man's Holy Book."

"We exist just like you."

"What of the town called Nazareth?" Ikenga asked.

"I worked as a waiter in Nazareth before I got this job."

"So there are restaurants in Nazareth?"

"Sure."

"And beer parlours?"

"Yes, just like in other towns and cities."

"You mean they also have prostitutes like we have here in Port Harcourt?"

"Of course there are brothels and prostitutes even in Jerusalem."

Ikenga halted his curiosity. He did not believe his friend and felt uncomfortable about hearing further blasphemous allegations about a city that Umuafor converts regarded as holy. Numerous songs by women groups upheld the notion of a paradise-like city where there was neither sin nor sorrow.

"That cannot be true," he reasoned. The Lebanese who professed another faith might be trying to pull him over.

Ikenga however maintained a warm relationship with his

foreign colleagues. Their weekends were spent in their best dresses in city centres and bars sniffing for better opportunities or money yielding contacts from white men. Although his salary was barely enough to pay his rent and sustain himself, he managed to squeeze and send a little money every now and then to support his father. Chinaza, unaware of those occasional goodies advised in one of her letters that he return to the village if the city was not profitable. But his persistence to explore his destiny far away from the village soon began to pay off and it did not take long before he realised that stories he had always heard about strange transactions going on in Port Harcourt were not superstitions; some white merchants were actually ready to pay good money for wooden idols and masks.

He concealed his excitement and tried to gather as much information as he could through the assistance of a good friend and fellow worker. That meant that his ancestors had indeed laid up treasures for him. Whatever the white men wanted to do with the old wooden objects was solely their own cup of tea. Besides, people would blame the dead for not stealing water from a fountain if he eventually died of thirst.

*   *   *   *   *

When he collected his fifth salary, Ikenga took an emergency sick leave, bought presents for Nne and Chinaza, and of course a bottle of foreign Schnapps for his father, and set off for the village. There was even an extra assurance from his contact who acted as middleman between him and the white merchants that if the items were over a hundred years old as he claimed, their hard times would cease to be. Thus, he went about consumed with fantasies of how he would prudently use the money when it eventually got into his hands; he would raze the dotted huts in his father's compound to the ground; erect a befitting *obi* for his father; build brick houses for Nne and his wicked stepmother; and still have enough to buy modern equipment like ploughs and harvesters which would enable him go into full-time mechanised farming.

Ikenga was in high spirits when he got off the motorbike that transported him from Afor Motor-Park to his father's compound. His family members warmly welcomed him and he handed out gifts of biscuits and loaves of bread to children from the neighbouring families who had come around to welcome the big uncle from Port Harcourt.

"I want to go with you to Port Harcourt," one of the smart young boys replied as his reason for rejecting the biscuit offered to him.

"You will come with me when you finish your primary school education," Ikenga promised.

"I have finished school."

"No, you have not," Ikenga objected.

"You can ask my sister," the young boy insisted pointing at his much younger and shy-looking sister.

"How old are you?" Ikenga asked him.

"I am eleven years old," the boy replied.

"Have you finished primary six?"

"I stopped in primary four."

"Why did you stop?"

"My father said that he has no money."

As one who had been to town and now knew the immense value of education, he felt pity for himself and all other children of Umuafor who had been denied a chance of acquiring basic education because of poverty.

"I will tell your father to send you back to school," he said to the boy.

"Will you pay my school fees?" the boy asked with a suddenly brightened face.

"Yes," Ikenga accepted.

"Thank you, Brother," the little boy said repeatedly before running off to tell his father that the big brother from Port Harcourt had accepted to pay his school fees.

Without wasting time, Ikenga set out on his mission the next day. His grandfather's *obi* had once housed some of the treasures but his father who was uncomfortable with the aged statues had gathered and sent them all to *Ogwugwu* shrine when Ikenga left for town. Chukwuma had also sold off the two sacred cows that the old man had reared, as there was no one to graze them. The dusty wooden objects which Ikenga had slept with for years since he occupied his grandfather's hut had never seemed to be of any material value until he went to Port Harcourt. His simple explanation to his family that he was going to meet a friend from the city and may return late had been enough to put the household at rest. Ikenga took a rather distant road that evening when darkness was about to set in the village to ward off any suspicions or speculations. The heavy clouds and scattered showers of rain had also done well to send people to their houses earlier than usual, with those returning late from the farm in a haste to escape the impending downpour, hence paying less attention to whoever walked past them.

He set off down the dirt-path, meandering first through the palm trees, next the village square, and then fields of cassava and maize before turning onto a narrow, shoulder-width path that took him through high grasses and crops and straight to *Ogwugwu* shrine. Whenever he felt that the pathways were rather deserted, he doubled his pace but observed occasional stops in silence, to ensure that exceptional noises and movements were only sounds from the whirlwind or nocturnal birds and rodents. The large *Ogwugwu* compound had also wound down in silence as Ikenga leapt up from a selected corner of the high-walled fence. The kerosene lantern burning in one of the huts belonged to the shrine keepers, and their movement indicated that they were doing some cleaning or preparing things for the activities of the next day and would be going to bed soon.

He knew his way around the shrine as he did his father's compound and knew that he needed not worry about the one eyed seer who was sure to have sneaked out to spend the night with one of his indoctrinated defenceless widows. The sky gave in when it could no longer withhold the heavy clouds and the rain poured mercilessly on the patient Ikenga who was overjoyed that the abundant treasures he was about to cash in on were just a distance from him. Gently, he dropped down like a big cat when he was sure that everyone had retired to his or her bed and tiptoed towards the secret entrance. His steps were frozen by few bleats from a ram that he had failed to dictate in the darkness but the bleats seemed to have not attracted any reaction from the shrine keepers and he managed to make it to the door. Quickly, he unfastened the knot, pulled the metal sheet to the ground, and while being careful not to slip due to his wet clothes, mounted the edge of the metal sheets, and crept into the one-meter square secret entrance leading to the inner chamber.

In the total darkness, he moved his arms around to navigate the tightly stuffed round chamber and selected four medium-sized statues. His selections were made so that suspicions would not be easily aroused as most of the idols in the inner chamber had been handed over by families or converts who were no longer interested in what they now regarded as "man-made-gods," plus the ones rescued from the crusade of Reverend Klaus and his followers. The *Ogwugwu* shrine located in Umuafor till today remains an abandoned house of the gods with only a handful of worshippers. Its devotees and deserters believe that the deity devastated the surrounding towns and villages with landslide and erosions as an act of revenge for their neglect. The desperate Ikenga was not totally ignorant of the perceived diminishing potency of the idols, but he upheld the notion that any idol, which possessed enough magical powers could escape from the white merchants after he may have collected his money and make its way back to where it belonged.

The way back was faster and shorter since there was no need to take a longer route. He slipped in unnoticed into the compound, stashed his loot under the spring bed and spent the rest of the night on the bed gazing into the darkness and recounting his steps. There was enough time to plan for his trip back to the city and how he would make good use of the money that was sure to come.

His heart boiled with the thoughts of uncountable wooden gods still scattered around Umuafor and the unchecked activities of many priests and priestesses. Some invoked spirits to kill unjustly when self-interest was at stake and would later come around with humans to mourn their deceased victims. Those entrusted with the sacred *Igu-Mmiri,* the Rain Stone, deliberately sent down rain whenever there was a feast if they were not properly consulted and appeased. Uzuaku, the poor widow who he had witnessed one among her litany of sacrifices, was yet to set her eyes on her only son. These injustices were beginning to eat into his bone, especially now that he had grown to understand what would have become of he and Chinaza if the coming of the new religion had been delayed. A bad habit that lasts more than a year may turn into a custom if he failed to act quickly.

As worrisome as the matter was, Ikenga understood that one needed a strong beak before going into a fight with a woodpecker. In a way of appreciation to Reverend Klaus and the new religion, he swore to secretly transport and dispose of the wooden gods in Port Harcourt for as long as the white merchants were willing to have them.

Suddenly there was a knock on the door. It was Chinaza who had taken over Nneamaka's morning ritual; knocking to inform her brother that water was waiting at their father's *obi.* Ikenga sat up hurriedly, threw his wrapper around his waist and shoulder, and spared a few moments to make sure that his wooden captives had not escaped before heading for his father's *obi.*

"I don't know when you came back last night," his father stated as Ikenga greeted.

"It was a bit late, Papa," he replied. "I had to wait long for the rain to subside."

"A heavy downpour indeed! Did you meet the friend you went to see?"

"Sure, he was insisting I spend the night."

"Everyone will insist that you sleep over because you came back from the city," Chukwuma remarked. "I don't need to tell you that Umuafor today is no longer the Umuafor of yesterday. Be careful with whom you eat and drink."

Chukwuma was genuinely concerned about the wickedness and jealousy that had almost overtaken Umuafor even as everyone was fast abandoning *omenani* for the white man's form of worship.

"I have not acquired any gold or diamond, Papa," Ikenga told his father. "Why should anybody harm me?"

"Living in the city could be a source of envy," his father told him.

"Has Chukwu-ma-onye-uka the son of Udeaja grown too old and weak that people can now dream of harming his son?" Ikenga asked.

"Nobody dares me!" Chukwuma replied. "But they might get you if your spirit is weak."

"Don't worry about me, Papa," Ikenga assured.

Nne came out from her hut shortly afterwards; the elderly women in the house were allowed to join the men folk when they broke the morning kola-nut. She had not had enough time to sit together with her son since he came back the previous day and the early morning get-together might be her only opportunity if Ikenga planned on leaving immediately as most city dwellers did. "How are you, my son?"

"All is well, Nne," Ikenga replied.

Chukwuma prayed over kola-nut and they all ate as they listened to Ikenga tell them everything they needed to know about Port Harcourt; the hardship, the multiple storey buildings, and the large number of people from far-away lands. He remembered that he had twice been to Port Harcourt during the struggle when his regiment was quickly drafted to help repel the enemy forces.

"It is such a big city," he recollected. "I am sure the whole ruins must have been reconstructed."

They discussed warmly and shared from a bottle of Schnapps till it was clearly daylight. Chinaza and her stepsisters also joined them when they were through with their morning chores and when Ikenga told them that he would be leaving early the next morning, they all prayed together for his safe return before going off to resume their individual daily activities. He insisted on following the girls to the stream as a precautionary measure to sniff through his footsteps and probably stop over at the shrine. The one-eyed messenger who had never wanted Ikenga to unseat him was particularly happy at first when he learnt that his young contender had gone to settle in Port Harcourt but now appeared happy to show the much grown Ikenga what was left of *Ogwugwu* shrine and state his disaffection with the job.

A universal acceptance and sense of oneness with regards to the new religious concept brought by the white Reverend had gradually swept across Umuafor and with this newly found identity, people no longer wanted to be associated with what the intruders described as barbaric ways. The remaining few who were mostly elderly champions of *omenani* were not only stuck with their oracles and deities but were always pointed accusing fingers at for any unexplained sickness, miscarriage, or sudden death. As aging and death took their toll on these *omenani* adherents, many who could no longer hold on gave up to embrace the new religion and these instances were normally followed by a noisy applause within the community in accordance with the story of the lost sheep. Hence, chief priests and priestesses who continued to enjoy secret patronage from those who claimed to have abandoned the *omenani* had cornered a number of shrines and deities, which had not been burnt down or sold into perpetual slavery in Port Harcourt.

An old tale has it that *Ichoku*, the parrot, who was made the mouthpiece of the sky birds once went out for an evening outing. His out-of-control way of talking landed him in a dreadful night meeting with evil folks. The gathering called by *Ekwensu* to reward his obedient servants went well and ended in time enough for both spirits and humans to disperse before daybreak. The Parrot flew a long way back to a weathered *uzuza* tree on the hilltop that shared a fence with an old chapel. But his wife refused to allow him in till he gave a satisfactory explanation about his whereabouts the previous night. As the Parrot stood motionless on the tree branch pleading for leniency, he noticed the very mortals that were present in the night gathering with *Ekwensu* filing in, in totally different garments into the church for morning service. The scene did not strike accord with his spirit and *Ichoku* immediately flew over to the altar crying: "*Ukochukwu na the same people.*" But that was all that the poor Parrot could mutter before the evil men sealed up his tongue.

Ikenga and the chief priest took a quiet tour of the *Ogwugwu* shrine premises, discussing in confidence some Umuafor religious practices. The chief priest then solicited Ikenga's help in maximising his income in the service of *Ogwugwu*.

"We can still work together," he offered.

"How?" Ikenga asked. "I now live in Port Harcourt."

"This is an opportunity for you to bring city dwellers to *Ogwugwu*," the chief priest explained.

"How do I bring them over to Umuafor?" Ikenga asked further. "Tell them that *Ogwugwu* has solutions for all their problems."

"And what if they don't have any problems?"

"We create one for them," he pressured. "We cannot abandon *Ogwugwu* shrine to be swallowed up by the white man's unseen God."

"Who are we to fight for *Ogwugwu*?"

"We are only making a living."

"The oracle might not be happy with that."

"Then it should show itself and protest."

"What will be my share if I have to dance to your tune?" Ikenga asked when he realised that the chief priest had sold his conscience to the devil.

"We will share equally whatever we squeeze out from them," the one-eyed seer answered frankly.

The conversation helped Ikenga put off whatever feelings of guilt that had weighed him down since embarking on his treasure hunt. He felt very much better after the chief priest revealed that the finger pointing he received from Reverend Klaus's followers would have discouraged him if not for the material sacrifices and offerings that came from secret worshippers of *Ogwugwu*. Pleased that his operations the previous night had gone undetected, Ikenga concealed his rage and maintained that he had just come to the village to see his parents.

"This fight is for *Ogwugwu*," he replied. "I have no strength of my own to engage in a spiritual battle or defraud my people in the name of the gods."

The one-eyed seer conceded defeat when Ikenga maintained his dissatisfaction at his offer and was pleased that the young contender had gone to city for good

\* \* \* \* \*

The next day was the popular Afor market day when the whole family would leave early to take their wares to the market. Ikenga had wisely chosen to leave that day to avert unnecessary questions from his curious sisters. He carefully packed the average size statues together with some long tubers of yam and other food stuffs in two sacs, loaded them into the family wheelbarrow to minimise breakage and headed for the Motor Park. Chinaza had agreed to pick up the wheelbarrow on her way back from the market.

The nine-hour drive to Port Harcourt through dusty and bumpy roads was far from smooth. He boarded an orient-painted Mitsubishi bus, which was originally designed for nine passengers but was packed with fifteen passengers excluding children squatting on the laps of their parents. The four wheels of the bus had almost disappeared under the fender, with luggage weighing far more than the mini-bus fastened on the top and sides of the overused commercial vehicle. It was a scene better described as a moving heap of refuse. Frequent police check points and the scorching heat of the sun made the journey lengthier while the passengers who had known no other luxury roasted in silence.

Halfway into the journey, they had travelled some few miles along the bushy road leading to Eziobe when a female passenger seated behind the driver pulled out a shiny .38 semi-automatic pistol. Two shots rang off through the roof and the smoking nozzle was pointed at the driver's neck, causing pandemonium with cries from women and confused children even as the overloaded bus danced roughly over the deathly potholes when the already shivering driver threw his hands up in surrender.

A self-acclaimed pharmacist who had been advertising and selling some locally made balm and herbal drugs was the first to be attacked. He handed over his purse when a slap landed on his face from nowhere and joined other passengers in the struggle to escape. Shouts of "your money or your life" came from all directions with no one caring to know who was issuing the commands as they all scrambled to exit the bus. The tiny windows intended as emergency exits were partly blocked by the goods tied round the bus and many who sustained injuries in the crazy commotion only began to feel the pain after they had gotten to the safety of the nearby bushes. Ikenga, who was seated on the last row had no chance of exiting through the side door but managed to force the rear window open. He squeezed himself out with few other passengers, and was lucky to have come out with only a minor cut on his forehead. The bushy highway, notorious for the rampant attacks by hoodlums, provided the bandits with ample time to carry out their operations with impunity.

The bandit group of two young men and a lady had separately boarded the bus at the park and waited for the right moment to strike. Speedily, they tore off handbags from passengers during the pandemonium, and tore down and ransacked the entire luggage before fleeing with the Mitsubishi bus and other items of interest. Traffic was frantically halted on both directions as other travellers who had unknowingly driven into the scene abandoned their vehicles and took to their heels. It took sometime before people started coming out from their hideouts to notice that the uniformed men manning the nearby checkpoints had also abandoned their posts and melted away.

There was a renewed outburst of tears when passengers discovered that their valuables were either missing or destroyed as bags had been torn apart, and other properties stained with palm oil. The self-acclaimmed pharmacist carried out first-aid on some of the wounded passengers before scurrying around to gather what was left of his stuff scattered around a fifty-meter radius. Apart from losing a polythene bag with minor belongings, most of Ikenga's items were lying around intact except for a few broken tubers of yam that had fallen off the sacs. He quickly gathered the yams and other foodstuff but distanced himself from the wooden statues.

Dealing on such items was seen as a despicable crime among communities and a criminal offence in the court of law. Another round of pandemonium ensued when people discovered that four strange *juju* were lying around unclaimed. Many grabbed their items in fear and moved a good distance away, leaving only two or three women who stood their grounds and rained down verbal fire from an unseen Elijah to consume the lifeless wooden objects.

About two and a half hours later, faint sounds of a siren were heard from a distance and soon, four black uniformed men jumped out of a black 504 station wagon with questionable roadworthiness which had "Rapid Response Squad" boldly inscribed on its sides, wielding their AK47 banana clips on everyone around.

"Where are the armed robbers?" they shouted with few frightening shots into the air.

A man who had lost a great deal of his electronic wares to the robbers approached them with fury not minding the risk of losing his life at the hands of a poorly-trained trigger-happy squad.

"You came at a good time," he shouted back in tears. "It is three hours already. Where were you when the robbers were on rampage?"

"We can't just jump out of the station," one of the uniformed men replied authoritatively. "There are procedures to be followed in matters like this."

"What other protocol is more important than protecting the lives and properties of the citizens?" the man questioned unrelentingly.

"Are you trying to teach me my job?" the uniformed man queried.

"Hand over the uniform to the government if you don't have interest in the job."

"Do you have a better job for me?"

"I hate you! I hate you all!" the man yelled through tears.

A handful of the confused crowd, inspired by the man's courage, drew closer and rained abuses on the police officers as well, and it took some reinforcement quickly drafted to the area to prevent the scene from getting nasty. The police was quick to assert their authority over the situation and insisted that whoever was involved must follow them to the station to make a written statement on what he or she knew about the robbery, the mysterious idols, and possibly, additional charges of insulting a police officer. They dragged and beat the man to submission, eventually taking him with two other men, the driver, and two of the praying women along with the statues they had wanted to destroy with Elijah's fire.

The skinny young conductor could not help but watch as the police bundled up his master into the car and drove off. They had suddenly become suspects, coupled with the unwritten law that once taken to a police station, whether guilty or not, one had to "settle," a local synonym for bribery. Besides, his master could be pinned down to the statues by the obviously inexperienced police officers that were likely to be in a haste to close down the case file of the robbery incident. It then suddenly occurred to the conductor that he had felt those wooden objects while arranging and fastening the two blue sacs on top of the mini-bus and he walked unnoticed up to Ikenga.

*"Mister, you sure say no be you get that juju?"* he asked softly in Pidgin English.

Ikenga stood motionless as if he had heard nothing trying to figure out the best way to frighten and keep the poor conductor away from him. Traffic had resumed normally and some passengers from the ill-omened mini-bus had boarded other commercial vehicles and continued their journey. He had deliberately stayed behind to see what would become of his treasured possessions and did not anticipate that the sacs would be traced back to him knowing how Motor Parks operated, especially on an Afor market day that was considered to be one of its busiest days.

"*Oga, you go follow me go station,*" the conductor pressed further when he received no reply from his passenger. "*Go tell them say na your property be that.*"

"I will chop off your head if I see you around me," Ikenga barked in a carefully controlled tone.

"*But na you get the juju!*" the emboldened conductor took a few steps backward and shouted louder as he sensed fear in the passenger.

"*How you know say na me get am?*"

"*I see you carry the Ijebu-bag for barrow come.*"

"*Na craze de worry you.*"

"*I no craze, Oga.*"

Ikenga had no other option than maintain his stand. An Umuafor woman had once said: "Instead of the piece of cloth around my waist to land me in trouble, I will rather swear with my life that it is not mine."

"That thing is not my own," he shouted at the hungry looking conductor.

"*I say na you push the juju for wheel-barrow come motor-park,*" the poor conductor maintained fearlessly.

"It wasn't me."

"*Oga, na you.*"

The encounter attracted the attention of the few remaining passengers who were still waiting for vacant oncoming commercial buses to continue their journey to Port Harcourt. As they drew closer, hoping to understand what the argument was all about, Ikenga responded with readiness to bail himself out with his foot. He had witnessed a number of cases in the city where jungle justice had been administered to alleged criminals by an angry mob. The same hardship that caused desperation had equally introduced a cruel system of justice as people apprehended for petty crimes like fowl stealing or pickpocketing were mercilessly beaten up and set ablaze by poverty-stricken mobs.

As the bus conductor explained to the closer audience how he had first noticed the wooden statues at the Umuafor motor-park, the athletic Ikenga dashed into the bush when the men tried to circle him. "Get him! Get him!" rang loudly behind him as he ran for his life deep into the bushy landscape, hoping that the men after him would not readily abandon their wares in the middle of nowhere to pursue a fast runner. The tall elephant grasses with its dried scratchy leaves also hindered navigation to his advantage, and luckily for him, they gave up the chase when their target disappeared from sight.

He did not stop running till he was absolutely sure that he had covered enough distance. Then he paused under a shady tree to listen for any movements or noise from those after him before heading further into the forest hoping that another village was close by from where he could continue his journey. As far as he was concerned, the wooden gods had fought back and made him lose everything. His tubers of yam and other foodstuffs would by now have been taken to the Police Station by the conductor to plead with the officers that the culprit had abandoned his goods and fled, and the case would be closed under the assumption that the escapee was also the leader of the robbery gang.

As Ikenga walked through the vast palm plantations surrounding the town of Eziobe, he slowed his pace and spent some hours on a treetop from where he sighted the next village and patiently waited for the sun to set. The small village bustled with activities and the bee-like sounds of Suzuki motorcycles that served as the major means of transportation. Stranded in an unknown town with no money left on him, he quickly thought up a plan on how to get back to Port Harcourt before dark.

A cyclist slowed down by his side as he walked briskly along the roadside. The rider had closed for the day but hoped to maximise his daily income when he sighted a man headed towards his direction. Ikenga quickly shed his run away act and boarded the motorbike when he discovered that it was just a lone old man. "Where?" the cyclist asked his passenger who did not name any village but pointed straight on. The worries to name a destination for the cyclist was taken care of when the soft-spoken old man opened up a conversation.

"I wish you are heading to the direction of my home," he said trying to adjust a shaky headlamp.

"Your headlamp is totally bad," Ikenga replied hoping to prolong the conversation.

"Yes!" the cyclist agreed. "Coupled with my bad sight, I hate working when it's dark."

"But we are safe for now?" Ikenga asked politely.

"Oh we are," the cyclist assured. "It's not yet that late but I was already on my way home when I saw you."

"This stressful job is definitely not for people like you," Ikenga advised.

"You are right, young man," the old man agreed. My son left the *okada* behind when he left the village for Port Harcourt and I found the business more rewarding than toiling at the farm."

"But why is my family insisting that I come back to the village and take up farming?"

"Remain in the city, my son!" the old man advised. "Do whatever your mates are doing and believe in your *chi* to open a way for you".

The old cyclist poured out advice, oblivious that his listener was busy calculating his next move. His chance came when the old man slowed down to dodge a palm tree uprooted by the wind. Ikenga moved his strong arm round his neck and mulled the man to the ground.

"This is one of the things my mates do in the city," he said to the old man.

"Please don't kill me!"

"I will not."

## WOES OF IKENGA

"I've got some money in my back pocket."

"I don't need your money!"

"Pity my grey hairs, young man!" the man pleaded. "I have a son of your age."

"Shut up, old man," Ikenga commanded. "Your motorbike is all I need. I will return it tomorrow by this time."

He dragged the man a few metres off the road and with precise force, covered his mouth and tied his hands to a tree. There was no sign of any human being as he rode out to the road. Hastily he cleaned the bike from the dirt gathered during its rough landing and sped off. It was not difficult to connect to the highway. The old fellow had already filled up the tank of the motorbike with more than enough fuel for the remaining one-hour ride to Port Harcourt.

# Chapter 4

When the attempt to raise money with the cherished treasures of his ancestors failed, Ikenga resumed contemplating abandoning his fatherland for the white man's land where he was beginning to believe his destiny lay. He was sincerely convinced that the spirits behind those statues were the architects of what had transpired on his way to Port Harcourt and that the statues would definitely find their ways back to *Ogwugwu* shrine. They had merely spared his life for the fact that he had never toyed with the *akpa-agwu* he used to carry or that his dead grandfather would not allow them, and going back to Umuafor to tempt the wooden gods again would mean extending a handshake to *Ekwensu* himself. As far as he was concerned, if the nosy white men would not travel to the interiors to gather the statues themselves, the treasures should all rot away in their respective shrines.

Ikenga would have preferred to fly through the skies into the land of abundance but his meagre savings from the fishing company could not have possibly procured the necessary documents as well as the flight ticket. His only option then was to join the mini-stampede of the young generation to escape the shores of Africa through its vast borders. Young men of Umuafor and neighbouring cities were on the move in search of greener pastures and many who had suffered devastation by the war were desperately embarking on any available means to get out of their immediate vicinity. What they hated about the beloved homeland they were leaving behind was the lack of opportunities. A decent number of men and women of indispensable quality indeed, determined to achieve greatness, strongly believed that the host country which they knew nothing of, would offer better opportunities and a brighter future. Undoubtedly, they presumed, the living standards would for sure not have any resemblance to what they were leaving behind. Umuafor men and women have been credited with turning dry land into vegetation, but one must first get hold of the desert to be able to turn it into a rain forest.

This phenomenon of illegal migration was not peculiar to Umuafor citizens alone. The early invaders of Umuafor whom *omenani* custodians claimed had brought calamity to the land and her people had also come from faraway lands without any invitation. In this era of modern voluntary feudalism, there was no shortage of people or group of individuals who facilitated these movements or encouraged people to migrate because they had a stake in the whole operation. Ikenga had barely aired his intentions to leave the country before offers of assistance started pouring in from different quarters with promises of a smooth passage and a pre-arranged path to citizenship in any foreign country of his choice. People who had enough money to spend on their travel expenses were packaged by these agents as students or businessmen to embassies of their destinations for visa and other documentation, thanks to the *Oluwole* gurus. But those who could not afford to travel by air were channelled through north Africa for onward journey to a new world across the ocean. When conventional means and outlets became tighter for the globetrotters and their agents following the growing anti-immigration policies of conservative governments of countries, Umuafor youths and their counterparts became desperate to take even more daring chances to emigrate, crossing the notoriously treacherous Sahara Desert on foot, or holding on to the scary legs of a flying vulture till it flew to the next dry land, thereby displaying bravery in the struggle for a better life.

Ikenga's intention to search for his *awele* in a foreign land met strong objections from Chinaza and Mr. Ubanese, the village headmaster who had received words that Ogbonnia his son may have abandoned school for debauchery. These objections however did not constitute any hindrance to Ikenga who now saw himself as not under any man's authority. His travel arrangements were almost concluded and he had only come to pay a last visit to Umuafor and say goodbye to friends and family. Nne did not say much but grieved in silence; Ikenga was the only son she knew and she would greatly miss him for as long as his adventure lasted. She poured out her blessings as Ikenga and his sisters sat round the muddy pavement of her hut late in the evening.

"The road and the seas will be obedient," she prayed. "Your journey will be a smooth one." There was a short interval as the old woman allowed her prayers penetrate the sky. She stood up and walked to Ikenga while adjusting her wrapper around her waist.

"Nne, can I get anything for you?" Chinaza offered.

"No, my daughter, I prefer to stand so that my words will stand." Before Ikenga, she stood for a while and continued. "Travel east or travel west, a man's own home is still the best. My bones are getting weaker by the day and your father's double barrel gun will not save him from old age. You must be back on time to sow our body with dignity back to Mother Earth."

"Nne, I will," Ikenga answered through drops of tears that made the passionate plea a "tear covenant."

"Promise me that you will not stay long."

"I promise."

Chukwuma, his father, actively gave his blessings to the idea because of the seeming hopelessness around Umuafor and his concealed wishes to drive round the village in a Mercedes Benz car. He had always hoped that the yoke of poverty that had tormented his family since the end of the war would one day be broken and if it would take his only son leaving Umuafor to achieve that goal, then so be it. Other family members and relatives were happy and excited when they heard that Ikenga planned on travelling abroad, and those who had a good relationship with him convincingly believed that their days of hunger and poverty were almost over.

*   *   *   *   *

Ikenga returned to Port Harcourt and set out with a company of other immigrants for the land believed to be flowing with milk and honey. The journey was agreeable through West Africa till they reached the north and proceeded towards the desert. Their supplies were running out and border agents and gangs of street marauders had become even more hostile and overdemanding. It

# WOES OF IKENGA

was dusk when they arrived at the no man's city of Ozalla, very hungry and exhausted. Migrants had renamed the dusty city, located deep into the desert off the northern borders of the desert republic, as it was best described as a wilderness or barren land. It was formerly a security control post but had gradually evolved into a mini-settlement and later into a city as illegal migration to the new world gathered momentum.

The original settlers of Ozalla were nomads, followed by deportees sent back from Libya and Algeria after successfully crossing the Sahara. These immigrants settled in makeshift muddy houses built by the nomads and engaged in legal or illegal activities till they could gather enough strength and resources to try their luck again. With time, the settlement became a major transit centre where migrants waited for their middlemen to arrange a means of crossing the Sahara, which was usually done in four wheelers or trucks.

The city always bustled with activities but at night, petty traders would pack up their wares and lock up their stores to give way to pimps and their corporate associates who usually took over the streets at night. Patchy brothel attendants and owners of *mama-puts* would then set up chairs and other paraphernalia to attract customers. Young beautiful girls would also be positioned in dark street corners, while older women would have marked out territories for themselves to fight off encroachers. The fight for territories and wealthy-looking clients had become a necessary part of the daily struggle because these women needed to make enough money to be able to settle their pimps or traffickers as well as fend for themselves. A minor wrangling often led to brutal exchange of blows and it was common during such ruckus, for the women to give up their credentials to prove to their opponents that they were not of the same category.

Such episodes grossly complicated the conventional public perception of the global prostitution business, as these women by their revelations turned out to not be young uneducated adolescents who had been sold into prostitution against their will,

75

but full-fledged ladies who were well aware of what they were going into and had agreed to pay a significant sum of money to whoever would teleport them over to *Terra-fantassimus.*

It did not matter to them what they would go through; focus was on the belief in the myth that success was sure once outside their home countries and more importantly that this success could be emulated regardless of those who had returned with nothing or worse still had ended up being beaten, diseased or dead. Whoever came back with enough money was respected and adored while those who came back poor and empty-handed were regarded as failures who had wasted their opportunity in the land of plenty. Their words and opinions never counted.

At Ozalla, Ikenga met Stella, a bright young lady from across the River Niger that linked Umuafor and a whole lot of other communities with its extensive tributaries and trade routes. She was in her second missionary race to get to the new world after a failed attempt. Their diversity found uniformity in their search for the good life and both were happy to meet each other and share ideas as people of the same extraction.

Stella, the oldest of eight siblings, had embarked on her journey with the full consent of her mother. Life had become unbearable when her father, the sole breadwinner of the family, was buried alive in a coal-mining accident. Thenceforth, she had grown up doing all she could to support and provide for her mother and siblings. Her education had been put on hold in high school when it was discovered that she was pregnant and their already dire financial situation worsened. She had carried the pregnancy to full term and agreed with her mother few months after delivery that the only way their family could ever lead a better life was if she toed the path of her mates. It was a rather open secret how she would make money when she arrived at her destination.

She had been overexcited when her mother told her that all necessary arrangements for her travel had been concluded as her mother had vended the only piece of land that her husband had been able to buy, after twenty-five years of working as a coal miner, to be able to raise the money. The deal with the supposed travel agent had been drawn, sealed with a juju ceremony to guaranty secrecy and ensure that both parties kept to their own ends of the bargain, especially as mother and daughter had agreed to make the balance payment of thirty-seven thousand US dollars as soon as Stella set foot in Italy.

"Our breakthrough has come, Mama," Stella told her mother. "Hold your excitement, my daughter," the experienced widow cautioned. "The road ahead is far from certain."

"I am going to make you a proud mother!" Stella happily reassured.

"Please take good care of yourself!"

"I will," she promised.

Her mother's fears were not unfounded. Girls had left for *Italo* only to fall victims of local occultists who killed and dismembered their bodies for money-making rituals. Many others had died on the way and many more who made it had returned with the dreaded *Obili-n'aja-ocha*, a sexually transmitted ailment that had stubbornly defied both traditional and white man's medication.

"I said take good care, my daughter," the woman pleaded once more.

"I will be very careful, Mama," Stella promised again.

"Don't forget the anointing oil Pastor gave," her mother reminded. This indicated that the woman neither had absolute confidence in the guarantees of the Juju Priest nor in the prayers of her next-door neighbour and self-acclaimed "man of god."

\* \* \* \* \*

Stella had set out with two other ladies and a man who had introduced himself as Osagie and they had travelled through Agades and Bamako, towards Morocco, while making occasional stops at bustling cities for the girls to work two or three nights of short-time prostitution to reload their pockets. Osagie had a good knowledge of the routes because human trafficking was his source of livelihood and he had for many years sent people up north for an onward journey to pastures across the ocean. He was also a member of cabinet of the Al-Khalifi Government of Ozalla, a sect comprised of a group of immigrants who after several failed attempts to cross over to Europe, resorted to forming and maintaining a secret government-like cult of their own to control desert resources.

Those who deemed Ozalla as pasture green enough had given up hopes of travelling and settled to obtaining money from whoever fell prey to their antics as the gang did not only wreak havoc in their host city but committed far worse crimes against their own compatriots who appeared desperate. They had become international criminals and outlaws, abetting heinous crimes including kidnappings and meting out inhumane treatment to their fellow fugitives. Stella because of her nature-endowed beauty had found favour with Erimoje, the President of the Al-Khalifi gang, after her dislodgment from Morocco when upon their arrival, she and some other girls had been distributed to the top leaders of the sect, as the norm was that women engage in prostitution while the men were deployed to do some other menial jobs to be able to raise enough money for the journey ahead. Eight months had passed and she was again gearing to try her luck. This time, through the open Libyan waters.

*   *   *   *   *

Stella was always the first to start up a conversation whenever she ran into Ikenga. She knew a lot about Umuafor and would not mind being married to one of her industrious sons.

"How are you doing, my dear?" she asked with genuine concern as she walked up behind him unnoticed.

"Oh! I am very fine for today," Ikenga replied cheerfully.

"You have not told me your preferred destination?"

"I have a cousin in Germany. That is my dreamland but any dry land across the ocean is also acceptable."

"We shall make it!" Stella encouraged.

"What of you, how has it been with you?"

"It has not been easy with me." She explained: "I have been

on the road for so long. The first agent abandoned us at Morocco, and we were handed over to the Gendarme by some wicked area gang when we could not meet their demands of fifty US dollars per traveller to free ourselves."

"Who is the Gendarme?" Ikenga asked enthusiastically.

"They are the no-nonsense law enforcement agents of the desert borders that hate to hear anyone speak English."

"And what did they do to you?" Ikenga pressed.

"We were grouped differently and locked up for three days, and after ensuring that they had extracted the last penny out of our pockets, they drove us in the night through the Algerian desert back to N'Djamena."

"Wow! That is disheartening."

"I will never lose hope," Stella continued. "My mother and the rest of my eight siblings are all depending on me. I must make it to *Italo* at all costs. That is why you see me here, to try again through Libya."

"What of these Al-Khalifi criminals?"

"Be careful with those men," Stella warned. "They are even more deadly than the notorious Gendarme."

"One tore my bag to pieces on my arrival and collected some of my belongings," Ikenga complained.

"And what did you do?"

"Nothing."

"That is so unlike men of Umuafor," Stella teased.

"I want to get to my destination alive."

She laughed at his retreat and led the way to a *mama-put* shack run by an elderly woman and her desert-begotten daughter. The woman had lost all hopes of making it across the ocean after several attempts and since going back to her country empty handed was not an option, she had decided to pick up the pieces of her broken life, right in the middle of the desert.

"Don't worry," Stella said to him. "I will take you to their president, he is a good friend and maybe you will recover some of your items."

"How do you know the President?" Ikenga sounded rather jealous. He could envisage what those mean looking desert monsters might have done with his beautiful sister and to imagine that the act of "good friendship" may still be ongoing saddened him the more.

Stella seemed to have been reading his mind as she suddenly quipped a defence in Pidgin English. *"This abroad tin sef ... but God dey."*

Ikenga on the other hand was already lost in thought. He did not pay attention to her explanations, which by the way would not have been enough to change the impression he already had of her.

Based on his traditional orientation on women, they were the very instruments of human life. A number of prominent tribes had their own jealously preserved body of myths, legends and oral traditions that featured women as the original mother of mankind. In line with this, the sanctity of a woman was well preserved and highly esteemed. Hence, prostitution was forbidden in Umuafor.

Many other myths also link humanity directly with God, and assert that the woman is His channel through which all people originate. The Umu-Ngene and their myths aver that before Olisa (God) made man, he first made a woman on earth and bore with her a child who became the first human. One other beautifully illustrated story of human existence featuring a woman is that of Umuchukwu, the self-acclaimed direct descendants of God. They affirm that a premier pair of humans were placed on paradise earth but were soon lonely and needed company. As they did not know how to make or where to find creatures like themselves, they pleaded with Chukwu-Okike to intervene. Chukwu in response to their request made a mixture of clay and His saliva, from which he formed a small human figure. He handed over the tiny human formation to the woman with instructions to preserve the figure in a clay pot and nurture with compassion for a period of nine months. She was not to take the figure out of the pot until it had developed limbs. The woman followed these instructions to the letter, pouring milk into the pot every morning and evening, until after nine months when she pulled out what had now grown to become human being.

The pot, signifying the womb of a woman wherein a baby takes shape, gave the woman positional advantage to share directly with God in a special way, the secrets and mysteries of life and birth. To crown it all, in what seemed to be more than a mere coincidence, Reverend Klaus had come from a faraway land, quoting from his Holy Book that the same Chukwu had mysteriously caused a virgin to give birth to God, the Messiah.

The discussion about Stella's relationship with the desert rogues was put on hold, as the two took their positions to enjoy the spicy *mama-put,* but she prayed that he would understand that their present predicament had left her with no better alternative.

*     *     *     *     *

Despite her ongoing affair with the head of the Al-Khalifi, Ikenga and Stella maintained a cordial relationship. With the few hundred dollar notes carefully wrapped in nylon sheet and safely tucked inside his shoes, he was surely not staying long in the filthy ghettos of the desert unlike Stella who waited for eight months to be able to raise enough money for the second leg of her journey. He therefore followed up on her line of contacts, and within a couple of weeks, his travel papers were ready for an onward journey to Benghazi.

As they had been told, the real adventure had just commenced. Convoy drivers waited till nightfall before commencing the seven hundred and fifty-kilometre journey to the Libyan border. The desert spawned from the houses and dotted shrubs ended on the outskirts of Ozalla to the newly erected outpost at the edge of the Sahara Desert. Ikenga had heard stories of the death of many who had being journeying through the Sahara, but had refused to allow it dampen his courage. For the journey, he had armed himself with enough water, bread and nuts before squeezing himself into the open rear of the four-wheel pick-up truck. The five-woman and eleven-man team of travellers had no information about what lay ahead in the course of their journey. All they knew was that they had paid money to someone they had not even directly met with and were now entrusting their lives to a driver who said little.

Stella, all smiles and all hopeful, had bought a lot of items and was now perched on Ikenga's laps as the Toyota truck with poor headlamps dangled through the dusty and rough paths of the desert. A pregnant woman was seated rather too close to the gallons of reserve diesel in one corner of the truck. She called out to the driver an hour into the journey when she could no longer bear the squeeze from the gallons.

"Please driver my legs are hurting."

"We all have to manage," the driver replied without looking back. He was also uncomfortable in the driver's seat as three adults and a six-year old child occupied the front row, which was meant to carry only the driver and a passenger.

"How long is this journey going to take?" Ikenga questioned the driver.

"Twelve hours, *Insha Allahu*," the driver assured in Arabic.

There was silence for a while and the only sound that could be heard was the roaring voice of the diesel engine. Neither the screeching sounds of nocturnal insects were heard, nor were owls and other night rodents sighted. Ikenga was still pondering on the driver's words when the pick-up truck pulled over at the first checkpoint. The security men who may also have a stake in the whole avocation had been hinted that two truckloads of immigrants had left Ozalla and had laid ambush to collect their non-negotiable "settlements." Otherwise, the whole journey with weeks of preparation would be terminated. The driver alighted to meet with the unidentified but heavily armed uniformed men, and in a couple of minutes, the truck was rolling again. Usually, the fee charged by the different agents included money for such "settlements", as bandits and security men alike knew very well that desert laws were non-binding declarations. There were also cases of different rifle-wielding groups randomly ambushing and ransacking travellers with impunity, collecting money or any item of interest they found in possession of the helpless crusaders.

The journey continued without any further hitches except for occasional stops for prayers whenever the driver and some of the Moslem passengers wished. Ikenga seized those intervals to implore his *chi*. He beckoned Udeaja his incarnate grandfather and all his ancestors to keep him behind when trouble loomed ahead and to keep him in front when troubles were behind. Stella on the other hand who had double protection from both the Juju Priest and her Pastor sprinkled a few drops of Olive Oil over her head and recited some prayers. The multi-coloured beads around her waist were to be activated only when she arrived Italy to guarantee constant patronage by wealthy white men. They were now in the middle of nowhere, and the dusty desert like the surface of the moon stretched as far as the eyes could see with no other sign of life.

As the darkness gradually began to disperse, Ikenga sighted people's belongings and scattered bones, and wondered what had happened to their owners.

"Those are not animal bones," Stella told him.

"Horrible!" Ikenga lamented. "They must have been eaten by wild animals."

"Certainly not," she replied. "There are no tigers or lions in barren deserts."

"How on earth will their relatives know what happened to their loved ones?" he asked in disbelief.

"They will hope for a juicy message through Western Union till tortoises start to grow hairs," the pregnant woman who suffered in silence threw in.

It was obvious that something tragic had happened to a group of immigrants very recently as the upper edge of the sun rose from the horizon with better visibility over the Sahara. Decomposing lifeless bodies of people who had tried to walk or run to safety could be seen as far as fifteen miles away slumped near their belongings. Also in sight were bodies of children half-buried by sand, lying face down near their parents or their empty water cans. There were no trucks or camels in the vicinity, and the fact that those people could not have walked that far into the middle of nowhere suggested that whoever brought them there had abandoned them to the mercy of merciless elements.

The driver sped through without stopping or paying attention to the corpses; the ugly sight was not new to him. Moreover, he needed to arrive at his destination before the Libyan border agents began their patrol. At last, the eleven-hour journey came to a stop at the Libyan southern city of Turzuq, from where the migrants would find their way individually to the port city of Benghazi. This was not a problem for either Ikenga or Stella who would leave him behind in Benghazi since the money she had would not be enough to transport them both across the Mediterranean Sea.

\*   \*   \*   \*   \*

For twelve months Ikenga survived on the little money he made from cobbling while trying to adapt in a conservative Moslem society. When the going seemed too tough, he thought to reach Ogbonnia with the number the headmaster had given him. He did not want to inconvenience his cousin financially, but a desperate person would even hold on to the edge of a knife. He dialed and was lucky to have Ogbonnia at the other end of the line.

"Who am I speaking to please?" Ogbonnia asked rather worried by the totally unknown number.

"It's Ikenga ... Ikenga Udeaja."

"Where are you calling from?"

"Libya."

"What are you doing in Libya?"

"Stranded."

"What! Why did you not bother to call me before embarking on your journey?"

"I never wanted to inconvenience anyone."

"You have made the worst mistake of your life, Ikenga,"

Ogbonnia declared. "I advise that you go back if you will listen."

"No going back! Moreover, I have covered more than half of the journey."

"This place is only a shadow of what people think of it."

"I don't want to believe that Ogboo my cousin would not want me to step my foot in the white man's land."

"Far from it, Ikenga!"

"But why have you people not run back all these while if it is that bad?" Ikenga asked.

"You will not understand, brother," Ogbonnia replied. "There is no way you will understand till you experience it."

"I cannot wait to experience it," Ikenga yelled. "Do something to rescue me from the heat I am taking here if you can."

On two occasions, Ogbonnia sent some money through a third party since Ikenga had no legal status or valid documents to directly receive such remittances, and no longer tried to discourage his cousin from his ambitions. Ikenga on his own took up some shameful employments that he would otherwise have been too ashamed to take up in his home country. He was ever determined to set foot on the dry land across the ocean and to prove to people that his destiny lay there. Within his seven-month sojourn in Libya, he was able to put together the one thousand dollars fee required by smugglers to guide them from the continent of hopelessness into the new world of riches and bounty. He and some other group of desperate travellers had barely been huddled aboard an ill equipped half-metal-half-wooden boat ready to dare the mighty strength of the Mediterranean Sea when armed men claiming to be royal coast guards stormed, dragging him and his co-migrants down the rickety boat by the riverside and chasing them back into town after a merciless beating.

That was his first experience of brutal manhandling since embarking on the journey. For all they knew, the thugs might have been arranged by the traffickers who had long vanished or could very well be one of the independent armed groups operating from across the country under the auspices of the fractured security system. Frustrated and in pains, Ikenga sneaked back into the neighbourhood he just said good-bye to–a three-room apartment rented by a Jordanian Jihadist and jointly paid for by immigrants who came and went through the passage lanes of the coastal town. His co-tenants welcomed him back after he narrated his ordeal and fed him for a number of days till he was healthy enough to fend for himself again.

The physical injuries and loss of money in the hands of the thugs did not stop him from dreaming that his *awele* lay beyond the deep blue ocean. Shortly after he recovered from his bruises and pains, he joined some group of immigrants running up and down the road, cleaning car glasses and mirrors whenever there was a traffic jam. This was somewhat better off than all his previous menial jobs though there were some occasional slaps from car owners who detested the sight of "unbelievers" from foreign lands sprinkling dirty water over their expensive cars.

To his greatest surprise one day, a car pulled up by the roadside on one of his busiest days and the driver asked if he was Ikenga from Umuafor.

"Yes, I am!" Ikenga replied, hoping that whoever knew him to be from Umuafor came in good faith.

"I have been looking for you all over," the stranger told him.

"Who are you, please?" Ikenga asked in disbelief.

"That is not important. Stella gave me your description and asked me to locate you."

"Stella!" Ikenga shouted. "Where is she? Was she sent back?"

"Take it easy!" the driver answered as he pulled out a cell phone from his leather handbag. "Your wife still loves you."

"My wife you said?"

"Yes! Many women abandon their husbands here as soon as they cross over. You are a lucky man!" he added.

Ikenga did not say or ask any further questions as whatever assistance even if from a presumed loving wife was welcome at this critical stage of his journey. The well-to-do looking man happened to be an agent from Stella's hometown with extensive knowledge of the desert routes. With migration at its peak, he had finally decided to settle in Benghazi and had made a fortune from facilitating the movement of migrants to the Italian Island of Lampedusa. He had narrowly missed death after a tragic mishap on the sea that claimed the lives of his wife and their five-year-old son and had since resolved to leave the land of the unknown to the unknown.

Stella who had maintained smooth relations with some of the bad eggs she met in the course of her journey had requested that Osagie help her track her husband, whom she had lost contact with. She believed his explanation that he was not part of the team that had defrauded and abandoned her first travelling company in Morocco, and so comfortably sent money with which the trafficker was to find and assist Ikenga with his travel plans. Osagie on the other hand had kept track of Ikenga and followed up on different leads until another traveller mentioned that the Ikenga he was searching for washed cars along Abdul Wajid Street.

Osagie touched some buttons on the cell phone and held it over his ears while Ikenga stared at his expensive outfit.

"*Italo babe*," Osagie called. "Please, call back immediately."

"Was that Stella?" Ikenga asked.

"Yea! She will call back."

In less than a minute the cell phone came alive with vibration and an Arabian melody. Osagie motioned Ikenga with his left hand to be still before pressing on the receiver button.

"How are you doing, girl?" Osagie questioned. "Your assignment has cost me a lot but I promised to locate him."

"I have an outstanding principle of fulfilling my pledges."

"Yes ..."

"That is I," Osagie boasted.

"I will give him the phone but don't forget my balance."

There was always an interval each time Osagie talked. Ikenga could not hear what was being said from the other end of the phone but was beginning to understand that Stella might have paid a lot to this stranger to search for him. Osagie handed the cell phone to him, cutting short his thoughts.

"Is that you, Stella?" Ikenga asked spontaneously.

"Yes, my dear!" the voice replied. "You have overstayed in Libya."

"The cricket is about to be blinded by the sand of it's burrowing," Ikenga revealed. "It is getting even tougher by the hour."

"It has always been like that," she remarked. "But I hope you are not trying to tell me that you are giving up?"

"Never!" he answered bravely. "The fight goes on. If the long legged *Atu,* the giraffe, does not succeed in killing Ikenga, Ikenga will definitely kill *Atu.*"

His words assured Stella that the man she had secretly fallen in love with was still within her reach.

"I've been trying to locate you. What is still holding you there?" she asked.

"They nearly tore my balls open when we boarded a boat bound for Lampedusa few months ago … "

Ikenga was about to narrate his ordeal and how hard he had been trying to raise money for the second leg when Stella ordered him to hand the phone back to Osagie.

At the end of their long discussion the man extended a handshake and introduced himself.

"My name is Osagiemwenagbon, you can call me Osagie."

"You did well to have found me," Ikenga told him.

"I am not through with you yet," Osagie maintained. "Throw away the sponge and your bucket of dirty water. Today you are coming with me to paradise."

Ikenga did not doubt or hesitate. Although he was not aware of what Stella had planned for him, he was absolutely certain that life in Osagie's world would surely be better than the insults and humiliation he received daily on Abdul Wajid Street. He handed over his working instruments to a comrade and working colleague and said goodbye.

"Don't forget me, Bobo!" the comrade who watched the sudden turn of events pleaded unconsciously.

"Have faith," Ikenga told him. "Your own messiah will one day appear from nowhere."

Osagie lived in an affluent and bustling neighbourhood southwest of Benghazi. The area was marked with spacious Arabian houses and tree-lined streets, home to several trading companies, government buildings, shopping malls and many illicit business activities. The Al Dawud area stood out because of its secret brothels and late-night shisha bars or water-pipe spots where night riders smoked flavoured tobacco from a water pipe called hookah, with multiple hoses to smoke from, so that up to four people could smoke from one shisha at once.

Osagie had secured an apartment in that area with his Libyan residential permit and the influence of his long-time friendship with a close confidant of the dictatorial regime. He took Ikenga in and lavished some Libyan Dinars on him with some of the money that Stella sent. Ikenga's last days in Benghazi were his first taste of paradise. Unknown to him, the money Osagie spent every evening in secret brothels, on his excess drinking, and shisha habits was actually money meant for his travel documents and air ticket.

"You are my best in-law," Osagie told him on one of the many occasions where they sat around in an Arabian restaurant dining like kings. "I hope you will not forget me when you get over."

"Certainly not!" Ikenga replied with his mouth stuffed with fresh fish. "A fowl does not easily forget the one who plucked out its tail feathers during the rainy season."

"I have helped many cross over but they forget me as soon as they taste the intoxicating fruits of the white man's land."

"The trend will change for good in my time," Ikenga assured him.

"You will be leaving Libya in a week's time," Osagie finally revealed.

"Wow!" Ikenga exclaimed, glowing with excitement.

"It took this long because I wanted to hand you over to the best water team," he explained.

"But Stella mentioned that I was to travel by air."

"That was her intention," Osagie admitted boldly. "But you cannot speak Arabic."

Osagie and his extensive criminal syndicates who were capable of packaging even chimpanzees with human travelling documents and seeing them through the ports of the bribe-stricken borders of the so-called third world countries had not bothered to render Ikenga the services which Stella paid for. The distance between he and the contract-giver coupled with the fact that cash was channelled straight to him had made this obtaining-by-tricks game a rather smooth one. Besides, Ikenga did not want to contemplate the alternative offer presented by Osagie—to stay longer than necessary and learn Arabic in order to pass through the airport. Instead he seemed genuinely grateful that Osagie had found him on the streets where he would have languished for months before raising enough money, and was now even more at ease knowing that his travel arrangements were underway.

* * * * *

The night crawlers were notified that departure time would be around midnight as the area was still in full swing. Instead of heading straight to the house, Osagie took a highway tunnel that led out of town, and their destination turned out to be a high fenced lonely bungalow on the outskirts of the city. An unidentified bearded gateman hurriedly entangled a rusty chain on a blue corrugated gate and closed them in as they drove into the compound. Ikenga followed Osagie in and stood quietly by the empty sitting room that had just a multi-coloured expensive orient rug on the floor while Osagie disappeared through a door. Darkness prevented him from studying the vicinity to at least identify an escape route should the need arise. The ghost compound had seen and kept a lot of secrets but had survived over the years because the powers that be had direct or indirect vested interest in some of the activities that went on there.

Osagie emerged with some strange looking men from the door who greeted him in low tones. Ikenga marvelled that such number of men were in the house, yet it was so quiet that one could hear the movement of an ant. They sat comfortably around a sparkling silver shisha on the orient rug discussing in Arabic. Ikenga was frightened because some of the men had revolvers and automatic pistols strapped to their waists but moved around as if nothing was amiss. He declined when the shisha was passed over to him and handed the pipe over to the next gentleman. Later, Osagie explained that he was to stay in the compound till the planned departure time, and disclosed some other necessary information before handing him a Libyan International Passport and some other documents.

The boys quarters behind the main building where he was led to was used to house ready-to-move immigrants by the smugglers. Ikenga was soon acquainted with his would-be co-travellers and was rather overjoyed to meet another young man from Umuchukwu who had just recently made it across the desert. They were all happy that their days in the chains and shackles of a poverty-stricken continent were almost over, and convinced of their immortality with an overwhelming faith and readiness to confront the treacherous sea conditions.

The twenty kilometre-square Italian island of Lampedusa had become one of the main entry points into Europe for the stream of economic migrants who crossed over from North Africa. The population of over five thousand inhabitants, which had long been outnumbered by aliens from across the Mediterranean, relied mostly on fishing and tourism for their income. Even though the open-sea journey had killed thousands, it did not deter the new waves of migrants that flocked in to escape intense drought, political meltdown and the consequent economic hardship that continued to plague their home countries.

The steady flow of humans and the concomitant revenue created an avenue for exploitation by human traffickers like Osagie and his associates. These smugglers had a fair knowledge of sea conditions and usually waited for bad weather to subside before moving their human cargo down to the overcrowded and noisy harbour.

There were still cars, trucks, and motorbikes everywhere when

Ikenga and his co-travellers were driven down to the harbour. Men armed with sticks and riffles roamed the area shouting at the already frightened travellers. In place of the custom agents who worked there at day, this gang of men had taken charge of opening the entrance barriers. At night, the rules were totally different because authorities changed hands, and a bribe of some Libyan Dinars or American Dollars was enough for anyone to pass through the barriers and do significant damage to people's properties.

The passengers boarded immediately they arrived at the harbour. Rather than take a second look at the death-trap with which they hoped to make the twenty-three hour journey across the high sea, the would-be travellers rushed in to secure a place in the worn-out vessel, and were all soon squeezed on the deck, from stem to stern. There was a mixture of races comprising mostly Arabs and nationals of Anglophone countries in West Africa. Ikenga, his comrade from Umuchukwu, and three other brave travellers who were probably on their second leg of the journey climbed onto a small open platform over the captain's cabin from where they had a clearer view of the ocean. When the anchor was disconnected for the boat to leave the dock, men armed with sticks brutally beat off those who were still clamouring for space amidst yells of "*Allahu Akbar*."

"*Italo*, here I come!" one called out standing on the elevated platform.

"It's still too early to say goodbye to Africa," Ikenga corrected.

"We are on the move man and nothing can stop us," another traveller from Banjul interjected.

"On the contrary," Ikenga insisted. "I was at this juncture some months ago, already dreaming of Italy before some men came aboard and dragged us off the boat with merciless beating."

"Those greedy agents are to be blamed," the Gambian explained. "That is to be expected if they refuse to settle the *area boys*. Look at them moving around with guns," he concluded by pointing at the rifle-wielding thugs.

Ikenga finally came to terms with what had happened to him few months ago from this explanation and closely studied some of the thugs roaming around to see if he could identify any of the men who had dealt with him.

"But how did you know that?" he asked his companion after sometime.

"This is my third attempt," the Gambian replied proudly. "I had a similar experience at my first attempt; the second was another horrifying adventure. Thank goodness we were rescued by a cargo ship in the middle of the high sea and handed over to the Libyan coast guards."

"Your corpse would have been useful to the sea creatures if you had been left to die there," another companion threw in jokingly."

"Death will not take me anytime soon since I have drunk from its cup and survived," the Gambian boasted.

"You wouldn't have made a third attempt if it was that terrible," Ikenga pointed out.

"I would have given up if I had a choice."

A few rounds of scattered gunshots to signal the departure of the overloaded convoy ended their conversation.

Again there were screams of "*Allahu Akbar*" as the two boats gradually drifted into the vast vastness of the sea. Even in their cramped positions, the occupants were cheerful. By faith, they would surmount this last obstacle before the Promised Land. They took turns to scoop out water splashing into the vessel and the waves did not sway their belief that troubled times would not last forever. The early phase of the journey progressed smoothly and in no time they could no longer see the dotted shining lights of the coastal towns and villages they left behind.

Suddenly, Ikenga's boat, which was a few hundred yards ahead of the second boat slowed down. Its old engine had had enough battering from the waves and decided to give up. The Bedouin captain, a big man with a long white moustache stepped on the jammed-in passengers without paying attention to their arms and legs as he went down to inspect the engine. With a hammer, his pocket torchlight and a screwdriver with which he unscrewed and re-screwed, he moved his fingers over the grease-stained cables to check if they were still intact.

The second vessel slowed down to find out what the problem was, and when someone suggested that the suction pump might be the problem, everyone nervously stared at the captain to do something as there was no more sight of land or green leaves.

The bashing sounds of the waves suddenly began to sound like death-drums, and all joy was gone in a minute as Moslems speedily counted their beads while Christians clutched whatever holy items they had with them. At the loud instruction of his co-captain from the other boat who seemed to have more experience, the Bedouin pulled off his windbreaker and fumbled with the engine. Soon, the vessel was miraculously revived with a wild applause from the passengers and the journey continued.

The sail progressed in silence and fear. Ikenga was for the first time in his life terribly afraid that if he died at sea, his people would not find his corpse to give him a proper burial. The open sea still had no end in sight and there was no reliable communication equipment, making it impossible to call for help should things go wrong. Suddenly there appeared a glimmer of hope as rows of light could be sighted from far away where the cloud seemed to descend on the water. It appeared to be coming from the shores of Lampedusa or from one of the floating offshore drills. The closer they advanced towards the source, the brighter it became and so their hopes were again raised.

The excitement was short-lived as the boat slowed down a second time. Obviously the problem had resurfaced and the captain again took up his instruments, and moved across the tailboard to the engine compartment but was unable to revive the smoking engine after a very long surgery. He went back to his cabin soaked in his own sweat and engine oil, lit a stick of Arabian cigar and closed the cabin door. The passengers waited patiently and those who could still muster an appetite ate whatever food they had left while those who had faith in the unseen did not stop praying. Both boats were dangerously overloaded and there was no possibility of transferring passengers. Ikenga and his group watched from above the cabin as the captain after a long discussion on his walkie-talkie with his co-captain, gathered his few belongings into a handbag strapped to his waist, and without saying a word to anyone pulled a long plank from the deck to make a bridge to the other vessel. When the passengers realised that the captain was planning to vacate the vessel, their sceptic murmuring boiled over to uproar and panic and few able-bodied passengers restrained the captain.

The ensuing physical tussle was ended by a gunshot from the other vessel. The Bedouin captain had clearly not adhered to the discussions and instructions from his more-experienced colleague. He was supposed to take a few belongings, dive into the sea and swim over to avoid prosecution. The intention had not been to completely abandon the travellers but to send a distress signal as soon as they were miles away from the stalled vessel. Fear was visible in everyone's face and nobody knew the next surprise that the Bedouin captain had in stock.

Since the passengers would not let him go, his colleague threw over a coil of rusty iron rope to be fastened by the tailboard of the vessel. The greater part of the journey was behind them and it seemed safer to tow the damaged boat for the remaining few hours instead of alerting the coast guards. The chain was fastened by the hack welded to rusty iron sheet just below the captain's cabin, and the Bedouin captain gave a thumb signal to his comrade that everything was in order. They were ready to move after a long delay, but when the co-captain accelerated the steaming engine to pull along the dead vessel, only a part of the rusted metal sheet responded, tearing off a long sheet of hardware in front of the vessel.

Seawater gushed in with an overwhelming speed and the anterior of the boat was suddenly overfloated and began to submerge, followed gradually by the posterior. Ikenga and a few others who were perched on the bare platform over the captain's cabin were the first to be swept into the water. There was no plan B and survival chances were pretty slim. People who wanted to shout or cry for help as was normal in such terrible circumstances took in more than enough water into their lungs. From the other boat there was panic and loud cries quickly swallowed by the ugly sight of death and helplessness. The other captain did not care to stop his already sailing boat, as his overcrowded vessel had not an inch more for another passenger and mounting a rescue operation meant that they would all go down. Some people who had managed to swim off the ill-fated vessel watched as their only means of safety drifted away while they made frantic efforts to get to it.

Ikenga was totally unprepared for a catastrophe of such magnitude. He was already deep down in the water before it dawned on him that it was a matter of life and death. With the experience gathered from the fishing company in Port Harcourt, he was able to swim up to the water surface to find out that the vessel he had been travelling with had almost disappeared into the water with most of its occupants.

The faces he saw in the water and that of those inside the unfortunate vessel were no longer perceptible. Their hands and feet seemed to be struggling in vain with terrifyingly indistinguishable swollen eyes and skull. When death comes for a man, it leaves him with no escape route; these expatriates clearly had none.

Meters away, the other vessel drifted from the people rumbling for any form of assistance or rescue. The rusty chain strapped to a metal sheet that had torn off the doomed vessel still followed the liner. Ikenga dived into the water and swam as fast as he could but the death that had trapped his co-passengers pulled the rusty chain every time he surged to grab the metal sheet that floated behind the moving vessel. He heard its rhyme clearly and it's beat more audibly.

*"Onwuuu ... onwu*

*Ogbu onye mgbe ndu n'ato ya*
*Omesuru onye di n'ula*
*Onwuuu ... onwu ..."*

His heart was already pounding with the murky rhythm but he refused to sing along. As he gathered all his breath and strength again to evade death, a sudden wave pushed his target further away from him.

"Death, you are not for me!" he rejected even as he trembled, but death did not relent in its quest to embrace him.

Umuafor men were known for their love and appreciation for life. Rooted in their *omenani* are occasional feasts, festivals and spontaneous merrymaking, in fullness or in poverty to cherish and celebrate life. Continually, they dared death while pretending to forget its sting until it would finally come uninvited. The claws of death, which he never expected so soon, were all around Ikenga and his heart pounded faster even as the fight for his life went on. While using up his last strength, he inwardly negotiated with death, with or without his *chi*. He clearly did not want to die; for the sake of the Udeaja family and Umuafor youths who were still preparing for their own adventure.

"How can I tell my story from the sea bed?" he loudly queried death.

It would take a while for the old engine to pick up its normal speed and Ikenga, seeing it as his only hope of survival, swam vigorously with his last strength till he was able to grab the rusty chain. Looking back at the gruesome scene of hundreds of his fellow migrants being choked by death, he had no doubt that the water had clearly been infested with death.

Back in Umuafor, it was believed that road intersections notorious for ghastly accidents and constant loss of lives were inhabited by death. Also, forests where people often fell from trees while hunting game or wild fruits were christened "forest of death." For Ikenga, the long stretch of waters off the coast of Lampedusa would forever remain the "Sea of death," as that was where hundreds of his comrades had perished before his eyes.

Along with the Bedouin captain who was also a very good swimmer, Ikenga was pulled aboard after a long distance before his strength ran out. They were the only survivors of the overloaded rickety boat. No one said much again till they arrived the shores of Lampedusa. Ikenga had been laid on the boat floor, bruised and in pain, with visions of his drowning comrades haunting him. He was sure to have seen those strange figures during his struggle for survival. They were very scary figures, to his right and to his left, not human figures but death itself, and had cornered him in the Mediterranean Sea but he refused to dance to its tune. That was what saved his life.

Once on the dry lands of Lampedusa, he did not care for the daunting protocols that accompanied refugee documentation and processing. It was evident that plagues of immigrants were about to overtake the tiny island and its inhabitants. Three major centres where migrants were kept on arrival had exceeded their capacity, and the hungry detainees sometimes had to jump over the fence to beg for food on the streets. He was diagnosed with broken ribs and flown to the Italian mainland with some other seriously injured refugees since the hospital could not cope with the stampede.

Stella was around to whisk him away from the hospital as soon as his conditions improved before the immigration authorities would come with their litany of questions. She was now married to a much older Italian man and needed to dance to the tune of the marriage for a certain number of years to get her *permesso di soggiorno*.

Initially, the marriage arrangement seemed too hasty for her till she began to understand the full rights of women in first world countries. Hence her decision to get pregnant for her Italian husband was to tap into the state-sanctioned means of nailing a man to a tree until the last penny dropped out of his pocket.

Ikenga was determined to travel to Germany. Ogbonnia could not have intentionally switched off his cell phone to cut off his contact. Meanwhile he could not continue to count on the kind hospitality offered by Stella's husband. Besides, things may take a dangerous turn if the old man found out that he was not in any way related to his wife. However, he stayed with them till Stella was able

# WOES OF IKENGA

to arrange fake travel documents that would take him to Germany.

# Chapter 5

As the pains of labour are forgotten when a baby arrives, so did Ikenga forget his numerous encounters with the angels of death throughout his rugged journey to the land flowing with milk and honey. He forgot the odour of decomposing bodies that had once filled the barren Sahara Desert, his handshake with death itself in the stormy waters off the coast of Lampedusa, the salty waters, and dirty food he had fed the worms in his stomach to prevent them from eating up his intestines.

Pain indeed nourishes courage. One cannot be brave if he has only had wonderful things coming his way. For a determined fugitive like Ikenga, the pains that had befallen him unexpectedly were less severe than those that were deliberately anticipated. Although he knew that the journey through the wilderness would not be easy, he had not expected such dreadful encounters.

The ordeal seemed to be over as the inter-city train pulled up at the Landesburg train station. Passengers alighted with their handbags and luggage. Some hugged relatives who had come to pick them up, while some others, who were clearly lovebirds, stood for a while and kissed their tongues out. Ikenga pulled his Montana synthetic bag from under his seat and jumped down the fast train. He was not expecting any welcome greetings from anybody and definitely not a hug. Ogbonnia, the only brother he had in Germany had switched off his mobile phone for reasons best known to him. He moved swiftly with the crowd to the direction where many of them were headed knowing that any hesitant movement would attract the attention of the on-looking security guards. This was one of the lessons learned in the course of the journey. He knew that he had to be composed despite his hunger-stricken look, and did his best to be.

The younger passengers moved down the steps while the elderly ones waited for their turn to use the escalator, and many headed towards the main entrance of the station. Ikenga without invitation offered to help a young student and his pregnant girlfriend carry three big boxes down the steps. The young man smiled warmly to the good samaritan as they descended the spacious station floor.

"*Danke sehr!*" he said as both men shook hands. Ikenga acquired extra confidence with the warm handshake from the gentleman. Even though he did not understand what the man told him, he could read appreciation all over his face. It gave him an added self-confidence that any one of the numerous station guards and stone-faced uniformed men who was watching would be convinced that he had come in good faith. He followed the majority carefully towards the entrance and adjusted his steps at intervals to look European while glancing around quickly to check if anyone was looking at him. The stories he had heard were confirmed when he spotted some black guys of about his age hanging around different corners of the train station, dressed in oversized jeans and hooded jackets.

"This is indeed the corporate headquarters," he told himself with joy.

He spotted two guys standing beside a bar close to the information centre, and his instincts told him immediately that they were from his part of the world, and most likely from his tribe. It took some level of expertise to be able to guess with ninety percent accuracy, a black man's nationality by merely looking at his face and his way of dressing.

"*Ndi oma*, I greet you," Ikenga said as he walked up to the two.

"Yeah, *nwa-nne!*" one replied confirming his assumptions. "How are you doing?"

"Please, I am just landing and have no idea where to go from here," Ikenga told them.

A fowl with ruffled feathers is never to be mocked because it might have won a fight. The two studied Ikenga carefully to understand what he meant. It could be assumed that the corps hunting for "dealers" in the station had given him a hot chase judging by his haggard looks.

"You came by air or what?"

"No! Far from it," Ikenga replied with a deep br<
very long journey with a very long story, but I just <
Italy by train."

Ikenga was still talking when a white lady in her early
with multiple earrings to the ears and nose staggered up \       _n
with tears dropping down her cheeks. He had always known that
*Ogbanje* existed in the white man's world, but what on earth could
make such a beautiful girl cry at this time of the day in such a
beautiful city? He wondered. One of the guys disappeared before
Ikenga could figure out the best way to offer his good samaritan
assistance and the young girl followed him immediately down the
underground station.

"We have to leave this place before you get yourself in
trouble," the other guy told him. "I will take you to an Afro-
restaurant close to the station. You can wait there till we are
through with the day's duty."

"I am in your hands, my brother," Ikenga implored.

"What is your name by the way?"

"Ikenga."

"My name is Mascot. We have to move, there is no time to
waste."

Both men moved down to the other side of the underground
station. Ikenga sensed danger from the alertness he read in
Mascot's eyes but he followed closely looking around with his eyes
and nose to see if he could identify danger if he saw one.

"Take this U-71," Mascot said to Ikenga as a light showed up
from one end of the tunnel. "Get down by the fifth station and
you will be standing in front of Green Garden Restaurant as soon
as you go up the steps. Tell them to give you food and something
to drink. I will be coming in a few minutes to join you." Ikenga
carefully listened and did as he was directed.

The Green Garden was bustling with people when Ikenga
stepped in. He had wished to enter unnoticed but that was made
impossible as people took turns to examine the new entrant and
make their judgments.

"It's like you've just entered town, boy?" Mr. Lasisi the owner of the restaurant asked.

"Yes, Sir!" Ikenga replied politely.

Mr. Lasisi was a kind-hearted old fellow who had bought over the restaurant when it was about to fold up. His life had been a rolling stone for a number of years until it had fortunately rolled into the bosom of his well-to-do Swedish wife. Psychological pressure and depression had caught up with him a few years after he entered the country when he had sadly realised that the certificates he hoped to find work with were not recognised. He had been denied a work permit and because he was too scared to engage in any criminal activity, his life had gradually deteriorated to a daily system of dressing up in a cowboy suit and taking long walks on the streets, talking and laughing to himself. Often he complained about his country's wealth, lodged in foreign banks by the past, present and future leaders. The goodwill of those that accepted such stolen funds from a nation on a relentless war against poverty has undoubtedly been bedeviled by *agwu*.

One memorable evening, Mr. Lasisi had positioned himself at a four-crossed road, directing traffic irrespective of the ever functioning traffic lights of Landesburg. Those who cared to listen to his numerous complaints afterwards either mocked or discarded his views as the empty words of a disenfranchised fellow. The Swedish woman who saved him from drifting away must have seen something unique in him to have made her move him to the comfort of her luxurious apartment. She had dished out money for him to pay for the restaurant and it did not take long before people began to realise that he was indeed a perfect gentleman being tormented by confusion and hopelessness.

"How are our people back home?" Lasisi enquired.

"It has been a while since I left them," Ikenga answered with respect. "But they should be doing better than me."

"Feel free!" Lasisi preached to make the weary looking Ikenga feel somewhat at home. "We were all once newcomers like you, from a distant land in search of illusive wealth. Your success will come if you persistently find your uniqueness and embrace it."

Ikenga stood by the counter listening to Mr. Lasisi. His first impression was that his countrymen were all cheerful and welcoming.

"Take a seat over there and let me offer you something to eat," Mr. Lasisi directed. "You have successfully scaled through the first hurdle."

Ikenga felt at home for the first time since he began this journey knowing that he was now in the midst of people he could identify with. He squeezed himself into a vacant chair in a corner close to the standing refrigerator from where he could have a good view of the whole restaurant. A giant Telefunken television hung over an elevated platform directly opposite him, booming with music. A fat woman busied herself behind the counter, which was well arranged with layers of assorted types of beer and hot drinks. The walls had nice decorations and tropical paintings that looked African. Some men noisily played snooker at another end of the restaurant. Ikenga fixed his eyes on the screen for a while moving his head slowly at intervals to the rhythm of the music till people withdrew their attention from him. None of the faces looked familiar but all he could tell was that they all looked good and nourished in their nice dresses with heavy bangles and chains round their necks. He silently prayed that Ogbonnia would make a sudden entrance but instead it was a waiter who stood before him with a plate of pounded yam and *egusi* soup, the kind of food he had missed for so long. Quickly he washed his hands when the waiter lowered the bowl and beckoned those around to join him as tradition demanded. He made heavy balls from the mountain of pounded yam, dipped into the *egusi* soup and threw down his throat, determined to deal with the hunger that had harassed him for years. A learned gentleman sitting opposite him in a worn out black suit and a dusty white shirt, occasionally drew people's attention back to him, hindering the smooth flow of the large pounded yam balls.

"Wow! Those balls are double the size of an egg in diameter," the learned gentleman said as Ikenga lifted the second ball. "Thirteen of such balls are enough to slow down your movement according to Professor Freeman's theory of gravity."

The people around the table burst into laughter, but Ikenga bravely put up a faint smile while doing justice to the mound of pounded yam before him.

"Leave the man alone, Prof!" a young man sitting right next to Ikenga interrupted. "Do you know what he went through before coming into this country?"

Professor Freeman had a long running feud with the young boys who made up the street clan. Though he had been advised a number of times by Mr. Lasisi to stay away from them, loneliness always sent him out in search of any one or group to have a word with. From his days as a student till the disastrous break-up with his third wife, the pattern of life he had been used to was clearly different from what was obtainable on the streets where ill-gotten wealth had deprived youths the respect for elders and the learned. The comment from the young man who was virtually new on the streets triggered a reaction from the nearly damaged neurons that transmitted signals to and fro the Professor's brain.

"From where did you get the audacity to talk when I am talking?" he barked at the young man. "Life abroad makes every Dick and Harry stand up against a Western-educated Professor."

"The street dwellers demand that professors respect themselves," the young man threw back.

"Be quiet, nitwit!" the Professor shouted on him.

"Call me whatever you like," the guy replied angrily. "But you are a disappointment to professorship."

"What did you just say?" Professor Freeman queried, moving forward with a clenched fist.

"You heard me," the young man maintained. "My country sent you overseas to acquire useful knowledge. You failed us all when you decided to stay a day longer after your studies."

The added explanation from the young street hustler was enough to unclench the professor's fists. Such in-depth analysis of his downfall was an exclusive preserve and not a topic to be discussed in public. Had he not gone into marriage in pursuit of the so-called resident permit, his success story would have been different by now. The thought of how low he had stooped –to the point of having such unhealthy associations with those he called nitwits or nincompoops–caused him to overreact whenever he felt that inappropriate words were being addressed to him.

"If I spare you for dealing in drugs in the train station," he threatened, "I will personally hand you over to the highest chamber of the country's law court to have you disciplined for insulting a law professor."

"Try the train station if your degrees and certificates cannot help you," the young man advised.

"Your generation will never smell any of my degrees."

"They are all useless degrees."

People who knew the man's aggressive nature intervened to prevent any exchange of blows. His case was well known and discussed in restaurants and beer parlours. Those related to him claimed that *agwu* was to blame for his failure while his fans that knew him to be well educated maintained that he had overstayed abroad and should work towards visiting his homeland.

Destitution indeed brings disdain, and on this assumption, the street clan argued that Professor Freeman's problem was entirely poverty as his story was clearly nothing to write home about after many years of schooling and working abroad. A German psychiatrist, who the professor had been referred to, gave a different diagnosis and continually gave drug prescriptions to the confused professor.

The long quarrel offered Ikenga some privacy and it did not take long before the mountain of pounded yam disappeared. A more relaxed Ikenga was helping himself to German beer when Mascot and his friend entered. They shook hands with some of their business associates, and greeted Professor Freeman with the honour due to him before joining Ikenga. Mr. Lasisi's wife followed up immediately with two bottles of Krombacher. She knew her regular customers from the corporate headquarters so well that she knew exactly what they wanted at any given time of the day.

"How do you see Landesburg, Boy?" Mascot asked Ikenga as he swallowed the first gulp.

"Excellent!" Ikenga replied with a smile.

"You said you had a long journey, which of the routes did you take?"

"I've been on the road for almost two years; I went through the seven forests and the seven seas."

"Thank goodness you made it ... a lot perished in the wilderness. Do you have any relatives in Germany?"

"Yes, I have a brother here," Ikenga answered. "His name is Ogbonnia.

"Is he aware that you are in town?"

"I have been trying his number for some time without success, I tried again this morning before I left Italy but his line was switched off."

"Could it be that he changed his number?" Mascot wondered aloud.

"It could be," Ikenga agreed. "I lost contact with him when I was still in Libya."

"It could as well be that you were overdemanding and he decided to sink your boat," Mascot said jokingly.

"I don't think so," Ikenga protested. "I tried not to inconvenience him."

"He has another name for sure?" Mascot asked in a more serious note.

"Ogbonnia Ubanese. That is the name he is known with."

"I don't know anyone like that. It could be that he is living with his *aduro* name but the most important thing is that you have arrived."

It was a sunny Saturday evening and everyone was wearing a smile. New arrivals hoped for a sweet encounter with a white woman so that their stay in the country could be cemented. Those who worked like donkeys through the week were relieved that another weekend was around the corner and those who had not tasted alcohol for five or six days because of their job restrictions, or were afraid of losing their driver's license were only too happy to be liberated.

The sun had started to set. Mascot and his friends were happy with the business of the day. There was a football match somewhere in the city and the Polizei had been deployed to the stadium to keep an eye on the hooligans and safeguard public property, and so there had not been many around to scare them from their illegal trade at the city train station. It was now time to go back to the house and get set for the night groove, and they gladly took Ikenga along. Already, Mascot had collected all his implicating documents, instructing that if the Polizei should stop them, he must maintain that he was just coming in from Somalia and that the two strangers with him had offered to help him locate the immigration office where he could lay his head for the night. Ikenga felt happy knowing that he was in good hands and that he would very soon be like them. The journey to Mascot's house lasted for close to an hour but that was not enough time for sightseeing for Ikenga who looked at everything a second time. The house turned out to be a row of twenty feet containers carefully designed and equipped to house refugees fleeing from persecution or war-zones across the globe. Occupants also included those who had lost the battle to hunger and poverty in their respective countries of origin and run away in search of greener pastures.

"This is my lodge," Mascot explained as he opened the door.

"Both of you live here?" Ikenga asked.

"I live alone," Mascot replied. "But most of the time I stay with my *Oyibo* babe."

"This place is not bad," Ikenga remarked.

Mascot and his friend laughed.

"*You just come, homeboy,*" the friend interjected in Pidgin English. "*This place na yeye.*"

Mascot hung his hooded jacket on the wall and brought out a bottle of Scottish whisky from the cupboard and gave it to his friend to open. His friend in turn handed it over to Ikenga, assuring him that a child's fingers are not scalded by a piece of hot yam which his father puts into his palm. Ikenga gladly accepted the honour as he took the bottle of whisky, raised it to the sky and offered thanks:

"*Chukwu Abiama,* we thank you," he prayed. "You said we shall live and that is why we are living. We thank you for our lives, and for the dead we thank you." He paused for a while to think about Udeaja, the grandfather that had given up life for his sake and his comrades that had perished in the "sea of death" off the coast of Lampedusa.

"A hungry man knows no peace," he continued. "From a distant land we have come in search of peace. We seek neither to kill nor to destroy but to fend for the stomach. *Chukwu-Okike,* You who created the coconut have provided it with water to drink. You that give itches to a child have also given him the fingernails to scratch. In unity with mother-earth we agree that wherever a he-goat is tied, may it feed from the grasses and leaves around." He paused a second time to allow his petitions ascend. That was when Mascot's friend remembered that his face cap was still on his head and hurriedly took it off.

"He who has got a drum will never beat on his bare chest," Ikenga continued. "Ancestors of our lands we beckon on you to remain awake because our enemies have not fallen asleep. If the wooden idols insist on tormenting us, let the termites never get weary of tormenting them. A person who chases a chicken is due for a fall because the chicken is a master of dodged escapes."

"My friends," he said turning to Mascot and his right hand man Santos, "kinsmen are born, but friendship is a gift of the gods."

Both men nodded their heads in agreement.

"The hinges of our friendship will never grow rusty."

"*Iseh!*" the two echoed in affirmation.

"Let the kite perch, and let the eagle also perch. Whichever begrudges the other the right to perch, it shall not break its wings but should show the other where to perch."

"*Iseh!*"

"That which we shall eat should come to us and that which will swallow us shall flee."

"*Iseh!*"

"We are strangers in this land. If any good comes to it, may we have our share and if any bad comes, let it go to the owners of the land who know what god to appease."

"*Iseh!*"

"May this drink double our joy and divide our grief."

"*Iseh!*"

"You will receive our prayers in heaven to rain down blessings upon good men."

"*Iseeehhh!*"

He lowered the whisky bottle, opened it carefully and poured few drops into a glass throwing it out to the unseen. This was an act of paying homage to the Great Being and to the ancestors; giving them the first taste of the drink before humans started to consume.

The two hailed and saluted Ikenga by his title name before pouring themselves some sizeable quantity of the whisky in the glass to drink. They discussed at length about the unspeakable atrocities taking place in their home country; the constant fear of armed robbers and kidnappers who were determined to face death if riches would not come their way; politicians who promised food to the hungry only to empty the food baskets when they stepped into power; the unworthy lifestyle of modern day self-acclaimed God's emissaries – those who claimed to be representatives of the Man from Nazareth; and preventable deaths caused by diseases that forced parents to keep on producing children with relatively no means of raising them up properly, while clinging on to the hope that few would eventually survive.

Their stories went on and on as the liquid content of the bottle before them steadily decreased. Mascot who was fond of joking with even grave matters advised his friends to drink and leave the problems of their home country to their home country as the host community in which they lived also had a litany of problems to deal with. He told them how men with healthy bank accounts and a number of houses would wake up in the morning and after looking down from their balcony over their fleet of expensive cars, go back to their bedroom to call the emergency medical unit only to complain that they had depression. There was the tragic death of a neighbour who had jumped to his death from a newly constructed highway bridge because his wife walked out of their marriage. "In a country where there are no problems, even a mosquito bite becomes a deadly worriment," he concluded.

Ikenga smiled to himself, knowing that mosquitoes had been biting him for as long as he could remember and no one in Umuafor had ever counted that as an issue.

Afterwards, they went down to a nearby supermarket to buy some foodstuff since their new friend would be staying in the container apartment for a while. Before catching a train back to the city, Mascot made sure that his guest got a good deal of revamping. Ikenga was now fully dressed in European ensemble and some who had seen him a few hours earlier when he walked into the Green Garden restaurant could barely recognise him. He was dressed in Mascot's oversize jeans trousers suspended above his stomach with a leather belt, and an extra-large t-shirt with the head of a late popular hip-hop icon boldly engraved on its front and back. Borrowed clothes are either too tight or too loose, but for the borrower, it is the fashion of the day.

Mascot seemed to have developed some likeness for Ikenga and was very eager to guide and spoil him. They spent some more hours at the Green Garden before heading to the main station to show their friend how beautiful the city could be at night. It was close to midnight and the train station still bustled with people, with fast food centres and restaurants making the best of sales. Tourists from all corners of the globe were dressed in their respective traditional garbs shouting on top of their voices in their own different languages.

"Wow! Everyone is friendly," reckoned Ikenga who had been counting the number of young men and women coming around to exchange greetings with Mascot and Santos. This was totally different from the stories he had heard about the German society and its conservativeness. Old and young men were out in frantic search of their lady of the night, while those who had found theirs proudly locked hands with them as they moved around. The ladies were not left out as they also emitted rays of attraction with the younger ones dressed as if their parents were not at home when they left the house. The older ladies of Landesburg who would like to remain eighteen till they die were garbed under layers of different forms of cosmetics on their cheeks and eyebrows to elevate their competitive advantage. Mascot and his friend were not on duty that evening but their business associates had taken positions in different corners of the spacious train station, signalling customers by nodding their heads when they spotted one. As trains from other parts of the city pulled up and people poured down into the station like soldier ants, the now relaxed Ikenga looked around in delight. The night was as bright and busy as the day, and his heart was filled with joy but he dared not let anyone notice that he was a *JJC,* so he composed himself as well as he could.

By the time they arrived the old city of Landesburg with the underground train, he could no longer hold his silence. After all, Umuafor people say, "he who is afraid of asking is ashamed of learning."

"What are they celebrating?" he asked Mascot.

"Weekend," came the reply.

All the buildings looked gorgeous with ancient designs, the streetlights were exceptional, and all lighted up like it was a night carnival in Rio de Janeiro. The city was filled up, as the rows of bars and nightclubs could not contain their guests. Everyone either had a bottle of beer in their hands or was burning their hearts out with sticks of cigarette and those who had had more than enough lay in different corners of the street in a pool of their own mess. Ambulances were overstretched transporting the drunk and the injured to the hospital and the Polizei were at alert to fish out troublemakers. The drinking code of Landesburg stipulated clearly that one could drink to death or till a doctor came to the rescue, but trouble would not be tolerated.

Three young girls walked up to them smiling, and one hugged and kissed Mascot. Santos was obviously not new into the game, so he cornered the second girl and opened up a conversation: Ikenga was left standing with the third girl while he contemplated how to make the first move. His timidity as a result of his cultural orientation did not allow him boldness in women affairs, but courage eventually came when Mascot gave him a knowing wink.

"You are looking good, girl," he said bravely to the third girl.

"Thanks!" the girl replied with a welcoming smile.

"What is your name?"

"My name is Alexandra."

"What is the country celebrating today?" Ikenga asked again not convinced with the answer he got from Mascot.

"Nothing," the girl replied. "It's just a normal summer weekend."

Alexandra was expecting more of the conversation but Ikenga was out of words. It had always been a problem whenever he tried to talk to the opposite sex. His *omenani* strictly forbade any intimate union of unmarried men and women, and the new religion from Reverend Klaus had also classified such union as capital sin with a one-way ticket to hell fire. He was rather perplexed as he eyed the two yellow mini mountains on Alexandra's chest piercing through her sleeveless blouse. Consequently he sensed a movement inside his oversized jeans and swiftly put his two hands in his pocket to hold down his magic stick.

"It's like you are new in the country?" Alexandra enquired.

"Yes," Ikenga replied. "I came in for a conference."

"Are you also Caribbean like Mascot?"

"Yeah, we all come from the same place."

"Welcome to Landesburg."

"Thanks, everything in this country looks beautiful."

"And me?" Alexandra corrected.

"You are the most beautiful."

Mascot tried to persuade the girls to come along with them but instead they wanted the boys to accompany them to another bistro of their choice. Mascot refused to dance to anybody's tune. Moreover, he wanted to take Ikenga to another nightclub where he would have better chances of getting a girl for the night if not for a long-term relationship.

He threw his hand around Ikenga's neck as the girls went their way and commended his bravery. "You have to be ready for a prolonged battle if you want to achieve those wild ambitions of yours," he warned.

"I am very much ready." Ikenga assured.

"I have to tell you all these things from day one," Mascot preached further. "In the jungle where only tigers survive, you have to fight every inch of your way for survival. Life abroad is not a bed of roses, but on the contrary, a battle and survival of the smartest. The goal is to achieve a good life, and of course the Resident Permit for easy travelling. For the hard currency, you collect from the train station, our corporate headquarters but for the *kpalli*, the permission to stay or work, you collect that from the girls since the jungle law leaves one with no alternative."

Mascot rounded up by emptying his beer and handing the bottle over to an old lady sitting by the roadside with a heap of empty bottles and recyclable cans. Ikenga nodded in agreement even though he did not clearly understand what his friend meant.

Oasis was one of the oldest night clubs in Landesburg known for oriental and black music. It was formerly owned by two German brothers who had sold it due to the unending trouble that came with the drug dealers and legion of junkies that patronised them. The new owner happened to be a Somalian ex-warlord who had fled his country after he fell out with his men, and had retained ownership of the club for a long time, against all odds. That was possible because of his connection with both the men of above and the underworld. Akim, the bouncer who had been hired to replace the former, was a no-nonsense man. With height that measured above two metres tall, he was popularly known as the strong man of Landesburg. His stony face and the breath that came out of his large nostrils were clearly enough to ward off anybody intending to make trouble. Monkey-man, the DJ, was in his best mood as well, with his long dread locks and bushy beard. He always sought to give customers a reason to come back to the club another time, and was successful at it.

Mascot jumped into the dance floor with his rude-man-style movements, shaking hands with friends and hugging ladies, and Ikenga followed closely shaking hands with whoever shook hands with his friend. The waiters noticed their entrance and quickly made a table ready for Mascot and his clique. Before long, the table was filled with glasses and different brands of whisky. Some friends joined the table and Ikenga got to meet and interact with many of them. He repeatedly asked if anyone knew Ogbonnia but no one seemed to. Whatever the case, Ikenga knew that Ogbonnia who had helped him financially through his rough journey would not intentionally avoid him now that he was in Germany.

He brushed the issue of his extended cousin aside and followed an elderly lady standing next to them to the dance floor. Monkeyman had just excited the ladies by playing one of their favourite tunes, and anyone watching Ikenga on the dance floor, draped in his oversized European outfit could clearly tell that he lacked European style. The lady took advantage of his obvious naiveté, and with her little knowledge of English, engaged Ikenga in a conversation to confirm if he was new in town.

"How long have you been in this country?" she asked.

"I am still very fresh," Ikenga answered honestly believing that his *kpalli* might come from her.

"I can help you with the Resident Permit so you don't suffer like others," she boasted.

Her words thrilled him, but he kept low his excitement. The dance floor was fully charged as Monkey-man played a few selected tunes that made people go wild. A giant mirror mounted on both sides of the dance floor multiplied the number of the dancers, and the disco lights of all forms and colours sent out their moon-like and star-like glows from above. As he began to rock the old lady, Ikenga noticed a vibration again down below. The more he tried to avoid body contact, the more the old lady drew him closer to herself. She moved her hands gently between his legs to feel the magic stick, while staring straight into his eyes and smiling through her cigarette-stained teeth. The young African boy felt shock waves as they rocked and rolled.

Both were sweating as they went back for a break. Their table had been doubled to contain glasses and bottles from more friends who had come in later with their girlfriends, including the old lady who had transferred to join Ikenga and his group of friends.

Soon she excused herself to go and use the toilet, Ikenga watched her disappear before pulling Mascot's shirt to whisper: "The woman said she loves me."

Mascot burst into a heavy and long laughter as he poured whisky into his glass with a bit of soft drink to dilute the solution before loudly addressing Ikenga: "You make me crazy, boy! How can somebody see you today and love you?"

Ikenga stared at Mascot confusedly. These were the same people who had been ringing into his ears that a woman was the only channel to cement his stay in the country.

"That shows you are a good hunter anyway," Mascot continued. "I will suggest you play along with the one-day love adventure. The patience of the hunter should be greater than that of the prey, though I am yet to find out which one of you is the hunter or the hunted.

Mascot's words always tended to be encoded with wisdom, and Ikenga who needed extra explanations to understand what was clearly meant threw out a question to get Mascot to elucidate. "Is it too early for a love adventure?"

WOES OF IKENGA

"No!" his friend replied. "These girls jumping around are all potential *kpalli*. If you are smart enough to collect your own on time, you sacrifice a cow to your *chi*: If you are on the other side of luck, they will run you mad before you lay your hands on the good-for-nothing Resident Permit."

"But this one is not too old to give me the *kpalli*?" Ikenga asked curiously.

"Not at all, we don't talk of age when it comes to *kpalli*, a goat that can give milk is far better than a cow that cannot. People with some degree of patience and tolerance have collected their *kpalli* from women old enough to be their grandmother. We are in Rome, homeboy, and we got to do just as the Romans."

Mascot was still delivering his alcohol inspired sermon when Ikenga tapped him – the old lady had showed up again.

"Hallo, lady!" he greeted staggeringly. "My name is Bob-Mascot Obiagu Chukwukadibia. I am the modern-day sole colonial master in the city of Landesburg, and I suggest that you enroll as a candidate for any upcoming dancing competition judging from your performance on the dance floor."

The old lady smiled warmly and raised her glass of wine up for cheers. Everyone around the table complied and she used this opportunity to study their faces as Mascot kept on talking without giving her a chance to introduce herself.

It was five o'clock in the morning and people were gradually leaving. Mascot and his friends had had enough of the night and he signalled to his girlfriend that it was time to go. Some of the guys who did not like to see a drop of whisky waste shared whatever was left of the last bottle. Ikenga also got a share as he was already used to palm wine and local gin from an early age, and the refined whisky from the white man's land had just done him some good. He staggered behind his new lover as the ladies collected their handbags that had been deposited upon entry with the keeper. The friends shook hands warmly and bade themselves farewell.

Ikenga had long forgotten that he entered the country just some hours earlier by the time they were headed to the lady's apartment in her BMW three series. Mascot had assured him that Germany was no country for rituals, and encouraged him to feel free while rocking and rolling with his one-night lover.

He watched as the lady drove professionally through the beautiful city and wondered what his friends back home would say if they knew that a white woman was already driving him around town. Next, he leaned backwards to have a second look at the lady through the corner of his eyes, while winding up the windows to ward off the cold morning breeze. From his assessments, the lady looked like she was in her late forties but was still very good looking even without layers of make-up.

"Are you married?" Ikenga asked bravely.

"My job would not allow me," the old lady replied.

"You should have gotten children at least," Ikenga asked further. "Ah! Children are very expensive in this county."

"Children are the fruit of life and the ones to help you when you can no longer help yourself," he explained based on what his *omenani* instructed.

"This place is not your part of the world," she corrected. "The government is there for everyone, old or young."

Ikenga felt ashamed of himself and his government. They were not there for Nne and Chukwuma his father, nor had they been there for he and Chinaza when they lived off refuse dumps right from a tender age, and were definitely not there when his mother and brother died during delivery. He felt saddened for a while but shook his head and smiled. His smile was not out of derision or whining self-pity, but a remedy or miracle drug to ease his pains and help him put in a positive perspective to the challenges he was sure to face in the white man's land. The years of poverty were over and so he had better free his mind to think clearly about how to tap into the potentials that awaited him.

"Marriage is not necessarily to bear children but to have someone around to keep company," Ikenga explained.

"Nicky keeps me company," the lady replied rudely. "I will not tie myself to any man."

"Who is Nicky?"

"Nicky is my big boy," she replied. "He is a breed from an Arabian mountain dog and an English sheep-dog."

"I see you get along well with your big boy," Ikenga mocked.

"Sure! We came back just recently from a two-week holiday in the Bahamas."

Ikenga did not utter a word from then on. If the old lady was wealthy and loving enough to take *Eke-uke*, the dog, on holidays to the Bahamas, then he who is human should be ready to visit the sights of the Seven Wonders of the World or to be invited for dinner at the Buckingham Palace. He resolved to maintain high spirits to properly harness all that the country had for him. When a goat goes to church, it does not stop till it gets to the altar.

Nicky flipped its tail around as a welcome gesture when the apartment door flew open but the long eared creature was noticeably uncomfortable with the new visitor who was also sickened by the sight of an animal enjoying such extravagance that many humans in his part of the world could only dream of. Dogs could be a man's best friend but they had no business whatsoever inside his house and certainly not on his bed. On this established order of co-existence, he insisted that the laboratory-manufactured pet be sent out of the bedroom. The old lady finally succumbed when Ikenga would not let loose his trousers, and Nicky was locked up in the kitchen against its will.

It was Monday morning before Ikenga could see the light of day again. He decided to not disclose what his eyes had seen to anyone until he saw Mascot. His lover dropped him off at the Green Garden on her way to work and the first thing he did was order a bottle of energy drink to salvage what was left of his strength when the waiter assured him that Mascot was around.

Mascot on the other hand was having a rough day at the City Station. It was almost month-end and all his customers had run out of cash. He had had to give free handouts, or up to fifty percent sales reduction in order to keep up the day's sales, or in some cases give a commission to whoever brought him a customer. By midday, he was tired of the game and took the underground train with two of his friends to cool off at the Green Garden.

Ikenga sprang up on sighting the three, and halted Mascot before he could enter the restaurant.

"Mascot ... " he called, taking him by the hand and leading the way a few metres from the entrance. "Mascot ... " Ikenga called again as he looked round to make sure that the walls and the trees had not suddenly developed ears.

"What's up, homeboy?" Mascot asked curiously. "Was there a problem?"

"That woman is an old vampire," Ikenga disclosed at last.

Mascot looked at Ikenga and burst into an uncontrollable laughter. He did not need to listen to the rest of the story because the old lady and many like her were well known for their insatiable desire for men with active magic sticks. They preyed mostly on newly arrived migrants with promises of marriage till they were through with their victims.

"This is not a laughing matter," Ikenga continued. "I would have called for rescue but you forgot to give me your phone number before we parted from Oasis."

Mascot laughed and laughed again and again till tears poured out of his eyes.

"Get yourself together, boy!" he said to Ikenga finally. "There are things I have to tell you, and there are things you have to discover yourself. Let's go in, that was a funny adventure you had this time. A lot have had very awful experiences in the race for Resident Permit. Santos's case was pathetic and horrible. He had a showdown in a guest house with two men who came to a night club dressed as pretty ladies but turned out to be something else as soon as they had their unsuspecting boyfriend in their shared bedroom. The intending love affair eventually turned into a blood bath and the hotel management had to call the police to quench the episode."

Mascot broke the news as he stepped into the restaurant and everyone laughed at the poor *JJC*.

Ikenga felt ashamed initially but as others narrated their similar encounters with those "old ladies", he loosened up.

"That is 'welcome to Germany'," Mascot told him.

Mr. Lasisi's wife who was pretending to be busy behind the counter could also not help laughing.

Ikenga's arrival at the Promised Land was well celebrated back home. He called the headmaster to inform him that he would be calling again at the same time the next day to speak with his father. When the call finally came, there was joy on the faces of Chukwuma, Nne and Chinaza who had already been waiting for the call three hours earlier. There was little time to explain to Nne what had kept him from calling in the past months but they were all happy that he was well, especially Chinaza who was extremely glad to know that the voice coming from the other end of the telephone was that of her twin brother.

"How is white man's world?" she asked cheerfully.

"Another world … " Ikenga replied frankly.

"I am glad for you, Ikem, please take care of yourself and don't run after those white girls I see on the television," she advised.

"I will not my dear," Ikenga promised. "All my ambition is to make my family proud and goodness will give me the strength to do it."

"You have done it," Chinaza said. "Just place my cell phone top on your list."

"Your prayers have reached the heavens," he assured. "Give the phone to Papa let me talk to him before my credit runs out."

Ikenga had vowed to not call home throughout his nineteen months as a sojourner because he knew that his people would be distressed and calling to narrate his ordeal in the wilderness would only make Nne break down. Besides, their tears or words of advice would have meant little to him during those deadly and critical moments as his father always told him that once the ship went afloat, what mattered most was the wise calculations and judgment of the captain. The old soldier had brought him up right from childhood to be the captain of his own ship and Ikenga trusted in his own ability to make right judgments when and wherever stormy waters turned up.

"Ugo-nnia!" Chukwuma yelled as soon as Chinaza handed over the old Nokia cell phone. That was the name given to Ikenga when he had taken his *Ozo* title at the age of seven.

"You gave me sleepless nights for a long time," he lamented.

"I've told you not to worry about me, Papa. I wanted to get to Germany before I called," Ikenga explained. "The ride was a bit bumpy and I did not want to bring more worries to any of you."

"You don't need to say much Ugo-nnia," his father calmed him. "Chukwuma, your father, has not been to Germany but I know you must have been through seven forests and seven seas."

"Goodness has been good to me, Papa."

"Yes!" his father answered in agreement. "Our ancestors have not fallen into slumber, and to Goodness you must be grateful. A good name is better than wealth. You have our name and blood in you and they must not get soiled. Always bear in mind that the wealth that takes only a market week to acquire is sure to contain in it things for which the gods will surely come to make claims. Mr. Maya, the German construction manager with Ronasko Company, once told me that Germans are hard-working people and that they work as fast as their machine. But still I taught him how to open a bottle of beer with the teeth. This is your opportunity to teach them how to break a coconut with the head."

The headmaster who was standing next to him burst into laughter and gestured to him that his time was up, but Chukwuma was not yet through with his advices.

"You must find Mr. Maya and greet him very well for me. Tell him that you are the son of Mayor. That was the name he gave me."

"I will, Papa."

"Carry along your bag of wisdom wherever you go," his father advised further. "And call me as often as you can."

"I will, Papa," Ikenga guaranteed. "Please take care of the family till I come back."

122

Chukwuma handed the phone back to the headmaster and happily slumped onto a wooden bench.

"How are you, my son?" the headmaster asked.

"I am doing great, Sir," the voice replied.

"You must have gone through a rough road but we are happy you finally made it. Have you seen Ogbonnia your cousin?"

"Not really, his lines have been dead since I entered the country."

"He might be having multiple load of work at school," the headmaster suggested unaware that his son had completely veered off the track. "I will let him know you are already in town whenever he calls again."

"That would be great."

"Try to get yourself a job and avoid the white man's way of life because times are hard back home and your people need your support."

"I will do my best, Sir. Goodness will surely use me to bless them."

"The ball is now in your court. All I know is that whoever steps into the white man's land is free from poverty."

The headmaster was still talking when the line went dead from the other end. Little did they know that Ogbonnia was about to complete an eight-month jail term in Balthazar, for attempting to collect money from a German community bank with a stolen credit card.

The news spread like wildfire that Ikenga was in Germany even before his family got back to their house. It was a rare privilege and honour to have a member of one's family in the white man's land. People who had issues with the family began to mend fences so that the wealth from overseas might trickle down to them when it started coming. The general misconception of life in the white man's land and total submission to the negative influence of wealth further aroused the runaway instincts among the poor youths of Umuafor.

# Chapter 6

Ikenga put up in Mascot's refugee camp for six weeks. He was very well content in the twenty-foot container with all its luxurious amenities, which had till now been only dreams, he ate and drank with hopes of recovering all the weight he had lost during his adventures in the wilderness. Chicken, which was exclusively a Sunday delicacy for the privileged few in Umuafor, was the cheapest among the edibles in the supermarkets. In different *Kebab* shops were also assorted oriental dishes with roast meat swinging with mouth-watering spices. Mascot's standing refrigerator was also stuffed with multivitamin drinks and assorted chocolate, while beer and hot drinks were loaded under the two-meter spring bed. Occasionally, Mascot came in to visit and they would go to the supermarket for shopping whenever there were excess coins from some of his poor customers at the City Station.

With all these goodies already at his disposal, Ikenga had no doubts about the enormous potentials and opportunities locked in the nooks and crannies of his newfound home waiting to be exploited. He was already the proud owner of a Nokia mobile phone, and living a life far different from what he was used to.

The *aduro* house was made up of rows of twenty feet containers but was extremely luxurious and very comfortable for an alien who had lived in patchy houses and slept on a raffia mat. Light came on at the mention of "let there be light," with a click on the switch. Tap water flowed at the touch of a joystick, and the buses and trains took him to his various destinations at the appointed time even if he was the only passenger on board. He told himself that only a greedy fellow would go on demanding for more with all these pleasures at his disposal. Although he had not started earning his own money, he was confident that his own share of the hard currency would soon start flowing in by the time he was through with the *aduro* process.

Migrants, asylum seekers and those with refugee status were generally and unofficially referred to as Aliens. Some in the Alien cartel were genuine political asylum seekers who had fled persecution from their various homelands, while a sizeable number of the crew were merely economic migrants who referred to one another as *Aduro*. Refugees could apply for *aduro* either at the point of entry or at designated refugee centres once they stepped into their country of destination. Political and economic migrants usually had their minds set on a specific country as preferred destination, and Germany took the lead as a magnet for economic migrants from Africa and Asian countries, apparently for the fast pace of their recovery after their own disastrous war and their continued economic dominance in the continent. That might have earned their industrious citizens and equipment the name "German machine" in the borrowed language of Umuafor.

Individuals who felt belittled by the *aduro* title or did not like to be classified as such carefully melted into the society when they sneaked into the country, avoiding those hot spots and trouble zones where the wide net of the corps might catch up with them. Some of them patronised fraudsters who arranged illegal documents for them and hoped never to get caught by the Polizei, but with rampant cases of apprehension and deportation, the Polizei and immigration authorities had proven that those with illegal papers would eventually get caught and many had come to realise that it was safer to apply for *aduro* and have all the necessary rights including a package of goodies and freedom of movement.

The direction which new migrants were likely to take upon arrival depended heavily on the first group of individuals they met, as very many left their home country for new life abroad absolutely ignorant of what awaited them. Ikenga had told Mascot about his background and semi-tragic adventure en-route his dreamland, and Mascot was in turn determined to see him through in the best way he could.

"If I should get one of these jobs that citizens reject," Ikenga suggested, "that would help me a lot."

"That is easier said than done," Mascot muttered. "Your adventure is not yet over."

"I know," Ikenga accepted. "But much of the bumpy rides are over?"

"One cannot tell yet," Mascot explained: "It is one thing to transport oneself over to this country, and another thing entirely to know when it is time to take one's bag and leave."

"I will definitely not be staying long," Ikenga announced.

"Those were also our wishes."

"How long have you stayed in the country?"

"I will clock six years by the end of the year."

"Have you visited home in between?"

"*For where!*"

"No!" Ikenga exclaimed. "I will not nail myself in this country like that."

"Get started first before you talk of that," Mascot instructed. "Your *awele* has a lot to play. Many blame the devil that stood against good governance in their respective countries, those who have been here for long will tell you about an unseen coercion by white man's juju that constantly holds them down each time they think of going back."

"That cannot be true or ...?"

"Not far from the truth I would say," Mascot expounded: "Everything is possible in the white man's land. The powerful deities and statues they snatched from the shrines of Africa cannot just be for mere decorations."

Memories of his encounter on the way to Port Harcourt came to Ikenga; the four wooden idols he had stolen from *Ogwugwu* shrine were to be sold to white merchants but he had not bothered to ask what they actually wanted it for. The fact that these foreign merchants only requested for the very old statues that still retained some degree of potency indicated that it had to be something about their supernatural powers. His Lebanese accomplice and middleman had tried to persuade him not to give up, that the incident along Eziobe dusty highway had just been a coincidence and not a counter-attack from the rotten carved woods.

"Could it be that they intentionally came over to steal our gods so they could extract their supernatural powers?" Ikenga asked in disbelief.

"That's the way I see it," Mascot answered. "They have the best sculptures and artists who can make better ones if it were to be for just beauty and decoration."

Ikenga was not sure how Mascot would react if he got to know about his encounter with the statues from *Ogwugwu* shrine, and so he kept that chapter of his adventure to himself and focused on his present worries.

"Where do I start with this *aduro* protocol?"

"I don't know what country is suitable for use now," Mascot told Ikenga as they approached Uncle Ray's house. "I came when the Juntas were on rampage in Liberia and we were warmly welcomed by the immigration authorities as sacred vultures of United Nations."

"I want to use Niger Delta," Ikenga announced. "The crises have surfaced again with arrests of all the village heads by government forces when they protested over the systematic destruction of their farmland."

"Nonsense," Mascot returned sharply. "Don't even contemplate using that to apply for asylum, unless you want to see yourself the next day at the Murtala Mohammed Airport or the Kotoka International Airport."

"Are they that strict?" Ikenga asked curiously.

"Not really."

"What is bad in using my country for asylum?"

"The name Nigeria makes no good rhythm with *ogene*, the music instrument."

"I would not want to deny my country for any reason."

"You will certainly do so before you realise it," Mascot informed him. "Going through those horrible encounters you narrated, it is evident that the *Lugardian* contraption has first denied you."

"They know not of my existence," Ikenga consented.

"Me, too."

"Which of the war-torn countries would you then suggest that I use?"

"Uncle Ray should know better," Mascot assured him. "That is one of his key areas of specialisation; you are lucky that the man was released from Balthazar a few days ago."

The two strolled and discussed till they got to Wincanton *Aduro* camp, a notorious refugee settlement in the industrial area of the city of Norsburg.

\*   \*   \*   \*   \*

Mr. Raymond Ogbonnia Ubanese was a promising and ambitious young man when he left Umuafor shortly after his college studies but not before he spent some years at a nursing school in a distant town. His father, the headmaster, had thought it wise to crown it all with the title, "Doctor", and used his influence to secure admission for his son to study a medical course in one of the German universities. There were no jobs for him in Umuafor and nursing was widely believed to be a non-demanding job meant for women. Raymond's pregnant wife had feared losing her husband to the white women she regularly saw on television and pleaded with her husband to stay back and manage the job of an attendant in her father's petrol station.

"Believe me, darling," he pleaded with his wife, "by the time I come back as a qualified medical doctor, we will build two or more petrol stations for ourselves or erect a town clinic near Afor market."

She finally gave in when all her efforts to persuade him to abandon his journey proved futile; said goodbye in tears, and begged him to come back soon to her and their unborn baby.

It was not wrong to dream of a better life, but "all that glitters is not gold" as Ray soon discovered. For the period of eleven years that he had lived in Germany, he had merely been holding his head above water while ruling out any form of retreat or surrender. His lectures at the Hamburg University barely lasted for a year before it occurred to him that Umuafor would sing praises of his money and not of his education. He then made up his mind to join the street clan instead of living from hand-to-mouth and draining his father's little earnings. Studies were then abandoned as soon as he discovered crooked means of making money, and soon, the little token regularly sent by St. Patrick's Mission to support him was declined. Hence, it was little wonder that Reverend Klaus had wondered what the young man was up to when he had sent the first Mercedes Benz 190 to his father, but Ogbonnia had put his father's mind at rest with the explanation that he combined his studies with a cleaning job.

Next, he changed his identity from a student of medicine to a political asylum-seeker running away from a country with a history of unending wars. The authorities had taken him to numerous embassies but all had declined issuing him emergency travel documents, with the last being the embassy of Sri Lanka where he had made his two security guards an object of mockery. Out of frustration, the foreign office had dumped him at the Wincanton camp and for long taken their eyes off him. With "unknown" boldly printed on the slot for his place of birth in the white sheet handed over to him as a temporary ID card, Ogbonnia could not legally earn a living and had thus devised alternative means of survival.

The endless trips to foreign embassies and unfulfilled threats of deportation had not only hardened him but also opened his eyes to more ways of tricking the authorities. He belonged to a group of aliens known as "*Aduro* of no Nation"; these were individuals who had sworn never to leave their host country till their financial situation improved for good. The authorities very much wanted to get rid of them but no country was willing to accept them as their citizens, including the ones they claimed to have come from. This group constituted a thorn in the flesh to the respective foreign offices that transported them from one foreign embassy to the other as they endlessly tried to obtain emergency travel document with which to kick them out. There were also cases where an alien would be flown back to a country thought to be his, only to be refused at the point of entry by hungry-looking immigration officers. Officers who normally accompanied such people to make sure that they were gone for good would have no other choice but take the alien back to their owner–the foreign office that would grudgingly receive them and wait till they got a valid proof of origin.

Another group of aliens to be pitied were those that called themselves *Ala-wu-otu,* which literally means, Mother Earth is one. These were individuals who had painfully accepted defeat either from the pressure of the ever-changing immigration laws of the host country or from the insatiable material demands of their family and relatives back home. They were too weak to jump through the hurdles set by their host country and too ashamed to return to their homelands empty-handed. Living one day at a time with a deep-rooted sense of guilt and dejection, they no longer thought about home and had consequently become like the multi-legged millipede that turned its death spot to its graveyard. It meant nothing to them if they were sheltered in the Ajegunle districts of Lagos, the shanty suburbs of Kandahar or at No. 10 Downing Street; they believed that Mother Earth would definitely provide them with a place to lay their heads as long as they were alive. Doctors tended to complicate their situation by prescribing a range of tablets for what was merely pure stress or financial problems. Thus, such people were often overlooked and left to sink in their own mess, in societies where economic hardship and unhealthy social order restrained each man to his own affair.

Ikenga and Mascot waited a few moments by the graveyard at the entrance of the Wincanton refugee camp. The old cemetery was very quiet except for the movements of rabbits and birds. Some graves were well kept with fresh flowers and freshly burnt candles, which indicated that their living relatives had recently visited. Ray showed up on his mountain bike from a pathway in exactly twenty minutes as he had promised.

"Ogbonnia!" Ikenga shouted with joy.

"Udeaja himself!" Uncle Ray exclaimed throwing his arms

open for a hug. "You made it at last?"

"Yes, big brother," Ikenga answered as he flew into his cousin's arm. "I almost lost hopes of seeing you again; nobody seemed to know anyone named Ogbonnia."

"I forgot to tell you," Ogbonnia admitted. "Everyone calls me Uncle Ray here."

"How could you have disappeared into the thin air all of a sudden?" Ikenga asked.

"You will understand it better now that you have arrived," Uncle Ray explained. "Life in a white man's land is a theatre understood only by the actors and not the spectators."

"What happened?" Ikenga demanded.

"These people wasted my precious time in Balthazar," Uncle Ray revealed.

"Where is Balthazar?"

"A dungeon in the heart of Landesburg," Mascot threw in.

"Why?"

"They called it *Betrug*."

"What is *Betrug*?"

"The language is not one to learn while standing," Uncle Ray said to curtail Ikenga's curiosity. "Have you applied for *aduro*?"

"Not yet."

Mascot, who stood watching the happy reunion with a smile, took it up from there. It had never occurred to him that Uncle Ray was the one Ikenga had been asking after. Raymond who was not only educated but had also undergone six months of intensive lessons in German, was like a big brother to many. People like Mascot who had not had the opportunity to go to school in their respective countries, ran to him whenever they received mind-bugging letters from the immigration authorities. Another source of daily bread for Uncle Ray was packaging intending asylum seekers with up-to-date information and suitable countries with which to apply for asylum.

"He is the brother I was telling you about on the phone," Mascot said to Uncle Ray.

"He is my little cousin," Ray told Mascot.

"That's what he maintained all along, I never knew that you were the said Ogbonnia."

"How was everybody when you left?" Ray asked his cousin.

"They are living as far as I know," Ikenga replied.

"I hope that there would still be enough men there. the youths of Umuafor have deserted her," Ray complained.

"Better to run away than be consumed by fire," Mascot declared.

"I wish I had stayed back," Uncle Ray lamented.

"You can still go back," Mascot teased.

"Where do I start when I get there?"

"From anywhere."

"Where?"

"You can start with your wife."

"Get serious for once, Mascot," Ray implored. Uncle Ray was a jolly good fellow on a good day but sometimes got bitter whenever he was reminded of where his decision to travel abroad had landed him.

"Look at me, Mascot!" he continued. "This is where I am practising what I spent years to learn in the nursing school. My little daughter turned ten three days ago, and I am yet to set my eyes on her. The thought of the numerous temptations my wife is avoiding or falling for because of my absence is one of my worst nightmares."

"That is why I said to start with her when you get back," Mascot concluded.

Ikenga looked at Ray with pity and confusion but Mascot who was used to his direct expressions and taunting jokes showed no mercy.

"You keep on pulling yourself down, Uncle," he said to Uncle Ray boldly. "Nobody forced you to come to this place. You are already useless to your family and your country but can still do something to pull yourself out of the mess."

Mascot was the only one with courage to talk sense into Ray

whenever he complained about his problems. Everyone avoided him either out of respect or the belief that "Big Uncle" with his level of education was old enough to take care of himself.

"Don't let the system run you mad," Mascot warned when Ray's agitation would not stop. "The resources of Landesburg are like a goat's udder. It does not yield milk unless you punch and squeeze hard."

Ray stared at his friend for a while, sighed heavily, and on remembering that his little cousin was watching, led the way to his apartment pushing his bicycle along.

He brought down an old leather bag hanging on the wall as he stepped into his twenty-foot container room, from the hand bag removed a silver snuff box and a long OCB premium Rizla, and offered as 'kola-nut' to the guests. It did not take Mascot long to prepare and light up the dried green weed. Next, he took a deep drag and held his breath for a while. An adage says, "kola-nut stays long in the mouth of those who value it." Mascot finally let out a thick white smoke and went on taking more drags. Ikenga watched closely and dodged his nose whenever the thick smoke moved towards his direction. He had avoided such hard substances and was still determined to stick to his vow. Mascot dropped the rest on a wooden ashtray and stood up to take his leave. His white lady had been complaining bitterly about his absence in the house and he needed to dance to her tune if he wanted his papers without complications. He handed Ray a hundred Dutch Mark note, and warmly shook hands with both comrades before leaving.

Raymond began by asking his cousin numerous questions about their hometown. He was sad when he got to know that the white Reverend who had been of great help to his family had passed away. Ikenga could not give any information about Ray's wife and daughter because he had not seen them since he left for Port Harcourt. As they discussed *aduro* matters which Ikenga would be facing the next day, Ray saw traits of bravery in his little cousin, and concluded that he was ready to dance to the tune since he had done all to come over.

"It's safe to use Sudan or Somalia," Ray suggested. "Those are the countries in Africa where lasting peace may not come in our generation."

The two finally agreed on Sudan and Ikenga received an hour lecture on the country's geography and current affairs. They also rehearsed some questions and answers that he was likely to encounter the next day. The lecturer picked up what was left on the ashtray when he was convinced he had done a good job and rewarded himself handsomely with a deep drag.

"There is no need for long stories so you don't complicate things and implicate yourself," he finally told Ikenga. "The key is to remember what you said during the interview and be able to know when a question is repeated in a different form. You will be issued a UN passport if your story is convincing. That will save you from the hell I am going through."

By seven o'clock the next morning Ikenga was at the entrance gate of a large building complex along Haven Street with many others of mostly African and Asian descent. The three-story complex was the central refugee headquarters in Landesburg. They were ushered into the waiting room shortly after eight o'clock by a warm-hearted gentleman who collected their names as they got seated. This routine had been on for many years with no end in sight or rather till the peaceful kingdom of the heavens would be established on earth. The interview candidates were to be individually questioned on why they were seeking asylum by the workers at the complex who had heard enough and no longer cared how horrible or strange an individual's story was, as majority turned out to be cooked up tales by economic gypsies.

Ikenga pulled up his trousers and put on a brave face when he was called up. He took his chair in front of a table facing a well-dressed and clean-shaven short man who was to interview him. The man dropped his glasses on the table, poured coffee into a teacup, and sipped as he examined the applicant from above the coffee cup. Ikenga who was also eager to win the short man's pity adjusted his facial look.

"What is your name?"

"My name is Hassan Ijenwata," Ikenga replied diligently.

"What country are you from?"

"I am from the Federal Republic of Sudan."

"Your place and date of birth?"

"I was born in Dafour but my birth was not officially registered."

"Why was your birth not recorded?"

"It was in a neighbour's farmhouse, my mother told me that the fighting was intense."

"How old are you?"

"I do not know."

"Where are your parents?"

"My father was taken away by the soldiers and my mother died during the war."

"Do you have any documents to prove your identity?"

"No, Sir."

"Can you ask your relatives to send them over to you?"

"I have no more relatives left."

"All of them died in the war?"

"Yes."

There was a short interval for recollection, the dialogue was going Ikenga's way and he was beginning to believe that his ancestors had sanctioned it all. His interviewer finished with the computer keyboard and maintained a prolonged gaze at him. The man seemed to understand what pushed these aliens to contemplate the unthinkable but he had his job to protect.

"Which of the local languages in Sudan do you speak?" he continued.

"None really," Ikenga answered. "I speak only English."

The interviewer raised his head abruptly, and tapped the pen on the table repeatedly. It was obvious that he was being presented with another tragic or comic story, which he was not in the mood to listen to, especially not on a Monday morning.

"Are you in any way related to the Queen of England?"

"No."

"You are not an English man," he told Ikenga emphatically "English language has no place in the local languages of the Sudanese. So where exactly are you from?"

"I was kidnapped when … "

"Hold on with your story," the man interrupted. "I want to know your country of origin?"

"I came from Sudan," Ikenga replied in a slightly aggressive tone. Uncle Ray had warned him not to give in to any form of intimidation; the workers at the immigration centre knew that migrants told series of lies to scale through and had also devised tricky means to make the soft-headed ones alter their confessions. "I know you are not from Sudan," the man accused.

"It's wrong for you to say that," Ikenga argued. "You don't know me at all."

"For the last time tell me where you come from."

"I am from Sudan," Ikenga stood by his words.

"You are not from Sudan," the interviewer challenged.

"If you must change my nationality," Ikenga replied after a while, "please make it German."

There was another period of dead silence from both men. The man ran his fingers over the keyboard while his short legs dangled in rhythm well above the floor. The interview had suddenly gone sour, and Ikenga's heart was beginning to sound louder and faster.

"It is always a problem dealing with short men. This one might not even have a wife or children and would not be willing to exercise leniency to the children of others," Ikenga thought to himself. "What is the ugly fellow planning to do next?" Ikenga wondered.

The man had not given him any chance to narrate what he had learned from his experienced lecturer, like how he had fought the Sudanese army alongside the People's Liberation Movement in Southern Sudan; his subsequent capture by the Janjaweed Militia and two years of untold horror in an underground detention facility in an unknown location outside the city of Khartoum; his miraculous escape and arrival in Germany by the help of a missionary who happened to be a good friend of his father; how he was picked up finally by a kind-hearted woman from the witnesses of Jehovah who had sheltered him for the night, and brought him down to the refugee centre that very morning. It could also be that the main interview had not yet started but whatever came out of this Monday morning showdown, Ikenga resolved that whoever was preparing to send him back across the Mediterranean Sea would only succeed with his lifeless body.

The giant cannon printer sprang to life and drew back his attention. The man rolled backwards on his office chair, picked a white sheet of paper from the printer and handed it over to Ikenga.

"You can go back to the waiting room Mr. Ijenwata," he said without looking up.

Ikenga went back to his position, studying the white paper to see if any of the strange words would reveal something to him. The only line that made any meaning was *Herr* Ijenwata Hassan, the *aduro* name that his lecturer had carefully chosen for him. When he realised that everyone who went in also came out with the same white sheet, he reassured himself that things had not totally gone out of hand.

They were all taken to a big dormitory after the interview and the embattled Ikenga was surprised to see some other refugees from his own country. Initially, he was afraid to join their conversation, suspecting that a spy might be mingling among them, but could no longer resist later in the evening when he listened to some who claimed to have fought against the regime of Omar Hassan Ahmad Al-Bashir exchange stories. The contents of the white sheet of paper that was given to him also became clearer to him; he had been posted to a small city of Rapsdorf in the eastern part of Germany, and booked for another interview upon arrival.

The dormitory was a transit camp with two house masters and a spacious refectory where inmates gathered three times daily for their meal and daily information with regards to their asylum status and possible transfers. Hassan Ijenwata was among the names called out the next morning during breakfast and told to be ready by 10 o'clock for their onward journey.

Uncle Ray was still in bed when his cell phone rang. He had awaited this call till late in the night before he went to bed. His mind would not rest till he was sure that Ikenga was permanently settled with a valid refugee status should he fail to bag a UN passport. He had packaged Ikenga with up to date facts and figures and was really hoping for the best for his cousin.

"You kept me restless, boy," he yelled on the phone. "I expected your call yesterday evening."

"There was no telephone booth around, Uncle," Ikenga replied.

"Where are you now?"

"We have all been taken to a transit camp."

"Have you been posted?"

"Yes, to Rapsdorf," Ikenga managed to pronounce.

"Were you fingerprinted?"

"No, I will go for another interview when I get there."

"Come straight back as soon as you drop the receiver."

"What?"

"Drop the receiver and start coming home."

Without any further questions, Ikenga complied, as Uncle Ray had instructed without caring to go back and inform his new friends about the abrupt change in plans. He had been in town long enough and knew the train and city bus connections to locate Ray's house where his cousin later explained why he had been asked to terminate the first asylum application.

Ray explained that parts of Eastern Germany were still regarded as poor states coupled with more than occasional cases of NeoNazism. Refugees were not particularly excited when posted to states of Eastern Germany, as there were less job opportunities, and the fear of attack by skin heads. Most importantly, since the law advocated interracial marriages or child bearing with a citizen as criteria for citizenship, the States of Western Germany were deemed to be more sociable and accommodating thereby giving an alien a higher chance of finding a partner.

"You have to keep repeating the journey till you are posted to any of the western states," Ray explained. "Then I will get you a nice job except if you want to run around the train station with addicts. I am too old for such a dirty game and I don't want to spend the rest of my already wasted life behind bars."

Ikenga helped himself to a bottle of beer, as he listened to Ray and his usual sad speeches. His father had often reminded him of the worth of a good name and he, being his grandfather's incarnate, was responsible for upholding the good name of the family. He was told that the old man had given up his life for he and his twin sister, and that he had also suffered a massive loss of wealth during the civil war but maintained his good name as his second inheritance. That made it easier for Ikenga to detach his grandfather from the evil atrocities going on in *Ogwugwu* shrine and greedy lifestyle that had overtaken those whom the gods had appointed to speak on their behalf.

"I will definitely look for a job when I am through with *aduro*," Ikenga said as Ray paused to have a drink. "My father will not forgive me if he hears that I deal in white or brown material."

"The decision is between you and your *chi*," Ray corrected.

"The old man you are talking about is thousands of miles away."

They talked till late and Ikenga seized the opportunity to share his life story. He told his lecturer that he would like to go back home someday as the only son of the family to take up his responsibilities. Since he came to understand why many aliens went into unplanned marriages in foreign lands, the so-called Resident Permit became meaningless to him. He was definitely not interested in wasting his time going into a cosmetic marriage just because of *kpalli*. He who brings in ant-infested firewood to his hut should not complain when lizards start to pay him a visit.

There was no place for divorce in Umuafor family composition and every grown-up had the moral responsibility of correcting a child when children went wrong regardless of who his or her parents are. Aliens normally carried along with them vestiges of their original culture and identity, which did not always tally with that of their host countries. Again, Ikenga clearly defined his mission; to make a little money that would help liberate his family from the chains of hunger and establish a small-scale business for himself in Umuafor or Port Harcourt. There were lots of beautiful women back home looking for suitors.

Two weeks later, Ikenga was on his way for a return match. One of the good teachings he accepted from Ray was to keep on repeating his asylum application till he got posted to any of the western states. He had shaved off his beards the previous evening to look a bit different, even though Uncle Ray assured him that thousands applied for asylum every month and that there was no way they would suspect him since they were yet to take his finger prints.

This time, it was a young woman in her thirties and the interaction seemed to have gone in Ikenga's favour. The lady began by asking him the colour of the Sudanese flag, the geographical location of the major tribes, the currency in use and the names of the former and current heads of government. Many of these were questions he had memorised and stocked in his fingernails, and so he poured answers like a freeborn Sudanese. He narrated his frightening ordeal as an unlawful combatant, his excruciating torment at the hands of Janjaweed Militia popularly known as devils on horseback, and of course his glorious escape. The young woman showed a great deal of interest when Ikenga pulled off his T-shirt to present scars from an old wound on his chest. The visible scar, sustained when he had fallen down from an *Udala* tree, was blamed on a government-backed militia and many ugly years in a torture camp. As for the mark on his forehead, he claimed that his head had been repeatedly hit against a wall till his skull fractured.

The interviewer was not ready to experience nightmares from Ikenga's wild stories; and halted it with a wave of her left hand. "Do you still experience pains there?" she asked.

"Yes!" Ikenga replied with a stimulated pain. "I have never been examined by a doctor."

"How old is the wound?"

"It's three years now since I escaped from Sudan."

"I have noted that here," the lady said to him. "That would make the welfare office arrange a doctor for you."

"Thank you, Madam!"

"Miss Merkel!" the lady corrected.

With that she handed over a white sheet of paper to Ikenga and asked that he go back to the waiting room. This second leg had gone perfectly well and from what he could see, the soft-spoken blonde lady was moved by compassion.

Ikenga did not wait for lunch when the luxurious bus brought the new candidates to the dormitory. He sneaked out immediately to call Ray. His destination this time turned out to be a small city called Bruggendorf and Ray told him to relax and play along since he was now in Western Germany. The *aduro* process was very smooth and another interesting adventure on its own. Ikenga and few others were arraigned for a second interview and thereafter taken to their permanent camp in Bruggendorf, a one and half hour drive from Landesburg.

Those who were unlucky or whom the authorities had found no element of truth in their wild stories were presented with letters of rejection immediately after their interview. Some candidates who believed their stories were convincing enough were also presented with letters of rejection after a thorough scrutiny from the Office of Foreign Affairs. On their arrival at the final destination, which turned out to be block building instead of the usual container heap, everyone was shown to his or her room in the extensive apartment block. While some had to share a room, depending on its size, Ikenga was lucky to have one to himself. He was provided with a brand new tabletop fridge, cooking utensils, beddings and toiletries while the sum of three hundred Deutsch Mark was to be paid into his newly opened bank account at the end of every month.

# Chapter 7

Problem silently crept in barely a year after he was posted to Bruggendorf when one of the Polish housemasters handed him a thick yellowish envelope. Since it was during the Easter holidays, Ikenga thought it was one of the many generous gifts he regularly received from the wealthy countryside dwellers. Those too busy to post their gifts to charity organisations usually went to refugee centres with their car booths full of fairly used clothing and other valuable handouts.

This was another sharp contrast to the general perception of the German society. With gratefulness, Ikenga proudly disputed any negative views by narrow-minded fellow aliens who inflicted havoc on the image of their kind host community by their unguarded utterances. Though there were no abandoned cars on the road as he had initially thought, his life had drastically changed for the better and the evidence was gradually being witnessed far away in his father's compound. The three hundred Deutsche Mark he received monthly from the social welfare went straight to his family while he sustained himself with earnings from a three times a week farm work which Uncle Ray had arranged for him.

The letter would have to wait till weekend when he normally went to nightclub in Landesburg or other big cities to scout for his would-be wife. With the look of things, he had eventually decided to not bite the fingers that fed him. Hence, he refused to accompany Mascot to the City Station for drug dealing. It is goodness that gives wealth and for that reason, he would keep an eye on the Resident Permit while doing whatever he could to support himself. His Saturday outing would also provide an opportunity to pay homage to Uncle Ray and hear what he would make of the letter in an orange-coloured envelope. His priority remained to transform the lives of his family members back in Umuafor and go back to take up the responsibilities that awaited him. He trusted Ray to help him secure a job with the strong conviction that if he worked hard enough, the Resident Permit would come his way.

Mascot who had unsuccessfully tried to recruit Ikenga at the City Station was beginning to believe that Ikenga had no interest in street life. Uncle Ray seized the opportunity to propose a working contract with an up-to-date working documentation. Although Ray was aware that Ikenga risked losing all his benefits from social welfare if he was caught working, he persuaded him to consider the opportunity, assuring him that no one would find out since he would be assuming someone else's identity.

In the end, Ikenga decided to be "fair to Goodness" in the words of his father. He chose to be productive to the society he lived in thereby holding up the family's good name. That way, he could reciprocate the hospitality shown to him by strangers, a decision, which he knew, would cost him his closeness to Mascot.

The mechanised farming system, which he had hoped for was far from mechanised in his own view. Although some heavy farming equipment did the tilling, selected harvesting, and spreading of fertilizers, the workers had more than enough to do every day. Mr. Meier, the obese farm owner, was a very hardworking and clever man who had met Ray some years earlier when he had come to the farmhouse in desperate need of a job. Then, Ray's first girlfriend had accepted his marriage proposal and he urgently needed to raise some money. Mr. Meier was not surprised when Ray did not show up after two weeks, but had instead sent for him to come and collect the money he had worked for.

He was a warm-hearted farmer who was not interested in cheating his poor migrant workers, though bitterly angry at the financial system that was bent on swindling off his meagre earnings in the name of taxation. Ray finally showed up one evening wearing a well-ironed white suit with a red tie, and Mr. Meier welcomed him warmly teasing him of laziness for running away from his job as he led him to the coffee table.

He offered Ray a cup of coffee and excused himself to go get the few hundred Deutsche Mark notes that was payment for the two weeks that Ray had worked. Ray in turn pocketed the few notes and presented a rather attractive offer to the farm owner as his reason for coming back to the farmhouse. It turned out to be an offer that Mr. Meier would not want to miss as German workers were proving to be too expensive. Ray would readily supply him with cheap labour, which would definitely go a long way in making up for the heavy taxes he paid to the office of finance. The two went into business for over a period of time, and Meier profited from cheap labourers channelled over to him, while Ray received a monthly commission of one hundred Deutsche Marks from anyone he sent to the farm for employment.

Ikenga arrived when things had tightened up, and Mr. Meier had started to insist that anyone seeking employment must possess a working permit. Photocopies were also acceptable so long as the worker had something to show to the Polizei who were bent on rooting out undocumented migrant workers and their employers. Ray made copies of his over-used fake documents and handed them over to Ikenga on the morning that he was supposed to follow an old worker down to the farm. The farmer immediately knew from whom the new worker was coming when he studied the documents and signed a six-month working contract for him. Those who were industrious and had not failed to show up due to sickness or any other flimsy excuse were regarded as permanent workers with a full-time working contract.

Ikenga's first day at the farm was a light warm up, seen as one of the easiest jobs, but entailed running behind a mega combined harvester and picking the potatoes that fell off the truck or left over by the monster-like farm machine. As he was well informed about the man's strategy, Ikenga did his best to impress the farm owner and foreman in a bid to secure a prolonged or permanent working status. He was very impressed seeing the wealthy farm owner toil with his workers everyday, share jokes with the few foreign words he had learned from them, and even drink from the same coffee pot with them at midday break.

Nonetheless, although he was energetic and hardworking, the man still fell short of Mr. Maya from the Ronasko Company, whom his father often talked about. His protruding stomach might be as a result of excess consumption but that did not impede his working strength, as he was always found talking and running around all day to encourage his workers and remark about those who were better off staying at home. Generally, the working conditions were favourable and this made up for whatever negative qualities Meier possessed.

One fateful Friday afternoon, everyone was happily rounding up for the weekend and Ikenga was in the warehouse washing a heap of harvested carrots with a fellow worker when Mr. Meier walked into the hall, and without saying much, motioned his two workers towards a half-opened iron door leading to the underground basement.

"*Da lang!*" he shouted as Ikenga hesitated to understand him.

Ikenga dashed through the door behind his much older fellow worker who had immediately dropped the plastic bowl in his hands and fled. The heavy slam of the door by their employer was enough to make him understand that something was terribly amiss.

"What is this all about?" he asked in a confused state in the safety of the basement.

"Control," replied the fellow.

"What kind of control in the farm?"

"Normal control."

Ikenga could not make any sense of the rationale behind controlling people who earned a living by toiling in the farm. He had heard of "normal control" at the train station, city centres and nightclubs. Also, he had encountered the same "normal control" occasionally inside the regional train on his way to Landesburg. Little did he know that waking up at four every morning and crawling around the vast farmland from sunrise to sunset to prove his capability was a criminal offence.

On one occasion, in the middle of a very uncommon winter season, when coaches were completely out of use because the emergency units could not cope with the heavy snow that swallowed its tracks. Ikenga however managed to make it to work with a mountain-bike he had bought from shoplifters, cycling a long distance in the freezing temperature in order to retain his job. It was in a bid to not to give himself up to the Polizei or give Mr. Meier a reason to terminate his appointment that he had quickly crawled into the bush when he was knocked down by a pensioner at a road intersection.

The old fellow and his wife rushed out of their car, having watched what seemed to be a rough frontal collision with a cyclist.

"Where is he?" the wife asked, visibly terrified that her husband had run over a poor cyclist.

"I am sure I saw someone on the bicycle," the man said still on his knees after checking for his victim under the car.

"Is he there?" the wife asked.

"I can't see anyone."

The terrified wife pushed her much weaker husband aside and went flat on the icy snow to possibly render whatever help she could. But under the car was clearly vacuous.

"Was that a ghost?" she managed to ask, surprised that a cyclist she was sure was under the car had simply disappeared. The pair reported the incident to the Polizei immediately and waited until uniformed men arrived at the scene to put down their own account of events.

With pains, Ikenga crawled away under the heavy fog that had severely hampered the early morning visibility. His bleeding knees must have known that neither the mountain bike nor the working documents in his pocket were genuinely his.

*     *     *     *     *

The two farm workers peeped through the ventilator hole and watched a green-stripped van rolling at a comfortable pace down the narrow farm road. Mr. Meier raised the alarm level to red when he sighted the van from afar and all the workers with fake documents quickly evaporated. The ones out in the field also disappeared into the thick green cornfield like chicks running away from a nursing kite, leaving their working equipment suspiciously

WOES OF IKENGA

lying around in the open. The mission did not permit the van and its occupants much time to sniff around, but they noticed a skeleton in the man's cupboard from his frenzied movements. They jotted down some information gathered from Mr. Meier concerning a wanted alien and left to plan for a surprise invasion another day.

Gradually, people began to reappear to tell stories of their escape in the recreation hall while the few workers with genuine documents laughed and made jokes of the "Mario adventure." The farm owner's oldest son quickly set the coffee machine in motion to ease tension.

"Next time, you play smart, young man," he said to Ikenga who was reappearing from the basement.

"I never knew I was committing an offence."

"You are all breaking the law," the younger Meier said. "Whoever gets my father into trouble will pay heavily."

"I played smart by turning down the illicit activities going on at the train station."

"Dealings in the City Station and illegal employment are both criminal offences."

"Then I need to review my choice of work."

"The former will fetch you more money," Meier's son explained; "But more time behind bars."

"Your father should wash his hands off cheap labour," an elderly man who had worked on the farm for years interjected. "This is slavery with a method."

"He washes his hands but they continually get soiled," young Meier replied jokingly.

The bottom of wealth is sometimes a dirty thing to behold. Albeit aware of his father's *modus operandi,* he was ready to play along so long as the long arms of the law did not fish them out. They took advantage of the helpless economic migrants who were fed up with being confined to their camps with stringent movement restriction orders by the authority. Fortunately, many migrant workers were happy to secure a job to help supplement their free monthly income instead of staying idle and decaying mentally in their various refugee camps.

The genuine workers hastily did the remaining work for the day as Mr. Meier decided to send the rest home earlier than usual for fear that the green-striped van might decide to make a surprise U-turn.

It was every worker's dream to close early on a Friday after the stress of the week. Ikenga who already had a line of programs was glad to know that his weekend had started as they finished from the recreation room. Topmost on his agenda was a return visit to a dark-haired beautiful girl he had met the previous weekend in a nightclub in Dortmund. He had resolved to make advances to a new girl every time he went out on weekends. His tactic was to follow up on his economic pursuit while casting a wide net for any girl who would fall by entering into a marriage with him. The girls deemed as potential *kpalli*, he kept in touch with, and serviced the relationship at intervals but those whom he thought had no material value; he cut off after a one-night stand if not immediately.

With a handful of other workers, he took the pathway to the small Bruggendorf train station and bade others a nice weekend. He stood for the three-stop drive to his station with his legs already aching for movement. In less than an hour, he was back at the same station in a rather groovy mood. Mascot had given him a lot of his extra-large fairly used American clothes when he was finally posted, so that he would not bother buying new clothes for some time. He decided to ride in a taxi to Dortmund immediately and then return to Landesburg later in time for Friday "singles' night," which normally started from midnight.

With regards to the orange-coloured envelope, which Ikenga gave him to go through, Uncle Ray prophesied danger: the immigration authorities had written to inform Mr. Hassan Ijenwata that his asylum request had been rejected because of conflicting accounts to his story and serious doubts with regards to his nationality. However, he had been given a four-week grace period to appeal the rejection, after which he should be ready to leave the country.

Ikenga was paralysed by these explanations, and even too afraid to imagine taking the powers that be in Landesburg to a law court. He had relaxed over the so-called letter of rejection issue, believing that he had made a convincing argument on the day of his interview. His thoughts flew round the globe in a fraction of a second.

"Where on earth was he going to go from there?"

"What if the appeal was also rejected?"

"Could any of his white girlfriends become pregnant from a one-night stand?"

He realised that many of the questions that flowed through his mind were without answers and bent down to scratch his bushy hair. Ray, who did not want what was part of a normal *aduro* procedure to dampen his cousin's spirit, assured him that all was well.

"How can all be well brother when I have only four weeks to leave Germany?" Ikenga asked vehemently.

"I will give the letter to my Jewish lawyer," Ray promised.

"Who am I to face a German Judge?" Ikenga wondered loud.

"The appeal process lasts for two years, by then you should have gotten your *kpalli.*"

Ray's assurances did not seem agreeable with the embattled Ikenga, and the rest of the weekend went on in shambles. His stay in Germany now lay in the hands of an unknown Jewish lawyer or in his determination to make a wife or mother of any of his girlfriends.

He needed not be told to reconsider his stand on marrying a foreign wife. Things were increasingly looking bleak and being sent back to Umuafor empty-handed was the most likely option for the immigration office, and the worst that could happen to him. Like his predecessors, he had to do something to lay his hands on a Resident Permit, since the hard currency was proving illusive.

Ikenga had actually doubled his efforts and was close to realising his dreams when he lucked out. He had arrived Mr.

Meier's farm to find that a good number of plain-clothed and uniformed men in combat outfits had besieged the farmhouse at a time when the farm owner had lowered the alert level.

Mr. Meier had gone with the driver on that fateful morning to make deliveries to the local supermarkets after dishing out the working program for the day and entrusting his son with affairs. The security agents suddenly appeared from all directions at exactly 9:15 am that Monday morning like rattled soldier ants, and all the workers were pinned down at their respective positions and stages of activity before they could realise what was happening. Those who had never encountered a well-trained German squad in action could feel their hearts drop to their stomachs as they were marched into one of the warehouses when the cops felt that they had the situation under control. The basements and the compartments were thoroughly searched and anyone found hiding was first given a thorough beating before being dragged out to join the others. They singled out Mr. Meier's son and demanded to know the worker that went by the name "Park Mungo" when he told them that his father had left with deliveries. The frightened young man did not hesitate to point at Ikenga, who was ruthlessly pounced on by three hefty men.

"Please don't kill me!" he screamed with his head held to the German floor, but his screaming did little to stop the men. He seemed to be the target of the border police who bundled him out in handcuffs into the car and drove off leaving the uniformed men behind to inspect the documents of the other workers. The proportionate brutality coupled with the rapid succession of events rendered the unsuspecting Ikenga deaf, dumb, and in total submission. As both male and female officers stripped him naked and searched him from head to toe, his only wish was for the ground to open and swallow him. The last among his marathon ordeal at the Central Police Station was a data-capture session, which included photo taking and fingerprinting of all his ten fingers before he was finally dumped in a small temporary cell compartment.

WOES OF IKENGA

The door flew open two hours later. Activities were now a bit more relaxed but Ikenga was still unable to digest what had happened to him. Meanwhile the officers who had scrutinised the documents found in his possession were grappling with the fact that their man might still be on the loose. Ikenga was later taken to an oval office for his first interrogation, after his rights to remain silent and the consequences of false testimonies were read to him.

"Your game is up, young man," the solidly built interrogator told Ikenga.

"I am not playing games," Ikenga replied politely.

"Yes, you certainly are."

His overwhelming assumption rendered Ikenga silent. An argument in the face of such overpowering authority might complicate issues for him and as such he preferred to not speak out of turn.

"It's only terrorists who maintain double identity in this country," the interrogator continued.

"I am not a terrorist."

"How can you be Sudanese and Nigerian at the same time?" the officer asked looking straight into his eyes.

"I am Sudanese, Sir," Ikenga replied albeit frightened.

"You are Hassan Ijenwata from Sudan and Park Mungo from Nigeria."

"No, I am only Hassan Ijenwata from Sudan."

"Who is Mr. Park?"

"I don't know him."

The man pulled his fingers from the papers he was going through, and turned in the executive office chair to face the suspect.

"We might as well call off this interview if you are not interested," he announced. "How can you tell me that you don't know Mr. Park?"

"I don't know him, Officer," Ikenga pleaded.

"How come you have been working in the farm under the name?"

151

"I picked the documents from the bus station."

"Keep the alibi to yourself, we know of an alien connection that runs an underground criminal network. I will crush all of you," he promised, pointing a finger at Ikenga.

His words forced out drops of urine through Ikenga's clenched pelvis. Only the gods could save him from this unidentified impending calamity. With fear and panic, Ikenga declared that he needed a lawyer, not necessarily because he hoped to be saved from the law but at least to have someone witness his execution. He was taken back to his small cell, and by the next morning arraigned before a make-shift judge who ruled that he be remanded in custody pending a hearing by the court at a later date, by which time the police was expected to have ascertained the true identity of their captive.

A young lady from Landesburg had been apprehended by the border control along the highway from Amsterdam with a large quantity of undisclosed hard drugs and had upon interrogation confessed to be a newly recruited courier for an underground drug syndicate headed by Mr. Park Mungo. Park, who was always at alert whenever a courier was on a mission, had taken cover when he sensed danger unaware that Uncle Ray had retained copies of his documents after arranging a contract marriage for him. The police who were surprised to learn that the name had not come up on their radar till then had then made straight to Mr. Meier's farm with enough reinforcement.

Ray engaged the services of his Jewish lawyer; but it took six months before Ikenga walked out of Balthazar, the maximum detention facility, with a one-year probation or suspended jail term generally known among the street clan as *anunu-ebe*. He was cleared of drug related charges but indicted for impersonation and working without a legal work permit.

# Chapter 8

To be served a jail sentence by a law court for no other reason than working hard on a farm to survive was another man-made law that proved difficult for Ikenga to digest. Law custodians argued that the taxes due for undocumented employments or "black jobs" were not paid to the Office of Finance, oblivious to the fact that migrants were forced to pick up "black jobs" because they were not legally permitted to work. The fair order of protectionism was to hand out fish to hungry aliens while lining up a range of tricky hurdles to be jumped before they became assimilated and issued with nets to fish for themselves. However, easy access to jobs would have saved a whole lot of moral and logistic issues and provided empowerment and dignity to individuals who had lost consciousness of their self-esteem.

The fit-in marathon and quest for a fishing net and identity thus became like a human version of the renowned Super Mario game and its adventure stages. Aliens who had been moulded with in-built shock absorbers to withstand challenges and obstacles scaled through while the unfortunate ones clung to hope or a sudden miraculous intervention. Their determination to keep on staying was fuelled by the belief that all would be well at the end and that if it was not well, then it was not the end. The *Ofeke*, those who left their destinies to chase shadows, were happy to settle for assorted affordable beer as milk and honey had run out and always praised their *chi* for bringing them over to the "Land of Canaan."

One's individual *chi* could also be influenced by other *chi* or semi-gods and gradually lose all its essential spiritual fortifications; that is to say that many of those who had fallen off track had not intentionally chosen to languish in a strange land but been overpowered by unforeseen circumstances. During a party session after a thanksgiving service organised by a well-known family, Santos had alleged that the law professor was the sole architect of his downfall, and Freeman had rightly responded to the challenge from the emerging street junta whose effrontery was boosted by the size of his wallet. The old fellow who was in a jolly mood during the service and after party had simply replied that it was only wise to wait till the evening of one's life to know what approbation to give to one's *chi*.

Those who had been destined to sleep and eat their lives away in refugee camps carried on while others searched for the socalled "black jobs" to free themselves from the imprisonment of their own conscience. The abuse that took place in such work environments by the dubious employers were left unchecked because the employees would rather forfeit their meagre earnings than take any matter to the authority. Employers were not the only ones guilty of abusing and cheating; aliens who had obtained their Resident Permit or citizenship status but chose not to work, usually handed over their documents to newcomers who did not want to indulge in criminal activities, and shared their employment benefits or sometimes deducted or withheld the entire salaries of their unsuspecting victims.

Ikenga came and had seen but needed to surmount those tricky hurdles before he could declare himself a conqueror. Life had become boring during his one-year period of *anunu-ebe*. He had gotten used to waking up every morning to go to work at Mr. Meier's farm, and the feeling of fulfilment that came with knowing that he had accomplished something for the day. Now, he missed the satisfaction derived from knowing that he had lost sweat for his livelihood and contributed to the welfare of the country in his own little way. These days, he was mostly confined to the refugee camp, where he spent time with friends in similar circumstances, going to bed very late and waking up at noon. Another big slap on his face was that the money he received monthly from social welfare had been converted to food vouchers, which could only buy him edibles from designated supermarkets, thus reducing him to the level of borrowing money from his friends every now and then.

Things had become really hard. Uncle Ray, who he normally turned to for help was also facing difficult times but Mascot sometimes came around to make his pocket smile while constantly reminding him that his benevolence was temporary. To overcome the situation, he resorted to handing out the food vouchers for real money below its value to migrants with family. That way he was able to feed, stock up beer, and afford weekend outings.

The Office of Foreign Affairs did not help matters either. After his release from prison, they continually sent letters with the usual frightening convoluted grammar and judicial lexis. They were increasingly getting more confident that Hassan Ijenwata might not have come from the country he had applied for asylum with. The immigration police had once paid him a surprise visit and he had had to accompany them to the Sudanese Consulate because they doubted his nationality. When he could not reply a common local greeting from an embassy staff, the embassy personnel immediately knew that another West African globetrotter had hijacked their country. He had however insisted that he was a Sudanese and accused them of being mercenaries of the Khartoum government who had unleashed terror on his community.

The verbal encounter ended without a win for either party, and the immigration police took him back to the refugee camp, notifying him of the date for a visit to the Ghanaian consulate. Those were clear indications that his time was no more; a situation that made Ikenga restless and anxious. He could no longer sleep at night because he was constantly haunted by the fear of being sent back to Umuafor, and the stigma attached to deportation, which sometimes resulted in a psychological damage of the affected individuals due to the deep resentment and verbal rejection that faced anyone who returned with a polythene bag.

Weekends were special for those who had just newly arrived, or were in desperate hunt for *kpalli*. That was the time to put on their best outfits, mingle in city centres and nightclubs in search of a lover. As bad as it seemed, the situation was definitely beneficial to some, like the obese or overused men and women of Landesburg who got to choose what alien to go to bed with. Some aliens also foolishly invested their energies hoping that such immoral unions would lead to marriage, only to find themselves walked out on as soon as their lovers had satisfied their sexual desires.

Mascot invited Ikenga on a special weekend when a girl he had met on a wild tour in Frankfurt promised visiting with her classmate. Ikenga highly hoped that it would work out this time. He had come across a number of potential *kpalli* but they had all slipped out of his hands in one way or the other. His cell phone rang shortly before the inter-city train arrived on the seventeenth platform at the train station. Ikenga hurriedly excused himself from the wayward station girls he was chatting with and withdrew to a corner to answer his call. It was the ladies from Frankfurt, calling to inform that they had missed their train and would be arriving in the next hour. Of course, that was no problem for a jobless civilian who was ready to wait for as long as it would take. As they say, a preacher never gets weary till he steps into Jerusalem.

"Was that your girlfriend?" one of the girls asked as he joined them again.

"No, my aunt!" Ikenga fibbed.

"You should not have run away to take the call then."

"She gets mad whenever she notices a female partner around me."

"Then we had better start leaving," the other one said.

"It's not like that, girls," Ikenga replied. "I have my life to live."

The station girls were as notorious as the drug dealers. They also got arrested by the police and were sometimes banned from being seen around the train station. These young girls in their late teens and early twenties from all racial backgrounds were hooked on the "piece of good life" from the bubble dealers. Many had abandoned their education at an early age and fallen victims of unripe marriages and uncalculated relationships. Their immaturity was made obvious as soon as the juicy lifestyle suffered a head-on collision, and consequently, those used to the extravagance offered by their alien lovers to secure their hands in marriage kicked them out immediately the running tap went off. The few committed to a decent married life walked out on the marriage as soon as they were matured enough to know that love had not propelled them into the union, thereby producing different children from different men. In the same vein, contract marriages suffered catastrophic ends when the agreed regular sum stopped flowing in.

Ikenga exchanged numbers with the girls before making up a lie to free himself for the rather important appointment. These girls had no destination and would have loved the conversation to go on but another hour was over and he needed to pick up the guests from Frankfurt as Mascot instructed. A pot trader whose fortunes are all invested in her clay pots is not much of a merchant. He immediately ran off to send a convincing message to the two that he was really about to miss his train. They had staged him for the whole hour and were ready to dance to his tune believing him to be one of the station boys with juicy wallets.

The train from Frankfurt pulled up on time and passengers poured out like bats dashing out of their caves. Ikenga waited in a corner for his cell phone to ring while stretching his neck to catch a glimpse of those coming out of the two nearest coaches. The girl easily recognised him from Mascot's description and moved with the crowd towards his direction.

"Are you Prince Hassan?" she asked in a gentle sweet voice.

"Yes, that's me," Ikenga answered with a quick involuntary movement.

"Sorry we kept you waiting the whole hour."

"It's my pleasure," Ikenga replied. "The fresh air did me some good."

"Mascot said he would be joining later. What's keeping him off?"

"Oh! He is a very busy man," Ikenga replied. "He had some things to tidy up when I left the studio."

"Is he really a musician?"

"He is a legend when it comes to music."

"I never believed it when he jokingly mentioned it in

Frankfurt."

"You better do, girl, we just came back from a two weeks AllStar Concert held in Amsterdam."

"Sure? You guys performed there?"

"For real!" Ikenga boasted.

"Do you sing or play any instruments?" she asked with excitement.

"I am the drummer boy."

"This is my best friend, Selda," the girl introduced. "We share the same apartment at school."

"Hello, Selda!" Ikenga greeted with a handshake and cheerful smile. "That sounds Turkish, am I right?"

"Yes, my mother is from Turkey."

"You are welcome to Landesburg."

"Thanks," both girls replied.

With that Ikenga led the two down the stairs to the taxi stand, replying greetings with just a wave of the hand as they walked through the train station. The crazy hunt for *kpalli* made people jealously guard their wives or girlfriends like golden eggs. A German proverb rightly says, "It is easier to guard against a bushel of fleas than a woman." Many unlucky aliens had suffered like the cheetah, which hunts down a game only to lose it to a marauding hyena. It was so alarming that even aliens who travelled to their home countries to apply for a marriage reunion visa also feared being abandoned by their wives. Indeed many had become victims of such cheetah and hyena affairs that even in the night clubs, people would rather go with their ladies to the lavatory than come back and meet her with another more impressive aggressor. Ikenga was definitely not ready to take chances with these two elegant queens. So, he responded to all greetings by waving.

The taxi driver switched on his metre and drove to a popular Chinese restaurant as the trio discussed.

"How does it feel travelling around as a star?" Selda asked as they waited for their menu in the restaurant.

"Great! It's a feeling one can only understand with

experience."

"That means I will never know it?"

"All hope is not lost," Ikenga assured. "We do allow some devoted fans come along when we are on tour."

"Wow! I can't wait any longer."

"Our next outing would be in few months time in Jakarta."

"I will be devoted and dedicated," Selda promised.

The wild laughter that ensued drew the attention of other guests. Ikenga had mastered the appropriate manner of approach and behaviour around white girls; Mascot had only given him few key words so that their words would not contradict when he later joined them. Everything seemed to be moving Ikenga's way, and by the time the waiter arrived with their food and drinks wearing a bold smile, only noises of cutlery could be heard from them.

"*Guten apetit!*" the waiter said warmly before leaving their table.

"*Danke!*" Ikenga replied.

He pulled out his cell phone to check the time halfway into his nutritious Chinese food; Mascot should be arriving any moment from now according to their arrangement. There was no way the girls could go back to Frankfurt that night. Although Mascot lived with his white girlfriend, he regularly slept wherever night fell on him, and was sure to have made plans to spend the weekend in one of the luxury guest houses as he normally did when the situation necessitated. Ikenga decided to flow in whichever direction the wind chose. Though he promised visiting Uncle Ray that evening, the visit could as well be postponed till further notice. *Ikikere-mkpo*, the wine loving ant, once told his kinsmen not to bother looking for him whenever he failed to turn up at the dinner table, because he might have followed *Di-ochi*, the wine-tapper, and his calabash home.

"This one must tender the *kpalli*," Ikenga told himself. "My *ofo* has got hold of her."

Mascot's girl was getting anxious by the minute. The whole show was not funny without her man by her side. What if another woman was holding him down in the studio? The thought of that possibility made her pull out her cell phone from her purse and dial repeatedly.

"His phone is switched off," she barked at Ikenga.

"Take it easy, baby," Ikenga replied softly. "Mascot is going to be here any moment from now."

Ikenga also tried reaching his friend with his own phone but the voicemail that replied did not worry him. Mascot would never disappoint in matters like this, especially not after all he had said about the sweet adventure with the princess from Frankfurt. Ikenga comfortably ordered his fourth bottle of beer and a second bottle of white wine for the ladies. He was sure that his friend had a good reason for the delay, but he just hoped that the girls were not contemplating going back to Frankfurt via the night train. "Can't we go to the studio?" the girl asked.

"That will not be of any help," Ikenga replied. "He must have left the studio by now."

"And where is he?"

"He should be on his way."

"But that's not fair," she lamented. "Mascot told me that somebody would meet us at the station but has not cared to findout if we arrived safely."

"He knows you are in good hands."

"That is no reason to switch off his handset."

"His cell phone might be out of service if he is coming with the underground train," Ikenga suggested.

"No," she objected. "Stars seem to take people's feelings for granted."

"Let's exercise a little patience," he pleaded with the girls. Meanwhile Ikenga was gradually getting nervous by the time he was done with the fourth bottle of beer. It was already three hours past the arranged meeting time and Mascot's mobile phone was still switched off. He would have paid the bills and taken the girls down to the train station to meet Mascot there, but he had given the last money on him to the taxi driver including the little change he was supposed to collect. What on earth could still be holding

Mascot from showing up till now? He normally did not keep late on weekends at the station.

To hold on to something, Ikenga ordered his fifth bottle because they had overstayed at the restaurant and the normal thing to do to pass time was to keep on spending. His cell phone rang just as the waiter lowered the beer before him. It was Uncle Ray.

"Have you seen Mascot?" the voice asked.

"No, I have been waiting for him the whole evening here," Ikenga replied.

"There is a problem, brother."

"What happened?"

"Somebody was just telling me the guy was picked up few hours ago."

"What? How? Who told you?"

"I will call you later."

Ikenga was not through with his questions before the line went dead. He stared at his cell phone as if it was part of the problem. The waiter who would not like to be reported to the management as being nosy abruptly dropped the beer and left. Ikenga grabbed the bottle immediately and went after him to whisper something in his ears and the young boy directed him to his boss. He silently explained that his wallet had gone missing and bargained to drop his cell phone for the bills and reclaim it the next day when he came with the money. The Chinese owner, probably a constant victim of OBT (obtaining by tricks) from hungry civilians who were capable of devising unthinkable means to quench their hunger, was immediately infuriated and told Ikenga to sit down and wait till he was through with what he was doing.

For a man to enjoy a banquet with two girls for more than four hours only to discover that his wallet was missing after he had filled his stomach sounded funny. The girls were very confused but they could sense that something was amiss. Mascot's girl maintained that men were heartless and that they had simply been brought down from Frankfurt to be messed around with. She was already raising her voice at Ikenga when three uniformed police officers walked in. It immediately dawned on Ikenga that he had

161

made a very big mistake. He should have quietly sneaked out after the call and left the girls to their fate.

The owner of the restaurant pointed at the three after a few words with the policemen who immediately walked to their table. "Is somebody having problems?" one asked amiably.

"Yes!" Ikenga replied. "I discovered that my wallet was missing when I wanted to pay my bills."

"Stop!" Mascot's girl shouted at him. "You can't take me for a ride. Have I told you that I am a comedian?"

She got up from her chair and stood few metres away from Ikenga to avoid the camera wherever it was hidden. Her actions indicated that she was still far from reality. The brain wash concoction, which Ikenga prepared for them, was an overdose and it would take some time to clear off.

"I am not interested in your search for superstars," she continued. "You have to ask for my permission before you can use my pictures and videos round the world."

Selda also got up and vacated her position with uncontrollable laughter. She had watched a lot of German comedy to see how people reacted when they were surprisingly caught up in a funny public comedy. This might be the very start, but she desperately needed to be counted as a devoted fan of the music band. The policemen were somewhat embarrassed as well. All they knew was that they were called for an emergency by a restaurant owner whom they knew very well, though the increasing number of street comedians had also not spared uniformed men.

"What have you got to say Mr. Comedian?" one asked Ikenga with a smile.

"I think I lost the wallet in the taxi," he managed to say amidst the laughter.

"You think or the wallet is lost?"

"Don't mind him, Officer," Mascot's girl interjected. "He paid the taxi fare from the wallet when we got down, even left the change with the driver."

The policemen did not know what to make of the funny episode but had to get serious to unfold the movie.

"Can I see your passport?" the youngest of the policemen stepped forward to demand.

Ikenga gazed at him. Speeding off when he was not sure of success did not appeal to him. Meanwhile, the officers had asked the owner to shut the entrance to bar people from entering.

"Your passport, please," the officer demanded.

"My passport is in the wallet," Ikenga answered.

"The wallet is in the taxi," the officer completed.

"Yes, Sir!"

"And where is the taxi?"

"On the road," Selda happily completed the puzzle.

"This comedy is not ending here," the young officer addressed his colleagues jokingly.

"You have to come with us to the station to establish your identity," another told Ikenga.

"That's alright," Ikenga accepted.

"Spare me the embarrassment, Prince Hassan!" Mascot's girl interrupted. "Is this what you brought me here for?"

At a point, one of the policemen turned to the girl to hear her own side of the story.

"They are musicians," she narrated. "My boyfriend was supposed to join us here since seven o'clock but he failed to show up."

"Who are you girls?"

"My name is Yvonne and this is my girlfriend Selda, they invited us over from Frankfurt to stage this show without our consent. I am sure that Prince has his wallet in his back pocket," she concluded pointing to Ikenga.

"What is your boyfriend's name?" the officer asked.

"Obiagu Bob-Mascot," she replied. "He is the head of the band."

"And the Prince?"

"Prince Hassan plays the drum."

The huge police officer that was jotting down the confessions of the girl put on his hand gloves and ordered Ikenga to be on his feet. Lightly he moved his palm over his body to ensure that he was not in possession of any weapon or dangerous object. The comedy was gradually unfolding and the girls were watching with interest to see what the officers would do with the supposed music star. Selda's excitement was now turning to concern but she was bent on seeing the end of the drama. It was obvious that the pathway to prominence, especially among black stars sometimes started in the most unremarkable scenarios.

A black overused leather wallet and a bunch of keys were pulled out from Ikenga's jeans pocket by the police officer. On careful examination and a short consultation to the white man's oracle– the computer, the police central database immediately revealed to the officers that they were dealing with an ex-convict who was a Sudanese refugee and not a comedian as the girls claimed. There was clearly no money with him to pay for the delicious banquet he had had with the girls and that meant he had to drive with the officers to the station for a minor interrogation and necessary paper protocol should the matter be referred to court. The girls were very ashamed on discovering the true identity of the man they had just dined with. Also, their expectations of a good time in Landesburg and hopes of touring round the globe with a popular music band had suddenly been dashed to the ground. They gave their names and addresses to the police as potential witnesses and left to find their way back to Frankfurt.

*     *     *     *     *

Mascot had intended to load up his wallet before going to meet with Ikenga and the ladies. The month had just ended and the overgenerous fatherland had paid the regular monthly salary even to its undeserving citizens. As the working population received their wages from the respective employees, so did cheats and drug users get paid from the well-structured social welfare system. This trickle-down effect at every end of the month could be felt from departmental stores to beer parlours, as well as the city station where drug users were stationed. It was a Friday evening and his plan was to round up on time, and take the girls round for sightseeing before they moved down to any club in the party arena.

The ever-busy train station was a major transit point for thousands of people who made their way everyday to and fro their working places. With the ever-increasing menace from dealers and users alike, the security apparatus was always restructured at intervals to counter the sophisticated nature of their conventional operations around the station vicinity. The Polizei had also devised a series of unconventional means to send kingpins behind bars since the users who were mainly citizens were sometimes not keen on co-operating with investigations. Stationary monitoring cameras, rampant harassment, and arrests of individuals loitering around by plain-clothed policemen helped to some extent but could not be the last straw that would break the camel's hump.

Mascot and some of his hard-necked friends resorted to breezing across the train station without hesitation. Like *enekentioba*, the ever-flying bird that mastered the techniques of flying without perching since men learnt to shoot without missing, they would briskly walk through the station in an overall working uniform, or neatly dressed as students with backpacks, pulling their customers like a magnet to a more secure and quiet zone. Mascot had till now avoided arrest due to his calculative timings and tactical manoeuvres. He always steered clear of the area as soon as he spotted an enemy in uniform or in mufti. Thus the police continually replaced the personnel stationed at the station whenever it was discovered that the dealers or the users, who patronised them, already knew the old groups.

Mascot touched down from U-Bann, the city service train, and walked down the station as drug users were already on the lookout for any dark-skinned passenger of the notorious train. That usually signified the arrival of the providers of their much-needed forbidden substance. He had seriously warned them never to approach him at the station to avoid suspicion, but to instead follow at a safe distance to wherever he was headed. Many who had lost control of their nervous system constantly flouted this order, which he always hammered into their ears. As they all knew, rattle-like movements and impatience to have their white or brown sugar could easily reveal to any onlooking undercover agent that the target of such advances was sure to be a dealer.

It had exactly happened as Mascot and other dealers feared, and set a whole lot of surveillance mechanism in motion. With his head, Mascot had just pushed off two limping users who were struggling with their pace to walk up to him. One of them, a haggard-looking woman stopped abruptly and pulled her colleague to a halt. She had suddenly remembered the instructions they had received a number of times. They followed at a very close distance putting together the little money they had on them while making sure they did not lose sight of their milkman. Some "gentlemen" around who still had their nerves under control followed from different directions including Gustav with his roommate and long-time best friend, an untrained German shepherd.

Although he had just alighted the city train, he took an alternative route back to the same platform and boarded another train heading back to the very direction he was coming from. His followers jumped in and took various positions waiting for any train stop that might be conducive for the street boy should he choose to not carry on with his illegal transactions inside the coach. The two plain-clothed detectives who joined the train had also already alerted their men to take positions at the first and second train stops. Already, one policeman was fully disguised as a drug user with a marked fifty Deutsche Mark note with which they planned to nail the dealer. Mascot had on the other hand decided to ride to the fourth station with his "students" to allow a good number of passengers get off the train.

The buying and selling commenced immediately they stepped off the coach with no regards for the staring eyes of confused passengers who got down with them, but briefly paused to wonder why a bunch of people were aggressively clamouring around a young black man.

"Give me three," one requested.

"I have only seven Mark, Mascot," the other pleaded.

"Where is my commission, man?" Gustav demanded. "I brought three customers for you."

"Be quiet!" Mascot shouted at them. "This place is not safe."

"It is very safe, brother," one limping woman responded in her poor English. "The police are not here."

Mascot was busy collecting money from the quiet ones and handing out corresponding number of white and brown bubbles that constantly popped out of his mouth, his eye coverage was well ahead of his immediate surrounding for his enemies or greenstriped vehicles. The undercover detective also came up with a well-rehearsed display of "student" character and collected three bubbles with his marked note. Mascot was somewhat suspicious of the new customer but quickly dispelled his fear since his trusted customers like Gustav and Anton did not raise an alarm. The old time customers and friends had saved him a number of times from trouble. As long-time addicts and "station emperors," they knew almost all the Polizei working at the station and always hinted their milkman whenever they were out on raid. In appreciation, the street boy always reciprocated with generous handouts and an offer of recruitment sometimes.

Anton was a seasoned truck driver who had given up his career and appetite to work when the Magistrate court ruled in favour of the children welfare which demanded that he must pay almost half of his monthly salary to his ex-wife and their eleven-year-old daughter. The court had already divided all he had saved for his retirement between both of them during their divorce, and the truck driver saw no more justification in paying to a woman who had every opportunity to pick up a job but refused to do so. That was when Anton decided to revoke the laid down culture of entitlement and dependency, as the authorities would stop at nothing for his pint of blood.

He had started with excessive drinking when he was driven out of his house and in no distant time graduated into hard drugs. Currently he was under the care of the welfare system since he was no longer able to fend for himself, and handed over his entire monthly allowance to people like Mascot to purchase his own destruction. The law, which knew not the difference between foreigner or citizen showed no mercy for men when it came to divorce or payment of child support.

*　*　*　*　*

As fast as his arms could move, Mascot grabbed money from whoever showed his note up without saying much to the poorer customers who were trying to make a good bargain. The agent limped closer to Mascot when he got information through the sophisticated communication gadget buried under his collar that the whole exit at the fourth station had been surrounded. From behind he grabbed his target by the neck and tried to pull him down to the concrete floor.

"Polizei," he shouted. *"Du bist verhaftet."*

A fierce struggle ensued. The second officer rushed forward wielding a handcuff and a round metal seal to indicate his identity. Mascot, an actor and seasoned street boy proved too strong and violent to be pinned to the ground by two middleweight officers. He made frantic efforts to free his throat, as that was the first target by the police to prevent suspects from swallowing the remaining contents in their mouth. With his two legs firmly dug to the ground, the actor muzzled the two men off him, and threw a rapid succession of successful random punches to any moving object in his blurred view before speeding off.

They chased after him while the penniless drug users who had joined the coach hoping for a free bonanza scrambled for the bubbles and Deutsche Mark notes that scattered over the station platform. Mascot ran as fast as he could toward the south exit from where he hoped to disappear into the heap of abandoned coaches. He was sure that his chances of going free if caught were minimal because the police might have arrested some of his customers who could be forced or frightened into testifying against him. But this time, police had no more interest in the users since they had material evidence and the double agent was sure that he had seen the culprit tuck the marked note inside his back pocket. Close to the overhead bridge at the south exit, another group of men raced towards him, and without a second thought, he jumped onto the rail track, determined to save himself unwanted time in Balthazar. The law agents would not give up, and the chase continued for a while along the rough rail tracks. Mascot would have made another triumphant escape if not for Marshal, the much active and intelligent German shepherd. The over-one-metre well trained dog was released to go after him when they realised that their reinforcement was no match for the street boy. The creature sprang from a distance on Mascot's shoulder and both tumbled to a halt at the rusty wheel of a rotten coach.

"I surrender," Mascot motioned to the glaring teeth of Marshal, its continued bitter roar was enough warning that slightest body movement would not be taken lying down. The motionless Mascot then realised that he had sustained a number of bruises on his elbows and knees as he lay on his back helplessly waiting for the officers to come and handcuff him. Careful not to make any moves that might offend the police dog, he gathered all the currency notes on him in a slow motion and tucked them into his mouth. To minimise material evidence, he hastily chewed and swallowed them all before the officers got to him.

Once inside Police Station, a thorough search was conducted and he was arraigned for interrogation before a senior officer with bushy moustache. Even though that was not his first visit to the police station, the advanced equipment and electronic gadgets were always for him so captivating and overpowering that he always played obedient boy once caged.

"I hate people like you," Moustache told him in plain language. Mascot stared at the officer expecting a real question.

"You were arrested for illegal drug dealings around the train station."

"No, Sir," Mascot replied gently. "Your men arrested the wrong person."

"You were caught redhanded with your white and brown packs."

"Your men have gotten the wrong person, Sir."

"What do you mean?"

"I have never dealt in drugs."

The officer dropped his pen on the table and relaxed in his office chair. He was a no-nonsense man who had been drafted to stamp out the menace of the street clan around the city station, when their illicit activity became blown to public consciousness. It drove him mad when people played on his intelligence or lied while staring him in the face. Smart criminals on the street made his work easy, while the foolish ones not only annoyed him but also complicated their chances of being set free. He swung the executive office chair sideways while gazing at the culprit before him.

"Do I show you my bad side?" Moustache angrily asked.

"First have a look at my good side before you show me your bad side," Mascot answered with a pitiable look. That was a simple request that sent the experienced officer rolling back on his chair. He had had enough with these African emigrants but would never miss an opportunity to explore their motivations and moral judgments.

"Tell me one good thing about yourself," he offered Mascot.

"My story is long," Mascot tried to explain.

"One good thing, I said."

"I was definitely not born a criminal."

"Were you born a saint?"

"No, Sir."

"What more can you say of yourself?"

"It's very long story indeed."

"Why did you decide to run away when the officers approached you?" the officer cut in.

"They grabbed me from behind," Mascot replied. "And I felt the explosive belt."

"Are you afraid of death?"

WOES OF IKENGA

"Yes, Sir."

"But your bubbles have killed many."

Mascot did not have much to say. He was inwardly guessing the number of months or years he would lavish in Balthazar as such carefully planned raids by plain-clothed police officers were aimed at taking an obstacle out for a while if not indefinitely. Normally it was carried out in broad daylight to send a powerful signal to the street clan who had refused to retreat or surrender.

"They had to let the dog on you when you refused arrest," the officer reminded him.

"They did not come for an arrest but to blow my head off."

These flimsy answers from Mascot were meant to buy time because he was convinced that he would be going in for a long time, and had nothing more to lose irrespective of whether or not he cooperated with the officer.

"What do you do for a living?" Moustache questioned after a short cigarette break.

"I am not allowed to work."

"That is no reason to deal on drugs"

"You are right, Sir."

"Do you know how many lives you have destroyed?"

"It is not in my nature, Sir."

"You have been operating for over three years now," the officer told him with certainty. "Have you not made enough money?"

"My father just died," Mascot pitifully replied.

"How many times will your father die before he is finally dead?"

Mascot pulled himself together. The only place he could remember to have used his father's death as an alibi was during his asylum interview. So how did Moustache come up with such a question when he was definitely not the man that had interviewed him on that fateful day?

The good-looking security agent was credited for cracking difficult puzzles and sending notorious criminals behind bars. His profession had exposed him to chapters of undocumented cock and bull stories whenever he conducted interrogations, and his attitude had earned him the name Moustache among the street clan. He was a rather amiable officer with a bulk of knowledge – thanks to foreign duties in the African and Asian continents– and would have sent Mascot to Balthazar as a repeated offender but his men had not recovered the fifty Deutsche Mark note and none of the users who could have testified against him had been taken into custody. Besides, he did not want to take the risk of the judge striking off the case for lack of sufficient evidence to please spectators who were beginning to cry foul at the alarming rate at which foreigners were being convicted.

"Have you got enough money to bury your father now?" he queried.

"Yes, Sir," Mascot answered.

"I don't want to see you at the train station again," Moustache sternly instructed.

"I will not come again."

With that he stood up and left without a further word. Mascot watched him disappear till a junior officer came over to escort him to the counter where his belongings were kept. It was difficult to believe when the remote-controlled door opened for him to leave. Hesitantly, he looked behind to get the approval of the man behind the counter.

"Get lost," the loud speaker yelled at him.

Once in the open and a free man, Mascot did not think of anything else apart from his two guests from Frankfurt. There was no doubt in his mind that Ikenga was going to do a smooth job, after all, he needed the *kpalli* more than anybody else. Happy that his cell phone battery had not run out, he quickly entered his, four-digit pin code, scrolled the contact list to Ikenga, and dialed.

*   *   *   *   *

That he allowed another potential *kpalli* slip out of his hand because of his cowardice left Ikenga wandering with self-indictment. The jest made of him by friends the whole night was not only well deserved but a wake-up call. Was it possible that the old woman did not know how to barb hair or that the blade was not sharp enough? Selda would have readily danced to his tune as a devoted fan of an abstract band till he could pin her down with marriage or pregnancy. Once a girl was hooked, another story was quickly configured if necessary to gradually disentangle the series of lies and deceit. Ikenga had however never made it to that level simply because there was no money on him to pay the bills in the Chinese restaurant, a level of poverty he had subjected himself to in order to maintain the good name of his family.

Mascot, who was eventually released from detention, did not talk to him for a couple of weeks. His actions were a total failure and mismanagement of a rare opportunity for someone who badly needed the Resident Permit.

If only he had known that the glittering colours of the white man's land were not gold. Reverend Klaus had tried to discourage him but the old man's advice had been regarded as the words of a wretched preacher who had lost touch with reality. Now that he had come, it would be difficult and humiliating to explain to the people of Umuafor why he had been thrown into a heap of palm kernel but could not pick a few to quench his hunger.

# Chapter 9

Ikenga finally gave in to hustling at the city station, thereby becoming an automatic member of the street clan. The decision was based on his perceived viable options, and because he needed to make a bold move if he was to be liberated from the chuckles of the welfare system.

Trying to preserve a good name had neither paid off nor placed food on his dining table or on that of his overworked father. He had come to Germany to improve his living standards and that of his family after all. The support program, designed to see people through temporary hard times, was not the solution to his longterm problems and since the authorities had a standing policy on work permit when it came to political or economic migrants, he made up his mind to explore his possibilities at the train station of Landesburg otherwise known as the Corporate Headquarters.

The ever-busy transit point accommodated the good, the bad and the ugly. Majority of the commuters were the industrious working populace who were always in a hurry to catch their trains or buses. Other visible occupants of the station were the secondclass citizens who for one reason or the other lived off social welfare and had no active engagements. They hung around for hours in the station vicinity or in the recreation grounds to escape the chronic lonely life that the state laws had thrown at them. The street clan represented outlaws like the drug dealers, pimps, pickpockets, shoplifters, and of course the sizeable number of patronage that they commanded.

Mascot was delighted that Ikenga had at last agreed to join them instead of living from hand-to-mouth at the refugee camp. He had a lot of catching up to do though, if he wanted to make up for the time wasted at Meier's farm and the few months in Balthazar.

The city station affair was one of the few businesses anyone could venture into without a start-up capital. There was no shortage of individuals at the background willing to give out grams of heroin or cocaine to any interested recruit. The stuff was wrapped in tiny bubbles of different sizes for different amounts and a new recruit got another batch after selling off and paying for the previous ones collected. However, the practice was later reformed to a cash and carry affair when stories kept coming from dubious individuals bent on acquiring wealth at all costs, who would pocket the capital and proceeds after sale, only to tell flimsy stories of police arrest or poor quality of the material to their suppliers. Another worrying dimension was when it was discovered that some members of the street clan when weighed down by the enormity of their problems resigned to the use of the drugs for their own consolation. There were also some, who might have deliberately started to take the dreaded substance as a way of proving their credentials as a strong civilian and their oneness with the street, but the hard drug tended to gradually pull them over the boundary and they were soon no longer able to disentangle themselves from the addictive nature of the destructive sugar. The subdealers who could not take any actions to retrieve their money or their high valued stuff in such incidents resolved in handing out the white or brown sugar to whoever had cash.

Mascot introduced Ikenga to his subdealer to guarantee that he got good quality and taught him how to make the bubbles, and the next day he was walking in a corporate outfit around the Corporate Headquarters with birds of the same feather. "The students" as they were normally referred to, who roamed the train station in groups of two or more with wretched wears or limping with their pets, were very easy to identify. They were being controlled by the drug and had no willpower of their own whatsoever. Whatever they received from the welfare at the beginning of the month was handed over to the street dealers to maintain their insatiable addiction. The men would then resort to petty stealing or pickpocketing to survive till the end of the next month while the women submitted to road-side prostitution. Another brand of users at the City Station were those referred to as "the gentlemen." These were well-to-do addicts whose consumption rate had not gotten to a destructive state. They had probably gotten their wealth via inheritance, well-paid jobs, or other alternative sources of income, tried their best to maintain a clean life, and were usually very clever about concealing their addiction from their relatives and friends. An experienced station dealer with a good strategy was likely to demand the contact numbers of a "gentleman," and the station affair would turn into home service with lesser risks of being picked up by the ever ready Polizei.

Ikenga could not do much on the first day but follow Mascot around as he struggled to speak freely with the few white bubbles concealed under his tongue. He had often been at the train station as a mere passerby but this was time to study and understand what actually went on within and without the monumental structure; memorise the plate numbers of the unmarked undercover police vehicles; and take cover or vacate the station vicinity if he saw any. He had been warned to be careful with the "students" at mid-month because they were likely to get one into trouble within their "dry period" out of desperation. The "gentlemen" were also not to be totally trusted because an undercover agent might pose as one. Above all, he was supposed to be able to identify the location of all the stationary surveillance cameras and be ready to swallow the mouth content should an undercover bystander suddenly dive at his throat. Those were the crucial guidelines that Mascot practiced and preached to him the whole day if he was to survive on the street.

The thirty-eight Deutsche Mark with which Ikenga went home the first day was a motivation that cleared all odds and propelled him to show up the next day as determined as ever. His street clan body language and the way he commanded the "students" exceeded the expectations of Mascot and the old boys. The cat and mouse game with sure periodic bonuses of hard currency was for Ikenga more enticing and rewarding than his experiences with squirrels and grasscutters in the swampy farmlands of Umuafor. It was not long before he ran into one of the girls he met on the day he had come to pick the two ladies from Frankfurt. "Wow! It's you again," he said to her boldly.

"Hi," Vanessa accepted with a warm smile. "I hope your aunt will not be mad at you this time?"

"Oh no, she is now of the opinion that I get married quickly."

"Why the sudden change?"

"She has realised that I am no more the little boy she used to know."

"Why do some of you want to marry European women when you already have a wife in Africa?"

"That's a very good question," Ikenga remarked. "Where is your girlfriend?" he asked trying to avoid her question.

"She was banned from coming to the station," Vanessa replied.

One thing Ikenga would later notice and hold dear about Vanessa was her free-mindedness. She opened her thoughts and heart to anyone who cared and hid nothing about herself or anyone.

"How can a citizen be forbidden from coming to the train station?" he asked immediately to change the subject.

She was the type that held one's gaze as she spoke, a warmly accepted Western culture that forbade undue royalty to anyone for reasons of age or wealth.

"Are you also married in your country?" she asked not willing to give in.

"Count me out of that blind culture," Ikenga answered with unsure sincerity.

He felt drawn to this girl; her young and innocent face gave her the appearance of one who would make a good housewife and mother.

"I want to settle down as soon as I meet my girl."

"Where have you written down the qualities of your girl?"

"Right inside my heart."

"Nobody can write on stone."

"I said in my heart."

"What do you think is there?"

"This is wonderful," Ikenga said laughing. "You have not even told me your name."

"My name is Vanessa."

"Hanging around the station is not good for you."

"Is it good for you?"

Her answers and questions came with ease. There was clearly no trace of malice and he had to struggle with structuring his own questions and answers while trying to keep up the momentum.

"It has always been the job of the man to provide for the house," he explained.

"And what if the man becomes incapable?"

"I am not afraid of tomorrow," Ikenga told her.

"Moreover whatever brings incapability must surely bring a solution."

His words sounded sweet to Vanessa, and reminded her that bravery was one of the qualities she looked for in a man. Ikenga who sensed that he had scored a point gently pulled her by the hand and headed towards a nearby *Kebab* shop. There would be no losses should the business of the day be held up for the day as his yam had grown two tubers and only an *ofeke* would harvest one and leave the other behind.

"What is your name?" Vanessa asked on their way.

"Ikenga."

"Is your country also engulfed in war?"

"Not really, I personally decided to embark on exploration."

"Exploration does not end at the City Station."

"I have to build my fortune independent of my father's empire," Ikenga told her with ease.

Boldness was also another quality that Vanessa looked for in her would-be man. She saw endurance and determination on the faces of these street boys and always wondered if things were really as well as they claimed in their land while comfortably braving risks on the street of another man's country. Whatever their thoughts or intentions might be, Vanessa had already made up her mind to build her broken life around one of them, and Ikenga soon became the treasure she wished for herself especially as he also possessed all the physical features that she cherished most; he was tall, handsome, and athletic.

With the massive influx of economic migrants, and the subsequent abuse of the assistance programs, the stringent regulations attached to the welfare system were gradually getting on Vanessa's nerves. The office of employment had written several times that she should take up a job they had reserved for her since she was unwilling to complete any of the available free programs. The young girl at her presumed peak of her life was still not ready to give up her freedom for such low paid jobs. Inwardly she had begun to realise that she was no match for her mates who had pursued a career but her good nature forbade her from blaming herself or anyone else, and so she sought for insurance coverage from members of the street clan.

Ikenga did not labour much to win her love. He simply loved her as he knew how to, and allowed her live her life the way she knew it. A nation known for its hardwork and care for the less privileged was bound to have among her citizens many who had been rendered useless by the loopholes in her uncompromising generosity and care. Vanessa had always had everything her way, right from the time she lived with her grandmother in her early age. Most of her mates had taken up a career or had steady boyfriends but she had refused to go for anything less than an already-made man.

Ikenga's solid body stature and juicy wallet was all it took. Vanessa took him to the *heim* where she lived and did everything necessary to suggest that she was available. They soon became a formidable pair and team at the train station. Ikenga sometimes slept over in her room instead of going back everyday to Bruggendorf, and with the proceeds he got from the illicit trade they rented an apartment in the city. She was delighted to leave the care centre that had been her home since she got separated from her grandmother.

Going home everyday with some hard currency renewed Ikenga's ego and resurrected his dreams of buying a car for his father and possibly one for Nne. But that would be the next priority as soon as their apartment was well equipped, to give Vanessa the comfort she deserved. Vanessa was not a complete novice to the activities that went on in the City Station and provided a wellmeaning logistic support in whichever way she could; always playing a love bird by the side of her man whenever he was on duty to scare off boyfriend snatchers and take the eyes of the undercover agents off him. As the money trickled in, she tucked it into her brazier for safety and would shuttle to and fro their house whenever there was a sudden shortage of supply. Her driving lessons, which Ikenga generously paid for, also emboldened her fantasies of living "happily ever after" with her dream man in a comfortable villa of their own. With the steady influx of money, she occasionally smiled to herself with a deep-rooted gratefulness that her patience had finally paid off. Indeed she had become an object of envy for many of her fellow station perambulators who had not been fortunate enough to have a brave hustler like Ikenga.

However, the vigilant station Polizei abruptly switched off the biblical manna falling from the sky. Their first attempt to have Ikenga imprisoned after a long surveillance had been thwarted by an over-lenient judge who freed him due to what he described as insufficient evidence and claims from Vanessa that the officers had simply cooked up the story to put an end to her relationship with a *nigger*. Her endless cries and readiness to be locked up with her man should he be falsely convicted had earned the pity of the spectators and the grey-haired judge. The next time, the officers had been very careful to strike when Vanessa was not around him, and when they were sure of an overwhelming proof of evidence.

One of his highly valued "gentlemen" had called to enquire about his location. Because he had just finished a short transaction few stops away and was already inside the metro heading back to the main station, he had directed the customer to meet him at a particular metro stop completely unaware that the long arms and ears of the Polizei still trailed him, regardless of the uncountable number of times he had destroyed and replaced his SIM card. The well-dressed drug user occupied a seat at Clemens metro station and calmly waited for his milkman as instructed. Ikenga, wearing a hooded jacket, stepped out of the underground train as the door opened and took his own seat close to his customer leaving a vacant seat in-between. Patiently, the user who was still conscious of the rule waited without a word until Ikenga was satisfied that the ground was level enough to strike. It was a normal working day and many who had come down the metro with him had long disappeared and they were left with only a few absent-minded commuters.

"How much do you have there?" Ikenga asked in a low commanding tone without looking at his customer.

"Two hundred Marks."

"What of the eighty Marks you owe me?"

"I will pay you next time," the gentleman who looked more like a beginner answered apologetically.

"That is what you have told me for three consecutive times."

"I will get my money next week or give you a nice cell phone for that."

"What type of handset do you have for me?"

"It's still brand new."

"Let me see."

The heavily built man who was seriously struggling to compose himself slipped the cargo on the vacant seat between them and Ikenga slowly picked the cell phone with his left hand while making sure none of the absent-minded commuters was paying attention. It was one of the latest Sony Ericsson phones and would serve as a well-deserved present for Chinaza if Vanessa did not grab it.

"I will take the phone," Ikenga said, cheerfully looking at his customer for the first time. The gentleman was glad that his milkman liked the present. He had been looking for a way to pay back for the bonus and bonanzas he received once in a while and was now presented with the alternative of coming with such cargo whenever he ran short of cash. Again he pushed over the tightly folded two hundred Deutsche Mark note over to Ikenga who tucked the note under the tight arms of his long sleeve pullover without a second look.

"But I told you never to come to the station," he barked in a low tone.

"Yes, but I live very far."

"That should not be a problem," Ikenga assured. "I will always come to your house whenever you need my milk."

"I will wait at home next time."

"You must learn to be good, Johnny."

"I will be good, brother."

The dangerous phase of the transaction was about to take place. The gentleman obediently and loyally answered all the questions while Ikenga bought time to make sure that he was going to get away with the action. When he was confident that all was well, he moved his left hand to wipe his face and with precise ease dropped a calculated number of white bubbles into his palm.

"Put them inside your mouth," he whispered; but the "gentleman" who had promised to be of good behaviour times without number wanted to know the number of bubbles he got for two hundred Marks and probably lodge a plea complaint if he was unsatisfied. He held his hand close to his chest to examine his much-cherished wares.

"Do what I told you, white monkey," Ikenga charged with a slightly elevated tone. Before he could realise it, an innocent looking young man who had been pretending to be occupied with a flat rear tyre of his mountain bike few metres away was already on his throat.

"Polizei ... Polizei ... Open your mouth!"

It was indeed an unexpected attack. Ikenga first struggled to free his neck from the young man's solid grip before smashing the large cell phone on his forehead when the officer did not let go. That was what gave him a breathing space to run for his life; aware that many policemen might be stationed upstairs or on the way down the metro station, Ikenga decided to bail himself through the extensive underground tunnel network.

A number of officers were pouring down the metro at the same time but none dared follow him into the tense dark tunnel, and instead seized the visibly shaken drug user with the white bubbles, which he had immediately abandoned with panic on the vacant seat. The long haired man was a newly employed junior staff at the management and consulting institute located a few blocks away from the City Station, and had decided to see his milkman briefly after work instead of driving all the way home and waiting for him to come over. The action-filled drama, which he had never witnessed, evolved very fast leaving him with no time to contemplate escape. Helplessly he accepted to cooperate with the police on the condition that he would be spared a jail term and the information withheld from his employers.

Ikenga, now deemed a dangerous suspect, was trapped in the underground tunnel for a good number of hours in the company of giant rats. Endless rows of motionless pillars, which represented the underground ghosts revealed themselves each time a train passed by, and almost frightened him into coming out and surrendering to the police if not for his firm belief that real ghosts only existed in his part of the world. The whistling noise of the electric train with its faint headlights made he and the mice scramble for cover, flat against the wall or dodge by the round concrete pillars to avoid detection. His willingness to keep a long lonely vigil deep down in the earth was to break the will of those after him, but he had poorly underestimated the determination and patience of the Landesburg Polizei. All the metro entrances and the exits had been sealed off with plain cloth officers and an intense manhunt initiated because of the serious head injury that he had inflicted on the undercover agent.

The incident had taken place at the metro station with few witnesses and no other member of the street clan had been around to dispatch the information. Vanessa called as soon as her driving lessons were over and immediately concluded that Ikenga was with another woman–the only reason according to her why a man would switch off his cell phone during the day. With concealed rage, she went over to the station trying to catch him redhanded and to tear whoever was playing second best into pieces. But not even Mascot or any close friends of Ikenga could give any information about his whereabouts. There was no reported incident of Polizei activity or arrest and so they all believed that their homeboy had gone for a quick spontaneous good time or was rather trying not to keep all his eggs in one basket. She bitterly went back to the house to restlessly wait for his arrival. The endless wait timed-out when some mean looking detectives arrived to ransack their small apartment in the early hours of the next morning.

She jumped off the sofa at the sound of a key being turned in her door lock, while shouting a whole range of questions without seeing who was behind the boor.

"What's all this?" she asked as the door, which was supposed to be locked with her keys swung open to reveal some group of men standing before her.

"Where are the rest of the drugs hidden?" one asked pointing a bright torchlight into her face.

"*Was soll das?*" she queried again. "What drugs are you talking about?"

"The *Koka*," the officer maintained.

"You have no right to enter my apartment."

"You have the right to remain silent," the officer instructed. "That will make our work easier."

"How can I remain silent when strange men have invaded my apartment in the middle of the night?"

"You have been aiding and abetting a drug dealer."

Vanessa relented immediately, knowing what it meant to be levelled with such allegations, and the fact that an individual's crime record stayed with the police for the whole of one's lifetime and might constitute an obstacle or a hindrance in one's future endeavours. The four men literally pushed her aside before she could finish any flimsy explanation, and made their way into the living room to commence their ransacking. Thankfully, she had been clever enough to send Ikenga's *akpa-agwu* down to the basement when she returned from the station. The frantic search lasted for less than an hour, and the police informed her when all her efforts to stop them yielded no results that her man had been arrested for unauthorised drug dealing in the City Station and seriously wounding a police officer. They seized some items of interest like mobile phones, an electronic digital scale, and a bottled transparent liquid thought to be ammoniac. A list of the items taken was handed to Vanessa.

Trying to build her life around Ikenga had been a strategy to evade work since she had no chance at the labour market. It was now clear to her that financial freedom would be severely ruffled if Ikenga were sent away for a long period. What would she then do with her life? She was already two months pregnant but had planned to tell him after the third month to minimise the chances of his opting for abortion. In tears she sunk into the sofa as the officers left, contemplating her next move. Going back to the child care centre was not an option and her aging father whom she was not on talking terms with because of his objection to her choice of life-partner would not be keen on welcoming her with open arms after many years as a prodigal daughter. Finally she decided to keep the pregnancy as the only way of clinging on social benefits and at least affording to retain the apartment for her and the baby.

For days she stayed indoors and cried. The information that Mascot brought from the lawyer was not promising. Although the Jewish advocate had promised to do his best, the evidences against Ikenga were overwhelming, coupled with a damning testimony from the fearful "gentleman" and another young girl who confessed to patronising the milkman for over two months.

Vanessa did not show up throughout the trial period because of her uncontrollable emotions and fear that her man would not be coming home with her. Their love had gradually developed over the period that she could not stand leaving her man behind at the end of the court hearing. It was after Ikenga had been sentenced to forty-two months imprisonment that she reluctantly accepted to pay him a visit with Mascot. She drafted a very emotional love letter, packed some of his favourite clothes with few edibles and set off for Balthazar.

They were seated in a round wooden table in the visitor's room discussing in low tones when Ikenga stepped in with a prison guard. Vanessa leaped up from the bench and flew into his arms; it was the first time they were seeing each other since the ill-fated transaction that led to his arrest. They held each other tightly for a few moments and when they let loose, tears streamed down her cheeks.

"No, darling!" Ikenga consoled. "This is not the time for that."

"Why did you let them catch you?"

"I tried my best."

"But your best was not good enough," Mascot who had remained unnoticed told him.

Ikenga extended a warm handshake and hug to his kinsman, and both men were exchanging compliments in their mother tongue when the guard who could not understand a word interrupted:

"You are only allowed to speak in German unless you want to call off the visit," he warned with an unfriendly look.

"Sorry, Mr. President," Mascot returned.

"You see why I always like to be with you wherever you go?" Vanessa continued in tears as both men cut short their conversation.

"It could also be the way it was destined," Ikenga answered. "It would not have happened if my *chi* did not allow it."

"What am I going to do now?"

"This is the time you have to be strong, my dear," Ikenga consoled. "How far have you gone with your driving lessons?"

"I stopped already."

"My goodness! Why?"

"I could no longer concentrate."

"You have to ... you must!"

"I was doing it because of you."

"You must continue with the lessons," Ikenga advised. "You are doing it for yourself."

"I don't need the driver's license anymore," she insisted.

"Then carry on for my sake."

"Are they going to send you back to Africa?" she asked sobbing.

"Most likely," he replied sadly. "Drug offences that merit more than four years jail term normally lead to deportation."

With the blunt answer Vanessa leaped a step backwards and lamented with her visibly distressed innocent face. "They can't do this to me, what am I going to do with the baby?"

"What baby?" Ikenga asked, looking at Mascot and pointing a finger at Vanessa's slightly protruding stomach. When Mascot nodded his head in affirmation, Ikenga broke the silence by proudly walking around the tiny visitor's room, pouring praises to goodness and his *chi* with words of salutation and appreciation for granting him his heart desires. In line with the beliefs of Umuafor, Ikenga saw his present detention as a grand design by his *chi* to avert a greater calamity or to preserve him for a better opportunity. The news became another beacon of conviction that his ups and downs in the white man's land had been predestined and triumphant victory awaited him after all the illusive predicaments.

"Clean your tears, Vanessa!" he said to her at last. "He shall be called Afamefuna. Udeaja's name will continue to live on."

It was a big relief for Vanessa when she saw that Ikenga was happy about the pregnancy. That might also help to secure his early release according to the assurances she got from Mascot.

She wiped her tears and placed Ikenga's hand on her stomach.

"How are you sure he is going to be a boy?" she asked.

"The spirit of my grandfather revealed it to me," Ikenga boasted.

"I love you dearly," Vanessa said to him with a prolonged kiss.

The jealous looking guard could not take that either. He could not understand why such a beautiful young girl chose to tarnish her bright future with a drug dealer, and chose that time to swing his baton and bunch of keys to indicate that visiting time was over. Mascot's plea for a few extra minutes fell on deaf ears and they were all sad that their moment of joy had been cut short while it was still gathering momentum.

"A part of me is with you," Ikenga told Vanessa. "That will be a fountain of hope and courage while I do my time. We are one family, and the system will not be able to tear us apart."

With the guard standing almost between them to drive home the fact that the time was up, Ikenga bade farewell to his visitors, collected the handbag that Vanessa brought and moved ahead of the guard into the long corridor leading to the D-section of the prison ward.

Back in the three-by-three metre cell, the news, which he had hoped would bring some comfort to his body and soul, became a source of anxiety and fear. He knew that Vanessa had no willpower of her own and might decide to do away with the pregnancy if there was nobody around to keep on telling her that all was well. Worse still, the goal, which he had perfectly scored, might be converted into a penalty shootout or throwing if the street gangsters began to notice that she was now alone. Evidently, his chances of staying in the country after serving his jail term would be hanging on a balance should anything happen to the pregnancy.

Apart from worries about Vanessa's pregnancy and its consequent impact on his refugee status, Ikenga also knew that years were counting on him. Since he had not been sending money regularly, Umuafor would only reconcile with him if he returned with plenty. The hunger, struggle, quest for wealth, undue loyalty for vanity, and unwritten discrimination that devoured Umuafor was visible and deep-rooted. Also, the post-war adverse effects of the struggle for survival, though swept under the carpet by Umuafor historians, had eaten deep into the bone of her sons and daughters. Judging by the number of years for which Ikenga had not been seen, any of his extended relatives who had not tasted from his easy wealth from the white man's land could be forgiven for expecting a triumphant return. For Ikenga and the young men of Umuafor who were literally scattered like the sands of the seas across the surface of the planet earth, failing to meet such expectations was seen as total failure or loss of one's manhood. It was the psychological effect of such disastrous failure that gradually caught up with him in his one-man prison cell.

As the hours turned into days and days into weeks, Ikenga was involuntarily drawn into lengthy hours of thinking and worries that yielded him no viable solution. At one time he lost interest in the recreational and sporting activities available to inmates, and preferred to spend the day in his cell. To him, the detention was unfair. After all, he was only a poor black man who came to take back his share of what the colonial masters looted from his fatherland, and justified his offence by continually telling himself that he was driven by hunger and quest for survival, and had neither killed, nor stolen from anyone to deserve such a harsh punishment. As the months crawled like a snail and freedom looked very far from sight, he resorted to his creator and his *chi* for divine intervention. Upon request he was given a Revised Standard Version of the Holy Bible by the prison's spiritual director. He remembered that the good old Reverend Klaus had referred to the Book as a complete spiritual armament and ever-ready consultant to all who sought freedom, but every time he intended to pray or read the Holy Book, his ever-present worries snatched his thoughts and concentration, and tears would roll down his eyes, until his intended prayer time was over. Probably because he was unable to communicate effectively with the unseen, the spirit beings decided to uphold his three-and-half years sentence.

*     *     *     *     *

He left Balthazar a different man, and in time to celebrate Afamefuna's third birthday with his family. Vanessa had kept the pregnancy because of her endless wish to have a "chocolate baby" and the hope that the welfare system would not fail in her time. Hence, she lived comfortably with Afamefuna as every other active single parent under the umbrella of the well-organised welfare network. As a mother, she loved her child, and in her free and lonely time consummated her smoking habit. The habit, which

Ikenga believed, had kept her going through the sad moments of his absence.

Few of his old friends came with some other new faces for the party. Apart from Mascot and his right hand men Santos, Iko and Andy, the other unknown faces that were introduced to him were new arrivals. This implied that the very same factors that drove the flow of human resources from the sweet shores of Africa to the Western world still had its wheels in motion. A happy Vanessa entertained the guests with enough food and drinks. Generally, her lifestyle throughout Ikenga's absence was commendable. With one or two abortions credited to her record, she had always carefully given Afamefuna the impression that his father travelled to a distant land and would one day return. Thank goodness the traveller successfully returned to his wife and beloved son, and after the "welcome-back to the free world" and birthday breeze were over, the two settled to pick up their lives from where they left it off over three years ago.

# Chapter 10

It was never the same again. The long and lonely days and weeks in the prison cell had made a lasting impact on Ikenga's ways of judgment and reasoning. After a rather strenuous process, a temporary work permit was issued him on assumption of a fifty percent joint custody of Afamefuna.

First, there were endless consultations with his lawyer on the best ways to declare his true identity. Afterwards, he renounced Sudan and the fearful stories he had stood by for many years. A light fine to be paid off in instalments was all it had cost him, and Hassan Ijenwata, an illegal alien officially became recognised as Ikenga Udeaja, a legal alien.

In no time, he secured a job through one of the employment agencies as a production helper. Okazi Foods & Services with its mechanically oriented working rhythm eventually became a safe haven from the periodic confrontations that constantly sprung up at home. Vanessa, who had lived alone with her son and presided over her own decisions, was irritated by Ikenga's complaints and restraints. Her welfare package had been slashed thin as soon as he started working and he no longer allowed expenditure for whatever he considered an unnecessary wish or pleasure. Money no longer flowed in as it used to and Vanessa who knew nothing about resource management detested the sudden control and restrictions. Although she managed to play along despite her reservations, Ikenga grudgingly went to work just to house and feed someone he now saw as an adversary because she was opposed to all his principles. The commonest fracas was about the number of sweets she consumed or allowed their son consume, her lack of willpower, and her inability to stock up grain for the rainy days. Both had been brought up in two different worlds with different views and their narrow-minded analyses of the problem had them quarrelling even more often and fighting for individual rights instead of the common good of the family. Vanessa was soon at the point of deciding to stop taking orders from an African and was beginning to seriously contemplate going back to single parenthood, which had a more attractive pay package.

Every morning, Ikenga left the house for work, praying that the day would never be over. His colleagues noticed that something was terribly amiss but nobody dared ask because of his sudden aggressiveness. Being a brother's keeper where community life had long evaporated was merely a topic for preachers and politicians. None of the workers really wanted to take over his burden because their own mountains weighed them down.

*   *   *   *   *

His nine-hour morning shift was over even while he still struggled to get himself into work mode. He had had less than two hours sleep the previous night because the greater part of the night had been spent quarrelling and yelling abuses. The heavily built Egyptian foreman and personnel manager had cautioned him twice to be up and doing in order to maintain the working frequency.

Long after the morning shift, he lingered in the dressing room unable to take off his work uniform. He was afraid of many things; going back to his house, breaking down in silence, becoming a prisoner of conscience, and mostly the idle queen, the mother of his son who had sworn to never take up any employment to help the family. The violent revolt from Vanessa the previous day was a clear reminder that he needed to start searching for the black goat while it was still day.

It started like every other day. Ikenga had just finished washing his work uniform and was waiting for the yam porridge on the stove to cook. He lay down on the sofa to catch a glimpse of what was going on on the television. "Inside Africa" was showing on Cable News Network with young students picking up awards for their immense achievement in their various academic fields. He smiled at the young stars as they filed out with prestige to pick their awards, and bemoaned the Civil War and its consequent economic hardship that had denied him of the white man's education. Then, he pulled Afamefuna close to himself, and gave him a kiss on the forehead.

"I will send you to the best school, my son," he said with the pride of a loving father.

"The education I missed is what I owe you. You will read and read until you are able to put down to paper what the birds are saying from the treetop."

The little boy was enjoying the joke and laughing his heart out. He hardly shared such precious moments with his father whose cheer seemed to die as soon as he stepped into their small apartment.

"Get ready to fly with your mates to the moon and stars," he said pointing at the ceiling.

His mother who was eavesdropping from the balcony quickly rushed in with a cigarette gummed between her two fingers and grabbed the little boy.

"Allow the boy to grow up before you present him with a litany of schools to attend," she shouted.

Ikenga was short of words. He pulled backwards and sat down to stare at the mother and her baby.

"I was just playing with my boy," Ikenga said apologetically.

"My son has the right to do whatever he wants to do when he grows up," she continued.

"If he doesn't want to go to school, he can pursue a career in any vocation."

"An illiterate has no chance in today's world."

"Who is an illiterate?" she queried.

"Take a look at yourself and tell me if you are happy with the kind of life you are living," Ikenga said.

"I am very happy with my life. I was getting enough money from the social welfare till you were released from prison."

"Why can't you understand me for good, this woman? We both owe our son a bright future."

"You talk of education all the time, nobody went to university in my family but they are all living fine. My father is a painter by profession and he is well off and comfortable."

Words poured out of her mouth, accompanied at intervals

with thick smoke every time she took drags from her cigarette. She had sharpened her tongue as a defence weapon and was ready for any confrontation, but Ikenga waited until the words started dying down.

"Goodness!" he shouted. This was an entirely different *Ogbanje* from the ones in Umuafor.

"Reverend Klaus should have finished with people like you before coming down to Africa."

"You have also not achieved anything in your home country or you would not have come over to Germany."

"But I have achieved a lot in Germany."

"The only thing you have achieved is selling drugs at the train station."

"With which I fed and sheltered you?"

"I am German," Vanessa boasted. "I always had shelter all along and will continue to."

"A German is not supposed to come to naught," Ikenga corrected. "There are many opportunities for you."

"And why did you decide to have a baby with a naught?" Vanessa asked.

He was silent for a moment. Her question had no easy answer. There had really been no time for courtship in his desperate search for a Resident Permit or citizenship. Besides, the long arm of the Foreign Office had been after him to send him back to Sudan where he claimed to have come from.

Many had been sent back to Africa or countries other than their own to face fresh humiliation from the hands of angry and hungry immigration authorities. He wished he had looked for a decent girl to bear his child, at least one who knew the value of education and a decent life. In the desperate attempt to navigate the stringent immigration laws of the countries, marriages were initiated spontaneously between prodigal citizens and aliens; the rejected old and the young; and ridiculously between stark illiterates and the very intellectual.

"I've promised you that I want to spend the rest of my life

with you," Ikenga said to her in a bid to remedy the situation. "We can make a better family if you put your hands in mine."

"You can't change me now," she replied still unwilling to relent. "This is how I am."

"On the contrary," he corrected. "The *Bekees* I know are very intelligent. With their knowledge and ability to invent things, my people refer to them as semi-gods. They make life easy for all but people like you who refuse to do anything are left behind. After all, there are cleaning jobs to be done, by the time you realise what you have done to yourself ... "

"Pack your things and leave this house!" she ordered. "If you think that I am not good for any other thing apart from a cleaning job. I am tired of you foreigners."

"Listen to me carefully!" Ikenga raised his voice assuming an authoritative tone. "I would rather kill you and go back to prison than to allow you ruin the life of my son."

With that, the young lady flared like wildfire. The period she had lived alone with their son had been an eye-opener, and she was able to gather enough in-depth information from her older associates about the lives of the so-called aliens, and the likelihood that most of them would eventually walk out of a marriage as soon as they obtained their Resident Permit. That had kept Vanessa agitated, especially since Ikenga returned from Balthazar and suddenly wanted to assert his authority.

She continued yelling till Ikenga fled to Afamefuna's room, and slammed the door heavily when he could no longer stand the abuses.

The peace of the evening had been devoured again. From under the blanket, Ikenga heard her rain curses that went on and on into his inner ears till his alarm clock sprung to life. He got up immediately, unable to tell for sure if he had slept or not, walked quietly to the sitting room to find mother and child sleeping on the sofa, and gently covered them with a duvet before going into the bathroom to get ready for the day's work. After scraping off what was left of his yam porridge from the burnt pot for his breakfast and lunch, he sneaked out of the house to catch the first bus.

Throughout the thirty-five minutes ride to work, he tried to understand or identify the *Ogbanje* element in his wife and its *modus operandi* in the white man's land. They had had so many serious quarrels in the few years that they had lived together, yet times without number she would fall on her knees and declare that she was unhappy with herself and unconscious of some of her actions. Vanessa's weakness was that she had gladly accepted that her broken life was irreparable and did not want to make any attempts to make a change or lift herself from the pit of depression, yet she refused corrections, especially from an African like Ikenga, even when it was obviously for the good of their small family.

Their lives had been full of white and red roses during the early stages of their relationship. He remembered how pretty she looked in her early twenties with long straight hair and big black eyes. Both had shown willingness to respect and accept each other's culture for the good of their new family and shared dreams and wishes to live in unity and love forever after. The steady inflow of cash from the city station had also been an added advantage but things had taken a drastic turn since Ikenga was released from detention, and the lifeline of their income became adversely affected.

Unknown to his parents, the little but sensitive Afamefuna was having nightmares due to the constant quarrels and fights he was now used to witnessing. First there had been a heated quarrel over amending the child's name, then circumcision, and also the invitation of Nne for *omugwo*. In his vicious quest to bestow an African identity on his first son, the boy was renamed Udeaja Heinrich Afamefuna and when he was rushed to the hospital a few days afterwards with acute diarrhea and symptoms of convulsion, his mother claimed that those native names may have played a part in her son's illness. Trouble pitched its tent in their two-room apartment for the three days they spent at the hospital unscarred by the lovely flowers sent by Vanessa's friends and family.

Ikenga made arrangements before they left the hospital to

secure an appointment for circumcision with the doctor's secretary. The tradition that he held so dearly had to be heeded. Vanessa like any loving mother did not want her baby going through what she saw as tormenting pain at such a tender age and took the baby to visit *Opa*, promising to be back early enough for the appointment. Reluctantly he allowed her travel with the baby due to his trust in the rapid response capabilities of the mobile medical unit should the symptoms manifest again. The appointment day came and went but Vanessa and her baby were nowhere to be found. Ikenga's anger boiled over in the house as he tried to reach her on phone, only to discover that the lines were dead. He could not go over because her father had never approved of the relationship and would definitely not receive him as a welcomed guest.

Though Umuafor tribe has till date not specifically pinpointed their origin or where their ancestors came from, their tradition had preserved for ages one of the oldest guiding principles from *Chukwu Abiama*; the circumcision of all free and slave born male children. This tradition and many other cultural similarities branded them as the breakaway lineage of the present day Israelites. He had sleepless nights worrying over Afamefuna's circumcision. He was sure that *Opa* who liked to oppose anything he stood for would likely team up with her daughter to challenge his decision.

"If only they would understand that this is not a man-made law," he pondered.

The problem that ensued few days later when Vanessa returned nearly left the relationship in disarray and Ikenga with a sense of guilt. He had for the first time raised his hands against a woman, smashed her cell phone, and locked up the apartment as she tried to ring the Polizei. The whole house had vibrated as free lying objects were turned to missiles by Vanessa who when yelling abuses in revenge, pulled down the room divider to the ground, sending the giant Sanyo television and all their electronic gadgets crashing to the floor. Ikenga, on the other hand quickly pulled their son away from the falling debris before seizing her again.

From the room where she had escaped to, she sobbed for the

whole day while Ikenga who was carrying their son slumped on the sofa to wonder why his *chi* had let him down. He had till now gone free with petty crimes but was not sure that the law would spare him for domestic violence.

By the next morning, the scars from his strong fingers were fairly visible and he could see them when they met by the kitchen door. She had woken up earlier than usual to tidy things up. The sitting room was suddenly well kept and the dirty dishes peculiar to the kitchen were all gone.

"I am sorry," he said to her while avoiding an eye contact.

"That's all right," she replied warmly. "It was my fault."

"You have made me beat a woman."

"I think I needed it."

"*Bekee* court will forget me in Balthazar if they find out that I beat up one of theirs," Ikenga said to her.

"I will tell them that I still love you."

"You woke up early today. Have you finally decided to help yourself?"

"I know I have to change," she replied. "I want my son to live a better life."

She talked nicely as if nothing had happened. The events of the night were soon forgotten, and the two put on bright faces as their eyes finally met and there seemed to be a genuine desire for reconciliation.

"But why did you take the boy away when you knew that I already made plans for his circumcision?"

Vanessa was not forthcoming with an answer. She rather turned over and continued her cleaning.

"You love my own, don't you?" Ikenga pressed further.

"I don't really know," she replied honestly." I feel like not to obey an African, I never obeyed anybody in my life."

"You don't have to obey me," he told her. "It's all about living a good life."

"This is the only life I know," she said at last.

"And now it's getting hard for me."

Vanessa sobbed as she opened up her heart, and despite her disobedience, Ikenga saw and cherished her good virtues. There was a moment of silence and they stared at each other. The only noise was that of the running tap water and the gnashing of the parrot caged on the kitchen wall.

"I am nobody," she said breaking down in tears.

Ikenga grabbed and held her close to his chest for a while. He suddenly saw the lovely Vanessa he used to know in the beginning of their relationship.

Destiny had denied them the care of a loving mother from their early lives. Vanessa had lost her mother at the age of four in a car accident and was brought up by an old aunt who lived in the family house. Her father who had cheerfully believed that work would set him free was rarely seen in the house. The tainted overall painting uniform became his everyday cloth since there was not much interval between removing them after work and putting them on again for work. There had been no in-depth communication or father-daughter relationship, and whenever they got together, it was to make sure that Vanessa had enough toys and other shallow objects that never inculcated any principles in a child. The aunt who was almost confined to the house because of age and other age-related factors showered love on the little girl, any of Vanessa's requests was a welcome opportunity for her much needed exercise or presumed housework. As the young Vanessa grew with audacity and began to revolt in school, her father decided to send her to *heim*, blaming Aunt Ute as responsible for his daughter's bad behaviour.

The authorities had a strict code when it came to the welfare of children but cared less about what they did with their lives as long as they did not break the law. This lack of motherly impact and direction based on the best quality of life for a child had cost Vanessa her education and most importantly the in-depth knowledge of womanhood and fundamentals of family values.

On the other hand, Ikenga and twin sister were about four years old when they lost their mother and the struggle for survival in the war-torn Umuafor had taught him a lesson he would otherwise not have acquired in any institution of learning. He had known famine and hardship just like *Okwa*, the wild bird that asked her chicks to always eat from the yam tuber and also from the root. So that when its owner harvests the yam, they would be able to survive from the root.

"I am in your life now," Ikenga assured her. "Everyone has his or her own story... this is not the time to dwell on the past but to focus on the future."

He held her cheeks up with both hands. "I love you, Vanessa, and we can still make it together," he said to her.

"But you might decide to leave me when you get your papers."

Ikenga found himself thrown off-balance because he had never expected this controversial allegation. Umuafor's culture and *omenani* did not advocate divorce once marriage rights were performed and no right thinking Umuafor man abandoned a son for a woman, but if the frog decides to leave the swamp for the mountains, it suggests that something is after its life.

"I have made up my mind to live with you for the rest of my life," Ikenga replied honestly. "But that might mean a premature death for me."

"What is that supposed to mean?" she asked.

There could be no other reason than the ones that led to their incessant quarrels and Ikenga ignorantly voiced it out unaware of the damages his opinions could cause.

"You don't play your part as a wife," he lamented. "For the years we have been together you have not tasted my food. My son has also started avoiding me each time I set my food on the table. I was proudly telling my people that I have found a wife not knowing that you will never go with me to visit my family in Umuafor."

"But I don't stop your son from eating your food," Vanessa protested.

"When you do not eat with me, he will definitely follow after your steps because he spends more time with you."

"I will help teach him to eat your food but please do not talk of visiting Umuafor. There are still a lot of diseases, violence and

WOES OF IKENGA

crime going on in that part of the world from what I see everyday on television."

"Take the food to Afamefuna," Ikenga told her at last. He had sensed that their quiet discussion in the kitchen was heading towards another quarrel. The emotional relationship that characterised a young family had disappeared after the short honeymoon they enjoyed after his jail term.

An inevitable clash of culture had set in because Ikenga and his partner totally lacked knowledge of how to deal with serious problems that were normal in long-term relationships. Two opposing cultures had been abruptly merged and were aggressively fighting for dominance. The wasted time in the prison had made Ikenga initiate a series of structural adjustment steps, which included giving his best to whatever he was going to lay his hands on and hopefully storing up a reserve for rainy days. His inherited cultural burden of taking care of his aged parents and younger siblings followed him through his endless journey in search of a better life. That meant that the little income from Okazi Foods & Services had to be slashed to achieve these goals, while Vanessa carelessly spent whatever came into her account by the beginning of the month knowing that another would come in the new month, as that was the system she was used to ever since she started taking care of herself. Her days in the care home had been no different. She received a little pocket money every Friday from the authorities and Daddy breezed in occasionally to visit her with packs of creamy chocolate and other goodies.

The cultural differences and upbringing between the two were just as far apart as their worlds. Thus it would be unfair to judge either of them as their coincidental union and the consequent cat and mouse lifestyle had been as a result of unhealthy immigration laws with their stipulations.

Ikenga had combed the city in search of *kpalli*, and had once been disappointed by a girl who could not cope with the speed with which he wanted the marriage. Vanessa had been in search of a good-looking negro to start a new life with as she had lost

201

interest in German men because of their retarded performance capabilities. Indeed, when a crazy chicken meets with a drunken wild fox, it becomes its destiny. The two had finally gotten together only to discover that they were too different to be united by the word "family."

The afternoon shift workers at Okazi Foods & Services were surprised to see Ikenga seated when they rushed into the recreation room to have their thirty minutes break. He put on a brave face and played few rounds of card with them till he successfully convinced them that he had only stayed behind to have a word with the management with regards to wage increment. They went back to their various positions when the half an hour break was over while Ikenga reluctantly left with them and headed for the bus station to board a bus to his house.

Life was gradually becoming meaningless from all points of view but he insisted on living since that was the only way to accomplish his endless goals. The gradual acceptance of the fact that he had let his people down and its psychological impact was building up pressure in his whole system. Letters in heavy German grammar and frightening colourful envelopes did not stop coming from different quarters. The supposed wife he had at home was bent on turning him into a lunatic. To be fair to fate, there had been some golden moments in his life but even those were shortlived and never lasted long. He had been bogged down with so much suffering and smiling and his *chi* had continually played along.

His *chi* may have actually tried to warn him through the dogged efforts made by Reverend Klaus to discourage him from travelling or the way the gods had betrayed him when he tried to dispose the four wooden totems in Port Harcourt to raise money, but he had simply been too blind to see then.

The bus finally pulled up at Bethel Station and Ikenga jumped down alongside some other passengers heading to their various destinations. It was an exceptionally cold Christmas eve and many were rushing to shopping malls to stock up for the long holidays.

## WOES OF IKENGA

Elderly men and women who had been rendered single by the divorce culture of the Western world pulled funny looking Chihuahuas behind them while many others clutched bundles of roses and other exotic flowers. Christmas trees and their coloured decorations came to life as darkness descended on the cloudy day even as Ikenga made his way through the roadside avoiding dotted mountains of snow and melting icy waters.

A neighbour walked past him metres before he got to the house door and gave him a rather cold greeting. It was unusual for the young German boy who normally saw Ikenga as a gangster and was always delighted to hang around him whenever he had the opportunity. As he held out his keys while on the last steps to the third floor, a big blue sac by the side of his door caught his attention. He guessed that someone was probably moving in or out of the house; it may be that the crazy next-door neighbour had decided to use his door as a refuse dump. Carefully he opened the sac to examine, only to find out that its contents were all his. He raised his hands over his head in shock, staring at the blue sac. It had finally happened.

Hastily cooked relationships and marriages blamed on immigration laws increased the number of bastards and family breakdowns. It had become a social norm, hence an unhealthy society was the order of the day. Ikenga had somewhat been looking forward to it but Vanessa had made it happen much earlier than expected. He tried opening the door with his key to convince Vanessa that the situation had not gotten to such an explosive level, but soon noticed after several failed attempts that the lock had been replaced. When he realised that he might be facing the biting teeth of the winter without a roof over his head, Ikenga banged repeatedly on the door. An old neighbour who had witnessed the arrival of uniformed men during the day peeped from a half-opened door and simply shut the door behind him, as he did not want to have anything to do with the case or to be called one day by the Polizei to testify to what he had seen. Ikenga banged louder and yelled abuses on Vanessa.

*"God go punish your Mama,"* he shouted. *"Me wey don de give you*

*chop since I know you, na so you wan pay me. You no go see beta, yeye woman."*

He was still cursing bitterly when two men walked up the steps to him. Vanessa had rung the police as soon as she heard his voice and from inside blocked the door firmly with a sofa to prevent him from forcing his way in and turning her into a punching bag.

*"Was geht hier ab junge man?"* one of the gentlemen asked.

A confused Ikenga turned round to face two young officers.

"What is your problem, young man?" the other one repeated in fair English.

"I don't have a problem," Ikenga replied as he regained composure. "I've not asked for your help either."

"Why are you disturbing the peace of the whole house?"

"I ... this is my house ... " Ikenga swallowed the other half of the answer as he heard the door open gradually. Vanessa had cleared her defence barriers when she noticed the presence of the Polizei.

"Who on earth advised you to change the locks in my house?" Ikenga demanded angrily.

The two gentlemen held him back as he advanced towards the door.

"You are not to be seen around this vicinity henceforth, Mr. Udeaja," they told him.

"But I pay the rent, gentlemen," he replied calmly.

"Your wife called that you threatened to kill her and her baby."

"You got it all wrong, people," he said to the two. "I am not a killer."

"You have ten minutes to go inside the house and pick up your belongings."

"Everything there belongs to me," Ikenga replied with controlled anger. "I bought the properties with my hard earned money and the child is mine."

"I got the vacuum cleaner from my dad," Vanessa declared from the half-opened door.

"Clap for yourself!" Ikenga shouted back. "And what can you

WOES OF IKENGA

boast of buying with your own money?"

"You have six more minutes left, Mr. Udeaja," one of the gentlemen reminded.

"Alias Hassan Ijenwata," the other one added.

They had made series of consultations on the computer–the white man's oracle–and found out everything they needed to know about the man they were dealing with.

"You are only allowed to take your personal items," the officer insisted.

"Keep them all!" Ikenga charged at the police officers.

"Oh! Thank you very much," one replied mockingly.

"Keep the 'thank you' and the 'very much' as well."

They watched Ikenga hop down the steps lightly as if a burden had been taken off his shoulders. He walked past two other cops positioned downstairs in a station wagon. They must have overheard the whole conversation or probably watched from their sophisticated communication gadgets.

Neighbours and onlookers also gathered to observe the episode from a distance with a mixture of pity and hatred. Pity that a man was being thrown out of his home in the middle of winter with no hopes of seeing his son again and hatred for an alien who paid back with crime and abuse of the system for the kind hospitality of his host nation. Whatever views they held could not have bettered or worsened his situation, as the Polizei were present to enforce the law and that was final.

Once into the open winter air, his problems overwhelmed him. Although he had jumped down the stairs lightly as if he had another apartment waiting for him in town, the trauma and psychological impact sank in when he stepped into the chilly December breeze. He had struggled and given his best to escape the *"Ofeke"* title, but the white man's land was determined to turn him into one. The thought of losing a son to a woman who had nothing but a useless life to offer him would always haunt him, as well as the possibility of never having the opportunity to visit his homeland with his son to prove to his family and kindred that he was not an *Ofeke,* or explain to those who cared to listen that life in the white man's land was far from what he had bargained for. Surely, his people would definitely not throw their arms open to welcome him if he returned with only bags full of stories after many years in the white man's land.

"No!" he shouted: "I have to end it all."

For the first time in a long time, he wished he could lay hands on his father's double barrel, to send dust to dust, and ashes back to the ashes if that would teach his ungrateful wife a lesson, or warn all "international mamas" who intended to kick the fathers of their children out of the house that the back door is never shut without a wrestle.

He collected enough bottles of Krombacher, from a nearby kiosk with the little money left on him, intending to drink up his remaining money and get ready to face whatever came next as Vanessa had emptied what was left of their joint account before taking her decision. He took a quiet corner under the iconic Ephizy Shopping Mall and cleared off the empty cans and blood-stained strings from drug users. Since he was not ready to face any of his friends, it would serve as his resting place for the night, if only the drug users would allow him.

Ikenga and his family became the talk of the town along with few others who had suffered a similar fate. Beer parlours and train stations were popular places to discuss aliens whose wives suddenly turned to scorpions or idle queens. The wives on the other hand converted the playground where they hung out with their children to a meeting point to discuss the fates of their alien husbands. Some who derived fun from displaying such dominance told tales of sending their husband down to the basement while they spent the night with another *kpalli*-hunting alien.

Others known as "international mamas" were bent on producing children from different men since the social welfare offered a luxurious life to their sort. Worse still, there were also cases of aliens who endured the compulsory three years of painful marital service and were due for Resident Permit but would be turned down by the Office of Foreign Affairs because their wives alleged that their husbands married them just for papers.

Every man had a story! Every alien had his or her unique comic or tragic story still waiting to be told.

The complexity of Ikenga's case so warmed up his nervous system that he removed his winter jacket to take in fresh air as he sat down to help himself to the chilled bottles of Krombacher. As he sat quietly consulting with his *chi* along the man-made illuminating beauties of Cardinal Josef Street, he knew that he had not much jokers left. The stench from the heap of dirty clothing by his side did not scare him off but instead reminded him of the resolute he-goat and his harrowing life ordeal.

*Nwa-mkpi*, the he-goat, ran to the soothsayer when it became obvious that men were determined to do away with he and his entire household. He had long complained about the ill treatment he received from women who always dragged him to the market against his will, and the fact that he was born free but was always subjected to slavery. Worse still, his horned head which was meant to be hung on trees to scare away evil spirits had been turned into a special delicacy by women who needed a male child from their husbands. *Nwa-mkpi* was neither the wisest nor the most foolish among animals, but for no just cause was made to atone for sins he knew nothing about as he watched his kinsmen being sacrificed to shrines and idols, or slaughtered mercilessly before sacred trees and rivers. His young ones were also snatched forcefully from their mothers and given away to human brides when they were married off. The perpetual agony and misery had drastically retarded his growth but *Nwa-mkpi* still found life sweet and worth living. From the soothsayer he had asked for life and not growth because, in his own words; "he who has life will eventually grow."

# Chapter 11

A neighbour's oversized cat usually visited his window whenever he retired to his exclusive apartment to muse about his boredom. The way it stuck out its wet black nose round the edges of the glass window with rhythm spoke volumes about life's unfairness to the poor creature. Its protruding stomach and unnaturally thick furs were its only weapon against the unfriendly climate, while a daily routine of sitting idle on its owner's balcony was its way of making the best of a bad bargain. The fat cat cried out loudly at night but the male partners she sought were either not around the vicinity or were also faced with the same unnatural isolation and confinement. Its owners, an elderly couple, lived in what seemed like a deserted apartment on the first floor of the opposite building. On the ground floor was a cold room powered by a large cooling system mounted at the backyard to support the business. These elevated cooling gadgets became a recreational ground and a pathway through which the lonely creature visited Ikenga's window.

The couple had a grown-up daughter who left the house in the morning for school or work and returned late every evening. The happiness that the cat enjoyed from the little girl's company had vanished as soon as she was old enough to have other interests and no more time to caress her or scratch her head whenever she dropped food for the feline. Canned foods had not only become tasteless with time but also deprived the poor cat of its braveness and nature-endowed hunting capabilities as there were no mice to hunt, and the birds were out of reach. Worse still, she watched powerlessly from the storey balcony as rabbits danced around everywhere.

Ikenga had enough to brood on in the comfort of his small room, but it was certainly not a good reason to stay away from the public. Vanessa had called several times for reconciliation but he refused to be cowed this time to the selfish desires of the inglorious idle queen. She had threatened to throw him out of the

## WOES OF IKENGA

house a number of times, and actually carried it out on two occasions only to initiate reconciliation whenever she needed his strong arms around her. When a bear cannot find flesh to feed on, it has no other choice but to eat grass.

"You tell me about Goodness every time," she pleaded with Ikenga as he sat watching the lonely cat from his window.

"Why can't you forgive me this time?"

"Stop calling my phone please."

"I have sent out some applications for a job," Vanessa revealed.

"I will start working soon."

"Don't work!"

"What of our son?"

"Keep him."

"Somebody from your country brought a letter for you."

"Keep the letter."

"Will you come around and visit us sometime?"

"I will when I have the time," Ikenga answered to cut short the conversation.

"Thank you, thank you *shartz.*"

Vanessa sincerely wanted to reconcile. It was just that problems always soon resurfaced. As for Ikenga, it had been a burial of his ego to swallow shame and move back those two times, but since she had emptied their joint account and invited the police to evict him this time, then she had better keep both the "thank you" and the "very much" as well.

Ikenga took ownership of a small room from a multi-storied block of flats on Robbin Street, some days after Vanessa threw him out. Rumours that it was a haunted house had driven off all the tenants, and the house owners had also abandoned the four hundred-metre property for pimps and homeless drug users. The city government seemed to have no immediate need for the acreage which was why they abandoned the small disgusting street to its fate. An elderly drug user he had met during his few months operations at the city train station had directed Ikenga to Robbin Street where he had taken ownership of one of the empty rooms.

Because he repeatedly failed to turn up for work without notification or any genuine reason, the employment agency that offered him the job terminated his appointment.

He could not have possibly continued with the job. Child welfare claimed to have written him immediately he separated from Vanessa to demand child welfare support. He did not know how that was possible, as he had left them no contact address. But when no answer came as they claimed, they had extended their arms to Ikenga's employer, and almost half of his monthly salary was withheld in accordance with child care regulations.

The personnel manager produced a letter when Ikenga barged into his office to demand why his salary was cut.

"They must have written you," the manager told him.

"Nobody wrote me," Ikenga replied.

"Did you remember to give them your new address when you changed apartments?"

"I am not paying a dime to anybody," Ikenga charged. "How do they want me to survive?"

The dedicated Egyptian who hated to distract the attention of other workers walked quietly and closed his office door. He had gathered from other workers what Ikenga was going through and it seemed that his employee did not clearly understand what he was up against.

"There is no way you can escape it," he said to Ikenga standing face up to him. "He is your son."

"The amount they deducted cannot be for Afamefuna alone."

"Is your ex-wife working?"

"No, she is not the working type."

"Mmm!" the manager sounded. "That is where you have a problem."

"I am not going to pay for any lazy woman," Ikenga maintained.

"Consult a lawyer and hear what he tells you," the Egyptian advised. "The system will destroy you if you approach it the hard way. You cannot believe what I have been paying to my ex-wife

WOES OF IKENGA

and our three daughters since we divorced eleven years ago."

"How are you surviving, brother?" Ikenga queried in despair.

Their discussion was now friendlier and less formal. The more experienced Egyptian was ready to give Ikenga the critical moral support every alien would need at this stage where failure to walk a fine line might have far reaching consequences.

"Their men are also not having it any easier," he said to Ikenga. "We both come from war-torn zones. In my own case, I would rather dance to the tune than go back and confront the Pharaoh."

His dismissal from Okazi Foods & Services became the last straw that broke the camel's hump, as Ikenga's only window to social interaction was completely closed off. He withdrew from his fellow countrymen because of their taunting jokes about his problems and state of mind. Many who cared to call and see how he was doing were greeted by the answering machine; yet, their uncountable messages did not move Ikenga to call back. When his cell phone was not switched off, he would watch it ring till it rang out if he did not want to hear from the caller. The few whose calls he cared to take, received a rather funny response that further affirmed their suspicions that he was battling with insanity.

Mascot continually called to warn him about jumping over the fence of sanity, which many had unknowingly crossed because of the enormous pressures and discomforts they had never anticipated in a white man's world. He clearly believed that the line Ikenga toed from the beginning contributed to his present condition. If he had followed him to the station from day one, he should have by now made enough money to pay for the Resident Permit by way of contract marriage or transport himself to another white man's country if his *awele* could not be found in Landesburg. Those who found their *awele* at the train station, *jugunu* or other areas of hustling had returned to their countries without having to go through the tormenting headaches and sleepless nights that came with getting a Resident Permit.

Painfully though, many older women who married their alien husbands for better, or for worse, till death did them part had fallen victims of such embarrassing and painful break-ups, as heartless alien husbands walked out on marriages immediately they obtained their citizenship without considering their partners' feelings.

The cat and mouse game had no clear winners or losers. There was the case of a woman in her late forties who out of sincere love had gone as far as reporting to the police about the sudden disappearance of her husband because the police was most likely the first port of call whenever an alien went missing. After consulting their oracle and going through their files, the officer at the counter categorically told the woman that her husband was not in their custody. She went around restaurants and meeting spots for Africans to see if she would get a hint of what had become of her lovely nineteen-year-old husband, but the few who knew his whereabouts were not forthcoming with information. Finally, the woman retired to her house in faith, when all efforts proved futile, waiting patiently for her husband to call for help or walk in through the door. The call finally came after some days, but from another continent, only for her husband to sarcastically tell her that the three-year-old marriage that she had nursed with affection was over.

Ikenga reluctantly received the call after a while because Mascot was not one to be ignored. The fear of the unknown sometimes made him contemplate the worst scenario. Deep down in his heart, he knew that Mascot would do everything humanly possible to ensure that his corpse got to his people in Umuafor should the unexpected happen. For that, he could not refuse calls from Mascot or even think of breaking up their long-standing brotherly relationship.

"Boy, how are you doing?" Mascot asked immediately without any formal greeting.

"Everything is alright," Ikenga replied.

"I know everything is always alright with you," Mascot teased.

"Vanessa told me she wants you back."

"You can take my position."

"This is clearly your cross, brother."

"Please take over!"

"That is not possible."

"Simeon helped out when it was unbearable for the Man from Nazareth," Ikenga pointed out.

"We have to talk things over then," Mascot suggested.

"The Book did not record any prior agreement before the takeover."

"Am I the Messiah?"

"A messiah in Landesbusg is long overdue."

"What of your son?"

"Give him your name."

"You can't be serious," Mascot got a bit louder and angry.

"Dead serious!" Ikenga yelled.

"Your Resident Permit is due in less than a year and you want to ruin it yourself? People who don't have money boast about easy movement with their *kpalli*."

"You can take the *kpalli*," Ikenga replied him. "Vanessa will help you make the necessary name changes."

"I don't need the *kpalli*."

"Give it to any Amanze he-goat if you have no need for it."

Mascot did not want to believe that the situation had gone that far. They had not seen since Ikenga left Vanessa's house but people reported that Ikenga's words were seriously jumping track and that his hair and beard were left unkempt. Nobody was sure where he came from every morning or where he lay his head at sunset. Mascot and Santos had tried to track him in the park or around Ephizy Shopping Mall where he was sighted a number of times but had not made any headway.

"Where are you living now?" Mascot asked started again.

"I have a house."

"You don't come out these days."

"I don't want to see anybody."

"Do you now see in spirit?"

"Some people I see in spirit, the rest, I rewind or fast forward my television to see whenever I desire."

Indeed, Ikenga actually did see spirits, in his long lonely hours, when consciousness took him back through the journey so far, and the horrible episode in the sea of death. The swollen faces of death often invaded. This time not after his life but to entertain him. He would often sit and gaze as zombie-like figures danced to the strange tune of *usurugede* that played from nowhere. Some danced around holding their severed head in their bloody hands, while others displayed paired tongues with a monstrous set of bloody teeth.

*Onwuuu ... onwuuu ...*

The tune would go on with perfectly combined drumbeats and the distant sound of *Oja*, the local flute. Performers included his long forgotten comrades and some people he knew in Landesburg. He clearly recognised the disfigured and scary face of Freeman, the confused law professor, deriving joy from chopping off the heads of any performer that went near him with a short oblong-shaped axe. The legion of dreadful dancers and performers clearly enjoyed the horror, as their headless bodies skilfully picked up the severed heads to continue with the entertainment.

*Usurugede*, the drumbeat of death, is as intoxicating as it is deceitful. Ikenga was confidently content with the people he saw in his everyday nightmare that he was no longer interested in going out to ask of anyone.

"What's the name of the street?" Mascot pressed further. "I want to come over and see you."

"The house is still under renovation," Ikenga replied. "I want to invite you all when I am through."

"I can help out with the renovation."

"That's nice of you, Mascot, but I am in the supermarket right now to buy paints."

"You will call me when you get back?"

"Sure."

"Then come over to Green Garden this evening."

"I don't like visiting there again."

"You are really not normal, brother."

"I will call you later," Ikenga said hurriedly. "I have to pay." Mascot accepted with skepticism and the call ended abruptly. His next move would be to find out where Ikenga lived, as he was sure that all his excuses and promises to call was just a way to end the conversation. It was obvious that the country and system had gotten hold of his thinking faculty and he needed true friends to help scoop the water above his feet before it reached his neck. Mascot was determined to help if Ikenga would let him. Indeed, to eat from the same pot with another man was to take an oath of perpetual friendship with him.

Ikenga removed the SIM from the cell phone immediately he finished talking with Mascot and pulled off the television cable to block out those he saw on air. Whoever said he was not normal was the abnormal one. How could a bunch of madmen in a mad society refer to him as abnormal? Anyways, he had finally made up his mind to disconnect from them all, so they could continue with their madness and leave him alone.

The involuntary movement of the cat's tail caught his eyes again. It had been squatting and listening to the whole conversation, and waggled its tail in agreement when Ikenga moved to disconnect unwanted people from his life. As the cat stretched its two forelegs in appreciation, Ikenga moved over to the glass window wondering how the poor creature coped with being confined to a space of five square metres. The dogs in the land were not finding it easier. Obviously, the body weakness and soft movements of the old men and women who owned them killed the agility of even animals that were born hunters. Instead of being an animal that confronted visitors and strangers alike, or keeping them at the entrance until their owner instructed otherwise, they ran to bed when there was a knock on the door. As for the mosquitoes and ants, they had probably been so fed with yoghurt and sweet jam that they had also forgotten how to bite and sting. Worse still, human beings, the most social of animals had also adapted to staying on their own, not because of insecurity but for fear of the law. Ikenga was not used to this order of things, yet everyone assumed that it was normal.

Locating Ikenga was no easy feat for Mascot. It would have been impossible if not for his street credentials, or if he had allowed the setbacks and responses he received from people at the initial stage deter him. All their friends had abandoned Ikenga to his problems and those who even remembered used him as reference when people gathered to discuss individuals with *psycho* problems. Mascot felt uncomfortable whenever such references were made. Many assumed they were related or from the same extended family because of their closeness ever since Ikenga arrived Landesburg. He had wanted him as his right hand man from the beginning and been ready to channel him to the fast lane but Ikenga had declined to come along.

With all ears on the ground whenever he was on the road, Mascot believed that he would one day stumble upon information that would lead him to his brother. Finally a hint came from the least expected source.

The wide central park runs from the major train station to the old city with a long row of shady trees and semi bushes along its path. There are three playgrounds with mini football fields and areas where families can hang out. Parallel to the motorway is a pond with a state of the art fountain extending towards an underground waterway. Hence, apart from the swan and the ducks reared by the city authorities, other water birds flock around to feed and groom themselves by the side of the pond. Rabbits, fearing no harassment from cats and humans, moved around as if the garden was originally intended for their specie. There were also footpaths in this extensive piece of vegetation in the middle of a big city, thereby providing the perfect environment for hide-and-seek games and dodgy deals.

Mascot was strolling down this park one evening when a drug user recognised him.

"Hi, Bob," the voice called. That was the name with which he was known at the Corporate Headquarters.

"Who could that be?" Mascot asked sternly.

"It's me, brother, it's Gustav."

Mascot halted at the familiar voice ready to take to his heels if it turned out to be an ambush by the Polizei. The illuminating effects of the streetlights were hampered by shady trees and bushy paths but still allowed visibility enough to make out figures from a close distance.

"Who is there with you?" he boomed.

"I am alone, brother," Gustav declared. "They have all gone."

"Who and who have gone?" Mascot asked with heightened alert.

"The Polizei," Gustav replied. "They have your brother."

Mascot did not care to find out which of his brothers was involved as everyone in the street clan referred to themselves as brothers. It was also not surprising to hear that one was picked up from the park as the new boys had extended their vicious business activities to the Central Park. He was keen on finding out what the station emperor was up to.

"And what are you doing here alone?"

"I can't move, Bob," Gustav replied in pain. "A brother crippled me."

Mascot pulled away a tree branch blocking his way, and looked around the shrub for any hidden figure or sign of movement. He finally went closer to Gustav when he was convinced that all was well but noticed no physical injury on the man lying with his back on the ground.

"What happened?" he questioned.

"The stupid boy gave me shit," Gustav said to Mascot in fair English.

"My legs are heavy."

"You will not listen to me, Gustav," Mascot lamented in a more relaxed tone. Apparently the poisonous snake had swallowed a female toad.

"Did I not tell you to stay clean?"

"I will be good from today," Gustav promised. "I will follow you down to Africa when we have made a lot of money."

"Shut up!" Mascot shouted at him.

"Can you help me up, brother?"

"Shhh!" Mascot motioned aggressively.

The police clampdown and the subsequent scarcity of the deadly substance on the street had led to adulteration. Mascot had once offered to help Gustav pay off his mountain of bills—a reason he gave that pushed him into the street. Gustav would in return give up using the drugs and instead channel his energy to marketing the bubbles to his co-consumers whom he knew better. It was a strategy Mascot had devised to alleviate himself from the risky job, when the presence of dark-skin coloured young men loitering around the Landesburg train station had increased to an alarming rate; but Gustav's addiction had gotten to such destructive phase that when they tried the joint venture a few times, he disappeared and reappeared after some days with such fables as those told in Umuafor in the days when animals could speak. Mascot got fed up after a steady loss, and called off the joint venture but still maintained a good customer relationship with Gustav. He was sure that Gustav had gotten the adulterated stuff this time around from any of the new boys, a mutual transaction which could be lethal if care was not taken.

"I will stop this time," he repeated with unsure sincerity. "I promise."

"That's your business," Mascot responded. "You are lucky to have a government that pays without labour."

Mascot held Gustav in both hands and pulled him to a sitting position. The long-time user, also known as the Station Emperor, was in serious pains. Whoever had done that to him was sure to pay for it. If Gustav did not set him up for security agents, he would dispossess him of the valued contents in his mouth with the jack knife he wielded at random.

"I am finished," he said painfully to his milkman.

"You are dead already," Mascot corrected.

## WOES OF IKENGA

"Do you have any good stuff for me?"

"My stuff is not for dead men."

"Make me live again!" the wounded Emperor pleaded.

Gustav was very happy that Mascot had walked by and dared not do anything that would make Mascot abandon him in the park. He knew Mascot to be one of the best milkmen, whose stuff could help him recover from the conquer mixture that had held him down for hours and did all to find a way of extracting the mineral deposits lodged inside Mascot's mouth without doing damage to his lips.

"Why did the police arrest your brother?" he quizzed carefully.

"Which of my brothers?" Mascot returned.

"Your brother, Prince."

"My own prince?"

"Yes, Prince Hassan."

"Where did the police arrest him?"

"I was here when they dragged him out with handcuffs."

"What has he done?"

"There was nothing I could do to help him," Gustav apologised sincerely.

"What happened?"

"How would I know, Bob?"

Mascot stared at his friend to make sure he was not hallucinating. Could that be true? What was Ikenga doing in the park to warrant arrest? There was no doubt about Gustav being sure of whom he was talking about. For the few months that Ikenga showed up at the station, Mascot had always introduced him as Prince Hassan to all his good customers and they were always seen together till the very day he had gotten the surprise attack from the law enforcers.

"You still remember Hassan very well?" Mascot asked to clear all doubts.

"Oh! You ask a lot of questions, brother," Gustav replied.

"Give me some good stuff to help myself."

"Was he arrested with any junky?" Mascot asked with much

219

curiosity.

"That I do not know."

"Uniformed Polizei or ...?"

"No, they were plain."

"Has it been long?"

"Help me up, brother, and stop your good for nothing questions," Gustav rebelled. "I want to get out of this place."

Mascot helped his friend to his feet and led him out of the park towards the station because he did not want to stop the flow of the much-needed information. Drug users and nonentities were also rightful citizens with unquestionable claims to their rights even in their depth of wrong. The Central Park was now deserted except for impatient lovebirds that could not wait till they got to their houses. Once out in the open, he made Gustav sit on a bench by the bus station. The valuable information was only good enough to help him out of the park but not for a handout or commission. Besides, walking around with a limping user, as a dealer would only bring him the publicity he was trying to avoid.

"Sit down here till you get better," Mascot instructed. "I will be back soon."

"You don't have anything for me?" Gustav demanded as his friend turned to leave.

"Get well from one before you request for another."

"Your stuff will help me get well, brother."

"Till you get well."

"Please, Bob."

The plea of the damaged man fell on Mascot's back. He was already off to make inquiries from the police post at the back of the train station.

He examined himself thoroughly before walking into the onestorey glasshouse to politely present himself to the officer at the reception. When his passport was demanded, he produced a white sheet of paper from his wallet and handed over to the young female officer wearing a headset fixed to her ear. The agent faced the monitor to consult their oracle about the paper in her left hand, tapping the keyboard occasionally. Mascot was getting agitated when the consultation took a bit longer, and carefully watched the lady's reaction and movement of her lips. He might have made the biggest mistake of his life by walking into the dreaded building should the oracle declare him a wanted man. It was foolish to even think of an escape route because Landesburg Police Stations, as he knew them, allowed free entrance but exit without authorisation was practically impossible.

"How do you know Mr. Ikenga Udeaja?" the police officer asked as she lowered the headset.

Mascot was relieved that the oracle had not demanded his head. Walking into that particular station as a notorious street boy was a calculated risk, a risk worth taking for Ikenga. He now had the audacity to boldly give his answers.

"He is my brother," he replied confidently.

"Where does he live?"

"He has a house with a family," Mascot answered after a short hesitation.

"No!" the officer rejected.

"He was evicted from his house, leaving wife and kid months ago after he threatened to kill them."

"So where is he living now?" Mascot asked returning her question.

"That is what we have been trying to find out."

"What offence has he committed?" he asked on noticing that the young girl was forthcoming with information.

The female officer pointed at the evidence still lying open on the table over the counter.

It was pitiful how far Ikenga had been drifted by loneliness and destitution. The park attendants had secretly spied on him when they observed a sequence of unexplained disturbances and disappearances of the big birds from the mini pond. Suspicion had initially fallen on the wild wolves that normally sneaked in at summer, but one would have noticed a trail of blood or scattered feathers. Since the parks were not fitted with closed circuit security cameras, they had decided to apply a conventional detective method.

Ikenga visited the park whenever his meat supply ran out. He had diverted to the fat sea birds and free running rabbits for his protein supplement when his means of livelihood became reduced to zero. His nature given creativity and adaptability that had been his tools for survival had never departed from him. With long strings extracted from a used bicycle brake system, he had made a crooked trap for rabbits and wild birds, and as for the lazy long-necked swan and ducks, he grabbed them by the neck from a short distance and squeezed life out of them with lethal force. He had meticulously drawn the master plan for attack on that fateful day. Wearing a hooded jacket, he had moved into a section of the park that was sure to have been vacated by families who had come for recreation, and walked casually to the centre with his eyes and ears at alert, before making an abrupt dive under a shrub and remaining calm for some time.

Time and patience are two qualities of a good hunter that Ikenga also brought along. The string traps had also been carefully positioned in marked places, and he necessarily had to remove them before leaving the park early in the morning whether they got a catch or not. Skilfully, he crept down the pond unaware that the eyes of the undercover security agents were on him with their night vision goggles. The city authorities had invited the police when they became absolutely sure that the individual on their radar screen was responsible for the disappearance of the big birds, and the security agents had been brought in to catch him redhanded so they could secure convincing evidence. Ikenga silently neared a sleeping duck standing with one foot on a dried piece of wood by the side of the pond. It seemed to have tucked its head under the feather for warmth, and was an easy target for an experienced hunter. He had simply raised the upper part of his body high enough to remove the thick hooded jacket and with that swooped on the unsuspecting creature.

The piercing torchlights and shouts that came from all corners had come too late to save the life of the big white swan. Ikenga was bundled down to the station with the lifeless bird and a row of string traps as evidence. Meanwhile, the police wanted to search his house to find if they could rescue any of the animals he may have captured and still be keeping alive, but the interrogation had not gone smoothly because he maintained that he lived in the park and train station ever since he was thrown out of his house. His appearance revealed that he was living rough but they were sure he had a place where he cooked the nature-given meat although he maintained that he ate them raw.

"With the feathers?" One of the experienced officers asked.

"Yes," Ikenga replied nodding his head in affirmation.

"Why did you resort to killing and eating these animals?"

"Hunger."

"Are you not working?"

"No, I am not."

"For sure you get money from the social welfare?"

"No."

"We prevented you from killing your wife and you are killing our animals?"

"I am not a killer."

"Do you know that this could land you in jail?"

"Better."

"Are you really normal?" a worried social worker that noticed some abnormalities in him asked.

"People say I am not."

"Are you?"

"Blame the country if I am not."

His answers were blunt and direct, and when he lacked an answer or chose to ignore, he stared around like a zombie.

The items recovered were listed down, including the dead duck, a hand-made catapult and a range of crudely fashioned string traps. Another marathon round of thumb printing and photographing was also conducted. He was a criminal after all, caught in the act. His clothing and other personal belongings were handed back to

223

him and he was told to expect a letter from the court in a couple of weeks.

Mascot waited by the long bench. The young lady had assured him that his brother would not be detained for the offence committed but that a hearing would be held when the court received an official charge from the public prosecutor. Vanessa had received a distress call by the police when they tried to ascertain the current address of her ex-husband and joined him as soon as she was able to arrange for a baby-sitter. She was overcome with grief when she saw a haggard looking man come out of the interrogation room half naked, and clutching his belongings.

The beautiful looking young woman, now in her late twenties, was not the bad sort. However, the heavy-handed means that her husband applied to make her a better wife had lacked meaningful compromise, probably because he saw his conservative culture as a life model and the only means of inculcating moral virtues and respect in their son. Vanessa who had always had her way and been bombarded from her early age with immoral exposure had refused to take orders from a primitive man and even though she was blamed as the architect of the whole mess, she had never wished to see the father of her child in such a bad state.

Ikenga shamefully accepted Mascot's handshake. His conscience always accused him of cowardice for not being brave enough to follow the path that Mascot had originally drawn for him. Disappointments had marred his good intentions to uphold the good name of his family, and his record in the files and computers of the law agents of Landesburg was nothing to write home about.

"Why have you decided to avoid me?" Mascot asked in a pleading tone.

Ikenga did not utter a word but kept on looking around as if he had totally lost his memory. Vanessa dared not go near him. Instead she handed over a letter to Mascot and followed the two at a safe distance out of the Police Station.

The ever-busy Landesburg train station was still bustling with life by two o'clock in the morning when the whole ordeal ended. Mascot waved down a taxi for Vanessa since the bus connection to her house might be difficult at that time, handed the taxi driver a note and bade her goodnight before he took Ikenga to a bar that offered twenty-four hour service in front of the station. The return of the prodigal brother called for a celebration.

He moved straight to the vacant section in a corner of the bar for fear of being driven out by the management because of the smell from Ikenga's dirty clothes. As soon as they were seated, a bottle of Jack Daniels was brought to the table as if they also knew his brand at any given time. Mascot brought out the letter from Vanessa. It was from Chinaza Ofojete. He read in silence, poured himself another glass of whisky, and handed the letter over to Ikenga.

"This is a wake-up call too late," he said to him.

"Is the letter for me?" Ikenga asked.

"I think so."

"From who?"

"Find out yourself."

Ikenga took a sip from his own glass and bowed his head to have a closer look at the rough sheet of paper in his hand.

Mrs. Ofojete Chinaza,
St Patrick's Mission,
Umuafor
P.O. Box 409.

Ikenga Udeaja, Germany.

Dear Twin Brother,

My greetings have been falling on deaf ears so I better go straight to the point.

I have not believed and would never believe that you would intentionally abandon your family. Papa has fallen a perpetual victim to all the shrines in Umuafor in his efforts to free you from the hands of white women or whoever has caged your destiny. His health has deteriorated because of your long absence and his family.

I am now married to the Ofojete family in Isiama village and I have six children if you care to know. Our family has also become a topic for discussion by the whole community, as they believe that your evil *chi* has influenced Ogbonnia, the son of the headmaster, to stop sending anything to his father.

You promised to be back on time but Nne died in agony without setting eyes on you. Her last days were full of misery. Arobinagu of Amanze accused her of having a hand in your destiny.

What is still holding you my dear brother? Have you forgotten that you are the pride of our family? Have you forgotten that you are my only pride? If that is the way you want to live your life, I wish you well. If it is caused by *agwu*, I reject it.

Forget whatever material thing still holding you and come back immediately. My greatest wish is to see you again. If I fail to do so before I die, don't mourn me.

Your Twin Sister, Chinaza.

Ikenga pushed away the table, sprang up like a robot and walked out of the bar without a word to Mascot. The night-shift bar attendant was not surprised when he heard the sound of glass breaking on the floor, as the spontaneous outbreak of fight among members of the street clan around the train station was a daily occurrence. The bar owner had also ordered his workers to not alert the police about minor fracas so long as their business was still profitable. Mascot who had managed to save the whisky bottle paid immediately and ran after Ikenga. The letter, which he had thought would call a dear friend back to order, might have done more harm than good.

Mr. Lasisi accepted to employ Ikenga in his restaurant as a way of rehabilitation and reintroduction into a normal social life. He did not turn Mascot's request down after the story of their brother's sudden reappearance was narrated to him. By the observations of Mr. Lasisi and his wife for the few weeks they took him in, Ikenga's self-imposed isolation had made him everything apart from a normal human being. Sometimes, he engaged himself in lengthy conversations and laughter but maintained a worrying silence and irritating behaviour with his black brothers, and when out in the open, he saw every white man or woman as an undercover agent and a potential enemy.

It did not take long before the impact of Ikenga's end-time acquired character began to be felt in the restaurant. He had been positioned at the bar but rendered a helping hand whenever his attention was needed in other areas of service. He would sometimes take orders from customers, only to forget them before he got to the kitchen or bar. His facial expression was far from welcoming, unlike that of an impressive waiter who wanted his customers to come back after the first visit. And when he was told to hurry up with drinking water, he would come back after the guest must have finished eating with a bottle of beer. The complaints lingered on till Mr. Lasisi could not take it any longer. He had also witnessed the extent of Ikenga's absent-mindedness and embarrassments, which had seriously damaged the reputation of Green Garden Restaurant.

Mr. Lasisi's actions showed that he had the interest and quick recovery of Ikenga and indeed the welfare of the Alien community at heart. Instead of a total dismissal, the restaurant owner restricted Ikenga to the kitchen as the only way to leave open the window of contact with his own people. Hence he was to help Madam Stella in whichever way he could especially in washing dishes as soon as they were brought in.

The much older and warm-hearted Stella had left her husband as soon as she acquired her Italian citizenship status. Then, she had suddenly realised that the Italian who had loved and supported her all through was too old and stingy for her liking. Up until Ikenga was taken into custody, she had maintained contact with him, desiring to have him as a future husband. She had made money from roadside prostitution but the unclean business and the effects of the excessive use of bleaching cream had left a lasting toll on her beauty. With her nine-year-old daughter and extra pounds she gathered over the years that added the madam title to her name, Stella was no more the best choice of a wife for any of the young stars. She had therefore gone to Germany hoping to start afresh in a new environment and possibly entice her dream man with money and the blocks of apartment she had built back home.

Ikenga with his presumed insanity preferred to rather remain single for the rest of his life than marry a woman who had been to *Italo*. His friends if he still had any would not spare him with gossip, Nne from the spirit world would also not give her blessings to such a marriage, and Chukwuma his father would see that as a disgrace to the entire Udeaja family. Such was the weight of cultural stigma and resentment attached to prostitution back in Umuafor.

Stella finally decided to apply for the job of a cook at Green Garden after all futile efforts to lure Ikenga into marriage with her wealth. She always opened up a conversation whenever they were alone in the kitchen to prevent his thoughts from drifting off, and took his dirty clothes home only to bring them back clean and ironed. She also suggested when there was no sign of improvement that a quick remedy would be to send him back to Africa where he would definitely get better in the hands of his people, with the social order and culture he was used to.

# Chapter 12

In Umuafor, the overall acceptance of Reverend Klaus's version of religion had not really brought about peace of mind or made everyone his or her brother's keeper as the late Reverend had always emphasised. It seemed that *omenani* had been quickly abandoned simply because the people needed a magical being that would rain down blessings as soon as they called. Umuafor frantically needed consolation and replenishment from whichever force that was willing to come to their aid. The secret patronages, which they later began to make to their rejected shrines and idols, clearly indicated that they were not keen on waiting for God's time or total discontentment with the slow pace at which their petitions were being met.

Thenceforth, the few remaining shrines and their keepers enjoyed steady and lucrative patronage from the very people who had turned their backs on the gods of their ancestors, and these gods' emissaries more often than not instead of interpreting the minds of the oracles, dictated their own judgments for their selfish interests or simply to punish those whom they regarded as deserters.

Umuafor with her twelve clans had for long cherished and applauded excellence. With the ever-dwindling interest in farming, and the increased joblessness coupled with the quest for wealth that was being born with every Umuafor child since after the war, young men were drawn back to the practice they had long rejected. Many went back to their traditional ways of worship and even cultism not because they had the interest of *omenani* at heart, but purely for power tussle and financial emancipation. This abuse of the *omenani* moral code generally resulted in a gradual degeneration of pristine values. Greatness and dignity was no longer rightfully bestowed on those who merited it but was simply assumed based on the amount of wealth that one was able to acquire and display. Paramount chiefs received money and vacated their positions while the *Nze na Ozo* titles meant for noble men were merely traded as commodities to the young, old, and even to many of questionable legacy and pedigree.

If one investigated Umuafor's history, it would be discovered that such celebrated names and titles as *Diochi* for a distinguished wine-tapper or *Omenka* for their reputable creative and innovative citizens were not conferred in vain. Nonetheless, wealth, along with its destructive influence, had dented Umuafor's moral garment, corrupted their priesthood and practically ruled in families, communities and the society at large.

The latter-day practitioners of *omenani* and these cultists went far and wide to acquire powers, knowing that the wretched and desperate people of Umuafor had become blind, and were mostly attracted to shrines and altars where supernatural powers were physically manifested. While pledging allegiance to the church of Reverend Klaus, many secretly retained *agwu* from different deities as their sources of power and wealth. Different altars with individual or group concepts of worship soon began to spring up in Umuafor with each group claiming to have received the staff of authority from Chukwu. Nevertheless, the gods were silent and Chukwu-Okike may have also left humans to tangle with *Ekwensu* and his legion of *agwu* for a while.

The ferocious competition for power and wealth quickly evolved into hatred and confrontation, with mortals ignorantly engaging into physical and spiritual combat on behalf of the spirits, and these battles became so vicious and deadly that people no longer felt safe to drink in the open, not to talk of sharing from the usual palm wine calabash whenever there was a feast.

It is said that *Ekwensu* and his legion of *agwu* began a second wave of vindictive colonisation in Umuafor after that of the white man. Evil men were believed to have poisons stocked in their fingernails, and could possibly send it to their enemies even from a distance. The kola-nut, which was the highest symbol of purity and hospitality, also became a medium to pass on poison and spiritual ailments. Moonlight gatherings along with many other cultural activities that were the beacon of good neighbourliness and a healthy society had vanished into thin air. This marked the destructive role anonymously played by religion in Umuafor and on the *omenani* that had once held her people together.

Mr. Arinze Ubanese was increasingly restless over his son Ogbonnia, and the medical studies that would not come to an end. Reverend Klaus's worries were now beginning to make meaning to the old headmaster. He may not have noticed that the medical studies were taking longer than necessary if the cars and money still flowed in but the tap had suddenly closed and worse still Ogbonnia no longer called as regularly as before.

Back then, the white Reverend had not stated specifically what the young man was engaged in, to have afforded to send a Mercedes Benz car a few months after he left, but had been absolutely certain that Raymond had gone out of track. Now that the white Jesus and his toolbox were no more available for consultation, the retired headmaster resorted to secretly consulting various power houses and fortune-tellers about the fate of his first son.

He was not expecting any surprises when he walked back from St Patrick's Mission one Friday evening clutching his hymn book and a wooden cross. His wife had displayed a bit of her arrogance at Afor market and her fellow market-women had verbally descended on her. Previously they had always condoned her pride as the wife of the headmaster and mother of a doctor until rumour gradually spread that her son had found refuge in the bosom of white women and might not be coming back soon. Hence, she was battered with words when she tried to belittle a widow who did not agree to her own offer over a basket of cocoyam.

There and then she realised that what she thought was a secret was openly gossiped about in the whole town. Not only was the Afor market ruined for the day, but her family would also remain a preferred topic for gossip and she would always be pointed at as the mother of a wayward doctor. She had wept all the way home, and was suddenly extremely angry with her husband who folded his hands in the face of such a grave problem.

The headmaster patiently waited for dinner assuming that it was delayed because of the extra business of Afor market days. When he did not perceive any aroma, he peeped through the tiny window over the kitchen and discovered no sign that the place had been used for the day. If Ugodi had bought *akara* with *agidi* for dinner as she occasionally did when she ran out of cooking time, his own portion would have been waiting on the table before he came back from the evening service. He was certain that he had overheard her a few minutes ago talking to Chinyere their youngest daughter.

"Are we not getting any meal for the night, Ugodi?" the headmaster asked, standing in front of his *obi*.

There was no reply from his wife. Darkness had gradually descended on the compound and surprisingly there was no sign that the *mpanaka* was still burning–a clear indication that Ugodi and her daughter had gone to bed. The only sign of life was the loud grunting and gobbling sounds of two giant male *tolo-tolo* as they constantly fought over dominance. The two turkey fowls had been given to St Patrick's Mission by a farmer as part of his tithe and had been handed over to the headmaster to look after.

The headmaster walked a few metres to the hut his wife shared with their grown-up daughter, and pushed aside the hanging colourful bead curtain.

"Ugodi," he called into the dark hut.

"*Onye?*" Ugodi queried.

"Are we not eating tonight?"

"Is the food ready?" Ugodi threw back at him.

"What?" the Headmaster asked in rejection.

"Let us know when you finish cooking," his wife maintained.

"Ugodi!" the astonished headmaster called again to make sure he was talking to his wife.

"Enough of the name calling!" Ugodi flared. "To be a woman is to take over the woman's role in the family."

"Who is the woman then?"

"It's you of course," she shouted as she emerged from the

dark hut pointing a finger with a push on her husband's forehead.

"You have lost the balls to free your son from the chains and chuckles of wicked people."

"Lower your voice, woman!" her husband pleaded. "The issue of Ogbonnia is a family matter."

"Count me out of the family affair," she shouted louder. "Your son's awkward quandary is already on the lips of every market woman."

The anger with which she returned from Afor market had not left her, and she was determined to offset it on her husband who without further words rushed back to his *obi* and grabbed a plastic water spray to disinfect the wife from whatever contrary spirit that may have taken hold of her. He was the type that shied away from trouble and definitely did not like the neighbours hearing the sound of quarrelling or fighting from his compound.

"Enough of your magic!" said the much taller and younger wife who seized the water bottle as soon as her husband raised his hand to spray.

"Your family has become an object of mockery," she shouted. "This water of yours has not helped us over the years."

"I have not known you like this, Ugodi," the defeated headmaster said to soften the situation, but his wife did not relent. She loudly lamented how the market-women had nearly trampled on her just because her fearful husband would not heed to her complaints and recommendations. The fruit of her labour was unjustly being denied her, and her dream to have her son who was a doctor take care of her at old age was increasingly looking bleak. Chinyere was also not spared from the ridicule as her fellow school children often referred to her as the sister of a prodigal doctor.

"You must do something to help Ogbonnia!" she cried out. "Why hasten to the mission when the missionaries are not leaving any time soon?"

"Calm down, Ugodi!" the headmaster implored.

"I will not," she insisted. "How are we sure their version of religion can be trusted? H ave our forefathers not been communicating with Chukwu-Okike before the intruders came? Have we not had sacred beings and statues before they presented us with their own fabricated heavenly creatures and pictures? Were we not conscious of *nso-ani* before religious houses began to sprout from all corners?"

"I have not known you this way," the defensive headmaster reiterated when the wife paused for breath.

"You left me with no choice," Ugodi explained angrily. "I must take the man's role in your weakness. How can you be going after a mouse when your house is on fire? Do Umuafor proverbs not tell us that a man who does not know where the rain began to beat him cannot know where he dried his body?"

Mr. Arinze Ubanese confusedly ran to the compound gate and bolted the entrance to keep away his intrusive neighbours from his private family matter. After the long verbal conflict, he eventually managed to send his wife and daughter back to bed promising her that he would be a man.

His wife's concerns had been a source of worry all along but he dared not make any move that would leave a question mark on the faith that he professed. As a young man, he was one of those who helped put up the structure now known as St Patrick's Mission and also helped to shelter Reverend Klaus in those early days when the *omenani* custodians had seen his teachings as a threat to their establishment. Ogbonnia's fate created more questions than answers, and was now threatening to undermine all that he had lived for.

He was beginning to believe that his son's destiny and present predicament might be the work of evil spirits and their human agents. There was no doubt in his mind about the potency of *Dibia* and various forms of shaman mysticism. Deeply rooted in tradition was the act of using the natural energies of roots, herbs and other mother earth given elements or objects in conjunction with personal powers deposited by one's *chi* to cure ailments, redirect events, or influence the state of affairs, but latter-day *dibia* had also come as things began to fall apart. They served as black magicians who drew upon malevolent gods or evil powers in order to invoke their image in a spell that could be used to destroy, cause misfortune, rewrite destinies or harm another person for the purposes of their personal gain. Unable to find answers to his worries or a solution to free his son, the headmaster went to Chukwuma who he knew was also facing the same nightmare.

If there were resources enough to sustain him, Chukwuma would have kept on marrying and producing children until he was confident that there were enough male sons to carry on the family name. He remained grateful to Chukwu Okike for his life but had not identified the hand of any lesser gods in his life's struggles and as such ruled out sacrifices, divinations and petitions. His argument was that the Great Being who knows everything had programmed human life from the beginning till end, so prayers and petitions could do nothing to change the laid down pattern of one's predestined life.

Confident that no evil man or woman would dare tie his son's destiny, he instead blamed Chukwu, the all knowing God, for giving him only one son knowing that he would eventually be held down in the white man's land. Ikenga, the son he knew too well, would not intentionally stay back there for any white man's sweet life or to punish the family.

"So what came over him?" he usually wondered.

The headmaster needed a great deal of perseverance and preaching to convince Chukwuma that their sons might be dancing to a different rhythm, as he carefully explained that greediness and jealousy could lead humans to invoke misfortune on their fellow mortals.

"I am in a position to know better," he concluded.

"Show me the shrine where the plan was hatched!" Chukwuma demanded. "And I will skin the *Dibia* alive."

"This is spiritual warfare," the headmaster corrected. "I have seen a lot over the years."

"What are you suggesting, Papa Ogbonnia?" his kinsman asked.

"We have to wake up from our slumber."

"I have been on guard all my life."

"The life patterns of our sons tell a different story."

"Then it is your turn to consult the magic box since your master is no more."

"I would have since closed the matter if the magic box had any solutions."

"The magic box surely has all solutions," Chukwuma corrected. "The white Reverend used it to locate my son when he ran out of the house for some days."

"Wrong!" the headmaster revealed. "The young lad ran straight to my house because you wanted to strangle him."

Finally Chukwuma learned where his son had taken refuge when he had run away from the compound for three days. He had always believed that the late Reverend must have had pity on him when he left and consulted the magic box.

"You hid it from me all this while?" he asked the headmaster.

"That was a small punishment for your actions."

"What other options have we since the magic box cannot help?"

"The solution can only be found in Amanze," Mr. Ubanese replied.

"Arobinagu, you mean?"

"Yes," the headmaster agreed. "My father when he was alive made several voyages to the oracle whenever he encountered a difficult puzzle."

"If your group has not destroyed it like they did to others."

"They did not succeed," Mr. Ubanese declared. "The oracle possesses invisible powers."

"Have you fooled yourself by running after a strange religion?"

"Ask me that again when we might have freed our sons," the headmaster replied, avoiding a direct answer.

"We have to take up the challenge," Chukwuma said. "I would not have been convinced if it was not you."

"There is no more time to waste, Chukwuma," the headmaster reminded.

## WOES OF IKENGA

"I am ready if we have to leave immediately," Chukwuma added. "If Arobinagu of Amanze has the answer to our worries, then I will sacrifice a ram to its shrine."

"A cow you should say."

"A woman can only rest the arm on that part of her husband where her hand reaches."

As the second in command at St Patrick's Mission since the death of Reverend Klaus, the headmaster would have wanted Chukwuma to go alone but his wife would explode again if he stayed behind. Besides, Chukwuma who he knew very well might overreact if things did not go the way he wished and that could throw their secret mission into the open. Both men later agreed to leave early the next day so as to be back in time for the headmaster to officiate during Sunday service.

*   *   *   *   *

Amanze was a land of industrious men. Though they possessed a regional network of oracles and shrines, the coming of Arobinagu was to them an acknowledgement of worthiness by the Great Being himself. The coming of the missionaries coupled with the brutal war may have desecrated the land and committed *NsoAni*, but the people of Amanze had jointly said no to any intruder trying to rob them of their *omenani*. Their resistance to foreign cultures had constantly kept them at loggerheads with any authority that tried to extend its influence over their way of life. They are till date famous for the mysterious coming of a stranger who was assumed to be mortal. The Amanze people offered the uninvited guest a land in the evil forest in an attempt to scare him away.

When the stranger did not die after the stipulated time for stepping into the evil forest where no one dared venture into, and still would not disclose his name, the dumbfounded elders of Amanze gave him the name Aro-bi-n'agu, which literally means "a being that dwells in the jungle." Soon the people and their leaders began to accept and adhere to his messages as divine guidelines from the Great Being especially as it enforced moral principles in

237

accordance with *omenani*. The well-established customary way of human coexistence and moral code consequently became a form of religion to the people of Amanze. From his wisdom bag, the strange being revealed to them that humans had limited knowledge of themselves and commended the noble men of Amanze for standing up to all forms of human domination. Contrary to the agenda of the foreign invaders to empty the earth's abdomen, Arobinagu proclaimed that Mother Earth did not belong to humans but instead all creatures belonged to her. As such, her valued treasures and resources should be tapped and managed properly.

The Outlander preached love and preservation of Mother Earth, which generously supported human life that Chukwu had entrusted to her care, and Amanze learnt from the strange being that life, in its diverse forms predates humans in the tiny enclave known as Mother Earth. According to him, this enclave is so tiny that humans have failed to make a cosmic fingerprint in the universe and as such were lost or completely left out in the unimaginable chain of celestial events. Therefore Arobinagu admonished them, never to bow to man's rule.

Another version from the few remaining elders of Amanze had it that Arobinagu came as an old man requesting a piece of land from the people. Since no one was ready to shoulder the responsibilities of an aged single man, they had showed him the evil forest. The stranger single-handedly made a pathway in the middle of the forest where he built a small wooden hut for himself. After the people of Amanze waited for the news of his death and it failed to come, they lined up around the edge of the forest with offerings, accepting that he was no ordinary man, and quickly embraced him as he began to cure people with different ailments and diseases. He was renowned for the mysterious ways in which he exposed evildoers and disputes were also taken to his court for his upright judgment.

That was during the peak period of colonial rule and apparently the white District Commissioner had not been

WOES OF IKENGA

comfortable with the rival authority of Arobinagu and had once sent the white army to the forest with orders to obliterate the shrine and execute the stranger from nowhere along with his co-conspirators for disobeying the orders of the colonial powers.

For three days and three nights, the band of colonial soldiers, armed to the teeth, marched around the seven-mile square forest unable to locate the oracle's shrine or its chief priest. It suddenly dawned on the invaders that the sacred shrines and statues scattered all over the twelve clans of Umuafor were not as ordinary as they seemed. As a result, Amanze narrowly escaped the invaders and the consequent slave trading through the supernatural powers displayed by Arobinagu.

The village heads, in a way of appreciation invited him to the palace and presented him with different kinds of sacrifices and again tried to find out where he had come from, his name, and his mission in Amanze.

"I was sent by Goodness," was his reply.

For every other question, the old man declined to give his name or reveal his mission but instead requested for someone to help carry the presents to the forest where he had built his hut, and the King had proudly sent his youngest son Onwuama, to assist without fearing for the life of the young lad should he step into the evil forest. The story had it that when they reached the entrance of the hut after walking all the way in silence, the old stranger handed his *ofo*, the symbol of authority to Onwuama and went in. That was the last that was ever seen of him.

\* \* \* \* \*

Chukwuma and his kinsman were on their way to meet the fifth generation in line of succession to Arobinagu chief priests. With his double barrel gun well oiled and well fed, and *obejili* fastened around his waist, he did not know what to expect but that he was ready to take war to anyone the oracle would say was responsible for his son's failure. Both men set out at the first crow of the cock to the land of Amanze as it was a journey that would

239

take a whole day of trekking if they were lucky to cross Ogba Bridge before market-women started to pour out with their wares. Of course they had to, because the headmaster would likely face disciplinary actions should news get to the church authorities that he was patronising the rejected gods.

They were neither to taste water or food, nor greet and accept greetings from anyone throughout their journey. Those were some of the information the headmaster had learned from his father as key to a successful consultation.

The journey continued with relative ease though the headmaster had to buckle up at intervals to catch up with Chukwuma. The old bushy track they had decided to take still retained ugly memories of the war with rows of abandoned trenches where the fighters of Umuafor had taken cover during the rebellion. While many records had been made of the bloody struggle, not much attempts were made at chronicling in details the scientific and technological ingenuity that had taken place in Umuafor during the arms struggle as their great thinkers had been the arrowheads of the scientific and technological innovations that had sustained the secessionist struggle through those years. An abandoned *Ogbunigwe*, the crudely assembled mass destruction missile that made the enemy troop jittery, had been left to rust at Ovuvu junction where the struggle had been bloodiest.

Both men decided to rest at the junction after a long trek and the headmaster brought out the roasted yam with oil bean that his wife had prepared for them, only to discover that his hymnbook and cross were still in the bag.

"But we should not taste any food," Chukwuma reminded.

"Indeed," the headmaster consented.

He carefully hid the roasted yam and the holy items in one of the dusty compartments of the *Ogbunigwe* since the latter had nothing in common with Arobinagu and his chief priest.

"Our children will never know the bitterness of the war," he said to Chukwuma as he pushed the items deep inside the chamber.

"The horror is not worth remembering," Chukwuma replied.

Seeing the dying *Ogbunigwe* evoked memories of the deplorable litany of brutality and death that he had witnessed.

"This is the very junction where Chinua's two sons were slaughtered."

"Were their corpses retrieved?" the headmaster asked spiritedly.

"It was impossible," Chukwuma responded. "I escaped with a bullet lodged in my right shoulder."

"No wonder he so much hated the invaders and their accomplices."

"The old man was strong to have lived through it all."

"May their souls find peace in the spirit world," the headmaster prayed.

"And Chinua's soul," Chukwuma added.

"Yes."

"Or do you think the old man is now in hell fire for not embracing Reverend Klaus?"

"The pass to heaven lies not in religion."

"Ogbuagu was a good man."

"Yes, he was."

The journey continued shortly after they had rested enough but this time on a relaxed pace knowing that they had covered most of the journey. As they got closer to the shrine, Chukwuma noticed that there was a big difference from the description he gathered from earlier pilgrims. A large chunk of the forest had been cleared to make way for the Amanze community hall and rows of mud huts also lined up to shelter the increasing number of *osu*.

Magnificent ancient trees round the shrine were regarded as the dwelling place of the spirits of the ancestors with their protruding overground roots which formed a sitting circle for pilgrims. Burning wax positioned at strategic corners of the forest engulfed the whole area with a strong unpleasant smell. Chukwuma and his kinsman walked past the community hall as they were directed and headed further into the forest.

Through his magical powers or human intelligence, the current priest of Aro with his charming personality had received word that visitors were coming. Just like many of his counterparts, the young chief priest who by virtue of inheritance had taken over the office had come to understand the power of wealth in the Amanze post-war era. From a distance he sized up his two guests to know the weight of their purse, as that would determine the nature and seriousness of drama he was going to display for them.

"Move no further!" he shouted loudly to his approaching guests. "Have you come to wage war against Aro?"

"How can humans wage war against spirits?" Chukwuma returned. "We have come in peace, *Ezemmuo*."

"Put down your weapons if you have come in peace."

"My assistance might be needed," Chukwuma insisted.

"No human assistance," the chief priest corrected. "Aro is a lone warrior."

"If Aro wishes so."

Chukwuma lowered his double barrel gun, unfastened his *obejili* and dropped it as well on the ground. If Arobinagu did not need his assistance in liberating Ikenga and his cousin Ogbonnia from whatever force that was holding them down in the white man's land, that was also acceptable. Both men watched the chief priest bring out a powder-like substance from his red overall mantle, pour enough onto his palm, and blow into the air. Then he sprung round his guests a number of times striking his *ofo* over their heads with strange incantations to ward off any spirit of doubt that might have followed the men to Amanze, as that would alter the potency of any charm or divination. When he was convinced that the spirits of his visitors had been lifted, he called on Aro to reveal the problem and the much-needed solution that brought his guests.

"You are the eagle that sits in his chamber while your feathers are being traded in the market," he praised the oracle. "When you can tell pregnant birds from the ground then their problems are minor." In the middle of his praises to Arobinagu, the chief priest turned to Chukwuma with a steady gaze and bulging eyes.

"What business have you got with water spirits?" he queried.

# WOES OF IKENGA

"I have no business with them," Chukwuma replied standing his ground.

"I can see wealth." He pointed down. "Aro has blessed you with houses and fleet of cars."

"You are right, *Ezemmuo*," the headmaster interjected. "But they are being withheld."

"They are being withheld indeed," the chief priest repeated. "He who chooses to remain silent will lose that which belongs to him."

"Aro, I implore you," Chukwuma pleaded.

"If you had delayed in coming, your life would be next."

"The land of Umuafor will not allow them," the high-spirited Chukwuma rejected.

"Arobinagu will not permit it either," the chief priest consented.

"*Ezemmuo,* what do we do?" the headmaster, who had merely been a listener inquired.

"It's not for me to say," the chief priest answered.

Turning away from the men, he made a series of acrobatic body movements like one having a difficult battle in the spirit world. "Arobinagu, I have come again," he cried loudly into the air. "Caught by a bush trap is a Chimpanzee but the Chimp will eventually go. We have the *ofo*, we have the *ogu*, whoever will deny us of our rightful entitlement, let his hands be soiled in the mud."

He stopped unexpectedly and gazed as if he had sighted the problem or its solution. His visitors also maintained calm hoping for a supernatural intervention to the problem that had given them sleepless nights.

"A barren woman," the chief priest screamed. "There is a barren woman."

"Yes," Chukwuma accepted.

"You must bring the barren woman here."

Chukwuma immediately knew that it would be close to impossible to bring his first wife to Amanze. Nne had accepted her fate and found happiness in the new religion she chose for herself.

243

Though she had occasionally been pressured to take part in her forsaken *omenani* if that would make people leave her in peace, under no circumstances would she accept to make a trip to Arobinagu's shrine.

"It's not about the barren woman," Chukwuma explained. "It's about my only son that has lost his way in a foreign land."

"My son too," the headmaster added.

"That is what I am saying," the chief priest took it up from there. "It took a while before the gods granted you that son."

"That's true, *Ezemmuo*."

"They were born twins."

"Quite correct."

"Another son died with the mother during delivery."

"You are right, *Ezemmuo*."

"That barren woman has tied up the two men in a foreign land."

"The barren woman?" Chukwuma enquired.

"Yes, the barren woman," replied the Aro priest. "Exactly the same way she tied up her womb."

That was a declaration Chukwuma could not bear. Nne, the wife he knew very well, was not capable of hurting an ant. She had regrettably accepted her barrenness as *onatalu-chi* when the best *dibia* in all of the Umuafor clans and the late Reverend could not counter the *agwu*. He had doggedly refused to be cowed into believing the unbelievable by the *omenani* custodians or their foreign rivals who had come with another version of religion to unseat them.

Instantly, Chukwuma made for his double barrel and pulled the trigger without hesitation. Before his companion could throw his weight on him, the damage had already been done. When the two got up, the left arm of the headmaster was completely shattered while the chief priest was nowhere to be seen except for his wooden *ofo* that lay motionless on the ground. There was a short pandemonium as the gunshot drew a number of people to the scene. Chukwuma, clearly agitated, stood his position ready to offload the remaining bullets on whoever dared near him. The smoking nozzle clearly scared people off him, giving him a good chance to drift backwards and look for his way back to Umuafor.

Chukwuma was for once frightened to his veins. Not because he had missed blowing off the head of the Aro priest or for what any man would do to him. He was terribly afraid of his longstanding ally, the double barrel gun that he had refused to do away with. He maintained a steady pace through his return journey but did not know that the news from Amanze, which had quickly spread like wildfire would reach Umuafor before him. Briskly, he walked past Ovuvu junction without a second thought at the pile of rusty war machines or the hymnbook that the headmaster had hidden inside one of them. His fear was that the gun had nearly killed his kinsman, and seven years of banishment would have befallen him.

Severally, he had been warned about his decision to retain the old ally. Reverend Klaus, when he was alive, had once sent a message through Nne, that the weapon with which her husband returned from the war was possessed by *ajo-chi*, the evil spirit. Udeaja before his death had also begged him to do away with the old double barrel because it carried curses from the spirits of those it had visited with death during the war. Chukwuma, then in his prime, had not been ready to heed those pleas and was consciously ready to die by the gun if that was the price to pay for standing shoulder to shoulder with his much-cherished musket, a weapon he had personally seized from a fallen enemy soldier. That had become for him and indeed the people of Umuafor, one of the material evidences of his bravery. Time and life's struggles had taken its toll on the aging man who was now beginning to see things the way his father saw them. He was now the living head of Udeaja family and would like to see his children get married and give him grandchildren.

When he got to the Ogba Lake area, Chukwuma finally made up his mind to dispose his long-time companion for good. The decision to part with the white man's death machine was in line with a popular Umuafor adage that "he who the gods protect must also protect himself." From a tree branch overlooking the lake that nourished the dense forest, Chukwuma sat and chewed his chewing stick. The white man's land had deprived him of sleep. Given a handshake, they demanded for a hug. Eloka, his elder brother, had been given to them during their father's lifetime and the white witches were now planning to withhold his only son? How was he going to handle a corpse that suddenly developed an erection while being taken to the graveyard? The gallons of precious palm oil and *okwoma* that Nne had wasted on smoky mountaintops of Ogba in search of a child had not yielded any positive results. He wished that the beast dwelling under the lake would for once show itself with any form of solution to free his son.

As the answers were not forthcoming for his numerous questions and worries, Chukwuma flung his double-barreled long gun into the middle of the lake and watched it sink before climbing down. He would plead with one of his remaining daughters to give up marriage and bear him grandchildren at home while he figured out how to take the war to the land of the white witches. As long as the headmaster was not dead, his injuries did not bother him much. That would serve as his reward for not taking him to a strong *dibia*. He could as well stay put in Amanze if he was not ready to come back and face his followers.

Chukwuma was very fast to have made it home before dark. At the intersection leading to Afor market, on the shanty road that led to his house, two women returning late from the market frantically threw away their baskets and ran for their lives when they bumped into him. Not ready to run for anything in the land of Umuafor, Chukwuma quickly drew his two-edged *obejili* but saw nothing as he jumped around. It was not yet dark and the women should have seen that he was not a ghost or any dangerous animal, but he sighed heavily for the little distraction and went his way ignoring the women and their wares. However, when the same incident repeated itself as he stepped into his compound,

WOES OF IKENGA

Chukwuma knew that it was out of the ordinary. *Eke-uke*, the family dog, also took to its heels as all the other family members ran for their lives. It was only Nne who mustered some courage and addressed her husband with tears from over the lower part of the family fence.

"Who did this to you, my husband?" she cried repeatedly.

"What is the matter with all of you?" Chukwuma queried moving closer to the fence.

Not only was the story of events in Amanze oversalted before it reached Umuafor, it had also warned people to run for their lives because Chukwuma had shot dead his kinsman and the Chief Priest of Arobinagu, and would keep on killing until the *agwu* that had taken hold of him was subdued.

"I have nowhere to run to," Nne continued. "Kill me but spare the rest of your family."

"Have I turned to a killer in your eyes?" he asked his wife.

"Yes, you have," she replied. "Where is the headmaster, your kinsman that went with you to Amanze? What happened to Aro chief priest?"

Chukwuma who hated to see Nne cry stared at his wife with pity while trying to make meaning of what she said. Whoever had brought down the story was determined to create terror.

"I have not killed anyone," Chukwuma said to her.

"Life has been so unfair to me," Nne bemoaned. "And you have just added 'wife of a murderer' to my list of names."

He leapt over the low fence and led his wife back to the compound trying to console her. "It was all because of Ikenga," he told her in a low tone.

"Arobinagu will rather compound your problems instead of solving them," she said to him.

"The headmaster came up with the suggestion that the oracle has the solutions," Chukwuma revealed.

"What happened to him, is he alive?"

"Yes."

"And why did he not come back with you?"

247

"He is ashamed of coming to face his congregation."

"He has sold his soul to the devil," Nne remarked.

The saga did not end there. The headmaster returned the next day with bandages on his swollen arm as the Aro priest had requested the services of *Okpo-mgbada*, the local orthopaedist, to fix his fractured bone before sending him back to Umuafor after a day's rest. He sneaked into his compound late in the evening and decided to lie low knowing that his secret mission would have become the topic of the day. To Ugodi who would not rest till her itching ears were appeased, he relayed all that had happened in Amanze, urging her to keep it to herself till he cleared himself from his superiors on why he made the trip to Arobinagu shrine.

Ugodi could barely keep it till the next morning. The barren woman had no son and would definitely not be comfortable seeing the progress of other people's sons. She therefore called together the leaders of the women's group to accuse Nne of tying up the destinies of her son and Ikenga. The mockery and finger pointing that came with it was a heavy burden for a woman in her old age who believed that life had not been fair to her. Resentment followed Nne everywhere she went, even to St Patrick's Mission where she thought she had found refuge. Life lost meaning for her and the appetite for living vanished too. Ikenga who she had nurtured into a man was for her the only son she would ever have, and now that he was held down in the white man's land for reasons she could not explain, Umuafor turned to blame and attack her as being responsible.

Majority demanded that she swear an oath before Arobinagu in support of Ugodi, some others instead preferred to have the oath done with the Reverend's holy book since she had no more dealings with idols. Other sprouting worship centres in Umuafor campaigned that *ajo-chi,* the evil spirits, which Nne must have dealt with in the past were still camped inside of her and to drive away the legion, one needed to pay or buy necessary materials and probably make pledge of royalty to the very shrine or altar.

Nne refused to be dragged anywhere for what they called

WOES OF IKENGA

purification or deliverance. She stuck to St Patrick's Mission and to the blameless white Reverend who shied away from scoring points when doing good. He was the one who should have detected and dealt with the evil spirits if any dwelt in her. Nne continually went to St Patrick's, not to ask Chukwu for blessings but for her death and in the privacy of her hut beckoned her *chi* day after day to take her life. Finally, her wish came to pass.

# Chapter 13

Mr. Raymond Ubanese flew into Germany when the immigration flow was minimal, with the authorities and the whole asylum procedure said to be at a blind stage. He had gotten his first three months visa from the Embassy of Germany as a businessman heading for an international trade-fair taking place in Hannover.

People from neighbouring countries like Ghana, Cameroon, Niger and Republic of Benin had flocked into Nigeria in search of survival at an alarming rate that citizens became worried that immigrants were about to hold the country to ransom. They had staged a mega demonstration termed "Ghana must go" to send especially the Ghanaians and other immigrants from West African regions out of the country. The poor Ghanaians who roamed the streets at day as barrow-pushers and shoe-shiners were also blamed for robbery and other criminal activities in the night.

Around that period, the Oluwole fraudsters originated and many of the early economic migrants from that region to the Western world travelled through Nigeria either with a tampered or genuine Nigerian passport. Oluwole became a notorious hotspot for document forgery and counterfeiting, a piece of territory that saw the west end of Nigeria into the Atlantic Ocean. The advent of the crime was blamed on foreigners and its perfection was partly done by talented men of Umuafor who were generally good in learning but best in perfection and deployment methodology. All forms of stolen and forged documents with unique technical knowhow were openly traded in Oluwole. They constituted a thorn in the flesh of the government and the law enforcement agencies, as they were capable of forging anything under the sun; they specialised in complex and advanced fee frauds, immigration scams, stamps, seals and printing of foreign bank cheques. University degrees and certificates from institutions of higher learning across the globe were also obtainable from Oluwole gurus.

A shocking disclosure at one point by the authorities revealed

WOES OF IKENGA

that a combined swift action by the State Security Service and the Army to dismantle the criminal enterprise netted about two thousand foreign passports, including those of African countries and the Western world. Also recovered from the raid were assorted foreign cheques, heaps of original blank airways tickets and postal money order from different countries. Dozens of arrests were made but those who knew the order of things walked out freely with the power of "settlement". A godly law agent lamented that the country would have been better off, if the skills, creativity, and imagination exhibited by some of the young suspects had been channelled towards lawful endeavours.

Ray joined the Oluwole business when he moved to Lagos after abandoning his father-in-law's petrol station in search of the proverbial greener pasture. Preferring to hang around and raise enough money for air ticket and basic travelling allowance instead of risking his life through the African deserts and rough waters of Europe, he was able to make a little money as an errand man, and his immense contributions to the game as a high school graduate was well appreciated.

The three months visa along with his international passport, which he intended to travel with as a business mogul was sold to another traveller who was ready to pay a good sum since he could always obtain another visa whenever he wanted. With the money realised from the dirty deals, he purchased a piece of land through his father in-law along a very busy highway with hopes of building his own petrol station. It was when they started running for cover every now and then from the police that he decided it was time to leave Oluwole in peace. One only tried to get what he could from the head of an elephant. No one ever carried it home.

After months of obedient service, his boss packaged him upon request as a senior clergy with the Catholic Archdiocese of Calabar heading for an inter-denominational Bishops' conference in Berlin. With all necessary documents on the table; a sealed and stamped letter of approval from the Archbishop, and an official letter from the Vatican to prove that Right Reverend Raymond Ubanese was

251

on episcopal assignment, the embassy issued him a multiple visa valid for six months and he was warmly welcomed as he landed at the Frankfurt Airport wearing a banded collar clergy suit and a spotless spectacle. As agreed, the return ticket and his passport were sent back to his boss as rest payment for the cheap visa he had arranged for him.

The *aduro* process during his time was not that smooth though he was armed with enough information before taking off. With all his experience, he had never imagined that the white men would have an accurate number of their citizens and know when an outsider came in or left their country. Germany had until recently not been listed among the top choices of destination for African wanderers because of the language barrier and perceived conservative nature of the German society. However, the country began to witness a steady influx of black Africans with the Nigerian exodus, which started in the early eighties and peaked in the late nineties. The trend was drastically slowed down as foreign Jihadists who sneaked into countries to carry out attacks constantly shook Western powers.

The overblown insecurity and security measures that followed, the bloody and costly wars against self-acclaimed freedom fighters, and the subsequent global economic meltdown made governments of those migration hotspots take a second look at their backyards. Ray had nobody to guide or direct him; the only contact he had was the phone number of a Ghanaian who had sought assistance from him at Oluwole before he travelled. He finally got him on line after some days of failed attempts.

"Why is your telephone off the whole time, Kwame?" he asked in low tones in the privacy of his hotel room.

"Who is on the line please?" Kwame asked from the other end of the line.

"It's Ray ... Raymond from Oluwole."

"Eee! *Charli*, is that you?" Kwame asked in his usual broken English.

"I came three days ago," Ray replied. "I've been trying your number the whole time."

"Sorry, *Charli.*"

"Have you got a job?"

"I am still battling with aduro."

"How is the *aduro* process? Where are you? Kwame … Kwame … "

Ray was still asking questions when the line went "tuun tuun tuun." Kwame probably did not want anything to endanger his newfound settlement. Illiteracy combined with his very poor command of English had robbed him of his ego. He had spent four years in Lagos with his wife and two children in an unpredictable and hostile environment since the "Ghana must go" uprising and had not failed to grab the opportunity when a passport with valid three months German visa was up for sale at a relatively fair price. He may have abruptly halted the conversation if he suspected that someone was secretly listening in or was fearful of being spied on by secret agents, as he could be sent out of town if the authorities found out that he was not originally from Liberia as he had claimed.

Ray was not satisfied with the haphazard information. With his three months visa and letter of admission at Hamburg University, which he retained all the while, he was not in a hurry. His academic pursuit was waived for quick money after some months of intensive German language classes. That was where his studies as a medical doctor ended.

He saw hustling as an easier way to accomplish his goals and return to Umuafor and his family in a triumphant style. It was clear that he needed to go for asylum so as not to have problems with the foreign office over his visa renewal. With the assistance of some birds of the same feather he had met in Hamburg, Ray applied for *aduro* and was posted to Zansberg, a small city a few kilometres away from Hannover. It did not take long before he discovered a lucrative deal along with few of his friends in those early days of migration.

A loophole in the country's asylum process gave rise to *Jugunu,* a process of applying for asylum with different names in different refugee centres and running round to collect juicy packages handed out by the immigration authorities every month end. In the small city of Zansberg, he was registered as Osman Sistani fleeing the Al-Shabab regime in Somalia, and in Bonn he applied as Gabriel Wiwa, a stepson of the slain activist from the Niger-Delta region of Nigeria. Yet in the famous Wincanton refugee camp in Norsburg, which he decided to call home, he was living as Nshiko Sankara from the war-torn Republic of Sierra Leone. He was actually able to send enough money to his wife to erect his own petrol station from the monthly allowances collected under those names, long after he sent the Mercedes Benz and a number of other vehicles to his father. Some of his overambitious co-plotters had even gone as far as travelling across borders to neighbouring countries with attractive refugee assistance schemes to apply and collect monthly payments from multiple refugee centres.

The certificates with which he had intended to continue his education were completely forgotten and the *Jugunu* practice lingered on for long till the authorities began to learn their lessons and introduced finger printing for old and new asylum applicants. Ray and his group knew that the game was over and devised other means of survival.

All efforts to cement his stay in Germany proved futile as rejection letters here and there threatened his peace in Wincanton. He would have been a father and in-line for a Resident Permit if the Turkish girl who abandoned her parents to join him at the refugee camp had not aborted her four months pregnancy. Some friends of his, eager to win over the girl's admiration, had revealed to the young unsuspecting girl that her husband-to-be had a wife and children waiting for him in his country. That was the kind of double life which some aliens painfully subjected themselves to in order to scale through the tricky hurdles of their host countries.

The unending disturbances and threats from the Office of Foreign Affairs became a major distraction whenever he tried to maintain a steady source of income. They had not only stamped his place of birth as unknown in the white paper they issued him but always came to pick him up every second month to visit another foreign embassy in search of his true identity.

Ray's cup filled up to the brim when he posed as the second son of the late President Mobutu of Zaire. He and his group had successfully convinced a greedy German entrepreneur that a huge sum of money stashed away by his late father was to be transferred to his account urgently for safe-keeping and he stood to gain twenty percent of the loot if he was willing to assist in the transfer.

The man had happily transferred an undisclosed sum to an unknown bank account for what the fraudsters had told him was a compulsory service charge that must be paid by the account owner. When Raymond and his group came again days later demanding for what they termed security fee from a Spain-based security company that was supposed to handle the transfer, the man became suspicious and alerted the law agents. A sting operation termed "alien connection" was quickly arranged by the ever-ready German Polizei.

The twenty-three thousand Deutsch Mark security fee was delivered in a hotel room to a gentleman who claimed to be from Credo Security Services in Valencia. Ray who was monitoring events from a kiosk opposite the five star hotel joined his friend as he left the hotel with the money, unaware that the man and woman loitering in the kiosk who had all the while pretended to be love birds were also interested in the action.

The Jewish lawyer could not do much as the evidence was overwhelming. He had instead pleaded for leniency on behalf of his client as a first time offender. The court found Ray guilty of fraud and impersonation and sentenced him to three years imprisonment along with some of his accomplices who also received different jail sentences. His time in jail was three long years of excruciating pain as his thoughts were focused towards his wife, their only daughter, and his aged parents who he had promised that he was going to come back soon enough to look after. The occasional telephone calls to his wife that the prison authority allowed once a week, always ended in tears for both of them. Eighteen months into his detention, his wife sent him devastating news; the government, to make way for an interstate highway, had demolished the petrol station that sustained the family. The state interior spokesperson had claimed that the piece of land was illegally acquired and the petrol station constructed without proper authorisation from the Ministry of Works, thus sending the issue of compensation to the grave and leaving those affected without any legal case before the court.

Ray contemplated telling the Foreign Office to send him back to his country but going back with nothing when the only means of survival for his family had been destroyed was not a sensible option. His time behind bars was gradually nearing completion; it would be better to endure for a year or two more and see if he would be able to make up for the loss when he got out. The Foreign Office was already waiting for him at the door when his time in Balthazar was up and took him straight to a deportation camp two hundred and sixty miles away from his home. This is a prisonlike facility where aliens are kept in preparation for their deportation. He wasted another eight months there and all efforts by the authority to secure an Emergency Travel Certificate (ETC) from any of the English-speaking countries in West Africa yielded no result. His lawyer stepped in again and argued that the Foreign Office could not continue to detain him indefinitely.

"The young man has gone through enough trauma," he charged at the court with few local journalists who usually came around to follow proceedings. Ray was eventually released, taken back to Wincanton Refugee Camp and left to fend for himself.

As security agents tried hard to root out bad eggs in the police-conscious society, Ray and his group devised more crooked means of getting around. He soon resorted to dating elderly rich women not because he was still interested in what he saw as "useless *kpalli*" but to complement what they got from their ever-busy husbands and collect any goodies that might come along with the game. Contract marriages were also arranged between aliens and citizens who wanted to earn a little more than what they received from the social welfare. Such arrangements bagged an upfront payment of five hundred Deutsch Mark for Ray and immediate completion of the agreed sum as soon as the marriage materialised. Thanks to Ray and his group, aliens also signed up for babies they had not fathered just to get the so-called *Vaterschaft* Resident Status; a latter-day introduced law that granted residency to an alien parent because of his or her fifty percent joint custody of a child. The new law that became a by-pass to the compulsory years of mandatory marital servitude created a baby boom for a country whose birth rate had drastically dwindled. With their unnatural energy, aliens who would stop at nothing to lay their hand on the shadowy resident permit were even more determined to impregnate trees.

His crooked means of survival in Wincanton did not end there.

From new immigrants who just entered the country with little or no idea about what life abroad was all about, Ray collected little money to give them lectures on how best and with which country to apply for asylum. His widely viewed assistance to new arrivals made him a big brother or an uncle to the second generation of fugitives in Landesburg and surrounding cities.

He stepped over his boundaries again when he single-handedly ordered a special printing machine from Amsterdam with which he entered into competitive business with the railway authorities. Monthly tickets for trains and buses were printed and distributed at very cheap prices to interested aliens and citizens who felt that the country and their politicians had not been fair to them. When the illicit activity boomed and money started flowing in steadily, the organisation quickly forgot that the security apparatus had not fallen into slumber.

On the day they swooped in on the one-room apartment, which Ray rented inside town for his printing machine, the neighbourhood was sealed off and anyone suspected of having any link with the small apartment bundled off to the Central Police Station. Two hungry looking black immigrants who were still taking lectures from Ray in preparation for their asylum process were also picked up from the small apartment but both denied knowing the real owner of the house and claimed to be totally unaware of any of the incriminating properties they were confronted with. The ambush to apprehend their lecturer was futile as he went underground for a while but was later picked up from the house of one of his wealthy concubines following a valued tip-off from a patriotic citizen.

It was clear to the authorities that Nshiko Sankara had a hand in the whole affair but there was no sufficient evidence to nail him. Those arrested with the forged ticket declined to testify against him and even the citizens did not have the courage to point at Ray in the court, not for fear of retaliation but for the fact that Ray was a good person and they would rather identify with him than with the court or politicians who cared less about their daily plight. Ray however was given a long *anunu-ebe*, a suspended sentence of three years should he commit any crime within a period of five years. This entailed that if he was to be arrested even for the least crime within the space of five years, he would serve all of the suspended three years jail term plus the time due for the fresh crime that he was arrested for.

With disgusting stories flowing out of marriages between aliens and citizens, Ray decided to wash his hands off the Super Mario game with his treasure hunt. The Foreign Office had lavished enormous amount of resources trying to send him out of the country. They suddenly got tired and abandoned him to fend for himself with his "no nation" status. Since he was allowed to live freely with "no nation" status, he made up his mind to abandon the issue of Resident Permit and the crazy Mario adventure. He had witnessed an unpleasant number of family break-ups and been called upon a number of times to settle differences by friends whenever their roof was on fire. A Gambian had confided in him why he had taken to his heels without second thoughts for his daughter from the day he received his permanent Resident Permit. He was then working fourteen hours daily in a cold room to make ends meet and with the tediousness of German work, could no longer perform satisfactorily on the bed. Aware that his wife made up for his inefficiency from somewhere else, the Gambian had painfully swallowed all sorts of unspeakable humiliation in the name of *kpalli* and had wasted no time to liberate himself as soon as the obligatory marital service was over.

Family is the fundamental nucleus of any community and a healthy family makes a healthy society. Many who endured the heartbreak came out of the treasure hunt with a retarded thinking faculty and a coloured sticker known as *aufhentalt* to celebrate. Those who broke off at the middle of the road lost whatever effort they might have made for the *kpalli* only to start afresh with another woman with no guarantee of success. Worse still, there were many who landed in psychiatric hospitals along the line because the data processing unit of their brain was constantly loaded with thoughts and its super hardware simply packed up.

Ray decided to leave the citizenship for the citizens since the Foreign Office had promoted him to the status of "*aduro* of no nation." He was no more afraid of being taken unawares back to Umuafor when no country wanted to accept him. Age was no longer on his side and that meant a change of strategy and extracareful calculations in his dealings to avoid more years of agony behind bars.

The three-year probation was enough time to evaluate his operational mode as the continually changing laws against crime and squeeze on the men of the underworld were getting tighter by the day. He needed to devise a legal means of survival otherwise the eyes of the law enforcers would always be on him. It was not easy for him to make ends meet without falling under the spotlight, and he neither received the normal monthly payment due a refugee, nor was he permitted to take up legal employment. The three years of *anunu-ebe* had left him surviving on the charity acquaintances especially those who had benefited from his asylum application lectures when the refugee flow was at its peak. With the ever-decreasing number of incoming asylum seekers and security tight ups, his family received less attention because they simply would not understand that the heat was much. Telephone calls from or to home countries were mostly with expectation from poor family or friends, a reason why many adventurers maintained long silence from their people instead of unnecessary explanations of hard time.

Life outside one's country can be adventurous but life as an economic migrant in the Western world is best understood by those who have lived it. Raymond Ubanese knew it all. His wife called and wrote a number of times to ignorantly blast him for abandoning them because of white women but explaining things to her made no sense since there was no way she would understand the situation. He wisely ignored her and searched further for his *awele*. She would understand by the time he was through with the obstacles and went back to join them as an already-made man. A latter-day adage in Umuafor says "he who refused to agree by sunrise will definitely do so by sunset." Wealth was the language that every Umuafor man understood and appreciated. The hunt for wealth knew no limitations or risks and the incredible sense of creativity deposited in every Umuafor man and woman helped them turn adverse situations to success stories. Empty-handed, they flourished with whatever minimal resources at their disposal and when given a stone, could turn it into gold.

Uncle Ray's face suddenly lit up with smiles as he walked home from a late night party. He had been clever enough to leave Green Garden Restaurant when he realised that his legs could no longer support him instead of disgrace himself in public. There was more than enough to eat and drink from an old friend who had invited all to celebrate his victory over what he called "injustice on child-for-resident policy of Landesburg." The guy had obediently complied with his wife's demand for over three years that they lived together. She had insisted that he hand over his monthly salary to her every month end, and even gone to the Foreign Office to report that her husband married her for papers. She had had every opportunity to pick up a job but refused to work and had made straight to the Foreign Office when she got an

WOES OF IKENGA

unpleasant reply after confronting her husband with rumours that he was planning to leave her. The young man had hired a lawyer after being turned down by the Foreign Office at the anticipated time for his Resident Permit. When the overdue permit was finally granted to him six months later, he threw a party at Green Garden to celebrate his victory.

Ray laughed loud and clapped his hand in excitement all alone in the middle of the night as he staggered to his house. He cared less about what anyone who heard would make of it. All he knew was that he had received a revelation from an angel. The revelation came even as he veered off the road to throw up the excess free alcohol that had made him leave the restaurant far earlier than scheduled. With blurred sight and sense of reasoning, he firmly held a tree by the roadside and vomited. While recollecting and smiling over the plans that had come to him, Ray wobbled till he got to his house and managed to close his eyes. When he woke up in the morning, he was weak but still able to remember what had happened to him and the revelation he had gotten on the way. It was obvious that he could not accomplish the assignment alone, and so he needed to consult one or two people whom the "spirit" might have touched.

The next morning he was standing in front of Mr. Lasisi's house, the family knew him very well that even Mr. Lasisi's Swedish wife would welcome him at any time of the day without prior notice. He greeted her warmly as usual and pulled Lasisi in his sleeping gown to the balcony. Lasisi's stepdaughter who was also fond of Ray came out of her room as she heard his masculine voice and joined them in the balcony.

"Oh! Have I disturbed your sleep, Sweety?" Ray halted his discussion and asked apologetically.

"No, Uncle," she replied. "I was already awake when I heard your voice."

"Can you help Mama out with breakfast in the kitchen?" Ray asked to keep her out of the conversation. "I want to have a word with Daddy."

261

The girl did not object, but hugged both men before disappearing through the corridor.

"As I was telling you, Lasisi," Ray continued from where he stopped, "the encounter was more ferocious than that of Saul on his way to Damascus. I held on to the electric pole by the side of the road for more than an hour till my sight gradually returned. The lightning was indescribable and the three men with sparkling white garment who spoke for a while with me were the ones that directed me to you."

Lasisi stood gaping. He had never been confronted with such mysterious revelations in his life and did not know how to respond. Though a low level believer, he always treated the things of God with a great deal of carefulness.

"What did the three men instruct?" he managed to ask.

"They instructed that we open a ministry."

"A church?"

"Yes," Ray answered. "A house of God."

"The churches we have are enough already," Lasisi pointed out.

"It can't be," Ray objected. "There is more than enough work in the vineyard."

"How do the beings want me and my family to get involved?" Lasisi asked enthusiastically.

"This is not a matter of you and your family," Ray cautioned. "Leave your wife and her daughter out of this, lest they dampen your spirit to the call. It's true that these white men brought down this religion down to us, but they have missed their track."

His eloquence and good command of English made Ray an orator with appeal, besides giving his companion an opportunity to contemplate might be risky.

"Satan uses doubt to keep us away from our blessings," he preached. "Check out your past before you ran into this woman. God is about to do a new thing in your life if you can only take a step of faith."

His last words were irresistible for Lasisi who had been praying and hoping for more and a better situation. He had managed

WOES OF IKENGA

Green Garden for three years but the activities of Mascot and his band threatened to drive away all his customers. They had turned the restaurant and its surroundings to a transaction venue whenever the heat was turned on them at the train station, often drawing the attention of the police. With random harassment and "normal" police controls inside the restaurant, many of his customers, mostly foreigners, now stayed away from the hot spot. This visit by Ray on a good Sunday morning might be the answer to his prayers but one thing still worried him.

"This is not as easy as you think," he voiced.

"With God all things are possible," Ray assured.

"All things are possible but not in this country," Lasisi insisted. "You do not have a good record in their files and computers; the white man's oracle does not know you as one of its best behaved refugees as to suddenly assume a Pastor."

"We are talking of spiritual transformation," Ray corrected.

"But the country deals with reality," Lasisi maintained.

"There you are," Ray replied confidently. "They are satisfied as long as the ministry is properly registered and pays income taxes."

With the last obstacle cleared, the two sealed their conversation and joined the rest of the family at the breakfast table.

*　　*　　*　　*　　*

The dwindling number of attendants on Sunday services in Landesburg made it difficult for churches with lesser number of worshippers to maintain the monumental houses of worship built and handed over by their grandfathers. Unlike Umuafor where dues and church levies were mandatory, the German government made church taxes optional and many workers who struggled to put bread on their family tables saw no further reasons to pay into what they saw as one of the world's richest organisations.

Those were the findings of Mr. Lasisi when he set out to look for a moderate sized hall as discussed with Ray. He was the type that was bound by his words and this contributed to his hopeless situation in the past because of betrayals by trusted friends.

263

Everything seemed to be working fine this time as the church authorities had gladly allowed them make a choice from two towering churches located in the city centre, an offer which Ray described as "God's doing." The registration and the whole paper work had gone on smoothly as well. It was no problem for Ray to arrange for various degree certificates in theological studies from Oluwole. When every other obstacle and area of concern was tidied up, they were left with fixing a date and making sure that the invitation cards got as far and on time as it could.

Ikenga was busy mopping the floor and doing some other minor cleaning in the restaurant before the day's activity started. He had been delegated to doing the least job in the restaurant because of unending complaints from the customers. Mr. Lasisi had offered him employment understanding his problem from his own experience and did not want to abandon him on the streets to be an object of mockery. With the assistance of his partner, he had tried to establish a forum to support migrants of all races who found it difficult to cope with the physical and mental challenges that confronted them in their host country. The unending paper protocol from the authorities was what made his Swedish wife give up and they had resorted to assisting individuals close to them with acute symptoms like dejection, depression, over-stay and psychological derailment.

One of the funny characters that benefitted from their daily free meal was the law professor, Freeman. The learned gentleman had come over to Europe in the good old days with a scholarship from his state government, and had moved over to Germany to pursue his PhD after a Jurist degree in Cyprus. His successful career had come crumbling at the centre of his life after his second bitter divorce, with all his five children from two marriages preferring to be with their European mothers. The first three from a Greek woman were already bearing the family name of their stepfather from the last information he gathered from the embassy.

Soon after the second wife left with her two children for what she described as her husband's abnormal behaviour, the community bank also stepped in to evict him from his bungalow apartment since he could no longer afford to continue with the agreed mortgage payment.

When the well-respected gentleman was often sighted at odd places with odd individuals at odd times, always in black suit and white shirt, the handwriting on the wall became clear. To compound it, he assembled some boys on a good sunny Saturday during a local inter-communal friendly football match to declare that all his earthly worries were over and that he, henceforth wanted to be addressed as Professor Freeman. While trashing out theories to back the freedom of his being in his usual black suit, he quoted from renowned scholars, to the amusement of those who gathered round him. Words never seized flowing from his mouth as long as there were people willing to lend their ears. Mr. Lasisi and his wife had stepped in when they saw the well educated man heading towards the boundary of insanity, as he moved from one park to another, sleeping around in his only known black suit. Whatever was left of shame had vanished and a man's self-esteem had deserted him.

Ikenga's problems were not limited to geographical boundaries and racial heritage. They cut across all spectrums and careers among immigrants especially those bound by the cultural burden of taking care of their old parents or relatives back home. In developed countries where a wide range of welfare packages are in place to support individuals and families, many do not find it easy either. A public health hazard has been detected in people born into the supposed "better side of the world." Citizens were constantly diagnosed with a latter-day ailment known as burnout associated with a stressful working atmosphere, distressful family breakdown and depression. In the words of Mascot who had no pity for such people, lack of butter could still pose a danger of malnutrition in a country where bread fell from the sky. Little wonder why a healthy family man with riches at his disposal would pick up one of his expensive cars, drive up to an expensive bridge and jump to his death inside an expensive man-made lagoon.

*     *     *     *     *

Mr. Lasisi stepped into the restaurant unnoticed. Ikenga had finished what he had to do and dozed off on the long sofa that had been his bed for the last few months. He went in to inspect the kitchen and the toilets, only to find out that a marvellous job had been done that morning. He knew very well that Ikenga was never found wanting in his duties and that strengthened his belief that there might be a spiritual dimension or hands of evil men to his affliction. Almost everyone that came at the same time as Ikenga had gotten their Residence Permit, the ones that were yet to receive theirs had a family and were coping with whatever challenges that came with the venture. Ikenga had done his best like others, and even got a son from Vanessa only to be chased out of the house before his permit materialised. It was said that when misery is highest, help is nighest but the gods had somehow withheld a ripe fruit from dropping for a good man.

The sound of Afro-rhythm filtered into his ears in his slumber. It took a while before Ikenga realised that the party he was dancing to, was not taking place at Umuafor village square, but rather Mr. Lasisi's favourite music. He opened his eyes and sighed heavily in disappointment.

"Where is Madam Stella?" Mr. Lasisi inquired.

"Not here yet," Ikenga replied still rubbing his fingers over his eyes.

"She knows we are having special guests today?"

"Yes, we discussed it before she left yesterday night."

"You have done a good job this morning," Lasisi commended.

"I did it all in the night, sleep left my eyes as everybody left."

"Have you slept at all, Ikenga?"

"I tried to close my eyes before I heard your music."

"Depriving yourself of sleep is not a healthy development."

"I did not choose it that way," Ikenga replied. "It is sleep that has chosen to depart from me."

"That is not normal."

"Ah! Normalcy! In this abnormal world?" Ikenga returned.

"Nothing is normal in Landesburg."

Mr. Lasisi pulled his chair close to the sofa. It was a good opportunity to have a word with Ikenga before the cook arrived. He lowered the music as he got seated by Ikenga and began to unfold the nylon bag with which he came in. Somebody needed to take the bull by the horn and this golden opportunity might be a remedy for all.

"I would have suggested you consult your father to perform necessary sacrifices on your behalf but the saviour has given us power to redeem ourselves from any bondage or spiritual chain."

"Nobody chained me, Lasisi," Ikenga rebelled. "Why are you always raising this flimsy topic?"

"But you are not behaving normal."

"I said you should forget normalcy," Ikenga revolted bitterly. "Tell me to stop working instead of these insults."

"I don't mean to insult you," Mr. Lasisi apologised. "We both know how you started working here. You also know the circumstances why I stopped you from serving the customers?"

Both men bowed their heads in silence. Mr. Lasisi was selecting the invitation cards and putting some into red coloured envelopes for special guests of honour. Ikenga who had had this kind of confrontation a number of times tried to recognise abnormalities in his behaviour. Apart from habitual gossip, people had told him jokingly that he was about to cross the psycho boundary.

"I am the one to tell you," Mr. Lasisi continued. "I was already eleven years in this country when you entered. He who has experience can milk a running cow."

"But nothing seems to be moving," Ikenga replied hopelessly.

"Throw not your nets away if you catch nothing," Mr. Lasisi warned. "You never know what the gods are planning next. This is the time to set our eyes on the ground and search for that which has fallen inside the water. If only you can surrender yourself with humility, the Almighty has the power to make a way where there is none. The cries of His people has made Him send the Moses of our time to lead us out of the bondage of Pharaoh."

With those last words, Mr. Lasisi handed a folded invitation card to Ikenga just as Madam Stella walked in through the entrance dragging a big Ghana-must-go bag with a bunch of fresh pumpkin leaves under her armpit.

"How could you, woman?" Mr. Lasisi bellowed as he rushed to help. "You also want to send our remaining customers away?"

"No! Not me," the surprised cook replied.

"Your golden armpits can reduce the nutritional value of the vegetable."

"Sorry, Sir."

"Sorry for yourself," Mr. Lasisi threw back. "Over-stay is also having its effect on you."

"Everybody is affected one way or the other," Madam Stella replied nonchallantly.

Mr. Lasisi carried the big bag into the kitchen without any further arguments. That Madam Stella, his long-time cook, was said to have abandoned her husband in Italy in search of a perfect man might not be far from the truth. The impact of the adventures across the Atlantic might be difficult to assess among adventurers, and those who made the journey and still lived to tell it admit that one or more of the software components in their cerebral hemisphere had been adversely affected.

Ikenga sat motionless listening to the faint voice of the two and the noise of pans and pots in the kitchen. He withdrew into the four-metre square room known as the VIP section and reluctantly unfolded the thick paper that Lasisi had just given him.

**Inauguration! Inauguration! Inauguration!**

Sankt Antonius Kirche          PLEASE JOIN US

29th August 1997               TO CELEBRATE
Service starts 10:00am.        THE GRAND OPENING
                               CEREMONY;

## RAY POWER MIRACLE FOUNTAIN

"And He hath brought us into this place, and hath given us this land, even a land that floweth with milk and honey."
… ..Deuteronomy 26:9

–Come and receive your instant breakthrough–

RSVP:

Mr. Lasisi Ubochi  Senior Pastor & Overseer:

Mr. Ayo Delenso  Apostle Raymond Ubanese

**Contact: + 49(0) 102273480 Mail- info@fountain.ray**

Ikenga who had lost appetite for laughter smiled to himself. People had not only soiled their individual names but also dared to involve the name of Chukwu, the Great Being, in their quest for material wealth. Ray, who he knew very well, was about to become the latest "man of god" like countless others who had been exploiting the business opportunity in a world where demand for all sorts of breakthrough was on the increase. His unofficial title as *"aduro* of no nation" was indeed about to be anointed and officially transformed to "holy man of no nation."

# Chapter 14

Deep in the interior jungle of Umuafor where folks lived as nature dictated, strange men had suddenly come from faraway lands with lots of enticing packages and hidden interests. They had asserted dominance over the defenceless folks and cut deep into that which held them together. Their virgin culture and ways of life became uprooted as their able-bodied men and women were taken to unknown lands to work in plantations. This sequence and fast moving events were witnessed simultaneously across different countries in Africa, and Umuafor and its neighbours bore a great deal of such human atrocity. The period was regarded as the dark ages and nations at the forefront of such man's inhumanity to man also brought their revised version of religion and method of worship. However, the unwelcome coming of these strange men was not totally a disaster as the enticing packages that they had brought along contained in them their system of government, modern education, science as well as their religion. Freedom and human rights, which later surfaced, were eventually used to evict the strangers who hurriedly left, leaving their broken tentacles and vestiges behind.

Among these foreign cultures and systems of life that invaded Umuafor and its twelve clans, religion was the only one that stood out in the lives of the people. Umuafor and its existence were fundamentally centred on religion and their strong belief in the Great Being but not only did they ignorantly abandon the religious practices of their forefathers, they also gladly embraced the foreign religion and excelled so well that they now had to export the practices back to the white men who were now seen as lagging behind. The explosion of religious norms and practices and everincreasing number of houses of worship, however, did not stamp out evil but rather propagated desperation and a steady increase of immoral atrocities among the rank and file of the society. A misfortune like financial hardship or an undiagnosed ailment was taken to an altar of worship as they were always blamed on evil spirits and their human agents.

The different religious theories in the world prove without doubt the existence of a Supreme Being that is the creator of all things. All creation stories started way before man, with nothing and He. Suddenly, mankind would enter the scene at a stage, and the original story would begin veering into different directions as a result of His wishes or man's error. Different ancestral and religious organisations have unique accounts of their existence in relation to the Great Being. Umuafor's version has it that the Great Being did not only create *Ani*–the Mother Earth–and many other gods, but also created for every human being a personal god (*chi*) to accompany one while navigating through life. One and his *chi* would also be arraigned before His presence for judgment as soon as death struck; where all the good and the evil things that one did during his or her earthly journey would also be called up as witnesses.

These stories were vivid in the mind of Ikenga when he was much younger; the scary sacrifices of different types and different intentions regularly placed at the marketplaces or four-cornered roads, the ever visible individual and ancestral shrines dotted around Umuafor, and the ancient magnificent sacred trees with the unique stories and powers they possessed. Myth has it that the early ancestors of Umuafor, in their quest to deal with death and its own mysteries, sent out two emissaries to the Creator with different requests. The dog was assigned to request that humans be sent back to life after death, while the slow moving chameleon was asked to tell Chukwu that death should be the end to physical life, and that humans should be held down in the land of the spirits when their life on earth was over. Because of its natural promiscuous tendencies, the dog made occasional stopovers wherever it saw species of its kind, but the slow and steady moving chameleon maintained its pace and became the first to deliver its message to Chukwu. Death was therefore upheld as the barrier between the living and the spirit world.

The religious practices of Umuafor were gradually swept under the carpet as the new version from Reverend Klaus gained momentum, and the sacred orders and powers that Chukwu bestowed on *Ani* and the other gods were then hijacked and abused by men devoid of scruples; oblivious to or contemptuous of what was right or honourable. The unexplained scientific endeavours which Udeaja and his forefathers enjoyed in their time soon disappeared or became mere folktales. Popularly referred to as half-man half-spirit, Udeaja had been widely believed to have travelled far and wide to distant lands through the sky in the form of a fireball. *Igu-mmili*, an oval-shaped water stone had been buried with him since nobody in the family was willing to take over the practice. He had used it to communicate with the Sky god to bring down rain whenever the land or the crops were thirsty.

Chinua, the greatest wine-tapper and a renowned hunter, never ran out of bush meat due to his magical powers that lured animals to his traps. His father, Nnamezue, when he was alive had been endowed with supernatural powers of hypnotism and would send the wildest man or beast to slumber by a simple touch of the hand or focused eye-to-eye contact. There were tales of many other noble men who had exhibited supernatural powers and Umuafor names like *Ikuku,* or *Agwo n'atu mbe* bore evidence to it. Most of these supernatural powers had sadly died out because of inadequate documentation and superstitions surrounding the transfer of such sacred knowledge. Few of these sacred practices, which survived the lengthy period of conversion, had been corrupted and interwoven with modern day religious practices to suit the popular demand of the people.

Ikenga had attended a number of local houses of worship in his early years in Landesburg but decided to confront the language barrier at that early stage. His intentions had been to make out a favourable environment for himself, from where his *chi* would be at peace while interceding on his behalf; after all, Chukwu is one and all worship belongs to Him. The hunt for material wealth and overemphasis on tithes and sowing of seed in some of the jet-age churches he attended had not gone well with his *chi* and his understanding of the Supreme Being. Though he sometimes

## WOES OF IKENGA

sounded extreme in his views about religion, he abhorred fanaticism notwithstanding. He admired men of every colour and respected everyone's faith, whether Buddhism, Christianity, Rastafarianism, Paganism or Hinduism. It was display of ignorance and mediocrity for an Umuafor man to claim that his religion was the only channel through which humans could get to the Creator or propagate violence in the course of spreading his own version of events. It was equally a sign of naiveté and deficiency when another group with a different account claimed superiority or initiated aggression in the name of religion. He was tired of the world's religions with their different interpretations and had decided to create a direct link to Chukwu for himself. Then, his load had seemed heavier than he could bear, hence the lingering perception that God had forsaken him–a move that contributed to the abnormalities in his behaviour to the eyes of the ungodly.

Even in his secluded one room in Robbin Street, he was constantly pestered by different sets of modern day missionaries who demonised others, claiming that their religion was the only solution. To the two Americans from an evangelical Christian group who had formed the habit of coming around every second day, Ikenga had blatantly declared that his problem was more financial than spiritual.

The men in their early twenties had been born into the religion and diligently carried out their spiritual duties. They had warmly and genuinely offered to help repaint his tiny room, which was in a very bad state, if he would buy a bucket of paint. Ikenga, who was in a very bad state whether financially, physically or mentally appreciated their kind gestures but would not buy their views, which originated from their own version of religion. Those from the witnesses of Jehovah had stopped visiting like a number of other groups that had also tried in vain. Gradually getting tired of their visits and wanting to put a stop to it, he picked his cell phone at the first ring and told the young missionaries that he was not at home, but the guys knew very well that he exhibited no more liking for the free society and hardly went out of his house. They knocked on his door an hour later, and Ikenga opened the door thinking it was Alfa, his friend from Zaire who had gone out to buy some bottles of beer.

"I told you people that I am not at home," he yelled at the duo.

The main entrance to the uninhabitable building was long broken and neither the owner nor the dejected tenants cared much. Instead of reacting, they walked into Ikenga's room with a ten-litre can of white paint hoping to surprise him.

"Sorry, Mr. Ikenga," one answered gently. "We don't intend to stay long."

"But I am not at home," Ikenga shouted.

"We are very sorry."

"You should have known by now that my problem is more financial than spiritual."

"Our material problems are all illusions," one preached. "We should seek first His kingdom."

"Eeh! That one is your own version," Ikenga returned. "My people say that no one sings 'alleluia' on an empty stomach."

"Then keep this bucket of paint," the other one asked. "We will come back when you are at home to do the painting."

"How did you get the money to buy that?" he questioned as they turned to leave.

"It's not that expensive," they chorused. "We get weekly pocket money from our superior."

Their simple act of charity was enough for Ikenga to give a thumbs-up to whatever group they belonged. His funny encounter with the Senior Pastor of Towin Tabernacle Ministry had been something else. The expensively dressed "man of god" had singled him out halfway into a heated prosperity prayer session and prophesied that he was defaulting in his tithes, and further proclaimed that the miracles which he had long waited for was just by the corner, and the only way to claim such God's unmerited favour was to sow a seed of faith. With those words, many had rushed out from the congregation to drop whatever amount they had at the feet of the Pastor, believing that they would attract

WOES OF IKENGA

favour from Ikenga's impending breakthrough. Yet, the words of the Pastor had made no meaning to Ikenga who was at the time surviving from hand-to-mouth and the lazy fat birds and rabbits he snatched from the Central Park. He was gradually beginning to question if he was the one going crazy or the free society.

Chukwu is an eternal being that surpasses all incredible descriptions, and a perfect being without mistakes who creates and controls everything. His nature is entirely beyond human comprehension. These features of His are commonly believed among almost all the world religions. It was this incredibility that led Umuafor to believe that the sun was one of His eyes. They also did believe that He lived on high while His garment glided through the earth surface, that His ways were not the ways of man, and his deeds solely at His own will. The expectation of an instant miracle or favour implied that Chukwu had some physical form or nature that could be understood by men. This widespread modern day form of worship was used by unworthy humans and the titled "men of god" who had hijacked religion to imprison the afflicted. It had eroded in their minds that Chukwu dishes out His favour at will just as He does by sending the rain and the sun to both good and the bad. It was in one of the worship services at Towin Tabernacle entitled "Instant Miracle" that Madam Stella persuaded him to attend when his condition worsened that the drama had evolved.

\*　\*　\*　\*　\*

Alfa, his friend from Kinshasa, who stammered when he spoke, returned with the bottles of beer while Ikenga was still standing at the door with the young missionaries. The thought of sharing the few bottles of beer with more people infuriated him when he saw the duo. He had completely lost out in the Mario adventure and resorted to drinking away his sorrows, and shuttling from his *aduro* camp to the ghetto-like apartment blocks at Robbin Street. The authorities had issued him a temporary United Nation's passport after a long asylum protocol when it was proven that his stories of imprisonment and torture in the hands of the late dictator and his

275

secret agents in DRC were true. But the psychological trauma he had gone through for twenty-two years in the country had taken hold of all or parts of his brain.

"Who are these small boys?" he stammered.

"They are my friends," Ikenga calmed him.

"We are missionaries from America," one tried to explain.

"A hungry man will have problems digesting the words of a preacher," Alfa remarked.

"Your bottles of beer are not the solution either," the evangelist corrected.

"The Holy Book clearly recommends that for people like me."

"On the contrary," the other interjected. "Our saviour came to take over your burden."

"If you say so," Alfa shrugged as he opened the first bottle with his teeth.

"My name is Elder Gardner and this is Elder Benny."

"My name is Sisse. Alfa Sisse."

"Are you also from Umuafor?"

"I came from Kinshasa."

"Can we also come around to share the word with you?"

"I am always available if you can pay for my time."

Alfa became more at peace when he realised that the duo were missionaries and were not there to share his few bottles of beer. His resources had also gotten to its limit and he depended on his friend most times to devise other means of survival.

Ikenga took a step backwards and allowed the three in but the missionaries refused to sit down as they felt that their host was not happy with their unapproved visit. It would also be hard to welcome the spirit when their listeners had their minds set on the beer bottles. They said a short prayer and left.

*     *     *     *     *

Ikenga's failure to attend the inauguration ceremony of Ray Power Miracle Fountain and his absence in their subsequent prayer meetings was enough to make Lasisi stop him from working at the Green Garden. Many concluded that he was possessed of a powerful evil spirit while the fools simply regarded him as someone who did not want to help himself. Lasisi who swallowed raw whatever fell out of Ray's mouth believed that a spiritual solution might be the remedy for Ikenga's problem and decided to wash his hands off the issue after Ikenga repeatedly turned down his pleas to come to the newly established church for deliverance. Ray was also not happy with Ikenga, not because he had any instant miraculous solution for his deteriorating psychological and financial problem but because his presence was needed to boost the number of attendants. It was not long before he devised another way to exploit the situation and display the needed miraculous powers that his sceptics were anxiously anticipating. Uncle Ray set off to Robbin Street after Friday prayer meeting. It became common knowledge that Ikenga lived on Robbin Street after his arrest at the Central Park. He had happily moved back there again when he was told that his assignment with Green Garden was over, and was relieved to be on his own again or with Alfa, a friend who best understood him.

Ray the latest "Man of God" went straight to the house number that Mascot had given him but there were no names on the door and not even a bell to ring. The filthy few hundred-metre close could be best described as a ghost avenue with paintings and drawing on the walls that reminded one of horror movies, and its occupants who were either coming in or going out from their respective quarters seemed as disgustingly dirty as the buildings.

He perched by the door, clutching his holy book and waiting for somebody to come out of the building as he was determined to talk to Ikenga and see if he could arrange a showdown for the powerful convention planned for the coming Sunday. Ray was indeed a courageous gentleman who had never lost focus of what brought him over to Germany. Many of his associates had fallen but determination had kept him moving even if he had to be the last man standing. The decision to cash in on the booming church business was not his best choice but all other alternative means of survival had either been blocked completely or met with long prison sentences. To worsen matters, politicians and lawmakers now used the activities of minority rights to attribute all kinds of survival mechanism to terrorism. A local dealer at the City Station was likely to face condemnation for aiding terrorism or serve a longer sentence because drug money, directly or indirectly helped procure weapons for extremist groups. Analysts had also directly linked passport forgery and document scams, which he specialised in, to terrorist groups.

The church game seemed to be the only available and safe means of obtaining money. Mr. Raymond Ubanese constantly nursed great fear in his private moments because of his long running religious background; afraid of the wrath of Chukwu that was sure to visit those who toyed with His name, or the deathly traps of *Ekwensu,* the tempting god. Silently, he beckoned his *chi* to be on guard believing in the mercifulness of Chukwu and his sure repentance once he had made enough money in the game.

He had barely finished the short prayer and a fast sign of the cross when Ikenga and Alfa appeared from the corner chatting and laughing aloud. His close association with the ex-rebel fighter from Kinshasa had turned Ikenga into a lunatic and they moved round shopping centres and supermarkets every evening collecting leftovers. Alfa was clutching two bottles of Vodka, the Russian whisky bought with money realised from selling the bucket of paint that had fallen from heaven while his friend was swinging a nylon bag containing cigarette stumps which they had gathered from ashtray stands outside shopping malls and drinking bars. The two-litre alcohol with its forty-percent concentration was sure to keep them lively and talking till morning before they retired and slept for the whole day. The two walked to Ray before Ikenga could recognise him.

"Hello, Uncle," he greeted.

"Hello, brothers," Ray replied.

"What brought you here at this time of the day?" Ikenga asked.

"I came with some good news."

"You know I don't want to be part of your good news."

"This is something else, Brother, and you will get some money out of it if you agree to the tune," Ray assured.

"Then let's break the proverbial coconut."

"Who is this friend of yours by the way?" Ray asked in their native language.

"My good friend, Alfa," Ikenga replied patting his friend on the back to assure Ray that his presence was not a problem.

"It is good that you did not start with us when the church was opened," Ray explained. "A good opportunity has surfaced for you to show up and grab your own cool cash."

"People have said enough about me and I don't want to give them room for more gossip."

"Be wise, Brother!" Ray corrected. "People can gossip, as they want as long as your money is flowing in. This is not something I want to do for a long time. You know I have a family at home."

"How is the money going to come my way?" Ikenga asked casually.

"Listen!" Ray pulled him closer. "We are holding a convention and deliverance service on Sunday, all you need to do is stage a good show with me and I will pay you Fifty Deutsche Mark for every hour you spend on the stage."

"That is to confirm rumours that an evil spirit from Umuafor is holding me down, right?" Ikenga asked.

"Far from it, dear brother," Ray lectured as usual. "Your problems culminated out of long years of stay in this country with nothing to show for it. That is everybody's problem as well but you have managed your own badly. The inherited burden, which drove us out of our fatherland, is still hanging over our necks, and our hopes have been confronted with disappointments and the uncompromising foreign systems. We all came to this place with the interest of our respective families at heart and the inherited cultural burden is going to live and die with us whether we have the means to deal with the situation or not, but money will go a long way in solving our individual problems," he concluded.

"Count me in, Pastor," Alfa said with a raised finger. "Fifty

Deutsche Marks for an hour is not bad."

"Both of you will benefit if your friend understands what I mean," Ray said to Ikenga.

"I understand very well, Pastor," Alfa pointed out. "You chase evil spirit from the altar, I manifest from the crowd."

"Exactly!" Ray agreed. "It must be a very serious and frightening display of an evil spirit."

"The fifty will be for the manifestation," Alfa negotiated. "Another Fifty Deutsche Mark if I have to fall down."

There was a brief laughter from the three but Uncle Ray who knew that his mission was not a laughing matter continued immediately. "Money will not be a problem as long as you both play your parts well."

"Count me out, Uncle," Ikenga replied angrily. "The land of Umuafor will not permit me to be a part of this dirty game."

"Umuafor has not sent us here to look at tall buildings and tarred roads either," Ray reminded him.

"He that runs faster than his *chi* will definitely retire before his *chi*."

"What you tried at the train station is also not a clean game."

"Yours is making money with the name of God," Ikenga reproached.

"Which is better?" Ray asked gently. "Making money with God's name or with the name of Satan?"

Alfa watched with dismay as his friend rejected the lucrative offer; all efforts to make Ikenga see reason fell on deaf ears. He even mustered the guts to walk out on them when he could no longer condone their preaching and suggestions that he had lost his sense of reasoning. Pastor Raymond had not expected a total rejection from Ikenga. This meant that his reputation as a selfacclaimed miracle worker was in jeopardy if Ikenga opened his mouth to tell anyone what had transpired that evening. Something had to be done to stop him or the promising ministry, which was barely six months old, could be heading to a closure. He stood face down with Alfa contemplating his next step, knowing that any wrong moves could be potentially catastrophic on his side. It was Alfa with his shallow understanding of the magnitude of their discussion that broke the silence.

"I am with you, Pastor," he said to Uncle Ray. "This brother of yours is mad."

Alfa, who was not far from a madman, would do everything possible to keep up his alcohol addiction. He had been apprehended a number of times for shoplifting with a range of pending court cases. People like him did their best in maintaining employment level for law enforcement agencies in law-abiding countries where the crime rate constantly fell below average. At one point he had put up a spectacular show with the authorities when he had occupied the complete coach of a regional train with his beddings claiming the right of a roof over his head. The drama, which propelled the authorities to consider his asylum application, had later landed him in a psychiatric hospital after he was dispossessed of his kitchen knife and empty beer bottles.

Deep into his world of thoughts and wisdom, Ray could not have heard what was said to him. It was a group of street dwellers coming down their direction that had distracted his concentration. Knowing that his presence in that kind of environment could be interpreted differently by different minds, he quickly collected Alfa's mobile number promising to call him the next day.

# Chapter 15

Landesburg is a city known for her ingenuity as well as hardworking citizens in all areas of industrial activity. The overworked population had limited time for themselves and many gave up marriages or any form of social life due to the rigid life pattern, and the sizeable number of its residents that reluctantly entered into marriage did so to reduce the tax burden imposed on singles.

The authorities were quick to react when statistics revealed a steady decline in birth rate. The aliens, otherwise known officially as political and economic migrants, were presented with an offer that circumstances made irresistible. Hence the rampant bearing of children with citizens in exchange for the so-called "Resident Permit" that eventually became a dissolute platform for unhealthy families and ultimately an unhealthy society.

These global stage actors who were eager to step out of their sticky situation became even more desperate. They had literally been made pranksters with a blank cheque to immorality, and so moved around with their out-of-control magic stick generating both wanted and unwanted pregnancies. It rained babies for some years in Landesburg as street girls and drug users soon became pregnant for a different man just after being delivered of another's child. There were also some women who pre-planned keeping the children to themselves and would move to kick out the fathers of their children when it was time for the signing of a joint custody agreement over the child. Since the law had made no provisions to protect fathers in such incidences or indeed in family decisions of moral sensitivity, the defeated alien ended up faced with no other option than search for another woman to bear him another bastard.

Umuafor had her share of abandoned children in various countries of the world where residential permits were openly traded for boosting the dwindling population or maintaining the workforce, and these broods who unfortunately may never have the opportunity to visit their fatherland lived the only life they

WOES OF IKENGA

knew in the countries where their fathers had abandoned them. Such abandonment in the case of Umuafor men was unprecedented because of the strong bond that held her people and families together. Overpowering circumstances, however, had made many men to pull off their heads when the centre could no longer hold.

Pastor Raymond Ubanese of Ray Power Miracle Fountain had profited immensely from the quest for a baby by most of his alien followers. The captivating power with which he preached love and procreation touched the hearts of the many young women who regularly attended his church. In these modern days when there is a raging battle for religious dominance, people like Ray delighted in laying claims to knowledge that they did not possess. He would meticulously paint a picture of the things of heaven with resounding assurance, like one who had just descended from an assemblage of the gods, and if one listened further, he would vividly be heard describing the geography of heavenly bodies and the centigrade at which hell's fire burnt.

The ministry upheld family as a divine institution and admonished young people to toe the path of procreation. Baby-seeking immigrants, who wasted no time in getting them pregnant, quickly chanced the women of Landesburg who had been drawn to the church house by the ministry's vibrant way of worship. Older ladies who had gone through several divorce protocols also came around hoping to catch a foreigner.

Pastor Ray would randomly prophesy seeing a baby boy or a baby girl and those who wanted those prophecies to be their portion claimed it with pledges of money or other material gifts. Uncountable bags of seed from desperate men and women hoping for a partner continually flowed to Pastor Ray's barn while elaborate thanksgivings were also celebrated in style whenever a child was born to any of the members.

People tried whatever they could to scale through the tricky hurdles of the laws of Landesburg in order to be eligible for Resident Permit. Voodoo and talismans of different forms and shapes were parcelled to those who had faith in them, and these baby hunters sometimes shared funny stories of women who had taken all necessary measures to avoid pregnancy, as they bragged that their herbal concoctions had neutralised the powers of the white man's contraceptive medications.

One of the intriguing characters of the time was an elderly vagabond named Eze, who was already very close to pension age. The sojourner left his hometown at the prime of his youth and spent a long transit period in a number of countries in pursuit of vanity. For years, he had stopped any form of communication with his relatives when he feared that someone down there was remotely controlling his destiny. Determined to lay hands on *kpalli* before paying a visit to his fatherland, the "child-for-residency" policy of Landesburg pulled him over from Poland where he had been struggling in vain for years.

Eze had given his best to win the heart of any woman that might bear him a child or accept a wedding ring, but his uninviting face scared off even the drunken partygoers and free-willed girls of Landesburg. He had gone into hiding after a narrow escape when the immigration agents turned their radars on him; on his way back to his apartment early one morning from a fruitless night outing, he noticed a strange car parked in front of the refugee camp. The parking lights and the heavily tinted windows had not allowed him see clearly but Eze was not prepared to take chances. Calmly, he had changed lanes to the other side of the street and dialed his roommate.

"They are looking for you," came the confirmatory reply after the first ring.

"How do they know I live with you?"

"These people are spirits," his friend returned. "Have I not told you to stop using a cell phone?"

"I saw a strange car downstairs," Eze silently said.

"Where are you?"

"I am just coming back."

"Better go back!" the voice advised. "Four of them are still

WOES OF IKENGA

combing the whole floor."

"Can you bring me down some money?"

"I am risking my own freedom taking your calls."

"Take care," Eze said and switched of the cell phone.

His nature would never permit him to indulge in any criminal activity, and he had all along believed that his good works would one day be rewarded. From his hiding location, he finally secured work in a family farmhouse around the neighbourhood. Thanks to his past nomadic lifestyle, the farm owner was quick to identify that his new employee possessed a rare expertise in animal farming, and confidently left Eze alone in the farmhouse whenever he had to distribute milk and homemade cheese to his customers.

His fourteen-year-old daughter was particularly fascinated by how Eze handled and communicated with the cows and horses. As her admiration grew, Eze began to visualise the *kpalli* that he had struggled over the years for, waiting for him in the farm. Catherina, the farmer's daughter, probably due to rapid growth and good nutrition looked fully mature at fourteen, and made all efforts to be accepted into the women folk, while refusing to allow anyone belittle her.

"You are still a small girl," Eze insisted as the two argued endlessly in the farm.

"If you don't stop that," she threatened, "I will stop coming to help you."

"We had better change the topic then," Eze suggested.

"Better."

"Why are you no longer interested in school?"

"Get another topic."

"Not before you answer my question."

"I hate school," Catherina opened up. "Miss Gonzales says that I am not intelligent."

"Who is Miss Gonzales?"

"My class teacher."

"Do you believe her?" Eze asked.

"She will not see me again in her class."

"Are your parents making arrangements to take you to another school?"

"They do not know that I stopped."

"Where do you go every morning when you leave for school?"

"To a friend's house."

Eze, instead of disclosing this sensitive information to his employee decided to exploit what he saw as an opportunity. From promising to teach the young Catherina all she needed to know about animal farming in preparation for eventual takeover from her parents, he soon began to take premeditated sick leaves to consummate her supposed school hours with her in his hideout. He would have pulled her from her parent's custody but that was not possible in the small ghetto-like room with no single piece of furniture.

Because of her rather large-for-her-age body, her parents did not recognise what was happening until it was too late. Her father insisted on terminating the six-month old pregnancy but his daughter had declined to either accompany him to the family doctor or name the man responsible for her pregnancy. She excitedly looked forward to having a "chocolate baby" for a black man with the skills and physical strength she saw in Eze. It had never occurred to the employer that the harmless-looking employee could be responsible till the baby was almost due. Since Catherina had not given up any clues, his leads and enquiries indicated that whoever got her daughter pregnant was part of the household. He clearly recalled that his daughter's sudden interest in the farm had begun shortly after Eze's employment. With no concrete evidence, the infuriated farm owner who would not leave any stone unturned went directly to the farm to confront his employee.

"You have overstepped your bounds," he barked.

"Is anything the matter, *Chef?*" the startled Eze asked as he turned to face his boss. It was a fight he was ready to finish, but he had to remain calm till the baby was born.

"What did you tell my daughter to lure her to bed?"

"There must be a misunderstanding somewhere," Eze returned sharply, as Catherina had assured him that she would never give him up.

"Are you telling me that you don't know of her pregnancy?"

"Is Catherina pregnant?"

"Yes, she is," the father replied. "And she could not have impregnated herself."

"Those little school mates of hers are capable of anything," Eze suggested. "I have seen them a number of times smoking *ganja*."

"My interrogations with her circle of friends pointed to a different direction," Catherina's father objected.

"Did it point to the angels?" Eze asked.

"Rule the angels out."

"Her school teachers?"

"No."

"Who could be responsible for the pregnancy then?"

"I am suspicious of her sudden devotion to the farm."

"Could a horse or any of those male cows be responsible then?"

"That, you can explain better," his employer told him. "You both keep long hours in the ranch."

"I took it to be part of her education."

"Have you turned from my employee to my daughter's educator?"

"No, *Chef*."

They stared at each other for a while, but the man who could read guilt written all over the stony face of his employee, only refrained from a violent attack because of his inward fear of black men. Although boiling with rage, the white farm owner felt defeated and stretched to point a finger towards Eze in his unmasked bitterness before turning to slowly walk away. His faith in the law kept him from collapsing and he wished that Catherina would agree to accompany him to the police station.

Eze did not wait for the man to reappear with a gun before

abandoning everything and taking off as soon as his boss went out of sight, because he had to stay alive by the time the Resident Permit would materialise. Through the carrot field, he ran towards the motorway and disappeared into the row of residential blocks.

Catherina poured out the whole truth when her father almost strangled her but refused to be dragged to the police station. By the time the police were finally invited, Eze was nowhere in sight to tell his own version of events. Until the man who impregnated the underage schoolgirl was found, the farm owner remained charged with the offence of employing an undocumented worker. As he was unable to produce a work permit or any form of identification of his employee, he also had no idea where Eze lived or any other information that could enable the police to carry out an arrest.

"That monkey made my daughter pregnant," he shouted as the police made his crime clear to him.

"What is his name?"

"Eze."

"Any copy of his passport or work permit?"

"He gave me none."

"Because you made no request?"

"I did, but he had none."

"And you offered him a job?"

"It was he who offered to help out in the farm."

"That is exploitation," the policeman explained. "The Office of Finance is surely interested in the taxes you avoided over the years."

"The man has not worked with me for up to a year."

"You can tell that to the court."

Father and daughter watched as the officer completed the paper protocol and handed out a sheet.

"You can keep that for yourself," the farm owner said, angrily rejecting the white sheet of paper. "I called the police for a rape case."

"The job would have been easier if your daughter would take us to his house."

"Why label me a criminal when I have only called you to a crime scene?"

"This is Landesburg," the police officer told him.

"The hands of the law will surely get the culprit when his identity is established, but you have also offended the law."

That was the case in Germany where citizens had no leverage when it came to the law and the no-nonsense law enforcement agents adhered strictly to their code of principles for the general good. Reluctantly, the defeated farm owner collected the white sheet of paper from the officer and slumped into the wooden bank. He was definitely going to pay a heavy fine if the court spared him from spending some years behind bars.

"You will receive a letter from the court," the officer added.

Eze had simply ended his working contract since no one had seen or heard from him, and the police went about other businesses since it was not in their powers to force Catherina to make confessions. They had actually emboldened the young girl when they warned her father in her presence about the implications of raising a finger on children, and her subsequent threats to run away from home had brought about a sudden change of heart from her father who did not want to lose sight of his only daughter. With his wife's support, the farm owner overcame the heartbreak and made necessary preparations for his grandchild.

The baby boy finally came three weeks earlier than scheduled through a cesarean section with minor complications. The grandparents were relieved that their daughter had made it and were truly overjoyed to have a grandson. The new baby brought a new life in the family, and even Catherina appeared to have developed some sense of responsibility and acted maturely with regards to taking care of herself and the little baby. Her father had sincerely forgiven her and did all he could to encourage her to go back to school when the baby would be old enough to be left with his grandmother. He believed that Eze was gone for good and was ready to help his daughter get back on her feet once again.

Catherina's father came back from his daily delivery one afternoon to discover an unexpected quietness in his house. Neither the music that usually noised day and night from his daughter's room, nor the cackle of baby toys were heard. His wife who had been busy at the ranch, a stone's throw from the family house, could not explain the whereabouts of the mother and child.

"Should we inform the police?" she suggested.

"But it is too early."

"This is abnormal," his wife persisted. "She does not go anywhere without informing me."

"For how long has she been away?" her husband asked.

"How would I know?" the wife questioned in return. "I went over to the farm as soon as you left."

The man turned away from his very emotional wife who dropped everything she was doing and followed her husband. They took a longer footpath to search the farm and nearby woods to make sure that their daughter had not gone for a walk with the baby. After combing the whole area and finding no sign of their daughter, the farmer became convinced about informing the police.

Meanwhile, Catherina who still maintained secret contact with Eze had arranged to meet him at the office of the child welfare to sign for joint custody of his son as they planned on securing an apartment and moving in together when he finally got full permission to stay in Landesburg. She had patiently played good girl before her parents, waiting for the day when the man she had fallen in love with would come out from hiding. Together with their baby, they went into room 29, when the number on their waiting tag was displayed on the electronic board. With assurances from Catherina to stand by him every inch of the way, Eze was prepared for this last encounter that would transform his status from a wanted man to a rightful citizen, with rights of employment and free movement. To his friends who knew what he was going through, he had given a hint of the day's plan to enable them know where to start searching from in case he failed to show up again afterwards.

The lady inside the office was wearing a pair of tiny spectacles that made her look very attractive. Her tender voice and kind hospitality was quite unlike those who Eze believed were usually specially selected for such positions of dealing with foreigners.

"Sit down please," she offered.

"Thanks," they replied jointly.

"What can I do for you?"

"My husband wants to sign the *Vaterschaft*," Catherina replied.

"Congratulations," the lady said with a warm smile. "How old is the baby?"

"Just two months old."

"Let me have your marriage certificates, the birth certificate of the child and your passports."

"We are not married yet," Catherina corrected.

"Then your passports please."

Eze handed over the passport that he had smuggled in from his country in preparation for this day. The date of birth in the passport had intentionally been reduced by half but still doubled Catherina's age. The lady collected the passports and bent over the monitor to enter the data. Their age difference was none of her business but the name, Eze Okoronta, from the red signal emitted by the oracle in front of her was a wanted man. As if that was not enough, Catherina's date of birth if what she read in her passport was correct deemed her a minor who was incapable of making her own decisions.

"Are you Catherina Müller?" she asked with a steady gaze.

"Yes," Catherina answered in her best composure.

"Your date of birth is … ?"

"26th of August, 1985."

The lady then realised that the huge figure she had taken for a grown-up was actually an underage schoolgirl with no knowledge about the implications of her decisions or actions. Initially, she had mistaken the minor's massive body size as maturity, and that may have also deceived the father of her baby. The officer turned to size up Eze. She read neither old age nor any sense of guilt on his face but could only see a desperate foreigner eager to live a normal life. Whatever the case may be, the laws of Landesburg had to take their course.

Unknown to Eze and Catherina, she had stepped on an automated alert signal that was concealed on the floor under her office table. The newly fitted security gadget was meant to send a signal to the police whenever migrants with their individual issues decided to transfer their anger on any of the defenceless office staff. Further questions and conversations with them were meant to buy time and keep Eze calm and full of hopes till the law custodian of Landesburg would arrive.

"You are still underage," she said to Catherina.

"But old enough to know what I want," Catherina replied.

"Are you sure you want the baby?"

"Yes."

"What class are you?"

"Tenth class."

"Should we seek your parents' consent?"

"That is not necessary."

"What do you think?" she turned to Eze.

"They hate foreigners."

"Could her age have a role to play in that?"

"I don't know."

Desperation for the right to settle in Landesburg was neither justification for criminal offences nor an excuse for any form of exploitation of underage children. The lady was convinced that Eze knew exactly what he was doing.

Before she could come up with the next question, the office door suddenly flew open with a single knock to usher in some plain-clothed detectives who in a commando-style operation, grabbed Eze without any questions and effortlessly chained his two hands behind. The action had been too fast to elicit any reaction from Eze. The police called to take out any foreigner from the particular office that had sent the signal. Whatever the matter was, it could be resolved at the station just behind the office block.

"Allow me collect the Resident Permit before sending me to prison," Eze shouted over and over again.

"You won't need it in Balthazar," one of the men answered before they whisked him away.

Catherina was short of words but recovered some minutes after the men left and coiled out from where she had taken cover by the side of a big flowerpot. It was difficult for her to comprehend that Eze's offence that warranted such a terrifying arrest was just having a baby with her. Tears dropped down her face as she gaped at the office girl. She was sure that such cruelty could not have been initiated by the friendly office worker and believed that the police must have overheard her telephone conversations with Eze and laid ambush for him at the children's welfare office.

"Where are they taking him to?" she asked.

"Prison."

"Why?"

"He is a wanted man."

"What has he done?"

"He is wanted for immigration problems," the girl replied. "Plus having an affair with a minor."

"He did not rape me," Catherina testified truthfully.

"But he committed a crime."

"That was with my consent."

"The law says below eighteen."

With that element of guilt that she had played a part in Eze's arrest, Catherina wept uncontrollably for the father of her child as the office girl tried to console her.

"Take me to the prison," she cried. "I belong to him."

"No," the office worker corrected. "You don't belong to any man."

Catherina refused to listen or stop crying but frantically cuddled her baby as she pushed open the office door and displayed awful scenes through the long corridors of the extensive floor. It was not until her actions began to cause embarrassment and distraction to workers and visitors alike that the police was called the second time. This time, it was two elderly uniformed men who after all efforts to persuade Catherina to leave failed, agreed to take her down to the prison yard to be with Eze.

*　*　*　*　*

A blue coloured police car drove towards the farmer and his wife as they stood in front of the house with the cell phone on his ears. The sudden disappearance of their daughter and her son meant that something was amiss and he feared for the safety of his grandson. Soon, the car approached at walking speed and halted few metres away from the couple, and Catherina alighted with her baby and without a word, walked past her parents into the house wearing a swollen face. She had finally given up when it dawned on her that the police car was taking her to her parents' house and not to the prison yard as they promised. Her father and mother watched as the door closed behind her and simultaneously turned to the police car for some form of information or explanation but the two occupants of the car simply communicated briefly with each other, reversed the car, and drove off.

"What is happening?" the woman asked her husband who was still gazing at the fast disappearing police vehicle.

"Not even a word," he muttered.

They hurried into the house to find that their daughter had retired to her room, sobbing uncontrollably. All efforts to get her to explain her sudden disappearance proved futile but they were delighted to have them back in good health, confidently assured that the police had taken care of whatever situation their daughter may be finding difficult to explain.

Catherina was up early the next morning, ready to leave the house again with the baby. Her refusal to share her burden had distressed her parents the previous evening, yet she was again getting ready to go out with the baby without a hint to her parents on where she was going to. Subsequently, her father, who did not want to lose sight of his grandson, put on hold the day's program at the farm and discreetly followed his daughter only to end up at the Ministry of Child Welfare. The farmer was surprised to learn that his daughter had been in touch with the father of her baby, and about the drama that had unfolded the day before. He grudgingly went back home, disappointed with his daughter's choice but relieved that Eze was going to be out of their lives for a very long time.

For four years, Eze Okoronta was locked away in Balthazar. Upon his release, rumours spread that his family had waited endlessly over the years, and performed his burial rites. Even as a living dead in Landesburg, Eze did not lose sight of the Resident Permit and all goodwill advices from well-wishers to visit home fell on deaf ears. Going back empty-handed after many years did not appeal to him, and he believed that it would be better to go back triumphantly, so that those who wished him dead would turn around to sing his praises. It is this same popular belief that has kept men and women of Umuafor under unspeakable conditions across all parts of the globe.

Eze joined Ray Power Miracle Fountain hoping for a divine intervention, and upon close consultation with the general overseer, was given a series of penitential and sacrificial rites to observe for the favour of God to locate him. Nevertheless, after sowing and making all the required seeds and resourceful sacrifices to the Miracle Fountain, Eze was one day rushed from the courtroom to the hospital for partial stroke when the mother of his daughter blatantly refused him the fifty percent joint custody he had so laboured for.

"The bigoted Judge ruled in favour of the wicked woman," Eze told Pastor Ray when it got to his turn for counselling.

"Are you telling me you don't have your Resident Permit yet?" Pastor Ray asked furiously.

"Yes, Pastor," replied Eze.

"What were her exact reasons?"

"You are asking as if you don't know these people, Pastor," Eze lamented.

"I thought I knew them," Pastor Ray said casually.

"She intentionally wants to ruin my life," Eze decried. "The only reason she presented to the court is that I used to be too aggressive."

"This is not fair," Pastor Ray grumbled.

"I made her pregnant," the bitter Eze recalled with his turbulent voice. "I stayed with her for nine months, but now I am suddenly too aggressive for my Resident Permit."

Eze had apparently gone to court not to fight for his rights over his daughter but to squeeze out the *kpalli* that had for long crippled his movement. Pastor Ray had also made repeated prophecies to that effect everytime he went up to the altar with an envelope containing his "seed."

"Calm down, Eze," Pastor Ray appealed. "God has his way of doing things."

"I am beginning to doubt your prophecies, Pastor," Eze declared.

"Believe His prophet and you shall prosper," Pastor Ray quoted emphatically to Eze who had always been an obedient follower but was now talking in a rather bold and offensive manner to the Pastor whose quotation had just added more insult to injury.

"You prophesied without mincing words when Astrid was pregnant that the Resident Permit would locate me in the house," Eze reminded. "I waited endlessly in my house and the pregnancy was eventually aborted. Your reason for my ill fortune was that I did not sow enough. This wicked woman has just refused me my entitlement despite the uncountable number of "seed baskets" I have brought to your altar."

"God is not a man that He should lie," Pastor Ray went further with his tactical indoctrination.

The words from the Holy Book were barely out of the Pastor's mouth before Eze seized him by the throat. Years of toiling and fruitless labour had made his hands as tough as crocodile skin and he had not much left to lose.

"Leave God out of this matter," Eze roared.

The two struggled briefly inside the Pastor's office. Pastor Ray

WOES OF IKENGA

was well aware of his status and the stipulations of the laws of Landesburg. The decision to become a self-styled "man of God" had been a calculated way to tap into the vicious demand for miracles and breakthrough. That was essentially up on everyone's lip and for him a clear economic pursuit for demand and supply of unnatural breakthrough softwares. Money had actually flowed in as his ministry grew, thanks to the seed sowing methodology, and cheerful givers who earnestly adhered to his spiritual guideline of storing up treasures in heaven. Even the authorities crowned it all by issuing Pastor Ray with a Resident Permit on account of his efforts to rehabilitate street youths and criminals. Hence he reasoned that fighting with a church member would not only tarnish his image but also undermine all his achievements.

"I rebuke you by the blood of the lamb," Ray tried to repel.

In response, Eze dished out a heavy slap from his very wide right palm whilst the left was still bolted tightly on the collars of Ray's white shirt. A second and third slap followed in quick succession, even as the Pastor continually rebuked an abstract demon.

"Stop this mess, Brother," the pastor pleaded at last, when the spirit he had intended to bind refused to give way. "We can talk things over as gentlemen."

"I am not a gentleman," Eze objected.

"Sure, you are."

"No, I am not."

"Let me make one out of you."

"A shaggy pastor begets a shaggy evangelist."

"Mind your words."

"I have not even started," Eze promised. "You are finished in Landesburg now that I know better."

"Are you going to kill me?" Pastor Ray questioned.

"Your life has no material value," Eze replied him. "Why should I spend my days behind the prison walls of Balthazar since your death cannot give me a Resident Permit?"

The pastor managed to put up an induced smile. He had never

witnessed such brutal confrontation throughout his many years of pastoral duty and was already seriously contemplating relocating or leaving the lucrative venture with the wealth already acquired should the handwriting on the wall get bolder. The grip on his collar gradually loosened as the confrontation wound down to a verbal one with the pastor trying to beat back the temptation like a "gentleman".

"Please sit down, Eze!" he pleaded.

"Do I sit down to renegotiate a new agreement?"

"What agreement?"

"Our contract has failed," Eze explained.

"You insisted that I sow seeds of faith throughout the nine months that the pregnancy lasted and I complied with all pleasure but your own part of the deal has failed to materialise."

"Where have I failed you?" the Pastor asked foolishly.

"I want my baskets of seeds back," Eze demanded adamantly with a bang on the office table. "I need my money back."

"Those offerings were not for me."

"Tell whoever has them that they failed to keep a promise."

"How do you want me to reach God?"

"The very way you got those fruitless prophecies."

"Fruitless prophecies?"

"Yes," Eze maintained. "You have always boasted that the Holy Spirit told you."

The Pastor had indeed been cornered as the devil-possessed member proved too stubborn to bow to any of his deliverance and evangelisation strategies. He was well aware that there were others still waiting to see him for counselling and knew that they might be overhearing the scuffles and was already making up an alibi as he pulled out his leather wallet.

"How much are we talking about?" he asked.

"You should know better," Eze replied. "I handed the envelopes directly to you."

"Remember that half of the money was used to purchase spiritual material," Pastor Ray explained. "And for nine times of the nine months pregnancy, I travelled to the wilderness to conduct fasting and prayers on your behalf."

"On the contrary," Eze interrupted. "For the bad luck that your prayer and fasting brought me, I demand compensation for damages."

The much-weakened Pastor had no further arguments or excuses. He was beginning to realise that he was dealing with the much talked about living dead of Landesburg. It would be foolhardy on his side to allow the fracas come out in the open and so he pulled out all the notes in his wallet and counted one thousand eight hundred Deutsche Marks.

"Take this and go your way."

Eze, who never rejected money, pocketed the notes and again spread his palms before Pastor Ray.

"What do you want from me again?" the Pastor asked.

"This is only a fraction from my baskets of seed."

"Go with your *agwu*," Pastor Ray implored. "Just go! A number of people are still in the waiting room."

"They are ignorantly waiting to enrich your pocket," Eze told him. "The wrath of those you have swindled will soon catch up with you. Alfa has told me the offer you made to him and Ikenga. Your cup has overflowed in Landesburg."

With those last words, Eze dashed out of the Pastor's office without a second look to those seated in the waiting room. That was the last he attended of services at Ray Power Miracle Fountain. The Pastor quickly rearranged his shattered office table, took a look at the mirror and followed up.

"God is real," he shouted a number of times to the waiting audience. They were for sure alleviated to know that everything was all right with their much beloved Pastor. The spontaneous loud argument that came occasionally through the office door had almost caused panic among them.

"Heaven is real," the Pastor roared again. "I have always told you that we are not fighting against flesh and blood; it is a spiritual battle, but greater is He that is on our side. Shout Alleluia somebody."

"Alleluiaaa!" shouted the miracle conscious followers.

"Today's counselling has to be suspended," he said to them. "The Holy Spirit instructed that I should devote the rest of the day for prayers."

No one doubted or questioned his instructions. They all left in a single file after a warm handshake with their Pastor.

The termination of the counselling visitation was suddenly hatched by Ray to get himself ready for any counter-action should Eze reappear in another style. He also needed enough time to figure out the best way to deal with Ikenga to stop him from wrecking his already sailing boat. Even as a "man of God," he was determined to take out any obstacle that would stand in his way and would not be cowed by any threat.

# Chapter 16

Ikenga was about to lay down his head early the next morning when Mascot called with news that Afamefuna had been rushed to the hospital with unexplained complications. Alfa had dozed off a little earlier on the sofa while they were still talking, leaving him to do justice to the remaining Vodka. Sleep vanished immediately the news came, leaving the drunken Ikenga panting in the tiny room.

The lovely little boy was evidence that he had not exactly wasted his life in a foreign country and the only proof of his enduring legacy. Therefore matters regarding Afamefuna always made him sit up regardless of the limited time that the system allowed for father-son encounter. Ikenga believed that if he would never be able to face his kindred back home in Umuafor to tell his stories, he would someday narrate the stories of his adventure to his son. He secretly kept his eyes on the small boy and jealously guarded him for the few hours every second week of the month that the children welfare office permitted him to see his son. All his hopes of a better life in a foreign land had been marred with difficulties and complications but to lose a son in the face of his predicament would add *Ofeke* title to his name, a humiliation he would regret even in the spirit world.

The plot was actually aimed at keeping a close eye on Ikenga or rather to render his words useless should he open his mouth to tell anyone about Ray's offer, but the oblivious Mascot, grateful to Uncle Ray for coming up with such a nice idea to save a brother, accepted to play his part as the only way he deemed necessary to help Ikenga out of his present deteriorating mental state. He was the only person who still commanded Ikenga's loyalty and maintained a warm contact with Afamefuna and his mother through regular gifts of children toys and birthday presents. That was why Pastor Ray went to him as the only person who could perfectly execute his plans.

Mascot arrived in a taxi with two of his close friends to Robbin Street to pick Ikenga who was already waiting downstairs to be taken to his son. The anxiety to set eyes on Afamefuna made him swallow his questions when the taxi driver drove past the normal route to the General Hospital. His silence was later broken when the taxi driver pulled up by the parking lot of the Kent Psychiatric Clinic.

"What is the problem with Afamefuna?" he managed to ask.

"I don't know exactly," Mascot replied calmly. "Vanessa told me he drank some liquid detergent."

"I will strangle that idle queen if anything happens to my son," Ikenga threatened.

"Nothing will happen to him," Mascot replied.

"When did the incident happen?"

"Early this morning."

Mascot quickly engaged the taxi driver in a conversation to prevent Ikenga from asking further questions and handed a note over to the man, asking that he wait to take them back. The three passed through a magnificent glass door into a well-decorated reception hall, as quiet as an abandoned cathedral except for the country music that filtered through the suspended loud speakers. Mascot motioned the others to sit down while he made straight to the receptionist who was half asleep in a secluded glass cabin.

The move, which lacked meticulous planning, had now come to its critical stage. Mascot was speaking in low tones with the receptionist, and pointing towards his friends at interval but Ikenga who could no longer wait for the paper protocol before seeing his son moved closer to the receptionist to demand why the process was taking ages, only for the receptionist to demand for his health insurance card.

"Give him your card," Mascot told Ikenga.

He pulled out a green coloured health insurance card from his wallet without hesitation and handed it over to the receptionist if that would hasten the process.

"Why my insurance card?" he questioned through the round hole on the glass. "In what room is the boy stationed?"

Mascot became disturbingly quiet; avoiding eye contact with

Ikenga but the unsuspecting receptionist took over from there.

"You must be registered before you see a psychiatrist," he told Ikenga as he pushed the insurance card into its slot.

Ikenga stared back at the man inside the glass cabin who seemed not to understand why they were there.

"Do you have a family?" the receptionist asked. "Do you experience sleeping problems at night?"

It was the man's focused gaze that made Ikenga realise that the questions were meant for him.

"What?" he shouted outrageously, frightening life out of the frail receptionist.

A spark of rage swept through his whole system as he realised that he had actually been lured to a psychiatric hospital without his consent.

"So this is the best you can do for me, Brother?" He turned to Mascot.

"The idea came from Pastor Raymond," Mascot replied truthfully. "There is no other way we can help you."

"He should have rid me of the *agwu* dwelling in me."

"Don't mind him," Mascot approved. "That *aduro*-inspired apostle is *agwu* itself."

Ikenga tore the card reader off the connecting cable and smashed the electronic equipment on the floor when his insurance card would not come out. Mascot who was forced to spring off quickly was also taken aback by the kind of animosity he saw on Ikenga's face. With his friends they tried to hold Ikenga down only to realise that they were dealing with a legion of more powerful and determined spirits. Within seconds, the hall was turned into a disaster zone as chairs and decorative objects were converted into weapons and missiles. The taxi driver who rushed in to ascertain the level of pandemonium was pinned down at the entrance by a flying flower pot that shattered the glass door. One of Mascot's friends who had shaky and problematic refugee issues ran out of the hall and disappeared as the situation escalated to save himself from double query should the *Polizei* arrive. Mascot also escaped

303

through a broken window with a serious injury on his elbow, leaving Ikenga to vent his anger on the properties inside the reception hall. The police siren and the ambulance did little to dampen his rage as he smashed the glass doors and windows into pieces.

"Freedom," he shouted. "I need my freedom."

The officers applied their stun gun on him since they dared not near him and he slumped to the ground like a lifeless clown. The panic-stricken receptionist emerged from his protective cabin to give a haphazard account of what happened and Ikenga was whisked away in a tinted Volkswagen van.

*   *   *   *   *

Many young black inmates see the notorious detention facility in Balthazar as a holiday resort. For those who lived by the "get rich or die trying" maxim, it served as a training camp for vocational courses. Also, one had to visit the camp at least once in the course of hustling at the City Station or other areas of endeavour to prove one's credential in the rank and files of the street clan. But for those who no longer had age on their side, it was a self examination camp in the heart of Landesburg. The reasons for detention among black inmates–individuals used to suffering and abject poverty–were easily predictable. Life in Balthazar was far better than being free men in their own countries. Hunger was not an issue, and there was the pleasure of having a television or a radio set for contact with the outside world. Beating or torture was out of question as they regarded themselves as sons and daughters of the United Nations, protected by human right decrees. These black inmates were mostly economic immigrants fleeing their countries in search of greener pastures, and motivated by the belief that manna fell from heaven on the streets of the Western world.

Thanks to the United Nations Charter that made it possible for one to dream of a better life in a foreign land and thanks indeed to the welfare system of Landesburg and countries that

## WOES OF IKENGA

generously welcomed and accommodated aliens from different races. It was left to time and history to judge the impact of the exodus that created a vacuum in a land of plenty as Umuafor and her entire clans had become like a basket being emptied into another world.

This trend started in the dark ages when humans were transported against their wish across the Atlantic to a new world through the most painful and agonising voyage the world would ever know, but with the advent of politics and uncultivated democratic principles in recent times, dubious politicians did all to empty the food basket of the people they were supposed to feed. Responsibility and accountability thence became merely decorative words borrowed from English, thus plunging a whole generation into a rat race, as survival of the wealthiest became the order of the day.

Umuafor was lucky to be one of the storage chambers where the generous Mother Earth stored her treasures. Blessings from *Ani*, however, turned to a curse to so many and since they had neither a say in the so-called government of the people nor a share in the mother nature-given national cake, they took their destiny in their own hands, risking odds to get out of their country in search of a better life.

It is hard to figure out the rationale behind a man abandoning his friends, relatives, and in some cases, wife and children, for an unknown world, armed with only his faith and determination to fight whatever obstacles that would come his way. Why would anyone risk his or her life and leave everything he or she is accustomed to, for a dangerous trip across the dry deserts of North Africa and the treacherous waters of the Mediterranean with very little or insufficient means of a safe passage? Why were these men, women and children ready to even walk on water just to escape the traumatised life that their country tossed at them? Why would any man look at death in the eye and dare to take his chances rather than live as a walking corpse? What would make a man confront the shame and ridicule that stares a wanderer in the face in a

305

foreign land?

Even the so-called intellectuals were not spared from the tempting exodus. The brain-drain was also given great impetus by wealthy nations through a series of arranged migration puzzles. Skilled labour programs and visa lotteries were all deployed to attract experts and professionals into joining the bandwagon while many who travelled abroad to acquire education were motivated to stay put after graduation due to chronic corruption and the stagnant pace of development in their native countries.

He who sees, knows it all. When stories of the recurrent tragedies of sea travellers and of people trying to make their way over to the "promised land" became rampant in the media, the world began to realise that even death could not stop a determined migrant who believed that since he had not made a change while living, the change would probably come with death.

As the heavy metal doors of Balthazar slammed behind him, Ikenga realised that he was caged again, possibly for a very long period of time. He could not believe that he was already in another timeless world of isolation, agony and soul searching. Like a time traveller with his travel machine, he could still see himself walking through the beautiful streets of Landesburg with people looking down on him and his abnormal lifestyle, but in reality, he was inside the prison command centre with four concrete walls and rectangular glass windows above his head criss-crossed by solid steel.

The six-storey complex, dating close to a hundred years, was built to house dissident soldiers that refused to comply with the orders of the then brutal regime. Its architectural design was one of a kind, built in the shape of a cross with the four ends of the cross marked sections A to D, with a clear view from one end to the other. The carefully designed protective steel made it practically impossible to move from one section to the other without falling under the watchful eyes of the guards. Inmates moved and played around in sections daily in the two recreation grounds within the prison compound. Guards were so unfriendly that it was assumed that they may have been given special orders to make the inmates regret every minute of their time, judging by how they walked up and down the long corridors and iron staircases with bunches of keys and batons dangling round their waists like good angels of Lucifer. Their duty was to make sure one did the time due for his or her crime, a duty they carried out with all patriotism.

From the mini white van with tiny tinted windows, four inmates were marched into the reception room for the normal check-in procedure. The other three were from Eastern Europe and confidently discussed in their native language, not minding if anybody was eavesdropping. Ikenga was third in the row and was still studying his new environment when the pot-bellied guard sitting over the counter roared.

"Hey, come over here, dealer."

Ikenga walked over to the counter, putting up a faint smile out of fear in order not to look rude or offend anyone. The shock of finding himself in this building a third time disorganised him. From Kent Psychiatric Hospital where the cops picked him that Saturday morning, he had been put through a marathon of interrogation sessions for over forty-eight hours and taken from one detention cell to the other before facing a magistrate court Judge early on Monday morning who recommended that he be held in custody till further hearing because he posed a threat to public safety.

"I am not a dealer," Ikenga replied angrily.

"That is what they all say," the guard said in a low tone as he bent over the monitor.

"You would be running naked on the streets if you were in my shoes," Ikenga remarked.

The guard looked up sharply to understand what he was being told and concluded that the words must be insulting judging from the tone and fury that came with it.

"Say that again," he asked.

"Your big head will explode if you have a slice of the load on my shoulders," Ikenga replied.

The fat guard, who was not so fluent in English, could not

make any meaning of what Ikenga said except for "big head" and was thrown off-balance by the second statement but would not take any insult from a drug dealer who was destined for time in jail. What he did not know was that the heart-broken alien had nothing to lose and could readily grab him by the throat and squeeze out his life the way he had done to the swans and ducks at the central park. Besides, the new inmate no longer cared whether he was sent back to Umuafor to face humiliation or left to rot in Balthazar. He considered his life a disgrace and was sure that his people would not welcome a loser with open arms.

"Keep quiet!" the guard roared with dots of foamy liquid raining out of his mouth. "You are all dealers. You will all go back to the jungle where you came from."

The room became still for a while but the guard continued until he was through with the four, promising to send them back to their various planets as if the power to send the aliens back to the mars and the moon were vested on him.

Ikenga returned to his memories, as his mind flashed thousands of miles back to Umuafor. He remembered the free and happy life he had enjoyed even in poverty, the suffering and smiling, and the close bond that had held his family, kindred and the entire community together. How could he have possibly known that he was giving himself up for a life of loneliness and an endless litany of laws in a land that was supposed to be flowing with milk and honey? He pictured the faces of Nne, Chinaza, and the rest of his many sisters. He tried but could not withhold the drops of tears streaming down his eyes when he remembered his father, Chukwuma. He cursed himself and the so-called land of Canaan that he had not been around to give Nne the befitting burial he promised. His family had become an object of mockery according to the letter he received from Chinaza, and the old woman may have lived longer, if only he was around. Worse still, strangers may have invaded their family to lay claims to the vast fertile farmlands and palm trees, the inheritance he abandoned in search of illusive wealth.

WOES OF IKENGA

"I don't blame you big fool," he shouted back at the guard. "I wish you could just take me back to where I came from."

"Take it easy, Mister Udeaja," one of the junior guards interrupted. "You are inviting more trouble to yourself."

Conrad Schwarz, a young prison guard in his early thirties, tall and good looking, interrupted when he felt that the exchange of words was becoming unbecoming. He was well admired by his superiors for his skills in exercising his duties and well respected by the inmates for his leniency in handling difficult issues and assisting people with various problems.

"Don't worry about me, Conrad," Ikenga said to him. "I am swimming in a pool of troubles already."

"That is not the proper way to talk to my boss," he cautioned. "Now sign here so I can take you to your cell."

Conrad handed each new inmate two pairs of bed sheets, a blanket and a set of cutlery.

"Be careful with them please," he warned as he passed the pen over to the fourth person to sign. "You may have to pay if any of them gets lost or broken."

The four gathered their belongings carefully, as those were the only possessions they would be entitled to for the years they were to spend in captivity. They held the properties to their chests and made way for whoever was to take them to their various cells to take the lead.

"Move it, gentlemen," Conrad, who had just cleared the counter and sent back some files to the shelf, commanded as he grabbed his baton and a bunch of keys. They made their way through a long corridor before climbing to the second floor of the prison complex.

"Do you all want to stay together in one cell?" Conrad asked knowing that there were still two vacant single cells for whoever would like to stay alone.

"Together," shouted the trio from Romania.

Everyone had disclosed their nationality as they were now discussing freely. The three had just been in town for few weeks

309

and were rounded up when they attempted to move some expensive designer shoes from an American boutique. They had abandoned their worn out shoes inside the small testing cabin and were marching out in the new boots when Onochie, the shop attendant, pounced on them. Since tearing them apart would bring him more trouble from the law-conscious state, Onochie decided to hand the shoplifters over to the police.

"I need a single cell," Ikenga retorted showing less interest in the discussion. "I just want to have some peace."

"I will give you your peace," replied Conrad as he turned around to read the expression on Ikenga's face. The three Romanians were shown into a cell with two sets of double beds and Ikenga was taken to the third floor.

Conrad tried to start a conversation to ascertain the nature of Ikenga's crime or any way he could be of any help but Ikenga was not ready to disclose much. As far as he was concerned, his actions had come back to haunt him. Sometimes he tried to make sense of his actions but could not understand why he did those things and explaining it to anybody was the last thing he wanted to do. It was gradually becoming clear to him that he had been wrong about the people who complained about his unnatural behaviour and the destructive power of his self-imposed isolation. They had even staged a plan to lure him into accepting a return ticket back to his country with a little pocket money to find his way home from the airport but his reaction when he discovered their plans had left all men running for their lives. That encounter had been the major reason he withdrew from everyone, believing they were all mad.

"You don't want to tell me what brought you here?" Conrad asked again.

"But I told you that I have done nothing," Ikenga insisted.

"The police cannot bring you here if you have not committed any crime."

"They sensed that I needed some peace," Ikenga answered casually.

The Landesburg *Polizei* are as good as German products.

Notwithstanding their unfriendly looks, they usually went the extra mile to ensure that law-abiding citizens were not harassed or innocently sent to prison. Like their counterparts in the construction and manufacturing sector, they tried their best to maintain the global perception of German quality. Also in a bid to achieve perfection in their combat against crime, they sometimes let go a suspect because of insufficient evidence or maintained prolonged surveillance to be sure they had the right culprit.

"I hope you are not one of the kingpins?" Conrad voiced. "I will eventually find out when I go through your file. Meanwhile, tell your people to get you a good lawyer. The situation has become very tense in the last few months, since the only daughter of a well known high court Judge died unnoticed in the park from drug abuse. Your brothers operating around the city station are also not helping matters. They have constituted a thorn in the flesh of the police and city authorities. Sometimes I think that those boys are entirely another set of human beings; you send ten to prison today and twenty will appear tomorrow."

"Survival," Ikenga whispered.

"They are brave men really," Conrad remarked.

There was some minutes of silence as both men stared at each other. They had reached cell number 306. Conrad was still studying his companion as he gently opened the door. Ikenga was about to tell him that he was not being detained for drug dealing but the guard interrupted:

"This is your single cell."

"I like that."

"It's no man's resting place honestly, and you can't have peace here."

"Can you please open the windows," Ikenga asked.

"A dirty junky left the cell this morning," Conrad remarked. "Press this button if you need attention, I've got one or two things to round up before I close for the day."

"That's alright, Conrad, I see you tomorrow then?"

"Sure."

Conrad closed the door behind him and rushed back to his post as Ikenga struggled to come to terms with his conscience. He would have proudly owned up if his offence was drug dealing or even shoplifting and friends would have judged him fairly as merely looking for survival but he had rather subjected himself to more ridicule and given confirmation to those who had long suspected that he was gradually going insane. Life had not been the same for him since the painful break-up with Vanessa and the subsequent refusals from the child welfare authority to grant him permission to see his son regularly. Hence, he had become a loner that had withdrawn from the public, and rejected calls and visits from friends. Crimes like rape and murder were deemed horrible and mostly not attributed to aliens whose major struggle was for a better life, but his offence this time was somewhat shameful and disgraceful and he might not be able to explain his way out the next day when he was sure to be confronted by Conrad or fellow inmates.

The risks of coming to that country as an undocumented and illegal alien had proven to be a worthless adventure. The golden fleece with all its imaginations had long been replaced with pain and frustration. Should one find a way to get to one's destination, he or she was likely to end up with psychosis due to pressure emanating from refugee status, insatiable demands of relatives back home, and the consequent pursuit of a non-existent treasure.

Someone needed to drum it into the ears of youths who at the prime of their lives tended to assume unimaginable risks just to get to a foreign country, that they would only be confronted with unbearable shocks and draconian immigration laws. Ikenga stared into the sky for a while through the iron-barred window, wiped his tears with the back of his palm and leaned backwards on the spring bed close to the wall.

A man does not cry in the face of a problem but struggles to find a solution. He dozed off before he could gather any instruments to dig out solutions to his numerous problems. He and his *chi* had been caught up in a cycle of problems that whether

WOES OF IKENGA

he was awake or asleep, were constantly in conflict. Something above humans must be against he and his *chi's* fortune as to why they were always on the wrong side of events. He had run his race as a strong man, and confronted obstacles like a warrior but things never went as planned. Umuafor believed that if a man said "yes", his *chi* also said "yes" in affirmation, even though in the case of the famous Okonkwo from Umuofia, a town that had borne much of the brunt of the white man's misrule, his *chi* had said "nay" despite his strong will and affirmation. Ikenga was beginning to suspect *onatalu-chi* in his destiny, an unexplained situation where an individual experienced steady failure notwithstanding all his determined or fervent struggles.

"Why will things never go as planned?" he asked unconsciously in his slumber.

"Your *awele* cannot be found in the white man's land," his *chi* replied.

"But didn't we embark on this journey together?" Ikenga queried.

"I never consented," his *chi* objected calmly. "You beings claim to know, not knowing that you know not. Humans who plan things have limited knowledge. Wisdom is reserved for spirit beings and humans who rightfully and fervently consult them. A little knowledge is dangerous to mortal man. Drink deep or taste not the puritan waters."

The short interaction with his *chi* was followed by visions of the scary episode in the sea of death with the swollen faces of his fallen comrades and sleep immediately vanished from his eyes.

The more he became convinced that his ups and downs were not his own making, the more he became desperate to get to its root. Apart from following the chief priest to various shrines whenever there was a sacrifice to be performed or to a native doctor if there was a need for consultation, he had also helped out during the Sunday church services as an altar boy and grown into a man with a fair knowledge of the gods of his ancestors. The Almighty God that the white man regularly talked about was also

313

not strange to him. He was the same as the revered *Chukwu Okike,* the God of creation, who the human eyes could not see and that explained why his forefathers preferred to reach Him through demi-gods.

His father, Chukwuma, had also tried to lecture him on a soldier's beliefs about Chukwu and His creations. From Chukwuma, he had learned that since He created and programmed all, worship and sacrifices from humans in times of difficulties could not change the already laid down plans drawn by the One who knows and foresees all.

Throughout his ambitious journey to the land of the unknown, Ikenga never expected to face any stumbling blocks when he got to the Promised Land. He had turned away from the gods of his ancestors after walking into a vault of sacred secrets, and cried foul as to why the gods would allow humans perpetrate injustice in their name, while the Supreme God that he claimed to have run to had also not extended a helping hand. The fear of the future became very visible in his distressed present state with worries of his past still haunting him.

He opened his eyes unable to tell if he was sleeping or not, while looking around to see if he had company. Visions of the dead that had been entertaining him quickly disappeared into the prison walls as their drumbeats ceased. He would gladly dance to their tune at this hopeless stage of his predicament if they were after his life, but it seemed death also had no use for a nobody. Again, tears clouded his eyes as he walked towards the window facing the sky with his eyes wide open. The tears did not stop flowing because he could clearly see the wrinkle-ridden face of Chukwuma, his father, with his usual chewing stick hanging out from one end of his lips, staring back from the sky.

# Chapter 17

Some days later, Conrad searched through Ikenga's file to learn the nature of his crime. Ikenga's queerness and unconventionality made him curious about the exact crime the young man committed. Throughout the week, Ikenga did not participate in the daily one-hour recreation time that gave inmates the opportunity to walk round the mini-field, do some simple body exercise, or exchange visits. The solitary life he had chosen for himself inside Balthazar was totally unlike men of his kind and race who usually dashed out of their tiny cells as soon as the doors were opened. He also did not seem interested in the weekly Wednesday public shower that prisoners endlessly looked forward to.

The breakfast wagon went round at 6:00 am, the much-loved lunch at 1:00 pm, and slices of dried bread with yoghurt or milk at exactly 4:30 pm. Those were the only times when Ikenga made himself available for contact with anyone at Balthazar. At other times, he preferred to be left alone. Occasionally, the guards peeped through the tiny hole on the door to make sure he was not attempting suicide.

On the sixth day, Conrad paid Ikenga a surprise visit. He had just opened the cells for inmates who were interested in going for the one-hour recreation and decided to stop over at cell number 306.

"Why are you not going for recreation?" he asked politely.

"I feel better in my cell," Ikenga replied.

"Is there anything I can do for you?" he pressed further.

"Anything like what?"

"Send a letter to a friend or relatives," Conrad suggested.

"No, that would not be necessary," Ikenga answered. "My relatives brought me here."

"Why, did you fight them?"

Ikenga had no reply to give. He had also forgotten his earlier claim that the Polizei had brought him over for no just reason.

Conrad was not going to give up, especially now that he had

managed to get his friend talking. Both from the society at large and the prisoners he was meant to look after, the obvious phenomenon with its symptoms were not strange to him. He also knew that an open conversation was a strong antidote for people like Ikenga.

"What happened at the Kent Psychiatric Hospital?" he asked.

"I am insane," Ikenga confessed.

"No, you are not," Conrad retorted immediately.

"If everybody thinks that I am not normal, it could either be that I am really abnormal or that every other human being is not normal," Ikenga tried to explain.

"Prolonged dejection makes people accept what they are not," Conrad corrected.

"You call it dejection?"

"Yes," Conrad answered. "The more you isolate yourself in Balthazar, the more your situation worsens."

"Dejection! I will add that to the list."

The guard looked steadily at the motionless Ikenga. What he did not know was that many people had differently diagnosed and labelled a range of conditions on him with the most common being that he was possessed by *ajo-chi* the evil spirit. Some chose to use English words like psychosis, melancholy, and dispirited, to qualify Ikenga's situation, and many others saw him as a victim of cultural burdens. As heavy and challenging as the burden was, material and financial assistance to his people was firmly rooted in Ikenga's beliefs and cultural practices. In the absence of any form of social support, that meant that assisting his family back in Umuafor was a burden that Ikenga could not consciously put down.

"I do not know for sure what you are going through," Conrad added after a long silence. "But self-imprisonment is definitely not the remedy."

"This country is hard," Ikenga admitted.

"Do not allow the system to hold you down," Conrad advised. "The citizens are not finding it easy either."

"Do you have a family?"

"Not really, but I come from one."

"Are they all dead?"

"Everyone went his or her way when Mum and Dad divorced."

"No contacts?"

"Sometimes," Conrad tried to paint a picture of his family. "My elder sister is on drugs. I heard that my mother has found a new boyfriend but there is no contact with my father since then."

"You are from a different world," Ikenga said to him.

"I see no difference in our world," Conrad objected.

"You will never see the difference because you do not know my world."

Ikenga would have been better off had he embarked on his adventure for his own welfare, with sound mind if not financially balanced but the quest to improve the living standards of his family had been the driving force, and once outside the borders of Umuafor, the praises sung for wealth and mockery accorded losers had made him ever more determined to return contentedly.

At the middle of the rough road when he had tried to distance himself from his people in Umuafor, fear and scary nightmares had greeted him. During his times in Balthazar, he had never stopped thinking about where he came from alongside the headaches associated with obtaining a Resident Permit. At the time when he was first released from Balthazar to join Vanessa and their son, when there was no regular source of income, his worries and sleepless nights had been mostly over the wellbeing of Nne and Chukwuma, his father. It was his sole responsibility to take care of them at their old age as was expected of him according to *omenani*.

\* \* \* \* \*

Following a detailed petition from his Jewish lawyer, Ikenga was taken from Balthazar to a state-employed medical doctor who specialised in the treatment of mental disorders. The experienced psychiatrist reported after several days of interaction, that Ikenga no longer posed any security threats and was consequently allowed to go, on the condition that he would provide his residential address to the court and immediately inform the Police whenever he changed apartments.

Ikenga returned to No. 4 Robbin Street. That was for sure the residential address he had given to the court. There he needed no key or permission from anybody to occupy a room in the abandoned blocks and life moved on as usual.

Mascot and some of Ikenga's friends hoped that the little incident would help their friend sit up. His participation to send Ikenga to the psychiatric hospital had been in good faith as that was what the authorities would have eventually done with his deteriorating condition. Pastor Ray who masterminded the plan to discredit Ikenga should he reveal their conversations took the glory for his kind gesture and dropped further negotiations with Alfa but looked far away from Landesburg for his stage actors.

Ray Power Miracle Fountain received the much-needed approval from its attendants when Pastor Ray successfully performed the well-rehearsed healing and deliverance sessions. He had been able to tap into the general problems of migrants especially when it came to attaining resident status, and with his ever growing eloquence and convincing power, being able to explain to the congregation of mostly aliens who constantly longed to go back to their roots that victory was on its way. Although Germans were unwilling to let go of any inch of their territory, he preached that the city of Landesburg in which they had stepped their foot was theirs. To those who had not gotten the Resident Permit, he underlined that the key to a breakthrough was to keep on sowing seeds. The skilful preacher though, avoided the fact that many in his congregation turned up every Sunday with a new partner and were breeding bastards out of wedlock in the name of Resident Permit.

Alfa was particularly not happy with Ray Power Miracle Fountain and its founder. Not only did they label Ikenga, his right hand man, a madman, the Pastor had also denied him the opportunity to make a living from the deliverance show business. All his underground and open campaigns to undermine the new church were rebuked as the empty words of a demon-possessed, and Ikenga who would have made his allegations believable preferred to leave everybody to his conscience and his *chi*.

"You see what I am telling you," Alfa ranted to his roommate as he splashed a bunch of letters on the floor. An ugly encounter with members of the Miracle Fountain on a Monday afternoon had kept him blistering the whole day, and he walked back to the house to discover that the postman who he had warned several times not to deliver letters to the building had dumped a number of letters on the corridor. The ghost building had no letterbox or names on the door, so letters addressed to the house number were dropped on the staircase or on the floor.

"Who owns these letters?" Ikenga enquired from his sleeping sofa.

"They all bear your name."

"All of them?"

"All of them," Alfa answered. "The Postman intends to give you a knockout this time."

Ikenga stretched out his left hand to pick the closest of the letters. It was from the Director of Kent Psychiatric Hospital addressed to Ikenga Udeaja at No. 4 Robbin Street, and contained a detailed calculation of damages and costs for the day their reception hall was turned into a disaster zone. That summed up to a total of sixty-two thousand Deutsche Marks, which he was advised to pay into a designated bank account within a space of two weeks. He passed the letter to his roommate and reached for another, which turned out to be from the children welfare centre. The letter accused Ikenga of defaulting in child support payment, even though its second paragraph acknowledged several unsuccessful attempts to reach him because of his undisclosed residential address. The authorities warned that he should immediately commence a monthly payment of one hundred and eighty Deutsche Marks to Vanessa, with an appointment date

319

when he was to come over to the office to specify his preferred terms of payment for the outstanding arrears. He threw the second letter at Alfa and coiled back under his blanket without bothering to pick up the rest.

"If you can still close your eyes after all these attacks," Alfa said to his friend, "then you are superhuman."

"They have practically made me a ghost," Ikenga consented. "If I am not wandering aimlessly on the road, then I am sleeping."

"How long are we going to live like this?"

"What do you want to do?"

"That pastor has to pay," Alfa insisted.

"You have not worked for him."

"Tell people about the offer he made to you if he is not willing to pay."

"Leave every man to his own," Ikenga advised. "We all came here to look for money after all."

"If you don't make money from the system," Alfa warned, "the system will make money out of you."

Alfa went on and on with suggestions and strategies to change their life but Ikenga was already snoring. An unqualified doctor would probably add sleeping sickness to the litany of his problems because since Ikenga returned from the short visit to Balthazar, he no longer needed to be drunk like Alfa before dozing off. His compound problems dissolved as soon as he laid his head on the comfort of the foul smelling sofa in his own corner of their room.

*     *     *     *     *

Ikenga Udeaja alias Hassan Ijenwata was how the German oracle knew him. The name had repeatedly surfaced on the radars of the immigration police and the Office of Foreign Affairs, and the oracle had suddenly started to emit red signals indicating that his cup was filled to the brim.

Hopelessness had made Ikenga forget that the German society known for hard work and resource management did not allow cups to overflow. First, Vanessa with the full backing of the children's welfare had stripped him of his joint custody of Afamefuna, then the deprival of his regular annual Residential Permit and the damming reports with video footage from the head of Kent Psychiatric Hospital. Hence, the relevant authorities concluded that the alien who was not contributing in any way to the country's economy was beginning to constitute a nuisance and their society would be better off without him.

Such decisions were final. The immigration police had an assignment that had to be executed swiftly before the Jewish lawyer could locate his case file. Besides, the true identity of the alien had been established and there was no need for emergency travel documents since Ikenga had already provided an international passport with which he was regularly issued a yearly visa.

Alfa saw three men lead his roommate away early one morning, but never imagined that he was seeing Ikenga for the last time.

The immigration authorities that received him back in his country simply kicked him out of the airport. That was after nobody turned up to ask for the sleepy deportee after three days in custody. They usually handled cases of deportees, and in most cases, obtained "settlement" from their relatives before releasing them. Ikenga's case was extraordinary; he had slept for almost seventy-two hours on the bare floor of the temporary detention facility, only to wake up at intervals and eat the watery beans and bread he was served without any complaints. Soon, the officers realised that feeding the sleepy deportee with no prospects of making any interest was not the best alternative.

"Wake up, young man!" one of the officers shouted at him.

Ikenga slightly raised his head from the synthetic leather bag he used as pillow.

"Sit up!" the officer shouted louder with a one-step-forward movement.

Sleep immediately vanished from Ikenga's eyes. He had always had a mild interaction with the agents and this sudden attack by one of them baffled him.

"What did the white man inject into your body?" the officer asked.

"Nothing, Sir," Ikenga replied politely.

"Is it not time to wake up after sleeping for twenty-two years in their country?"

Ikenga stared at the officer like a zombie while holding close to his chest a medium sized synthetic bag, the only possession he came back with.

"Where are you from?"

"Umuafor."

"You don't have family or relatives?"

"I do, Sir."

"Why is nobody coming to ask of you?"

"I don't know, Sir."

"Nobody kisses a loser," the officer explained angrily. "Better know it now."

The sleepy deportee still maintained a steady gaze. He knew what the officers wanted from him but decided to play calm since he was not ready to "settle". The man's angry expression and explanation reminded him of what he was going to face in Umuafor.

"Not only have you succeeded in tarnishing the image of the country," the immigration agent charged again, "you came back a failure."

"I was not a failure before I left," Ikenga objected calmly.

"Shut up there!" the officer barked. "Will you be able to find your way back to Umuafor?"

"Yes, Sir."

"Follow me!"

A form was handed over to Ikenga to append his signature. Ready to hand over himself to whoever was interested in having him, he signed without hesitation.

"Now get out of here!" the agent ordered.

"Can you help me with transport money?" Ikenga asked gently, to make sure that the men would not like to have him for another second.

"Out!" the officer shouted pointing at the door. "There are still vacancies under the bridge if you cannot transport yourself down to Umuafor."

At last, a free man in his own country, Ikenga greeted his fatherland with a sigh of relief. He seemed not to mind the noise pollution and the lousy life patterns that he was no more used to. Ultimate survival meant that he must immerse himself again in the system while standing up to the abuses and insults that awaited a loser. He was lucky that those money-conscious immigration officers had not discovered the two hundred Deutsche Marks with him. The money was a humanitarian handout given to every deportee at the point of departure.

From a taxi driver who talked all the way to the central motor garage, Ikenga gathered the necessary information he needed. His attempt to catch up with the last of the long distance passenger buses to Port Harcourt was smashed to the ground by long traffic and police checkpoints.

"Look at what is happening here," the taxi driver remarked as he wheeled into the noisy motor garage. "Those of you living abroad are having an easy life."

"Have you been abroad before?" Ikenga asked reluctantly.

"No, Sir," the taxi driver replied. "My life savings went with my first attempt."

"Better not go for a second attempt," Ikenga advised.

"I have no other option," the driver complained. "Two of my children were sent back from school because of school fees. This taxi has only made me older than my age and cannot sustain my family."

Ikenga who was not in the mood to correct the widely held impression handed out a little more than the agreed fare and alighted.

"Thank you very much, Sir," the taxi driver shouted at his back.

The quest for wealth epidemic directly or indirectly made night travel a risky venture. Horrific attacks by young men and women who would go to any length to acquire wealth just for its glory had made commercial vehicle owners have a rethink. As a result, passengers like Ikenga had to hang around in the garage till the next morning to continue their journey. With overgrown hair and unkempt beards, Ikenga was not much of a target for the night racketeers who constantly lingered around the garage.

The night at the central motor garage was one of the best evenings Ikenga had had in years. It was a night of a thousand laughs with his countrymen who did not have everything to enjoy life but had life to enjoy everything, a total recall of the system he used to know.

Darkness was visible in the noisy garage with scattered patches of electric lights and local lanterns. Car horns did not stop honking while people roamed like rattled soldier ants. Record sellers pitched their external speakers at positions of their choice lambasting everyone's ear with music. Rows of bars and open-air restaurants popularly known as *mama-put* bustled with activity alongside their own music tunes. To interact or discuss in such an environment, people pitched their voices above every other source of noise in order to be heard. There was no visible sign of the law or its agents to scare people who went about their normal daily activities with relative contentment.

Ikenga chose a vacant seat in one of the lively *mama-put* joints and ordered a bottle of cold beer. Travellers waiting to continue their journey the next day seized such opportunities to liven up. He was barely seated when one of the guests, a co-traveller, confronted him with an expensive joke.

"What of a fowl sacrifice to have your hair shaved?" the man offered.

There was a round of laughter from the animated guests and he managed to respond accordingly.

"A cow, if you insist on shaving my hair," Ikenga responded. "My female cow is pregnant at the moment."

"That will do," Ikenga accepted. "The calf will go for my bushy beards."

The heat was turned off him when he managed to repel a number of taunting jokes with consistent ripostes. The noisy showdown went on till early morning when the church bells and calls to prayer notified travellers that the ticket office had opened. The restaurant owner handed out a complimentary shot of *kai-kai* to travellers who he thought made the night with most applauding jokes, and Ikenga with his exceptional facial look received one too before leaving for the ticket office.

The bus driver sounded a warning horn for the road hawkers to clear their wares out of his way and used the short interval to take a last shot from his own locally made cocktail, a mixture of *kai-kai* with roots and herbs. The bus, packed with travellers, dangled its way through potholes out of the Ojota Central Motor garage with thick black smoke pouring out of its roaring engine. It did eventually make it to Port Harcourt from where Ikenga took another mini-bus to his town.

He was increasingly delighted about setting eyes on Umuafor even though he was not expecting a grand reception from his people. Celebrations and merrymaking thrown by the sons of Umuafor who returned with success stories had made those who came back empty-handed to virtually sneak in without telling their own side of the story. Since the war ended, Umuafor wanted and only heard success stories from her adventurers. Many who lost their lives along the seven forests and the seven seas were left for the wild beasts, and those who encountered untold challenges and came back half alive or with sicknesses were swept under the carpet. Words from their mouth carried less weight since it lacked backing with money or material wealth, and therefore made no impact. That meant that the children of Umuafor, although from a land blessed abundantly by goodness, were ever ready for blind adventures, generation after generation.

The *Ogbunigwe* skeleton at Ovuvu junction reminded him that they were getting close to Umuafor. The heavy equipment had long been overgrown by elephant grasses but was still recognisable at the strategic position where it was hurriedly abandoned.

Noticeable changes along the way demanded that Ikenga must change his orientation after twenty-two years of being away from home.

"The forest is gone," he said speculatively to the female passenger sitting right next to him.

"Which forest?" the much younger lady asked. She may not have been born or probably too young to know what forest he was referring to. Meanwhile, Ikenga was sure that that was surely the hilltop where *Eke-Ogba* rested her head, the place where he had escorted Nne a number of times in her quest for a child to sprinkle palm oil over the rising white smoke every harmattan season. The lake was still recognisable as it ran parallel to a newly constructed highway but the little mountain with its vegetation had completely disappeared. The area that was once the forest was now ringed off with multiple structures towering over the high concrete fence, but one particular observation that made him quite uncomfortable was the irritating open sewage that was channelled from the premises right into Ogba Lake.

Turning over to an elderly man next to the girl, Ikenga carefully persisted in his quest.

"How are the fishes coping with this rate of pollution?"

"They have all died out," the man returned sadly.

"This is surely the location of Ogba forest?" he persisted pointing at the complex.

"Oh, that was long ago," the co-passenger answered.

"Unbelievable!" the startled Ikenga exclaimed.

"You are not from the area?"

"I am from Umuafor."

The man took a second look to see if he could recognise Ikenga. He was not from Umuafor but knew quite a lot of Umuafor natives from many years of business dealings in Afor market.

"How come your face is so unfamiliar?" he demanded.

"I left Umuafor a long time."

"Where have you been?"

"Overseas."

"Are you just coming back?"

"Yes."

The man did not believe it. Nobody came back from overseas with just a handbag. He took Ikenga to be one of those fraudsters that cooked up unimaginable stories to extract money from their victim's pocket and became more conscious of the little money with which he intended to buy wares at Afor. To subsequent questions from Ikenga, he supplied direct and prompt answers.

"Have they managed to drive out Eke-Ogba?" Ikenga asked with more enthusiasm.

"The beast transformed into national cake."

The ambiguous reply from the man halted the remaining questions on his lips. The explanations he needed might not come from his co-passenger and the remaining drive to Umuafor Motor Park was a very short time for the long clarifications he needed. He drew fortitude from the contentment of being back in his beloved fatherland, and brightened up to the warm realisation that destiny had been waiting for him back home while he had gone abroad in pursuit of shadows. In the face of Umuafor *Onuku* who would surely make jest of him for coming back empty-handed, he remained steadfast that the soil he was stepping on had a lot to offer.

Chinyere was the first to recognise him when he stepped out of the mini bus at the Afor garage. The headmaster's daughter was now married with children and ran a provision store at Afor market to support her family. Ikenga who wanted to enter unnoticed could not hide his discountenance when a full-fledged woman ran towards him with open arms. He reluctantly accepted a hug but did not recognise the woman at the first instance.

"It's me, your cousin," Chinyere reminded.

"Which of my cousins?" Ikenga asked. Anybody who knew that he was just returning from abroad could claim to be his relative or long forgotten friend just to be eligible for a present.

"The headmaster's daughter."

"Is this you, Chichi?"

"Yes."

"Oh, forgive me," Ikenga apologised. "You have completely changed."

"Life in Umuafor has turned me to a sandbag."

"How is my headmaster doing?"

"He is strong," Chinyere answered skeptically. "Your absence all these years has taken a toll on him."

"That was not our fault dear cousin."

"What of my brother, Ogbonnia?"

"He is doing well."

"When are we expecting him?"

"Soonest."

The headmaster's daughter did not bother to ask about his luggage when Ikenga walked off the bus with just a handbag. She believed that he might have loaded his luggage separately inside another vehicle.

"I spent the whole day with Chinaza," Chinyere continued. "She came to the market today."

"I cannot wait to see her," Ikenga yelled.

The news of his arrival spread quickly from the market as many who saw his interactions with Chinyere from a distance would later find out that it was their son who had left for the white man's land a long time ago. Those who did not have much to do in the market joined the escort to Udeaja's compound.

Ikenga did not recognise his compound. The spacious family fence now looked different, as it had been restructured. He would later be told that Eloka, the uncle he never knew, had returned some years ago, as a Western educated engineer who had been particularly selected because of his exceptional performance to oversee the construction projects at Ogba. The beast of Ogba had turned out to be one of the largest reserves of precious crude elements the world had ever discovered, and Eloka, with his education and wealth had practically pulled out Udeaja's

328

compound from below the level of poverty to a height far above. He had put up two modern duplexes for his family and his brother Chukwuma. The smoky *mpanaka* had been replaced by a heavyduty Yamaha generator to power the compound and those of the immediate neighbours since an unknown *agwu* had obviously crippled the national power supply.

While he struggled to make meaning of the changes, neighbours gathered to welcome him. Chinaza and her children were already waiting as news of the return of her twin brother had also reached her. Youths who were not yet born when Ikenga left Umuafor also came to welcome their "big" brother while the ambitious ones hoped to solicit his assistance to travel to wherever he was coming from.

As if he had informed the elders of his return, a small number of men were sighted round the modernly furnished *obi* that Eloka had symmetrically positioned between the two structures. They had converged to discuss with the chief engineer, the meritorious system with which appointments in the new construction site must be distributed. Eloka had given them hope that their voices would be heard and their concerns addressed in all areas of governance. Unlike many who went in pursuit of knowledge in foreign lands that returned with a number of degrees and certificates but forgot their common sense, Eloka seemed genuinely concerned with helping his people forge ahead.

The men rose in unison at the sight of a stranger being accompanied into the compound by a cheerful crowd. Ikenga halted a few steps from the colossal *obi*, and as if he ordered his congregation to be still, the chanting and loud voices subsided. Eloka boldly stepped forward, zipping up his jeans trouser. The qualities which Udeaja family members were made of could not be found wanting in him, even after years of schooling and working experiences abroad. He knew immediately that his nephew was back for good and rushed to hug him. He had never met Ikenga but the striking resemblance to Chukwuma that he saw on the face of the bushy-haired young man answered all his questions. The other men filed out to hug their son as Chukwuma threw away his chewing stick to sing a song of liberation and freedom after a warm embrace with his son. The crowd rejoined and the welcoming went on.

Although people had not seen any luggage with the big brother, they waited for presents from the white man's land. Some who noticed the lack of freshness and unhealthy looks not common to people from abroad quickly dispelled their fears. Coming back from abroad was not something often witnessed in Umuafor. The journey was also not considered a spontaneous one for Ikenga to forget buying gifts for the people he left behind and the long travel might have contributed to his haggard appearance. Besides, it was part of the *omenani* to come for presents when a family member or relative returned from a distant journey.

Jealously proud to have come from Umuafor and very happy to be reunited with his fatherland and the culture he knew, Ikenga came out to the grand *obi* after a well deserved welcome from his father. He was definitely not a loser and to shy away from comments or people's expectation would make him an *Ofeke* before his own people. Had any of the so-called "losers" who returned from abroad been brave enough to tell their stories, Umuafor's youths would think twice before embarking on a blind adventure.

"I greet you all, my people," he greeted.

"You are welcome," they replied. Many wanted to cut short the welcome protocol for merrymaking, but he stood still till their noise subsided.

"I have held on to life just to tell you my story," he continued.

"A travelled child knows better than the old man who sits at home."

"Our ancestors say so," one of the elderly men supported.

His kinsmen were rather startled with such unwarranted comments at a time of jubilation. They however remained calm for the big uncle to throw more light on whatever he had to say.

People were still trooping into the compound to share in the

## WOES OF IKENGA

presents and rejoice with the family for their son's safe return. Ofoma, the village drunkard, would not be left out. He also staggered in expecting a gift. Memories of the fiesta he had had when Eloka returned made such calls to Udeaja compound an honourable one. The news came to him on his way to the village square and he quickly decided to abandon the village brand of *kai-kai* for the foreign one. Till he got to Udeaja's compound, he complained to passers-by and stationary trees how he had looked after the community year after year while Ikenga was away.

The sun was fast disappearing, leaving a golden shadow over the landscape and flourishing vegetation. A gentle breeze filtered through the mango and *Udala* trees that shielded the compound from excess sunshine during the day. Nocturnal ants made their presence felt from treetops and cracked walls, as if to tell the silent crowd that they were also waiting for presents.

"I have not come back empty-handed," he said. "I came back with my story. Losers are those who perish in the battle or lose the effrontery to tell their own story."

"Are you saying that you have no schnapps for home-branch?" Ofoma threw in from behind.

"Shut up! Keep quiet!" a number of voices shouted at him. The offensive reactions he received pulled Ofoma together, supposedly because his system was not yet saturated with enough alcohol or he feared that this adventurer had something more interesting to offer which was why everybody wanted to eat him alive. In any case, the boozer backed down with the determination that if the piece of yam on the fire would not get done quickly, he was ready to wait indefinitely.

"I lost my target," Ikenga admitted boldly when the noise died down.

"*Ani* will not permit me to keep the informative adventure to myself," he continued.

"This is my experience and story… "

Umuafor was all ears.

* * * * *

Ofoma sang about the chronicles from one beer parlour to another and from one village square to the next. Most times, depending on his state of consciousness from excessive drinking, he would sing Ikenga's praises for his courageous spirit with which he narrated his ordeal to the people of Umuafor. Other times, he would reduce the adventurer to a mere object of ridicule for wasting those long years in a white man's land but could not afford a bottle of whisky for "home-branch," people like him who looked after the village while they were away.

The story of Ikenga travelled far and wide. Blown by the wind and dispersed by sea waves to the end corners of the globe. Those yet to master storytelling techniques added salt and pepper to get their audience laughing whenever the legendary tale was told. The tragi-comic storyline, however it was being told, maintained the indispensable fact that Ikenga was happy to be back in his home land. To millions of Umuafor explorers and wanderers trapped in solitude and servitude round the globe, the woes of Ikenga were similar to theirs. As they pictured themselves in the factual story, there was a sudden realisation that milk and honey flowed in Umuafor while they went into the wilderness in search of an illusive greener pasture.

# GLOSSARY

| | |
|---|---|
| *Abacha* | –Cassava/Tapioca |
| *Aduro* | –Assylum / Assylum seeker |
| *Agbala* | –Female deity |
| *Agha- elinam* | –May I fall not in battle! |
| *Agwo n'atu mbe* | –A title for extraordinary gallantry |
| *Agwu* | –A possessing spirit |
| *Ajo-chi* | –Bad luck/ill fate |
| *Akara with agidi* | –Bean cake and bread |
| *Akpa-agwu* | –Shrine's handbag or a bag containing illicit materials |
| *Akpu, Ofor, Ogilisi* | –Trees |
| *Ala-wu-otu* | –The land is one and same. |
| *Alu* | –Taboo / Abomination |
| *Amadioha* | –God of thunder |
| *Ani.* | –Land |
| *Anunu-ebe* | –Traditional talisman / runic tree |
| *Anyanwu* | –Sun |
| *Area boys* | –Street gangs |
| *Atu* | –Giraffe |
| *Aufenthalt* | – Permission to stay / resident |
| *Awele* | –Destiny |
| *Bekees* | –Whites/a couple of white men |
| *Betrug* | –Fraud |
| *Charli( e)* | –F riend ( Ghanaian exclamation) |
| *Chef* | –Employer / boss |
| *Chi* | –Personal god |
| *Chukwu* | –Supreme Being |
| *Chukwu-ma-onye-uka* | –God knows the true worshipper |
| *Chukwu-Okike* | –God the Creator |
| *Da lang* | –This way |
| *Danke sehr!* | –Thanks a lot! |
| *Danke!* | - Thanks |
| *Dibia* | –Traditional medicine man |
| *Diochi* | –Palm wine Tapper |

| | |
|---|---|
| *Du bist verhaftet* | —You are under arrest |
| *Egusi* | —Melon |
| *Eke Ogba* | —Python/Anaconda |
| *Eke-uke* | —Skinny dog |
| *Ekwe* | —Wooden gongs / slit drum |
| *Ekwensu* | —Devil / Satan |
| *Enekentioba* | —A bird |
| *Ezemmuo* | —Chief priest |
| *Ezi-oyi nno* | —Welcome, Good friend! |
| *Ganja* | —Weed / marijuana |
| *Guten apetit* | —Good appetite |
| *Heim* | —Care home |
| *Ichoku* | —Parrot |
| *Igu-mmiri* | —Rain stone (used by traditional rainmakers) |
| *Ikuku* | —Wind |
| *Insha Allahu* | —God willing |
| *Iseh!* | —Amen! |
| *Italo* | —Italy |
| *J J C* | —Johnny just come ( a new comer) |
| *Jugunu* | —A trick |
| *Juju* | —Talisman / gods |
| *Kai-kai* | —Schnapps / Locally made hot drinks |
| *Kebab* | —Turkish dish |
| *Koka* | —Cocaine |
| *Kpalli* | —Generally referred to resident permit/green card/visa/passport |
| *Lugardian* | —C reated or made by Lugard |
| *Mama put* | —Local restaurant |
| *Mbaaa!* | —No! |
| *Mpanaka* | —Oil lamp |
| *Ndi oma* | —Good people |
| *Ndi-ichie* | — Traditional titled men |
| *Ndi-Ozo* | —Group of titled men |
| *Ndubuisi* | —Life is foremost. |
| *Nna anyi* | —Our father [with respect to an elderly man] |
| *Nna m Agu* | —My father the lion![depending on the context, the meaning varies ... it could be an insult or a praise] |

# WOES OF IKENGA

| | |
|---|---|
| *Nso-ani* | –Taboo |
| *Nwa mkpi* | –He-goat |
| *Nwa-nne* | –Child of my mother/ sibling/cousin |
| *Nze na Ozo* | –Traditional titled men cult |
| *O k p o- m gba d a* | – T r a d i t i o n a l orthopedic |
| *Obejili* | –One-edged sword |
| *Obene* | –Wine calabash |
| *Obi* | –Men's hut |
| *Obili-n'aja-ocha* | –HIV/AIDS disease |
| *Ofeke* | –A fool |
| *Ofo* | - Traditional symbol of authority and honesty |
| *Ofo and Ogu* | –Traditional symbols of justice and truth |
| *Ogba-agu* | –Masquerade |
| *Ogbanje* | –Possessing spirit |
| *Ogbuagu* | –Lion killer |
| *Ogbunigwe* | –War machine |
| *Ogene* | –Metal gong |
| *Ogilisi* | –A traditional tree |
| *Ogudiegwu* | –War is terrifying. |
| *Ogwugwu* | –Deity or a god |
| *Oja* | –Traditional flute made of wood |
| *Okada* | –Motorcycle / Motorcyclist |
| *Oke na ohia, ngwere n'uzo* –Helter skelter, to your safety | |
| *Okwa* | –Wild chicken |
| *Okwoma* | –Traditional balm |
| *Oluwole* | –Fake / fraud center |
| *Omenani* | –Tradition |
| *Omenka* | –Creativity (Blacksmith) |
| *Omugwo* | –Babysitting |
| *Onatalu-chi* | –God given |
| *Onugbu* | –Bitter leaf |
| *Onuku* | –Stupid / idiotic |
| *Onwu* | –Death |
| *Onye?* | –Who |
| *Opa* | –Grandfather |
| *Osu* | –Outcast / one consecrated to a deity |
| *Oyibo* | –White man |
| *Ozo* | –Traditional title |

| | |
|---|---|
| *Ozodimgba* | –Chimpanzee |
| *Papa bikoziooh!* | –Please Father! [a plea] |
| *Permisso di soggiorno* | –Resident permit |
| *Polizei* | –Police |
| *Shartz* | –Treasure |
| *Sofort!* | –At once / immediately |
| *Terra- fantassimus* | –Fantastic land |
| *This place na yeye.* | –This place is messed up |
| *Tolo-tolo* | –Turkey fowl |
| *Udala* | –Local cherries |
| *Udo* | –God |
| *Ududo-Nka* | –Deity |
| *Ukochukwu* | –A Priest |
| *Usurugede* | –Traditional fetish dance |
| *Ututu Oma* | –Good Morning |
| *Uzuza* | –Medicinal leave |
| *Vaterschaft* | –Paternity over one's child |
| *Was geht hier ab junge man?-* | What is happening, young man? |
| *Was soll das?* | –What's all these? |